CATNIP JAZZ

by Marilinne Cooper

...BAJA SUR, MEXICO...

You could have fried an egg on the sidewalk. If there had been a sidewalk. She tried to remember whether she had encountered any sidewalks since crossing the border, but her brain did not seem to be functioning properly. Removing her straw hat, she used the hem of her dress to wipe the sweat that kept dripping into her eyes from her brow. The damp hair plastered to her scalp seemed to momentarily cool her as it dried in the scorching sun, and although she longed to leave her hat off, she knew better.

Was she hallucinating or could she actually see the mid-afternoon heat? It rose in waves over the sweeping landscape of hard red soil and sagebrush, the emptiness broken only by a random mesquite tree or saguaro cactus. The mountains in the distance mocked her with memories of shade and clear air.

It was quiet. Too quiet. How long had she been standing here? Time passed so differently when you were not in a vehicle, barreling along at high speed on an endless thoroughfare without shoulders, dreading the next double sixteen-wheeler that came charging at you in the other lane. It was hard to imagine this well-surfaced road had been just a short detour off Mexican Federal Highway 1, the main route that ran north to south through the Baja Peninsula. Why would this road be paved if nobody ever used it?

She could not believe it had really come to this, that he had actually dumped her out on the side of the road and driven away. She kept expecting to see the familiar silhouette of the van appearing out of the melting apparition that was the horizon, making a U-turn and then coming to stop beside her. The door would be flung open, accompanied by the usual choruses of "I'm so sorry, baby" that followed his abusive tirades. For nearly two thousand miles he had repeated the threat of throwing her out, but not until they had hit Baja with its kilometers of uninterrupted desert had she actually begun to worry.

As the days fell into a pattern, she learned to anticipate the rise and fall of his moods. In the cool of the early morning as they cooked breakfast and cleaned up, there would be pleasant banter. If they were staying put and not breaking camp, their relationship was usually fine. They would relax on the deserted beach by the Sea of Cortez, smoke a joint, drink a bottle of Jose Cuervo, maybe have a little "camper sex." If he consumed enough tequila, he would pass out shortly after dark and snore drunkenly until dawn, leaving her to enjoy the starry beauty of the desert night without having to endure his company.

But if it was a day for moving on, the tension would begin to rise even as they packed the van. He would deride her for not tying a knot perfectly or for putting the wash basin some place other than in its customary location beneath the ice chest. Things would chill for a little while once they got on the road, but after an hour or so they would disagree on what music to listen to, and then they would come to a crossroads and argue about which route to take, and soon it would be past lunchtime and hunger would begin to overshadow whatever fractional good humor might have been left between them. A short time later he would be swearing at her, calling her contemptuous names and threatening to hurt her if she crossed him in any way. Once he had backhanded her across the side of her head as she clutched the steering wheel. There had been profuse apologies that night, a meal at a nice cantina and even some make-up sex that, for once, focused more on her needs than his, but after that she always made sure her suitcase and carryall were totally packed and easily accessible – just in case.

The strain between them had actually begun in Mexicali, after the momentary high of passing easily through customs, when she had realized that, not only did he not read or understand Spanish, but that his eyesight was seriously lacking.

"How could you not get your new glasses before we left on this trip?" she asked in disbelief. "You're nearly blind in one eye and can barely see out of the other!"

"You want to drive, bitch? Let's see how well you do!" Before she had realized what was happening he was out of the van and opening her door. "Move over. And I'll fucking kill you if you fuck up my vehicle."

She should have left then, but at that moment she felt unprepared to negotiate the dangers of an unfamiliar foreign city. Instead she chose the devil she knew, or thought she had known for six months in New Orleans. She'd been so in love with him when they planned this trip. At the time she'd been the one in charge, the powerful woman who'd engineered their relationship, who'd overcome her own demons to make a new life with this man.

So she had been the driver for the next seven hundred miles, thinking at first she would be more in control behind the wheel. But each day she seemed less and less in command of her own situation, although she tried desperately not to let him know how well he was eroding the foundation of her usual cocky and confident self-image. She began to make an emergency plan, feeling redeemed when they passed a rough-hewn shelter where a few dusty locals awaited the arrival of a once-daily bus. If he threw her out into the desert, eventually a bus would drive by. Whether it would stop for her was another issue entirely. She comforted herself with the thought that everything would be all right when they finally got to Cabo and settled in for the winter.

The first time he had yelled at her, "Stop the van. Now!" she thought he was joking; then he grabbed the wheel and forced her to pull off into the dirt. "When I tell you to stop, you stop, understand me? I'll throw you out right here in the desert, you just watch me!"

She bit her lip to keep from telling him what an asshole he was while she waited for the tirade to stop. He had not apologized or attempted to make it up to her and she had shuddered for days afterwards when she recalled his mistreatment of her that night. It was the first time she realized she was truly scared of him and how crazy he was becoming. The moody spontaneity she had considered passionate and sexy was morphing into a dark and unpredictable lunacy. It reminded her of her childhood, and before long she was reacting the same way she had as a girl, mentally shutting down to cope with unpleasant situations.

By the time she got the van stuck up to its wheel wells in sand on a beach somewhere north of Loreto, she was so accustomed to his explosive behavior, that she found herself cowering defensively on her knees before he even began kicking at her. Luckily another four-wheel drive vehicle showed up moments later and helped pull them out. He had acted instantly contrite until the other truck had spun off down the seafront, which was apparently inaccessible with their kind of tires.

But after that he had insisted on driving and once they were alone in the cab, his ranting began to crescendo again. When he yelled, "Get out! I mean it. GET OUT NOW," she closed her eyes and leaned her head against the window, trying to put as much space between them as possible. Then suddenly the van veered sideways and came to an abrupt halt. Before she realized what was happening, her door had been flung open and she had tumbled out onto the ground, his dark shape looming over her.

"Believe me now, bitch?" he shouted, kicking a shower of red earth and stones into her face as he moved swiftly back to the driver's side. With a desperate flash of reality, she quickly reached behind the seat and pulled her bags out into the dirt; her straw hat which had rested carefully on top of them sailed through the air to land several feet away.

And now here she was, alone and dehydrated in the desert, on the side of the road with all of her belongings. A giant bruise was rising on her left butt cheek, and her lips were growing increasingly cracked and dry. If someone offered her a bottle of water right now, she would gladly have traded her entire emergency fund of five hundred pesos that was hidden in the interior pocket of her duffel.

She tried to remember how much five hundred pesos was at the current exchange rate. A dollar? Ten dollars? Wait – seventeen to one...she could not do that kind of math in her head right now. Or ever really.

Why had no cars driven by? Somebody must use this road. Maybe she should walk. It could be no more than ten miles out to the main highway, but she could not remember any turn offs or side roads at all on the last stretch. She recalled that she had convinced herself (was it hours ago?) that anybody who left the main route would probably be going all the way to the end. Or vice versa.

Was she imagining it or was the temperature actually growing cooler... Disoriented as she was, the harsh realization that the sun had actually moved to a lower position in the sky brought her situation harshly into focus.

She was alone in the desert, and night was coming.

CHAPTER ONE

Baja Sur, Mexico
September 2017

"What the…"

Blinded by the rising sun and still half asleep, Myles didn't see the woman until he was only a few feet away. Backlit by the glare of dawn; he thought the unusual shape in the middle of the road was a wandering cow or a runaway horse. Then a thin arm emerged from the dark silhouette and began to wave frantically in his direction. Reflexively he slammed on the brakes, and the truck squealed to an unceremonious stop, just barely missing her.

Exhaling deeply a few times, he shifted into reverse and slowly backed up until he was alongside the apparition approaching his passenger door. He lowered the window and stared openly, trying to make rapid sense of the situation. Where could she possibly have come from? There were no buildings in the surrounding desert, at least none that he knew of.

The first thing he noticed as she leaned into the cab was how filthy her arms were. Like she had spent the night lying on the ground or something. Then he realized that if she was out here on the road to nowhere, she might have actually slept in the dirt. Beneath the brim of a crushed straw hat a pair of startling blue eyes ringed by dark smudges peered anxiously at him. Black streaks ran down the hollows of her cheeks besides pale chapped lips that moved soundlessly.

"You want a ride? Quieres ir a …" At this time of the morning his rudimentary Spanish failed him, but words were clearly unnecessary. She had already opened the door and was pushing a dusty duffel bag onto the floorboard. Hastily he cleared the accumulated debris off the seat; he couldn't remember the last time anybody had ridden in the truck with him.

As she climbed in, he found himself looking for clues and cues about her. Her knee-length attire could have been a man's ribbed cotton tank top if not for its curve-hugging shape and elaborate tie-dyed pattern. Bare legs with skinned-up shins emerged from a pair of turquoise cowboy boots that probably cost more than a full set of truck tires. Silver bracelets and bangles adorned both wrists and several pendants and chains hung around her neck. He noted the elaborate tattoo that seemed to crawl out of the low neckline of her dress, around her bicep and up one very tan shoulder.

As she folded her frame into the seat, he saw she was almost as tall as he was, and maybe leaner, with almost no breasts to speak of. Her chest looked like maybe it had thought about growing and then changed its mind, the slight swelling of the nipples being the only visible protrusions against the stretchy fabric. A throaty, smoker's cough alerted him to the fact that he was staring.

"Water? Agua?" Her voice was no more than a hoarse whisper.

"Oh, yeah. Absolutely. Here." Quickly he handed her a liter bottle that he kept in the compartment on the side of his door. As she gulped it down, she flashed him a look of gratitude that for some reason made his face grow hot with emotion. "Can I – uh – drop you somewhere?" Although it was the appropriate next thing to say, the question seemed absurd.

She wiped her mouth with the back of her hand, and somehow succeeded in making her face even dirtier. "Bus station?"

He snorted before he realized she was serious. "Huh. Really. And you're headed where? North? South?"

Beneath the grime her expression seemed to sag with exhaustion. "I don't know. Any place but right here will do. Someplace I can get a meal." She coughed deeply again and then finished off the rest of the water. "And someplace I can buy you another bottle of agua."

Myles shaded his eyes and squinted at the clock on the dashboard. There was no way he could take her with him and there was nowhere he could drop her off that wouldn't make him late, even by Mexican time standards.

Making a wide U-turn into the other empty lane, he headed back the way he had come.

"Thank you so much," she murmured, removing her hat so she could rest her head against the frame of the open window. Long strands of hair in some indeterminate shade of blondish-brown whipped out into the wind as the truck picked up speed. From beneath eyelids heavy with fatigue she seemed to be assessing his appearance now, and he glanced down at himself, unsure of what she was even seeing.

He was wearing faded green board shorts covered with salt stains, and a weather-beaten rust-colored T-shirt that would soon be more holes than fabric. He couldn't remember how long it had been since he'd looked in a mirror or when he had last shaved. He leaned out of his own window, pretending to adjust the side-view mirror and tried to catch a glimpse of his face.

Bleached almost white from the sun, his chin-length hair, still too short to pull back with a rubber band, was tucked behind his ears. The taut skin over his cheekbones was so brown it could have belonged to someone else with a different heritage than his. A pair of women's sunglasses with white plastic frames hid gray eyes that, these days, appeared both haunted and distant. He'd found the shades abandoned in one of the palapas on the beach; they were high quality and did the job. Lifting his chin he checked out his beard growth. Gnarly, he thought. In ways both good and bad.

Embarrassed by the idea that anyone, even a hitchhiker, might catch him checking out his own looks, he shifted his attention back to the stranger beside him.

9

"So can I ask you – where were going that you ended up back there?"

She tensed up for a second and then relaxed and shrugged. "We were lost. Took a wrong turn. Obviously."

"We?" What had he missed – did she have a pet with her?

"My boyfriend and me."

"Your boyfriend. Who is where..." Myles lifted his foot slightly off the gas pedal, thinking maybe this had been a bad idea.

"Fucking bastard. I would say he's probably in Cabo by now, except that the man can't find his fucking way out of a fucking paper bag." She crossed her arms over her chest and gnawed on her cracked lower lip.

"So what – he just left you there?"

His open disbelief seemed to validate her anger. Appearing to blink back tears, she sat up straighter and pumped a fist in the air. "Damn straight he did. Who does that, right?"

Myles shook his head, judgment clearly passed. "And when was this – that he abandoned you in the desert?"

"I don't know – yesterday afternoon? After I got the van stuck in the sand. I – I – thought he would come back for me eventually."

"You could have died out there. Your boyfriend is an idiot."

"Ex-boyfriend. I've taken him back for the last time." She coughed violently and then asked, "You don't have a cigarette, by any chance, do you?"

"I don't smoke. Sorry." He instantly regretted that he had apologized for not smoking tobacco.

"Anything? I find that hard to believe." She flashed him a grin and for a moment he saw the possibility that she was actually beautiful in a raw-edged way.

He dug in his pocket and then laughed with her as he handed over his pipe and stash. "Hold on," he warned. "Wait till we get through this intersection and are up on the carreterra. The federales sometimes have a checkpoint just north of here."

As they turned the corner, he was not surprised at how quickly the weed disappeared into the space between her thigh and the seat cushion. When her gaze lingered for a moment on the shell of a pink concrete building that had at one time been a taco cantina, he realized that she was probably starving.

"What's your name?"

"Kit."

"Like a cat?"

"Or a baby fox." She gave him a sly smile. "Or a foxy babe. Ha, ha, sorry. I use that stupid line all the time. And you?"

He didn't answer for a moment, pretending to concentrate on shifting the gears of the truck as he accelerated to a nearly unsafe speed. "They call me Coyote," he replied finally, still staring straight ahead.

"Like a dog?" This time she threw back her head and laughed heartily at her own joke.

"Yeah, a wild one." There was nothing lighthearted about his tone and they settled into a guarded silence. Eventually she fished out the weed and they shared a few tokes.

By the time the truck began bouncing down the rough road to Playa los Cocos, Kit had fallen asleep sitting up, but the erratic bumping of the final stretch jerked her rudely back into tense wakefulness.

"Where are we?"

"Almost there." Myles steered around the deeper ruts and potholes before they emerged onto a flat sandy surface that ran parallel to a placid cove. A row of seemingly empty, thatch-roofed palapas stood open to the sea. They passed by a half dozen of these crudely built structures until Myles pulled the vehicle up to a space that was clearly inhabited.

He watched Kit's eyes take in the place he called home. From this view all that could be seen was a battered truck camper supported by cinder blocks and connected by a green tarp to a wooden building with three walls that sat on the edge of the sand.

"Welcome." He climbed out and put his hands on his hips, and stretched his lower back.

"You live here?" With surprising speed, she materialized beside him, surveying the landscape.

"Something wrong with that?"

"Not at all. It's…" She ventured towards 'the front yard' and then stopped to use a corner of the palapa as a boot jack, removing her hot and inappropriate footwear before stepping barefoot onto the beach to see the inside of the shelter. A smile spread across her dirty face. "It's perfect."

Ducking under the webbing of a hammock that was strung between two poles, she studied the furnishings of his domain. A plastic folding table served as his kitchen with a two-burner camp stove above and a couple of coolers below; a wooden shelf built along the back wall held a few pots, plates, and other utensils. On a woven straw mat, there was a camp chair with a broken armrest, and next to it sat a small round end table painted red with a folkloric pattern of green and yellow flowers; this actual piece of furniture seemed out of place in such a rustic setting. One corner of the interior was partitioned off with bright sarongs hung on a length of clothesline. Snorkeling equipment, fishing poles and a boogie board were piled against the far wall. Other assorted gear and tools filled the space beneath the tarp that hung between the stationary camper and the outside of the palapa.

"What do you need first – a sandwich or a shower?" He rummaged in one of the coolers, pulled out a couple of tangerines and tossed one to her. "And by sandwich I mean beans and avocado between two tortillas."

"Oh my god, that sounds divine. You, Wild Dog, are a godsend. Do you mind if I sit in your one seat?" She dropped herself onto the worn canvas chair as she tore the skin from the fruit, all the while staring out at the mesmerizing surface of the water.

"Make yourself comfortable. And here." Myles poured some water out of a gallon jug onto a washcloth. "You might want to wash your hands before you eat. This may be paradise, but it's still Mexico."

"Gracias, senor." Even in gratitude, her tone was a bit mocking.

By the time he had finished assembling the simple tacos, she had devoured the tangerine and was watching his every movement hungrily. "You remind me of my cat when I'm cooking fish," he said handing her a folded tortilla.

"You have a cat?" she asked incredulously between mouthfuls.

"Diva! Here, Diva!" he called. There was a soft thwacking sound and then a slim striped feline streaked across the sand floor and rubbed up against Myles's ankles. "There's my best pal. Sorry I woke you up from your daytime nap." He cradled the cat in his arms for a second before releasing her to the ground.

"Not just a cat, but one that comes when a Coyote calls," Kit remarked with teasing admiration. Myles could sense her true personality beginning to emerge now that she had a little sustenance.

Squinting at the sun, he wondered what time it was and how long Ernesto had waited for him before leaving. On the far horizon he thought he could make out the shape of a small boat.

"So nobody else is in residence in your neighborhood right now?" Kit peered up and down the quiet shoreline, the buzzing of flies being the only sound other than the noise of food being chewed.

"Dean and Diane are down at the far end. They've been here for six months. But that's it. Sometimes campers show up for a night or two, but it's been too hot for most people until recently. Dean says they'll probably move when it starts to fill up with snowbirds in a few weeks." Myles shaded his eyes and looked in the direction of the campsite he was referring to, but there was no sign of life from the small motor home of the retired Californians. He wondered if they were even up yet.

"So when you say shower, what exactly do you mean?"

"Huh?" He looked back at Kit who was examining her dirt-encrusted limbs as though she was just realizing how filthy she was.

"You mean, like take a swim and wash off, right?"

He chuckled. "Actually, if you look around the corner you will see my solar shower bag hanging from the clothesline. And if you wait another hour or so, you will have to be careful, because the water will be hot enough to burn you."

"Really? That is so brilliant. I haven't had a hot shower since Bahia Los Angeles." She stood up almost gleefully. "But I should probably take a swim first and rinse most of this dirt off so I don't waste your water. Let me put my suit on."

As she headed back to the truck to find her duffel bag, Myles almost called after her to say she didn't need one, but thought better of it. He didn't want her getting too comfortable here. Later, at some point, he was going to have to drive her up to Mulege where she could probably actually get a bus to wherever it was she was headed.

Kit returned wearing a purple bikini that was so skimpy she might just as well have been naked for the amount of skin that the triangles of cloth and strings covered. He wondered if she was aware of the large bruises that were now exposed, one across her back and another on her upper thigh, and then remembered the boyfriend who had dumped her in the desert. He watched her as she waded out through the wide expanse of shallow water and then glanced questioningly back at him over a bony shoulder blade.

"Keep going!" he shouted. "It gets deeper!"

At the end of the beach he could see the gleam of Dean's long white hair and the curve of his large tanned belly as his neighbor peered curiously out the open door of his RV. He wondered how long it would be before the gregarious old man found a reason to mosey down the sand and check out who his antisocial younger friend was talking to. Maybe he could get Kit back on the road before then. And if he was going into town, he might as well make a list of shit he needed to buy.

Ducking into his own camper to look for paper and a pen, he was embarrassed to realize it looked like the scene of a burglary or looting. Clothing was strewn everywhere, along with empty gallon jugs and other debris. His bedding was bunched into a ball at the foot of the mattress that filled the front width of the space. Diva's food and water dishes took up most of the tiny kitchen counter that he no longer used since his expansion into the palapa. The only improvement he had made to the camper since parking it was the cat door he had installed so that Diva could find safe refuge from animals of prey when she needed it. He knew it had saved her life on more than one occasion and he always made sure it was in working order. That and the propane refrigerator.

For a moment he considered straightening up, but decided that was unnecessary and extreme. He never did anything in here anymore, except sleep, so what difference did it make? It was just a place where he could lock stuff up. It was not like he was going to invite Kit in for tea or something.

Reflexively he lifted a cushion and made sure his fiddle was in place and then checked the coffee can in the back of the fridge where he kept his cash. Getting low again; he would have to do something about that soon. Removing a few thousand pesos for purchasing supplies in Mulege, he escaped back outside.

Kit was emerging from the water, her hair slicked back and dripping, a beatific smile on her face. Myles thought she was maybe the skinniest woman he'd seen in a long time, and she didn't look bad in a tiny bikini. And maybe she wasn't as old as he'd thought she was when he'd first laid eyes on her exhaustion-etched features. He

15

suppressed the urge to find out what the rest of her story was — if he asked questions, she would too, and he wasn't about to answer any inquiries regarding his past.

"Let me show you the shower," he said, trying to hasten things along. He lead her around the side of the palapa to where the black bag was suspended above head level and heating up in the morning sun.

"Not very private, is it?" she laughed.

"Yeah, a frigate bird might see you. I don't think you have to worry. I'll take a walk down the beach until you're done." Like it mattered to him whether or not she was wearing the little wet scraps of cloth that drew the line between naked and not naked.

"Okay. Thanks, I appreciate this," she called after him.

As he wandered slowly along the edge of the water, he saw Dean watching him from the shade of his own thatch-roofed shelter. "Coy-boy!" He motioned him over. "No work today? Want a breakfast empanada or some coffee? Diane just heated some up."

"Uh, no thanks, Dean." He knew it would only take seconds for Dean to get to the real point.

"How about your friend down there? Maybe she'd like some."

Myles couldn't help but laugh. "You are a piece of work, D-man. You're so bored you would probably pay me to tell you who she is and where she came from."

"Now you're hurting my feelings! I'm not bored, I'm just curious. It's not like you ever have any visitors." Behind Dean, Myles could see Diane moving closer to the window of the RV so she could hear the conversation better.

"Hi, Diane." Myles acknowledged her presence and a second later she came to the door, a purple sarong covering her solid girth and tied around her neck, soft, wavy white hair flowing loosely over her bare shoulders. She smiled but said nothing, waiting as expectantly as Dean for Myles's reply.

"I don't know who she is, all right? I found her out on the road to Playa Bonita. I think she spent the night out there. Her name is Kit. She was thirsty, hungry and needed a bath. I did my humanitarian act for the day. In a little while I am going to take her into Mulege and drop her off. End of story. You guys happy?" Myles was aware that he sounded like a plaintive teenager trying to put off his parents, but he didn't care.

"I'd say that story has a lot of holes in it," Diane commented, leaning against the doorway and crossing her arms.

"Sure does," agreed Dean. "You didn't ask her how she ended up on the road to fuckin' nowhere? Even you would have asked her that."

"She said her boyfriend abandoned her there. Apparently, it wasn't a great relationship."

"Oh, the poor woman. Why don't you bring her down so I can feed her some breakfast?" Diane was already in compassionate supporter mode.

"I fed her. She'll be fine." He didn't want to explain to them that he did not really want Kit hanging around any longer than she had to. There were places he was supposed to be, things he should be doing. "I just walked down here to give her some privacy while she showered. I better be getting back now."

"Maybe she can stay for a few days. The two of you can come to dinner tonight!" Diane shouted as Myles strolled away, trying not to appear in a great hurry.

He did not like to admit to himself that he enjoyed the attention and care of the older couple. Being family-oriented had been a big part of his previous lifetime, but there was no place for it in his current existence.

He walked slowly, hoping he'd given Kit enough time to finish bathing and get dressed. The temperature was already climbing and he didn't really want to be in town during the hottest part of the day. But he could see no movement as he approached his campsite.

17

"How's it going?" he called in the direction of the shower but there was no response. His heart beat faster as he thought she might have invaded the sanctity of the camper. But as he turned slowly in a circle, he saw what he had missed before. Under the shade of the eaves, his rope hammock was stretched taught with the weight of its contents. Wrapped in a beach towel, her damp hair falling through the loosely woven mesh, Kit snored lightly, dead to the world.

That night, when he'd told her she couldn't stay past morning, her eyes had narrowed slightly. "Really?"

"Yes. Really." He was trying to clear a space for her to sleep on the narrow bench seat of the cramped camper. There was no way he was going to share his bed with her.

She stepped outside and for a while all he could see was the outline of her gaunt shoulder blades as she stared at the vast starry darkness of the moonless sky. "You mean here, in your campsite, right?"

"What?"

"I mean, there's nothing stopping me from moving into the palapa next door, is there?"

He froze, bed pillow in hand. "Why would you do that?"

"I like it here. It feels safe. And I need to regroup."

Myles didn't know what to say so he said nothing. It had been the way their conversation had been going all evening, since she had finally awakened after sleeping well into the afternoon. Dean had eventually wandered down, his curiosity having eaten away at him all day, and the sound of their voices had roused her from the netherworld she seemed to have fallen into. Grasping the towel to her chest, she had tumbled out of the hammock and onto her feet, staring at them with a dazed lack of comprehension for a few seconds. The ropes of the hammock had left deep creases in her back and arms and along one side of her face.

"You okay, darlin'?" Dean had asked, and Myles could see him making a quick assessment of her looks. "Coyote, get her some water. She should keep hydrating."

In the half minute it had taken him to retrieve a water bottle, Kit and Dean had already become best of friends and cemented plans for a cozy barbecued supper for four at sundown.

"What the hell..." Myles had mouthed silently at him from behind Kit's back, but Dean had just grinned broadly as he turned to walk back up the beach.

But it had not been an unpleasant night. Dean and Diane, delighted to have some fresh company, had been contagiously upbeat, and Kit had fulfilled all their social needs and then some. Dressed in a skin-tight tank top and a colorful flowing skirt, and adorned with multiple beaded necklaces and silver bangle bracelets, she provided the evening's entertainment by producing a deck of tarot cards and reading their fortunes in her lyrical Louisianan accent. Apparently she was a "professional," working the tourists on Jackson Square, selling handmade jewelry as her legitimate business with fortunetelling on the side. Myles was completely skeptical of her actual abilities to read the future, but admired her well-practiced approach as he watched Dean and Diane fall under her spell.

It was not late when they made their way slowly back to Myles's campsite, and by then, loosened up with cheap tequila and good weed, Kit had engaged him in some companionable chit-chat, asking him personal questions about his past that he skillfully deflected, learning way more about her life than he revealed about his own. Although she'd grown up as rurally as he had, her childhood in a backwoods bayou town was as different from his own quaint New England village as anything could be. From her description of life on the streets of New Orleans as a young runaway, through a narrative of rough jobs and skanky boyfriends, to the part where she met Denny the charismatic con man who had helped her establish herself as vendor and entrepreneur before luring her into traveling to Mexico with him, Myles gauged that she was in her early thirties, which made her more than ten years his senior.

"Okay, if you're going to be mysterious, let me read your palm then and I'll tell you about yourself." He stiffened as she reached for his hand, running her fingers over the rough skin on the underside. "Relax, I'm not gonna jump your bones. Come over here under the solar lantern so I can see your life line."

In the battery-powered half-light, her face was eerily etched in shadow as she studied his palm, and for an instant Myles had a sense of what she would look like as an old woman.

"I can see that you are from New Hampshire..."

Despite his suspicion of her, he laughed aloud. "You read that in my hand?"

"No – on your license plate, silly." She laughed with him. "Fortunetelling is mostly about awareness." She traced a line with her nail that sent an unexpected shiver down his spine. "You're kind to animals and humans..."

Okay, it didn't take a psychic to figure that one out, but he kept his sarcastic thought to himself.

And you had your heart broken by a beautiful woman..."

"True enough," he admitted. "Although I think I broke her heart worse." He pulled his hand away. "And actually I'm really from Vermont."

"New Hampshire...Vermont...they're kind of the same place, right?" She followed him back to the camper.

"Not if you're from there." He opened the door and then turned to her. "Louisiana, Mississippi..." He mimicked her drawl. "Y'all are the same, right?"

"Oh, y'all are so bad, boy." She gathered up her skirt and stepped up behind him. "Yowza. What hurricane hit..." Her comment trailed off as he glared at her. "Sorry. I know, beggars, choosers, and all that. And I am truly grateful for your hospitality."

But when, a few minutes later, she made the comment about moving in next door, he began to worry that his basic sense of humanity may have betrayed him. He did not want or need his privacy invaded; he had way too much at stake.

"I'm going to sleep. I have to leave before dawn, so you have a choice of a ride to town at that time or not staying. But I lock up the camper when I leave, so either way you will have to be out." His tone of voice indicated that he had shut down the companionable tenor of the conversation.

Although Kit did not respond, in the closeness of their confined quarters, he could sense the shift of her mood from amiability to apprehension. What was her problem – this was his space and he was not threatening her, just stating the facts. Angrily he tossed her his head lamp. "I'm turning out the light. If you need to see, you can use this."

"Thanks. I do need to pee and get a few things out of my bag." She flinched visibly as the cat door flapped open and Diva slipped quickly inside. "You scared me, kitty," she murmured before stepping out into the night. "Ooh, it's getting chilly out here."

Myles felt badly about his attitude, but he was just not accustomed to having anybody share his personal environment. He dropped his shorts onto the small rectangle of flooring that ran down the middle of the camper and hoisted himself up into the double bunk. He wasn't really ready for bed; normally he would have read or played his fiddle for a while, but it seemed like the only way to retreat right now. He slid under the quilt and threw an arm over his face as Diva curled up on his chest.

He pretended to be asleep when Kit came back, but he was really covertly watching her beneath his elbow. Illuminated by the headlamp which hung around her neck like a medallion, she appeared to be wearing only a long sweater and a pair of socks. Shivering, she picked up the blanket he had given her and folded it in half before laying it on top of herself as she tried to get comfortable on the thin cushion of the bench. Finally she flicked off the light.

After a while, she said, "You're still awake, right?"

He hesitated for a beat before answering. "Yeah."

"So what are you running from?"

21

"Who says I'm running?"

She snorted. "Everybody here is running from something. Even if it's just the weather."

"Okay, then. Maybe I'm a murderer."

"And maybe I'm a bank robber. What'd you really do?"

"I killed a librarian."

Kit laughed loudly. "Oh, come on. That's the best you can come up with?"

From somewhere just beyond the campsite, the eerie howl of a coyote echoed through the vastness of the night.

"Okay, how about I not only killed a librarian, I had an affair with my best friend's wife who was pregnant with twins?" Why was he even talking to her? But what did it matter, she would be gone tomorrow.

"Coy-boy, I love it. Your imagination is as wild as you are." His vision had adjusted to the dark enough now that he could see her sit up and lean against the wall, the sweater falling open so that the white expanse of her bare chest was visible as she tucked the blanket around her waist. "So now tell me – how'd a kid like you earn the money to get all the way here from Vermont? Come on, make it good."

"Buried treasure?"

"Not bad. Give me another."

"How about a rich uncle who died and left me a map to his buried treasure?"

"What did he leave you – gold and diamonds? Damn, I wish I had a cigarette. This is almost as good as sex."

"Nah, fifty dollar bills in Chock-full-o'Nuts coffee cans." The more truth he told her, the more fantastic he realized it sounded.

"Excellent. I can totally visualize that." There was something inexplicably erotic about the little sigh of satisfaction she gave, and Myles ignored the warning bells going off in his head. "So somewhere in this camper is what...like fifty thousand in cash?"

This time he laughed. "Not a chance, sweetheart."

"What – you already spent it all? No, let me guess – you gave it away."

He was stunned into silence for a second before rising to the bait. "Oh, you must have seen that in your crystal ball."

"Well, it doesn't surprise me. So what do you do for work now?"

"Let's see...maybe I steal from the rich so that the poor can find better job opportunities in other countries?"

Kit made the sound of a buzzer. "Ehh. Okay, Robin Hood. You can do better than that. Try again."

"And then I help supply the fishing boats that they escape on?" The more he told the truth, the more he appeared to be lying.

"Oh, that's way too serious. Tell me something I can believe."

"I play music on Saturday nights in a bar in Mulege for cervesas and a few pesos?"

"Oh, my god. Tell me you're in a mariachi band and I might come in my pants. If I was wearing any. Sorry, that was crude."

This time Myles hit the imaginary buzzer. "You lose. I'm not a mariachi. I'm a fiddler and I play with an expat guitarist."

"Wait – that's kind of boring. When did this conversation get real?"

Myles could not keep the grin out of his voice as he answered. "What do you mean? It's been real the whole time. Good night, Kit," he said.

Then he lay there for a long time with his eyes open, stroking Diva's fur and trying not to think about the unbuttoned sweater of the woman a few feet away.

CHAPTER TWO

Baja Sur, Mexico
October 2017

The sun was already setting behind the mountains as Myles pulled the truck up next to the camper. He was disturbed to see that two more sites along the beach had been occupied since morning. In addition to the four luxury motorhomes that had arrived together a few days earlier, there was now a white van and an old-school Airstream trailer. Dean had been right – snowbird season was definitely creeping closer.

Kit was sitting in the camp chair by the water's edge, smoking a cigarette and watching the shifting colors of the early evening sky. When she saw Myles approaching, she quickly stubbed out the butt and slipped it into the pocket of her dress before blowing a kiss in his direction.

"I brought you something." He dumped a cloth bag out into Kit's lap. Several tarnished spoons and knives clanked unceremoniously together into the open space between her knees. She looked blankly at the gift for a few seconds before shrieking in delight.

"Are they real silver? I love you, Coy-Dog! Now I can actually get to work making some jewelry."

Myles put a finger to his lips and looked around uneasily. The new neighbors weren't quite within earshot but you never knew.

"Where did you – never mind. I don't need to know." He noticed her hand was trembling as she reached for the half-empty bottle of tequila that sat in the sand at her feet. He thought the bottle had been nearly full when they went to bed last night, but it wasn't like he was keeping score. On any given day, she drank way more than he ever did

24

and the truth was, she was actually way more mellow when she was drunk.

"Looks like you've been getting a little buzz on this afternoon?" He saw now that her cheekbone was scraped like maybe she'd had an unsteady run-in with one of the corner posts of the palapa.

Ignoring the question, she nodded towards the hand he was still holding behind his back. "What else do you have for me, lover boy?"

He revealed two shiny fish dangling from a line. "Dinner."

Kit had not even lasted a whole night on her own in the 'palapa next door.' When Myles had returned that first evening, part of him was still hoping that maybe somehow she'd be gone and his existence could go back to same-old/same-old. But with the help of Dean and Diane and their guest air mattress, she'd set up a makeshift camp and was already up the beach, sharing cocktails with the old Californians by the time he arrived home.

Despite their group protests, he'd declined a second night of socializing, preferring Diva's undemanding company. He'd already said way too much to Kit, even if she didn't believe most of what he'd told her. He sat in the canvas chair under the stars, working out a new tune on his fiddle, when suddenly she materialized out of the darkness, tapping her foot and listening.

"They told me you were good, but y'all are genius. Where I come from, you could make a lot of money with that talent. You ever been to New Orleans?"

"Nope." Despite the fact that he'd traveled over four thousand miles to get to Baja from northern Vermont, he didn't feel like he'd really ever been anywhere. It wasn't like he'd been sightseeing along the way. He'd driven nonstop for four days to get to the border, stopping only to crawl into the camper and sleep when he became too exhausted to keep his eyes open. Before she could ask him about that trip, he changed the subject. "But I have been to

Europe." He thought that would be the end of the discussion because he was sure she'd never been there.

"So y'all are a privileged white boy, just like we suspected." Her raspy laughter rang out into the rapidly cooling air of the fall night.

"We?" He stopped playing.

"Dee and Di and me. We were speculating about you."

He gave a snort of disbelief. "Privileged, oh, yeah, that's me, all right." He stood up abruptly. "Now, excuse me, I'm ready for bed and I have to ask my butler to lay out my pajamas and fill my marble Jacuzzi tub for me."

"Don't be such an asshole!" she called after him. "Mysterious is not a becoming color for you!"

Fuming, he sat in bed with a book propped up on his lap, not even seeing the words. "She won't last more than a few days," he whispered reassuringly to Diva. "No worries, right?"

At some point in the night, his covers resisted the tug he gave as he rolled over to sleep on his side and he realized that something much larger than Diva was sleeping beside him on top of his quilt. After a brief flicker of fear, he knew immediately that it was Kit.

"What do you think you're doing?" he mumbled angrily. "Kit. KIT."

She threw an arm over him and answered drowsily, "I was scared. And cold. Now go back to sleep."

With what he was beginning to recognize as her amazing capacity for narcolepsy, she was dozing again in a matter of seconds. As his initial fury wore off and the heat of her lanky limbs began to seep through the layers of batting that separated their bodies, he realized that he had missed the coziness of another human being sleeping next to him. While the hours crept towards dawn, he allowed himself to indulge in the memories of Chloe and the amazing pleasures of their physical closeness. In the darkness, without actually touching, it was easy to imagine that it was Chloe snuggled up against him.

26

Just as it began to get light on the horizon, he drifted off into a dream that was a muddle of eating pancakes on Chloe's enormous naked pregnant belly in the comfy bed in the cabin loft and licking the maple syrup off of her soft hot skin...

So he was already on fire, when Kit slipped under the covers and into his fantasy. He tried to keep his dream going but her wiry body did not feel anything like falling into Chloe's lushness. But it did feel really good.

"Oh my god, what was that...besides amazing..." Kit slid off of him and fell onto her back, still breathing heavily. She turned her face towards his and then propped herself up on one elbow. "Wait – I hope these are tears of joy." She brushed her lips against the salty wetness running down one cheek.

Myles covered his eyes with the back of his arm, but his chest heaved a couple of times, giving him away. Kit used the edge of the sheet to wipe his face and nose, but the gentle gesture caused a fresh outburst of emotion. "Sorry, I just haven't felt – anything – for so long..."

She stroked his hair as he sobbed against her shoulder for a few seconds before shuddering into silence. Between the sex and crying, he'd released more pent-up tension than in all of the last six months. Wrapping himself around her damp body, he felt himself falling into a deep and dreamless abyss.

When he woke a few hours later, still in the same position, he had a momentary sense of revulsion. What had happened here – he hardly knew this strange older woman – but then remembered that for a few brief minutes he had forgotten the void he carried inside. Suddenly he was aroused again by the possibility of escaping once more into that enjoyable mindless pleasure.

His fingertips searched out her nipples – small but sensitive under his exploratory touch. She shivered and rubbed against him in response. Her breasts were so different from the soft fullness of Chloe's that there was no point in comparison. He compartmentalized his mind and

27

then shut off the parts he could not think about. It was time to just be an animal in the desert.

"Aren't you supposed to be somewhere this morning?" she asked a while later, her lips pressed against his shoulder blade, one hand somewhere between his thighs, another running along the coarse hairs of his abdomen.

"Here is fine." He felt incredibly spent, almost empty, and there was something liberating about it, he wanted it to go on forever. He reached behind him to touch her bare skin and pull her closer. The air in the camper was hot and still now; he could feel the sweat running down the small of her back.

"How about I make you breakfast?" She straddled him as she tried to make her way off the bunk but he grabbed her around the waist and pulled her down.

"How about I make you my breakfast?"

"Let's have some food first. You're gonna need all your vitamins, baby." Somehow she slithered out of his grasp and onto the floor. "Where do you keep the coffee? Wait – oh, my god, don't tell me that you don't drink coffee..."

Once they laid down the ground rules, it became their own unique version of paradise. All Myles required was no questions – about his past or present – and all Kit needed was a trip to the closest mercado every few days for cigarettes and tequila. She respected his privacy and kept up a one-sided conversation when he didn't feel like talking. When he left to "go to work" she didn't inquire about his day or where the money came from. And at night she gave him the kind of carnal comfort that kept him both satisfied and wanting more.

"Can we go to a bank or cambio?" she asked after a few days. "I need to get some more money out – I'm not going to be your kept woman."

After he reminded her she would need some ID, he found her dumbfounded, sitting in the sand with the contents of her purse dumped out onto her lap, holding up two passports. "I forgot I had both of them..."

28

"You have multiple identities?"

"No, I always kept both of our passports in my bag. Mine and Denny's. I've got everything – his visa and his Mexican car insurance papers. Oh, and look. One of his credit cards. If he gets stopped by the cops, he's totally fucked." Her brief flash of concern turned immediately into a fist pump of victory. "Ha. Too bad for him."

On Saturday night she went with Myles to the gringo bar in Mulege where he played music. She used Denny's card to buy them both dinner and a lot of drinks and at one point, beers for everyone in the bar. As they staggered back to the truck, she tossed the card into a drainage ditch. Myles was too drunk to drive well and after he had weaved down the highway for a while, he finally pulled off the road and Kit spread a rough woven blanket in the open bed of the truck and they stretched out on it, the stars overhead spinning like an amusement park ride.

"Oh, my god, I want to fuck you out here," she said, unzipping his jeans and hiking up her dress.

Even in his nauseatingly dizzy state, her raw sexuality turned him on. "You want to fuck me anywhere."

"I do and I will. Oh, how I love you, Coy-boy," she groaned as she settled herself on top of him. As always, at her declaration of devotion, Myles felt his mind and heart shutting down and he said nothing as he gave into the magnetic pull of physical attraction.

He awoke stiff and cold a few hours later. Leaning over the side, he puked in the dirt and then got into the cab and drove the truck home, with Kit still asleep in the back.

It was not the lifestyle or relationship he might have dreamed of, but in its own weird way, it worked for now.

"I like that you are almost as tall as I am," he admitted to her one night, as their long limbs entwined in a comfortable sleeping position. "We fit together well."

"And I know you like the idea that you can probably wear my clothes. I think you would look great in that long black dress with the cutouts on the side."

"Don't even think about it."

"Afraid of our feminine side, are we? Wouldn't I love to dress you up and take you out for Halloween back home. I could make you so beautiful. A little eye make-up, some jewelry..."

He'd learned to accept and even enjoy the weird and wildly erotic imaginings she so frequently threw out there. There was no one in his previous life he could equate with Kit and that was what he liked about her. She reminded him of no one he had ever known before.

"At least let me pierce one of your ears," she whispered, taking his earlobe in her teeth and biting down softly. And by the end of the week he sported a silver hoop with a couple of dangling seashells. "And now you are officially the sexiest man alive," she had declared before going down on him in the hammock in broad daylight.

After it had become clear that Kit was sticking around for a while, Dean and Diane had beamed at him for several days, as though he'd made them proud. "I get a vicarious thrill knowing you are getting some every night now," Dean told him, sucking on a joint before passing it over. "You deserve it." He coughed harshly as he exhaled and then added, "And besides, we're leaving soon for more remote parts, and I'm glad you will have someone else here with you to fight the turistos off."

"Ohhh, don't tell me this, dude. I'm suffering separation anxiety just thinking about it." The prospect of life at Playa Los Cocos without his surrogate parents was almost too bleak to contemplate. "Will you keep an eye on her for the next couple nights? I need to be away."

Dean raised an eyebrow but knew enough not to probe. He'd been the one to introduce Myles to Ernesto and Myles knew that Dean was aware of the kind of work detail he'd gotten involved in.

Kit had been a bit edgy when he told her he'd be gone for a few days and then would not elaborate. The more he shut down, the chattier she became until finally he slipped his hands under her dress and did the things to her that he knew would make her breathe heavily and stop talking.

He returned from that trip to discover she'd spent the time cleaning up the camper like it had never been cleaned since he'd owned it, scrubbing the walls, counter and floors, even washing (by hand, no less) the funky bedding they slept in, and which had been growing funkier every night.

"Shit, you didn't have to do this for me," he commented, trying not to complain that he had no idea where to find his belongings since they were not in the usual heap on the floor.

"I didn't do it for you, baby, I did it for me. I don't like livin' frat house style. And those sheets – well, they smelled like a bunch of animals were sleepin' here."

"Well, they are. A couple of kit-cats and a wild dog." Much as he didn't like her moving his shit around, he had to admit the place looked super nice. "Thank you."

He turned to grin at her; her hair was pulled back from her face in half a dozen little braids that were braided together in the back into one fat braid, the sun-bleached strands mixing with the darker blonde ones that didn't often see the light of day. She wore a thin stretchy white dress that showed off her Baja tan and pretty much everything else that was under it, from the darkness of her areolas to the narrow arrow of pubes. For a moment he felt light and lucky that this was what he had come home to instead of a fusty closed-up camper and a can of refried beans.

"Why are you even wearing that – you can see everything through it."

"Because I knew it would give you a hard-on? Am I right?"

He reached out and pulled the straps of the dress off her shoulders. "Honey, I'm home," he murmured.

But as the days passed, living with Kit was not always a honeymoon and after Dean and Diane departed, the only thing they shared for half a week or so was a dark mood. Some Midwestern fundamentalists moved in a few sites down and then a quartet of loud Canadians arrived and their own private paradise seemed much less than perfect.

"Take me with you," she begged him as he prepared for another overnight excursion. "I don't care about whatever it is you do."

"There is not even a remote possibility that will happen so don't even ask again."

"What am I going to do here – with *them*?" She nodded towards the strains of country music that drifted up the beach.

He shrugged. "You don't have to stay. I can take you to the bus." His tone was hard and indifferent.

They glared at each other for a long minute before she stormed off towards the rocks at the end of the cove, stopping only to retrieve her cigarettes and a nearly empty bottle of tequila. At that point in time he had been ready to be done with her drama and thought about packing her bags for her. They had not spoken again until late afternoon, when he tossed his backpack into the cab of the truck and started up the engine. Just as he put it into gear, she appeared by his open window, out of breath from running, reeking from an unattractive mix of smoke and alcohol.

She put a sweaty hand on his upper arm and squeezed. "Bye."

"Bye. See you in a couple of days." Gently he took her by the wrist to break her grasp. Before she could say anything else, he left her behind in a cloud of red dust.

He returned three afternoons later to find her wearing her purple bikini and drinking beer with a couple of Dutch bicyclists who had pitched a tent for a few days under one of the nearby palapas. When she stood to greet him, he felt a warm rush at the familiar sight of her crooked teeth, jangling jewelry, narrow hips and long legs.

This last time when he'd left, there had been no conflict between them. She'd strung tiny silver and lapis beads on a piece of fishing line and then hung them around his neck and said, "For good luck," before kissing him goodbye.

Now, as they ate barbecued fish and drank cold beers, he thought she seemed quieter than usual after so many hours apart. Inquiringly, he touched her bare foot with his own. "You okay?"

"Mmmm. Fine. Just tired. I think I spent too much time in the sun today." Her leg began to move up and down in a nervous gesture and she pulled her foot away from his.

"Well, let's go to bed right after we wash the dishes," he suggested.

Her expression relaxed and she reached over to brush his unruly locks behind his ears. "What happened to that manly braid I made to keep the hair out of your eyes?" she scolded jokingly.

He ran his fingers over the cut on her cheek and she winced. "You should put something on this so it doesn't get infected."

"I've heard a dog's saliva is the best thing for a wound."

"Even a wild dog?"

"Being licked by a wild dog is even better." She laughed a little and then picked up their plates. "Okay, I'm making myself hot. Maybe we should just leave the dishes for the wild dogs to disinfect."

"Just bring them into the camper with us." He suddenly felt as eager as she was to skip to the good parts.

She was still getting undressed by the time he was stretched out naked and ready on top of the quilt. He watched her slowly undoing the intricate lacing that held her shirt together. "What is that thing you're wearing, some kind of corset?" He had not really noticed her attire until now. "And that's some honking necklace you have on." He stared at the wide metal choker that seemed to be made of heavy chainmail links. "Looks like some medieval torture device."

"Thanks for your educated fashion commentary." She had finally freed herself from the blouse and was trying to undo the catch on the necklace.

"Come here, let me help you."

"You don't have to," she said as she reached up to flick off the light. "I've got this." He heard a clank on the counter and then felt her warm body covering his own. "Oh, baby." Her wet tongue lashed out playfully at his nose. "I've got this place down here that needs some serious attention from a wild dog..."

The sex was erotic and energetic and afterwards he felt marvelously unwound and stress-free as the cool air of the desert night drifted soothingly across their bodies. He was almost asleep when he felt Kit disengaging herself from his embrace.

"Go to sleep," she whispered. "I'm going out to have a smoke and use the john."

With great effort in his semi-conscious state, he wrestled the quilt out from under himself and up as far as his waist before drifting off again. He could smell Kit's cigarette and hear the sounds of her fumbling around in the stillness of the campground. Almost asleep, he was startled into wakefulness as one of the other vehicles on the beach revved its engine and pulled out onto the road. Cursing angrily, he put the pillow over his head. He hated sharing his paradise with assholes.

He didn't know how long he'd been sleeping when the sound of an explosion woke him. "Kit?" He sat up in the dark, disoriented, not sure if he'd been dreaming.

"I'm right here." Her breathy voice came from a few feet away. "What do you think that was?"

He could see her silhouette as she kneeled on the cushioned bench and peered out the window. He twisted around to look out the screened opening at the head of the mattress. "Something is on fire. Out by the highway. Maybe there was an accident." There was another loud pop and flames shot towards the horizon.

"Do you think we should go check it out?"

34

Lights were going on in the motorhomes parked down the beach, people were shouting and doors slamming.

"Sounds like Russ and Phil from Manitoba have it covered. I say let's stay out of it. Come back to bed."

"Alberta."

"What?"

"They're from Calgary." She was still staring out the window, fixated by whatever horror was happening on the horizon.

He leaned over and touched her arm. "Come on. We're safe. Keep me warm. I'll even sleep on the inside." He tugged on her sleeve. "What is this you're wearing? My hoodie?"

"One of us had to start the cross-dressing trend." She climbed up next to him and unzipped the dark sweatshirt. "But I am wearing my own leggings." She cocked her head, listening to the Canadians getting into their SUV. "Maybe I should see if I can go with them."

He tugged at the Lycra around her waist. "Leave it be. Take these things off and I promise you a better show right here."

Despite his exhausted state, it was hard to sleep with all the unexpected excitement going on nearby and Kit seemed exceptionally wired. He stroked her in all the right places, trying to release her tension but his efforts seemed to have the opposite effect, bringing her to some ongoing plateau of pleasure.

"Jesus, how many times have you come now?" he whispered into her ear as she arched and moaned again.

"I've lost count. You're like catnip to this kitty, babe. Oh, my god, I love you so much, I can't stop..."

"What's this?" He could feel the tears on her face.

"I'm so happy you're here with me."

It was mid-morning when an insistent banging on the camper door finally woke them up. Through the open screens of their windows, Myles could see that the sky was a strange shade of gray, heavy with thunderclouds, and he could not guess what time it was. It had only rained maybe twice in the all the months he'd been in Baja and the change in weather was oddly disorienting.

"Hello! Buenos dias! Anybody home?" A deep voice in heavily accented English accompanied the knocking.

"Si. Coming," Myles called back, sliding to the floor and searching for his shorts.

"Policia. Open up, please."

Kit bolted upright, holding the sheet to her chest. Myles looked around trying to find something for her to put on quickly, but all he could find was the complicated garment she had discarded the night before. "My kimono," she hissed at him and he tossed her the silky robe that hung next to the door before he opened it just a crack.

"Hola, senors," he said cheerfully to the two uniformed men glaring at him. Out of the corner of his eye he saw Kit sweep the pot pipe off the shelf next to the bed and conceal it under the pillows.

They looked behind him with undisguised interest at Kit sitting in the loft holding the kimono closed with arms crossed over her chest.

"Sorry to bother," one of them apologized. "Su esposa? Your...," he searched for the word, "... wife?"

"No, no, mi amiga." Myles stepped outside and moved a feet steps away, hoping they would follow. Behind his back, he heard a snicker and thought he heard the word "puta" which he knew meant "whore."

"Can you come too, missus?" They waited patiently for Kit to tie the belt of her robe and emerge onto the beach.

"What's this about?" Myles demanded.

"We are just asking the people here about the incident last night. It is our job." It seemed that only one of the men spoke English well enough to actually communicate. The other took a few steps back and watched from behind polarized sunglasses, which were completely unnecessary on such a cloudy day.

36

"The explosion? What did happen last night?" Myles asked them curiously.

"Did you or you see a white van that was parking here yesterday?" He ignored Myles's question.

"Yes, I saw it when I came back at sunset. It was down there." Myles pointed to the last campsite on the beach, which stood empty now. He realized that all the occupants of the other motorhomes and truck campers were gathered outside their vehicles, observing the interview taking place.

"I saw it too," Kit volunteered, moving closer to Myles.

"Bueno. Did you see a driver or passenger?"

Myles shook his head. "I didn't, but it was almost dark when I got here. How about you, Kit?"

"Umm, yes. When I took a walk that way in the afternoon, I did see a guy. I said hello to him." She waved one hand in a southerly direction, the other hand hovering protectively at the neckline of her robe. "Did you ask the people in those mobile trailers? They must have seen him."

"Si, gracias. We talk with them before you. They say they see you talk to him."

Kit shrugged. "I talk to everybody on this beach." Her Southern accent was more pronounced than usual, perhaps on purpose. "I'm a friendly bitch, ask anybody here." She laughed. "Especially when my boy is away, I visit with all of them."

"So you speak to this man then?"

"No, he was not very sociable. You know, not welcoming. Unfriendly. I just said, 'hey y'all' and finished my walk." She shaded her eyes and peered down the beach. "So he's gone now?"

The two uniformed men exchanged a glance. "Can you describe how he look, missus?"

"Kinda big. Muscle-y. He was wearing a blue hat and sunglasses. But he had this honking moustache." At their blank looks she demonstrated with her hands what she meant, drawing imaginary handlebars over her lip and twisting them. "Comprende?"

Myles was surprised to see the policia actually smile and nod. "Oh, si, si, mucho gracias." The atmosphere became more relaxed and he thought maybe the interview was over and then the English-speaking one turned to him. "Where were you yesterday?"

"Fishing." His one word answer did not seem to be satisfactory. "Would you like to see the bones from our dinner?" He started to move towards the camper.

"Not necessary. If we can just see your passports and tourist visas, we will leave you alone and be on our way."

"No problemo." Kit disappeared quickly into the camper to retrieve her documents but Myles continued to stand there, an empty smile frozen on his face. What was he going to do here...

When Kit came back out, he ducked inside and covertly watched the interaction between her and the Mexican cops. She was actually laughing with them — holding her passport up next to her face and mugging, already best of friends, the way she was with everyone. These guys were not writing anything down, they would not question his passport, but his visa had expired a few months earlier.

He saw her glance back in his direction and then she continued to chat with the two men in her appealing and flirtatious way. He knew she was stalling to give him time, even if she didn't know what the problem was. He dove into the small fridge and retrieved the Chockful o'Nuts can. His cash stash was getting extremely low.

When the policia retreated a few minutes later, Kit turned to stare at him in astonishment. "Did you actually bribe them?"

"That's how it works here. My paperwork is expired. Live and learn, sweetheart." He shoved his passport into the front waistband of his shorts and turned away, having a sudden and uncomfortable realization. Although they had shared every crevice and orifice in the most intimate way, he did not want her to know his personal identity info.

"So they never told us about the explosion, did they?" he mused. "Maybe Russ from Manitoba can enlighten me."

"Alberta," she called after him.

By that afternoon they all knew the sketchy details; the white van had driven out of the campground around midnight and blown up on the side of the road before it reached the highway, the cause not exactly clear, possibly a leaky gas can or propane tank. The big deal was that in its blackened remains was the charred body of an unidentified man. When the police had arrived in the morning, they discovered that the license plates had been stripped off the vehicle, which everyone agreed was suspicious and which led to lots of speculation. "Probably cartel-related," was the conclusion that seemed the most satisfying.

But all group conversation curtailed with the arrival of the rain. It poured from the sky like a torrential waterfall, transforming the dry arroyos into rushing streams, dripping through unseen cracks in the palapa roof, and soaking the edges of the mattress before they had time to shut the windows, skylights and vents. The tarp that connected the thatch-covered shelter to the camper buckled under the weight of the gushing water, creating a deep washout that divided their kingdom in two halves, making it necessary to wade through knee-deep run-off to get back and forth as they tried to protect their belongings from the fury of the storm.

Wet and miserable, they finally huddled inside the moist and stifling camper, the pounding of the rain on metal making it impossible to even converse. Diva crawled into a cupboard and curled up in a protective ball. As darkness fell and the storm showed no signs of abating, the pressure in the small space began to rise.

"Don't even think about smoking one of those in here!" Myles snapped as Kit drummed a cigarette against her knee. He had no sympathy for her when she came back inside drenched to the skin. "Next time take your clothes off before you go out. It's damp enough in here already."

For dinner they ate cold leftover rice and beans and drank warm beer. Myles played his fiddle and Kit tried to read a paperback. The solar lantern overhead threw an eerie light over her, reflecting off her blonde hair and casting her body into shadows.

"Looks like the weird horse collar you were wearing last night left a mark on your neck," he commented in a confrontational tone.

Immediately self-conscious, Kit dropped her book and put a hand to her throat. "Fuck."

"Why would you even wear something like that?" Using his bow, he poked at the offensive piece of jewelry which still sat on the counter where she had tossed it the previous night. "Looks kind of S and M to me."

In one fluid angry movement, she picked up the choker and threw it out the door into the rain. "There. Gone."

"You didn't have to..."

"Denny liked it. I never really did." Rummaging in her duffel which shared part of the bench with her, she drew out a long flowered silk scarf and wrapped it around her neck. "So you don't have to look at it."

"Whatever. You don't have to be so extreme." Shaking his head, he returned to playing again.

"Is that her?" Kit was staring intently at his fiddle case, which sat open at the foot of the bed.

"What?"

"This pretty chick with the luscious boobs. Is that the one who was your pregnant girlfriend? Oh, wait – and that's you with the impressive dreadlocks, isn't it?"

He'd forgotten that he'd taped the Polaroid photo onto the red velvet lining. Chloe wearing only a smile and a little white lace dress that barely covered what needed covering. His own clean-shaven face radiating an innocence that was long gone. Two happy kids in love, sharing a pitcher of red wine in the glow of a Greek island sunset. It was his private memory and he did not want Kit looking at it. With a flick of his foot, he kicked the case shut. "Yeah."

"Sorry. I know you don't want to talk about her. But...you. Why did you cut that hair?"

His expression faltered between grin and grimace. "It was time for the locks to go. I told you, I was a murderer on the run."

"You?" One of her long fingers traced a line from his temple to his chin and then came to rest on his lips. He closed his eyes and savored the sensation. "What did you ever kill besides time?"

CHAPTER THREE

West Jordan, Vermont
Mid-September 2017

"You did what?!" Tyler's voice thundered across the small kitchen causing both Athena and Artemis to burst into tears. Angrily he stormed towards the six-month-old twins, swooping them both out of their high chairs, bouncing them up and down to try to soothe them. "Sorry, girls. Just trying to protect you from your crazy mother's ideas."

"Your grandfather is a bigoted, narrow-minded old man," Chloe called over her shoulder, as she rinsed the dinner dishes. "Did you even read the story I wrote about George for the paper?"

"Of course I read it. There were so many letters to the editor that came into my email as a result, I couldn't ignore them, even in Greece. It was the most controversial article the Jordan Times has ever published." Tyler settled the babies into their canvas infant seats, gave them each a soft rattle to hold, and then straightened up, groaning with a hand on his lower back.

"And we sold the most copies ever. Besides exposing a decades-old injustice. The truth is, George is a great babysitter. He actually knows how to entertain the twins." Her pointedly sarcastic remark was clearly a dig at Tyler's awkwardness around small children, but he was too astounded by what she had just said to send a barb back.

"And how is it you know that our neighborhood registered sex offender is a great babysitter? Are you telling me he has already been here? In my house with my granddaughters?" Tyler couldn't remember the last time he'd been so worked up.

"Just sit down and listen to me for a minute before you have a heart attack or some other old person thing." Chloe spoke in a low, controlled tone that wouldn't disturb Athena and Artemis, whose eyes were still round and watchful. Tyler remained standing, glaring at her silently, waiting for the explanation to come. "While you were off, gallivanting around the Greek islands for months looking for your sleazebag wayward son–"

"Who also happens to be your quote husband unquote..."

"I was here, not only taking care of these babies, but running your business. When I interviewed George, I don't know... we just clicked." Chloe sat down cross-legged on the floor next to the girls. "He was a victim of circumstance in a different era. The man never molested a child in his life." She picked at a loose thread on the rug.

"How can you be so sure of that?" he demanded, running his fingers through his unruly gray curls in a nervous gesture. "You can't know everything about him."

"Well, I have some empathy. Technically I could have been arrested at one time for having sex with a minor." She looked up defiantly at him. "I was eighteen and Tucker was still sixteen. And you were an accessory to the crime because you condoned it and allowed us to live here with you."

"Don't throw that back in my face. We were all in agreement that it was the right thing to do at the time." It had only been a few years ago that Tyler had returned from the Caribbean vacation that had turned his world upside down when his son had run away with an "older" woman and subsequently fallen in love. He could never have pictured then what his life would have become now – surrogate father to his own irresponsible son's children, his daughter-in-law living in his house with the babies after leaving Tucker for his best friend, Myles. Both of whom had apparently disappeared off the face of the earth.

43

Mentally exhausted by the complicated relationships in his life, he sank down onto the couch and put an arm across his eyes. "I can't deal with this right now."

"Exactly. You can't ever deal with it. Which is why I hired George."

"Fine, fine, you win." Tyler picked up the television remote and clicked the power on.

"I can't believe how much TV you watch these days." Chloe abruptly got to her feet and moved towards the kitchen counter. "Does that mean you aren't covering the zoning board meeting tonight?"

"Shit." He stood up. "I've already missed the beginning of it. Guess I'm out of here."

As he headed for the door, she waved an envelope at him. "By the way – this came today." Now she was the one glowering. "Maybe there's something you'd like to share with ME?"

He looked at the return address; the results of the expensive DNA testing he'd had done to determine who the twins' father really was. He'd sent it off months ago, after secretly collecting all the necessary samples from the involved parties. Hair from a brush he'd found in Tucker's drawer and more that he'd stealthily clipped from Myles's head when he'd been residing with them after the birth, along with downy blonde wisps from the babies themselves. If Chloe had been honest with him in the first place he wouldn't have felt the need to know definitively if the girls were actually Mackenzies. But his obsessive curiosity could not be satisfied without knowing the answer.

"Maybe." He tucked the envelope into his notebook and walked out.

By the time he walked into the town hall, the meeting was almost finished. He managed to pull together a quick summary on the contentious ongoing argument about landfill expansion, which Chloe had been covering in his absence. When he got back into the car, he stared for a while at the long-awaited envelope, still unopened, unsure if his stressed mental state could handle the news, whichever way it went. He decided to head over to the West Jordan Inn and do the honors with Sarah. Either outcome affected them both.

It was quiet for a Monday night in the height of foliage season and Sarah was able to come out from behind the bar to give him a quick hug of greeting. "Welcome back, stranger. How long have you been home?"

"A few days. Still waking up at 4 am and I haven't been going out much."

"The trip was that good? Or that bad?" He knew that Sarah had already been filled in by Chloe on the results of his search for Tucker but assumed she wanted to hear it from his perspective.

"Tucker left Skyros a few months before I got there." He gratefully accepted the beer she put in front of him. "He was crewing on a yacht that was doing an Atlantic crossing, bound for the British Virgin Islands."

Sarah nodded. "I heard that. So why'd you stay over there so long? I figured you'd move on to the Caribbean."

When he didn't answer immediately, she looked up from the bill she was totaling. "Shit, you met someone, didn't you? Don't even try to deny it, it's written all over your suntanned face."

It felt good to laugh for probably the first time that day. He told her about sailing to Amorgos with Kristina from Croatia and how he'd shut himself off from the news of the world, his own life, and from his conflicted emotions, enjoying a month with a beautiful blonde and a few cases of Greek wine until finally his guilty conscience had caught up with him and he'd flown home only to find Chloe, at twenty years old, was running the newspaper better than he ever had. Which had plunged him into an even deeper depression.

"So are you moving to Croatia?"

"What? No, god, no. That was just a consensual fling. I'm done with real relationships; I'm clearly not cut out for them." He didn't want to discuss his failures with women,

45

especially not with Sarah, who'd been his most catastrophic long-term love affair, back in the days when her long braid had been black, not silver, and her last name had been Scupper, not Scupper-Adams. She'd left him for Hunter, a younger man with a laid-back outlook on life, and then for the next two decades had raised a mixed family of natural and adopted children, while Tyler continued to pick the wrong partners. One of whom had been Lucy, Tucker's mother. Tucker had been best friends with Myles, Sarah's oldest son, until a mishap in Istanbul involving the two of them and Chloe had split them apart.

Now, for different reasons, both boys were missing. Tyler hadn't seen Tucker for almost two years and had lost contact with him nearly a year earlier, when Chloe had abandoned him in Greece to his single-minded pursuit of learning to sail. Previous to that, the young couple had been backpacking around the world and had secretly gotten married in Thailand.

Myles had vanished for more sinister motives. Having indirectly caused the death of two women in New Hampshire, he had fled under the misimpression that he was wanted on two counts of manslaughter. The story was more complicated than that, stemming from a financial miscalculation on the part of his parents that led to the loss of a music school scholarship and some misdirected resentment on Myles's side that started him on a path of petty crime. But since his disappearance half a year earlier, no one had ever been able to contact him and let him know he was not actually a wanted criminal.

And then there was Chloe.

Which reminded him of the reason behind his visit to the inn. "This came in the mail today."

Sarah's eyes widened when she realized what he'd slapped down on the bar. "And?"

"Nothing. I haven't opened it yet. I thought I'd rather do it with you than Chloe. She doesn't even know I sent the samples in for the paternity testing, although I think she suspected when she saw the envelope."

"No doubt. Well – let's open it. Find out who the real grandparent is here." Sarah gave a quick glance around at the bar patrons to make sure they were all happy, and then came around so she could read over his shoulder.

As he ripped the letter open, Tyler's trembling fingers gave away all the anxiety he was trying to hide. Two pairs of eyes scanned the information as quickly as possible. Eventually Sarah let out a long breath and closed her eyes for a second.

"Well, congratulations, Gramps. I always knew they were from your side of the family – no one in my history ever had blonde curls like those two. Even if it was my son and not yours who attended the birth and acted like a father." Tyler wasn't sure if she was really relieved; he thought she might have secretly been wishing for some surrogate children to replace the one who had turned his back on his loving family and run away. "So what does this change?" she asked as she returned to the other side of the bar. "Wait – would you really have thrown her out if the paternity test had come back in favor of Myles?"

Tyler shrugged. "Guess that's one decision I don't have to make now." As his apprehension over this issue was finally resolved, he felt his body relax – until he remembered the other impetus for his tension. "But I might throw her out for other reasons. Has she told you about George, our new babysitter?"

"George?" she asked innocently, suppressing a grin.

"Damn. You know about it. What do you think?"

"Actually I've known George for years. He's a sweet old man. He and his partner, Robert, come in here occasionally. I always thought it was just a rumor that he was a registered sex offender; I had no idea you could look it up online and see all of them in any town. And you know, it's the kind of thing that once you see it, you can't unsee it." She shuddered a little. "There were a few other real creeps listed in our area. Poor George. I feel bad for him."

Tyler shook his head. "You are such a bleeding heart liberal. Would you want him to babysit for your daughters?"

47

Hunter and Sarah were very protective of the two Chinese orphans they had adopted the previous year, worried about adding any trauma to whatever the girls had gone through before arriving in the United States.

She was silent for a moment. "I don't know. That's different."

"How is it different?!" He snorted and drained his mug.

"Because we've never let anybody babysit them. Except Dylan. And only when one of us is nearby." She turned away to refill his glass.

"Well, no one has ever stayed with Athena and Artemis either. Except for Myles in the beginning." He regretted the words as soon as they were out of his mouth. "Sorry. I didn't mean to..."

"Look, have you ever even met George?" Sarah deftly dodged the topic of her oldest son. "I didn't think so. So you're just a judgmental, conservative old homophobe, Tyler Mackenzie." She turned her attention to a customer at the other end of the bar. "Can I get you anything else, sir?"

Her words stung, mostly because he was afraid she was right. He drank the rest of his beer silently while he watched her work and reviewed what he knew about George, looking him up in the Jordan Times online archives on his phone. According to Chloe's article, George had lived on a large communal farm in southern New Hampshire back in the early seventies with about thirty other adults. Some of them were couples, some were not, and there was a certain amount of partner swapping and "free love." But there were also ten children under the age of twelve. George was quoted as saying something along the lines of, "We didn't wear clothes in the summer. It was too much trouble and we weren't afraid of our nudity."

Another reason Chloe related well to him, Tyler mused. She was also a nudist at heart. The summer that she and Tucker had lived in the tree house behind his bungalow, they got dressed only when they had to leave their little home.

But the nudity had backfired on Sweet Dream Farm and in the summer of 1974, the authorities had arrived at the commune to find the only adult in residence was George, swimming in the pond with five children, three of them little girls. All of them were naked. George was arrested for indecent exposure and corrupting the morals of minors. When the other commune members heard, they put on clothes and went to the police station to pick up their naked kids; not one of them stood up in George's defense.

"There was no crime but they weren't my children. I was the lifeguard, making sure they didn't drown. I've never molested a child in my life, but I took the rap for the whole farm and I've had to register as a sex offender ever since." At the time of his arrest, George had not come out yet as gay, even to his farm "family." "In my experience, it turned out that most of the hippie men I encountered were actually extremely homophobic. So the truth is, I never even had sex with any adults during my days on the commune. But nobody believed me."

Tyler realized he was skeptical also and wondered where that put him on the scale of bigotry.

"Which island did you say that Tucker had sailed to?" Sarah's voice interrupted his thoughts.

"What – oh, the BVIs. You know, Tortola, Virgin Gorda..."

She looked at him uncomprehendingly and then said, "No, I've never been there. But you do know, don't you, that while you were blissed out in whatever idyllic Greek place it was, the Virgin Islands were pretty much devastated by Irma a few weeks ago?"

It was his turn to stare at her blankly. "Irma who?"

Sarah could not believe that he had totally missed the news about Hurricane Irma. He tried to explain to her that not only did he not have any internet or watch TV for a month, but weather stories from the Western Hemisphere did not make big headlines in Europe. He realized now that he had been hearing some updates on the hurricane that had hit the Caribbean, had read about the island of Barbuda being completely wiped out, but somehow had not picked up anything regarding the Virgin Islands. With his third beer, he devoured everything he could find on his phone, was horrified by the pictures of denuded trees and ravaged homes on St. John, and by the photos of hundreds of yachts piled up on top of each other in the bays off Tortola. There was no power, no water, no communications and no flights in or out of the damaged airports.

By the time he looked up, Sarah was shutting down the place and pouring her nightly shot of tequila. "So what do you think?" she asked.

Tyler took off his glasses, rubbing his tired eyes. "I have no idea. And did you know there is a second hurricane headed for that area right now? Maria." He shook his head in disbelief. "Those poor people."

"And that's where you think Tucker is?" She took a long sip of her drink. "At least you have some idea of the geographic location of your son. That's more than I can say. Myles could be anywhere in the world." Her shoulders sagged momentarily, and then the strength came back to her posture and she shot back the rest of the tequila.

"All I know is the name of the boat Tucker was crewing on and the first name of the woman who owns it. Melania."

"Despite her weariness, Sarah could not keep from laughing. "Like Mrs. Trump?"

"Yes, exactly. Perhaps even as wealthy." He emptied the cash in his pocket onto the bar. "Unlike me. I'm hoping I can track her yacht down through some online message boards or something similar. I haven't explored that yet; I will, but not tonight."

"George is coming over this morning," Chloe announced from the couch, where she was nursing both infants at once while scrolling through the newsfeed on her IPad. Tyler still marveled at how she managed the trickiness of this maneuver, but obviously she had grown pretty experienced at it. Her physique had already returned to its usual size and now she seemed to have trouble keeping her weight up with the round-the-clock breastfeeding of two babies. But unlike the postpartum weeks when she first came home from the hospital, these days she seemed continually wired, a high-strung archetype of efficiency. She was no longer a dark-eyed, dreadlocked waif floating from pursuit to pursuit; she was a lush young woman with short, unevenly cut brown hair that rarely got combed and did not get in her way. Every movement had a purpose, each minute had a goal, and there was rarely a breath of relaxation.

"So are you saying you want me to leave?" Tyler stirred milk into his coffee and decided that the headache he had was probably more of a hangover than jet lag.

"No, I'm saying you need to meet him and talk. Without me there. I'll be in the office, working." One of the twins had stopped sucking and had turned to look at Tyler with a bright smile. "Artemis wants you to pick her up."

Tyler was still not entirely comfortable with being in close proximity to Chloe's naked breasts which were exposed so much of the time and so much larger than they had been pre-pregnancy. And he was still not used to sharing his house with his daughter-in-law (he still had trouble thinking of her as married to his son) as well as the babies and all their paraphernalia. And he was definitely not used to the responsibility and non-stop demand that went with the whole parenting thing.

"Artemis would be happier if I drank some of this coffee first," he said bleakly as he came forward. "Wouldn't you, sweetie?"

"Actually I think Artemis would be happier if you changed her diaper." As Tyler lifted her sister off the couch, Athena also decided she was done nursing and reached her chubby hand out towards him. "Sorry, Athena, you will have to wait for Grampy Tyler's attention." Chloe stood up and without bothering to button her shirt, walked into the kitchen.

51

Was she going to act so casual when George was around too, he wondered, and would Tyler be the only one who felt awkward about it?

"Nice to meet you finally. I've read about your exploits on and off for years." George extended his hand to Tyler and sat down at the table.

"Really?" Tyler was embarrassed; George only appeared slightly familiar to him. He looked like any other older man from northern Vermont, wearing a plaid flannel shirt and blue jeans. His white hair was swept neatly back from a pleasant face that was still quite handsome and unlined, even for a man who had to be over seventy by now.

George laughed. "Don't feel bad. I keep a low profile. Thank you." He accepted the cup of coffee that Tyler offered him. "I moved here over forty years ago, as soon as I was released. I used to go to the West Jordan Inn when Woody still owned it."

"Wow, you do go back here a ways." He wondered how George could act so normal when he was such a stigmatized community member.

I remember when you nearly died in that hotel fire. And I actually saw you perform with the infamous Double Phoenix theater company." For a fleeting moment, George's eyebrows raised suggestively. "That was quite a scandal."

Tyler felt his cheeks actually flush at the memory. "More than anyone will ever know."

"They never found that guy's body in the lake, did they? I still get the creeps when I go out there fishing." George shuddered a little.

"So what did you do for a living in this neck of the woods?" Tyler was actually more than a little curious.

"Well, I've pretty much been a kept man for the last quarter of a century." He grinned and made a little over-the-top, movie star kind of gesture. "Robert had a good job teaching law at the state college, so I could stay home and keep house and care for our dogs. Before that – well, let's

52

just say I've done every minimum wage job around, from shoveling manure to cleaning the local auto repair shop."

Chloe appeared in the doorway to the office. "Sorry to interrupt – Tyler, have you really not contacted Lucy since you've been back? You know she must be desperate to find out about Tucker if she's actually taken to texting *me* regularly."

"I suppose you know who Lucy is also?" Tyler rolled his eyes and looked over at George.

"The dragon mother-in-law who lives in Burlington? The short one with that stunning headful of long white curls? She stopped by one afternoon while you were gone." George took a sip of coffee as Tyler gaped in amused disbelief. "She's a pistol, that one. But you can't blame her for worrying about her son."

Tyler's friendly co-parenting relationship with Tucker's mother had taken a serious nosedive when he had "lost" their son on the Caribbean camping vacation and then returned with Chloe, the wild older girlfriend who moved in with them and who had taken her son's attention away.

"Yeah, well, she could have gone to Greece herself if she wasn't so wrapped up in her entrepreneurial life. At one time she was a better investigative journalist than I was. Tell her to stop bugging you and I'll call her later." Tyler's attitude about Lucy's after-the-fact urgency was clear.

Pursing her lips, Chloe shut the door and left them alone again.

"So it seems like you've pretty much got the story on everything. By any chance, did Chloe mention who the twins' father really is?" Tyler asked casually, glancing back towards the office. If Chloe was eavesdropping, his comment would probably flush her back out again.

George looked at him quizzically. "Was there ever any question?"

"She never brought up the fact that it was Myles who she came back from Greece to be with and who lived with us after the twins were born?"

He could see George struggling with betraying Chloe's confidences in him. "Well...she told me about Myles. But it made her sad so we didn't talk about him much. Is..." George lowered his voice. "Is he the father?"

"Actually not. But I'm sure Chloe wishes he were."

"Does anyone know where he went? I feel so bad for Sarah and Hunter." His expression became so compassionate that Tyler decided that either George was a very good actor or a very good man.

Tyler shook his head. "But he's very resourceful, shall we say. I'm sure he's okay, wherever the hell he is." He stood up. "Well, I guess I ought to get that call to Lucy out of the way. So welcome to our incredibly dysfunctional family, George. Maybe you can bring some sanity to our household."

CHAPTER FOUR

Baja Sur, Mexico
October 2017

Less than twenty-four hours after the visit from the policia, Myles's already fraying world began to truly unravel.

After a day spent reconstructing the campsite from the destruction of the storm, he was late to his Saturday music gig. Almost immediately he had to plead Kit's case with the manager when she was busted for bringing her own full bottle of tequila into the bar. After slipping the owner a few pesos, Myles was carrying the liquor back out to the truck when someone stepped out of the shadows directly into his path.

"Coyote." The voice was unfamiliar but chilling enough to make him stop and pay attention. "I have a message for you from Ernesto."

Myles stopped breathing. Ernesto had never sent any communication this way before.

"He says to tell you the supply chain has been cut. Your services are no longer needed."

"What? What do you mean?" In the unlit street, he could not even see the face of the person speaking to him.

"It's over. Playa Bonita is off limits. He also asked me to warn you that the federales are looking for you and the others."

Although he'd known it was a possibility, Myles could not believe this was actually happening. "Wait! He owes me for the last run."

The answer was a harsh laugh fading into the distance that haunted him for the rest of the night. His playing suffered from the distraction of this disturbing turn of events and his tips decreased accordingly. "What's wrong with you?" Kit whispered to him during a break. "All of the sudden you look like a hundred miles of bad road."

But what he couldn't tell her about before he damned well couldn't tell her about now. Back home in bed, she became frustrated by his preoccupied unresponsiveness to her advances and finally fell asleep coiled around him, exhausted by her failed efforts to satisfy either of them. He lay awake, gazing unseeingly at the ceiling, absentmindedly fondling one of her small nipples into a reassuring hardness that he could stroke his thumb over while he thought about the future. When she moaned in her sleep and unconsciously writhed against him, he moved his hand down between her legs, expertly bringing her to a swift and intense climax, enjoying the brief rush of power it gave him to be able to have command over something when his life had suddenly spiraled out of his own control.

But whatever small primal comfort he had achieved in the night disappeared in the morning when he stepped outside to pee and saw two police cars pulling up to the end of the beach by the empty campsite where the white van had been. "Shit." He looked the other direction and was equally disturbed to discover that, overnight, four new RVs had moved in to the remaining empty spots.

"If you want to come, I'm hiking over the rocks on the north side to the next cove for the day," he told Kit. "I need to get away from all these people so I can think clearly."

It took her only a brief glance in the direction of the cops for her to make the decision to go with him.

"I'm bringing Diva," he announced, scooping the cat up under his arm. "What?" he demanded at her questioning look. "She always comes with me when I go up there. I put her in the backpack when I go over the cliffs."

Still agitated from the storm, the usually placid sea crashed over the craggy path making the rocks slippery and difficult to navigate, especially since neither of them had thought to put any footwear on. Myles had to grab Kit's arm a few times to steady her as the water swirled around her legs, but unsurprisingly, she was quite agile and maintained her balance.

Finally they stepped onto the pristine sand of their destination, a small, unspoiled crescent without another human being in sight. Myles released Diva onto the beach and she scampered a few dozen feet before stopping to wait for them to catch up. "Is this perfect or what?"

Kit breathed deeply before untying her sarong and spreading it out on the sand. "Totally." She flopped down, her arms and legs spread-eagled under the sun.

"And did I mention you don't need a swimsuit here?" he said, dropping his shorts and diving into the surf.

Satiated by a snack, another swim and then some uninhibited outdoor sex in the privacy of their peaceful surroundings, they smoked enough weed to sustain an ongoing shimmering buzz, before Myles finally broached the topic that had been on his mind.

"I'm thinking it's time to move." Scooping up a handful of sand, he sprinkled it slowly up and down her bare back.

"I'm not ready to go back to camp yet."

"No, I mean get out of Dodge. Like get on the road."

She sat up and stared at him. "What are you thinking? Where would we go?"

"I don't know. Some place less crowded." He dribbled more sand over her chest and it stuck to the sun-burned nipples that seemed to point accusingly at him.

She lay back and shaded her eyes with the brim of her straw hat. "You have somewhere in mind?"

"Sort of." He stretched out next to her and closed his eyes. "I'm out of money and I need to find some."

She giggled. "I know the feeling. It's hard being penniless."

"Hard? Like this?" He put her hand on his crotch.

"Again already? You teenagers."

"Hey, I'm almost twenty."

She stopped mid-stroke. "Wait, for real? That's only how old you are?"

Before he could reply, a muffled shout caused them to pull apart and look guiltily over their shoulders. Someone was staggering down the beach, waving a beer bottle and yelling. Kit gave a small shriek and sat up, hugging her knees to her chest. "Shit, it's Canadian Phil. What's he doing here? Where is my bikini?"

"Fuck him. We can be nude on this beach." Being stoned usually made him either paranoid or rebellious and right now he was feeling very defiant.

"Well, there are the outlaws, wearing only their God-given birthday suits!" Phil's slurred triumphant announcement sounded like he'd consumed way more than just the one beer he was waving. Kit tried to hide behind Myles as he staggered closer. "Pow!" He pointed the end of the bottle at them. "You are under arrest. Or at least you should be."

"I don't know what the fuck you are talking about, but leave us alone." Myles's voice was way more confident than he felt. "We're not bothering anybody."

"You're. Not. Bothering. Anybody." Phil emphatically panted each word, out of breath from his headlong journey across the treacherous cliffs and over the sand. "Right." Uninvited, he plopped down next to Myles. He reeked of alcohol, as though he'd been drinking since the night before, perhaps on a twenty-four hour bender. "Russ didn't think I should say anything, but I wanted to prove to him that my theory is correctomundo."

Beneath the brim of his Edmunton Oilers cap, Phil's bloodshot eyes tried to focus on Myles's face but kept traveling down his naked body. "It's hard for me to talk to you with your dick hangin' out like that, man." He said "out" like "oot" and normally Myles might have snickered a little at the Canadian pronunciation, but right now he was too annoyed.

"Then leave. No one invited you 'oot' here." Myles leaned back against Kit and spread his legs wider, hoping Phil would take the hint.

Phil turned his gaze to the neck of the bottle in his hand, apparently trying to see how much warm beer still swirled in the bottom of it. "Not until I get your confession."

Behind him, Myles could feel Kit squirming to pull her bikini bottom up over sandy legs. "Fine, I confess. Now go."

"No, hear me out. Both of you!" he shouted angrily as he saw Kit stand up and step away, bathing suit top in hand. She froze in place and turned slightly, the outline of one sand-encrusted nipple defining her feminine shape. "What's your name – Kitty. I saw you, Kitty."

Phil was red in the face now, seemingly worked up in so many ways, and Myles looked back at Kit questioningly. For a few seconds she was deathly still and then, assuming the same insolent attitude as Myles, she whirled around and gave Phil a full frontal view. "Well, see me now, Phil."

He squinted at the prepubescent appearance of her breasts. "Underwhelming," he remarked unkindly and turned his attention back to Myles. "I saw your 'foxy lady' here talking to the guy with the white van on Friday and she was saying more than just 'hey.'"

Over the sound of the surf, Myles could just barely hear Kit suck in her breath.

"So she's friendly. What's your problem with that?"

Phil gave a fake guffaw. "Guess your definition of friendly is a little looser than mine. But it doesn't matter now anyway, right? Because he's dead."

"So what are you saying?" Although his mind was racing, Myles rose slowly to his feet with an intimidating nonchalance that he didn't feel. A moving shape in the distance caught his eye. "Looks like someone's looking for you, Phil."

"Shit. Goddam it." Phil began to speak faster. "I told Russ it was better if I did this alone."

Kit tugged at Myles's arm. "Let's get out of here, Coy-boy," she murmured in a frightened voice. "We don't need a confrontation out here."

He shook her off. "No, first I want to know what he's trying to say. Are you accusing Kit of something? And what gives you the right?"

"I was an eyewitness to her behavior that afternoon. And I think you know what I am talking about."

"You saying she had something to do with him being dead?"

Phil stood up unsteadily and then with a surprisingly strong gesture, poked Myles in the chest. "No. I think you did."

Fueled by the stunned silence that followed his allegation, Phil began laughing almost maniacally. "Am I spot on, or what? Last night, they were all putting their money on it being her, but I said no, that's too obvious, look for the jealous boyfriend. He's the one burned that dude up."

"This is what you came out here to tell us? Some ridiculous story you made up because you were bored and drunk out of your totally whacked-out mind?" Myles was the one yelling now, waving his arms around. "You're bumming my high, man. Now get the hell out of here before I call the police myself and have you popped for harassment!"

As the sound of Myles's voice reached him across the empty expanse of the beach, Russ broke into a run, arriving at his friend's side before Myles had even finished speaking. Now his bellowing joined the fracas, as he tried to drag Phil away. "What the hell is wrong with you, you drunken fool!" He began pushing and pulling him back towards the rocks, but somehow Phil managed to slip from his grasp.

"Lemme be, I gotta take a leak." He unzipped his fly and shot an arc of piss over the sand, forcing Russ to back up several feet.

Russ looked at them apologetically. "Sorry, folks. As you can tell, he's way over his limit." Then a frown furrowed his brow as he took in the odd pair; Myles, buck naked and wild-looking, hovering over Kit who was on her knees and sobbing as she tied a sarong around her neck and stuffed belongings and gear into a bag.

"Kit, just wait a minute. Let them go back first. I have to find Diva." Myles grabbed his shorts and headed for the sagebrush at the edge of the beach.

"I think I need a nap now," Phil announced loudly and Russ raced to propel him forward before he sagged to the ground. "My work is done here. Book 'em, Danno. You'll be hearing from my lawyer!" He continued shouting crazy non-sequiturs as Russ guided him off, finally turning back and shouting, "Murderer!" the last word resonating like a clanging echo through Myles's head.

Myles watched them grimly, wondering how long it would take Russ to navigate Phil over the slippery cliffs. They would have to give the Canadians an extra few minutes so as not to overtake them on the way back.

"Why are you still crying – it's over. They're gone now." His nervous rush of adrenalin was quickly being replaced with irritability and a lack of understanding about what had just taken place.

Kit hiccupped a few times and then finally sat back and lit a cigarette, taking a few puffs to calm herself down before silently fixing a frightened and inquiring gaze on him.

They stared at each other for a long minute, each waiting for the other to speak first. "You know," Myles said at last. "I don't care if the guy fucked you in the ass in broad daylight while Phil watched but– "

Her gut reaction was so swift that he felt the sting across his cheek before he even realized she had lifted her hand to smack him. "I love you more than any man I've ever known! Why would you even *say* that?" she hissed dryly.

He touched the burning sensation on his face with detached wonder – no woman had ever hit him before. Then he continued, "...but does he really think I would kill that guy over it?"

"So what are you saying – that you don't care that much about me? That even if a man defiled me against my

61

will – which, by the way, didn't happen, – you wouldn't defend me?" She glared at him angrily.

"That is a totally twisted point of view." His stoned brain seemed to be drifting from the original thread of the argument. "What are we even fighting about?" he asked distractedly as he saw a flash of striped fur behind a rock. "Diva! Here, girl!" The cat ran forward and rubbed against his legs.

Kit's expression contorted through a wild range of emotions before she seemed to gain control of her facial muscles. Myles watched with distant fascination as she forced her features to soften and relax. She reached out for him and, taking his cue from her, he tried not to flinch as she touched his bare torso. "Don't you see, this is how it starts. Rumor mill, gossip, hearsay... before you know it, people are calling it truth. They're fabricating stories and telling and retelling until they believe it's real. I didn't do what they say I did, you didn't do what they want to believe you did, but they need answers so they made some up."

Her trembling fingers set off a tremor in his own body. He didn't need anybody taking a closer look at his past. Or his present. "We need to get out of here." He was whispering as though they were not alone on this deserted stretch of shoreline. "Tonight. After dark."

"Okay." She leaned her forehead against his chest. "You just tell me what to do."

Kit was a fast and efficient worker. Without any unnecessary chitchat, together they broke down his camp and packed up the equipment into and on top of the camper, which they hitched back onto the truck bed.

"You know they're watching us," she murmured to him, as they folded up the blue tarp.

Myles glanced down the beach to where the Canadians had gathered with a few of their neighbors, enjoying sunset cocktails in a circle of folding canvas chairs. He moved to the back of the palapa, out of their line of sight and motioned for Kit to follow. "Go down there and talk to them.

Mention that we're thinking about heading south. To join Dean and Diane near Loreto. And then going on to the beaches beyond La Paz. Charm them. The way you know how."

She folded herself around him and kissed him deeply, rubbing against him in that feline way of hers that she knew aroused his animalistic hormones. "I'm all over it, lover boy."

For a moment he felt himself falling into the magnetic abyss of the sexual attraction between them before remembering the emergency of the situation was more important than the urgency in his groin. His tongue was still intertwined with hers as he pushed her away. "Go do it. Now."

Myles watched her adjust her dress over her hips and run her fingers through her hair like a comb. Then, throwing back her shoulders, she strolled boldly down the beach. He leaned his head back against the rough siding of the building and closed his eyes, suddenly exhausted. What had he gotten himself into here... there was no turning back now. As soon as darkness fell, they were driving out of here. Headed north.

He fell into the hammock, the only thing to sit on that had not been packed yet, and ran through the plan he had formed loosely over the course of the last few hours. They would not go too far, roll into Santispac in the wee hours and head for the deserted beach around the corner, all the way at the end of the road. Spend a day or two there, he'd scope it out, "pick up" some cash and supplies, and then they would head up to Gonzaga Bay. That was as futuristic as he could be right now.

The sound of an approaching motorcycle broke into his thoughts – it must be Diego, the "manager" of the beach palapas. Even after six months, Myles had no idea what Diego's relationship to the property actually was; all he knew was that Diego collected the money from people who camped at this deserted site with no services. The rate was definitely adjustable depending on how long you stayed and how much money it looked like you had.

He heard the unmuffled engine cut off and then the crunch of feet on gravel. "Coyote. Buenos noches," he heard a low voice call.

"Que pasa, Diego." A shadow, short and stocky, emerged a few feet away out of the growing darkness.

"I come to tell you – some people in the village and some policia, they are asking about a gringo."

"The one in the fire?"

"No, a young gringo working in Baja for some months now."

Myles tried to sound casual. "Huh. Okay. What are they saying?"

Diego's shoulders moved up and down in a shrug. "A lot of talk. But I think they will be looking for this man soon." He turned away. "I don't want no trouble here."

"Diego, no problema. Mira." Myles flicked on his flashlight and swept the beam around the empty palapa and then trained it on the camper.

The man gave a big sigh and then extended his hand. "Gracias, amigo. And good luck to you."

Huddled beneath a blanket and uncomfortably wrapped around each other, Myles and Kit stayed in the hammock until nearly midnight, when they were sure that everyone else on the beach had gone to bed. Then, unhooking the last piece of "furniture," they climbed quietly in the cab of the truck. Myles drove slowly down the dirt road, trying to make as little noise as possible until they were out of earshot and onto the highway.

The night was clear and quiet and because it was Sunday, even the long-haul truck drivers were few and far between. After a short while, Kit dozed off, leaving Myles alone with his thoughts and fears.

Somehow, in just a few short days, his peaceful existence on the Sea of Cortez had imploded. He felt desperate and confused and could not picture what the future held beyond the next twelve hours. He'd always known the whole illegal immigrant operation with Ernesto was incredibly risky but it had made him feel good, that he was actually helping people, even saving lives, by aiding them in their struggle to get to a place where they could have better lifestyles and livelihoods. But now he was afraid that he might not even be able to save himself.

He cut the lights as the truck rolled into the Santispac campground; the moonlight would have to be enough to guide him. He was stunned by how many more RVs had arrived since the last time he'd been here and breathed easier when he had passed them all by and was heading out to the end of the point. As the road became rougher, Kit was jolted awake and stared blankly around before reaching out to touch Myles's arm.

"Where are we?"

"Almost home, babe."

It was past noon when he finally awoke. His senses were momentarily assaulted – the brilliant light of mid-day, the sound of Kit's off-key singing, the overwhelming smell of coffee brewing a few feet away. The pressure of Diva's paws against his chest.

"Ready for some breakfast, sleepyhead?"

Sitting in the camper doorway, eating scrambled eggs with salsa and tortillas and gazing out at the sea while a woman brushed the tangles out of his hair, his life felt like it should be perfect. Only it wasn't.

Later in the day, they took a stroll down to the campground to look around, hand-in-hand, trying to appear like just another American couple on vacation.

"Act like we're on our honeymoon," he said as, from behind his white plastic sunglasses, he assessed which of the motorhomes was the most expensive and which of the tourists looked carelessly wealthy.

"That's easy." Kit stopped walking and pulled him towards her, slipping her hands into the back of his board shorts. "Kiss me like you can't get enough of me."

As he made a public display of their prolonged lip-lock, Myles watched a tiny blonde woman emerge from a 42 foot Winnebago carrying two white Chihuahuas wearing rhinestone collars, one under each arm. "Ronnie, we're out of Grey Goose again!" she shouted at a man who was reclining in a state-of-the-art cantilevered lounge chair. "And the antenna stopped working!"

"This is making me hot. Maybe we should go out in the water and have sex," Kit suggested. "Isn't that what newlyweds do?"

"Not here." The last thing he wanted to do was call attention to himself by doing something outrageous and memorable. "Let's keep moving."

At the far end of the beach there was what looked like a private cove that he hadn't noticed before. Four large RVs formed a semi-circle like a wagon train around an elaborate outdoor party set-up. Although it seemed impossible to imagine, next to this collection of outsized vehicles, a seaplane was parked on a small stretch of flat sand.

"Okay, I've seen enough," he announced. "Let's go back."

"I'm tired. This is like a friggin' hike," Kit complained as they trudged back. "Can't we just stop and take a honeymoon swim?"

But the tide was out and the water was so shallow that they had to kneel down to even get their whole bodies wet. As Kit splashed around happily, Myles kept his eyes trained on the shore, observing a trio of girls trying to set up a tent in an improbable spot on a very public part of the beach. At first their ineptitude was humorous but after a while, it was embarrassing and he waded out of the surf to offer his help.

"We're bicycling this part of Baja," one of them explained. Petite, tanned and wiry, her short curly hair was held back from her damp face by a wide stretch headband. "And we've only had to sleep in the tent once and we're just not very good at this."

"Especially not the ones of us who are cranky and tired," snapped a muscular brunette with a pair of thighs that looked strong enough to crush rocks.

"A swim will fix you right up," Myles assured them, not wanting to get into the middle of a travelers' squabble.

"I'd give anything for a hot shower right now," said the third one, holding the waistband of her tight spandex biking shorts away from the sweaty skin of her belly. Myles was more mesmerized by the size of the breasts contained by the elaborate crisscrossed infrastructure of her sports bra top and could not help but compare her shape to Kit's. He didn't know much about cup sizes but these were definitely a double something.

But what he did know something about was the value of sports gear and clothing, at least enough to recognize that their bicycles, camping equipment and clothing were top tier quality and probably added up to more than a Mexican family earned in a year. Realizing that his unchecked resentment for opulent excess was quickly rising to the surface, he busied himself with replacing the poles into the correct loops so that the tent could pop right up. "So you three felt safe enough riding alone down here?"

"There's three of us – we're not alone." The irritable one with the rock-crushing thunder thighs sat down heavily in the sand.

"Somebody give Arlene a granola bar or something. Her blood sugar must be low. So far everyone's been very friendly and helpful." The little one handed him the last of the flexible tent poles. "We're gonna stay here for a couple of nights and rest up. We're having a bonfire party this evening, if you want to join us."

Although he thought he sensed an ulterior message, Myles realized the main impetus for the invitation was that the girls were probably sick of each other's company already. "Thanks, I might actually be out this way tonight. Maybe I'll stop by."

"Is that your girlfriend?" She was watching Kit wade out of the shallow water towards them.

He hesitated, not knowing what to call Kit. "She's...uh...yeah, my partner for now. We're traveling together." Uncomfortable with the topic, he walked away and waved over his shoulder. "Maybe see you later."

"Thanks for your help!"

"They're cute," Kit remarked as she fell in step with him.

"Rich girls."

"Unlike me, you mean?"

"Unlike both of us." He forced a laugh. "Look, there's a little cantina here. Let's stop in and get some fish tacos."

"And hopefully they've got some cigarettes too. I'm almost out."

By the time they got back to the camper, it was almost sunset and Kit proclaimed herself completely exhausted. They sat in the canvas camp chairs (Dean and Diane had contributed the second one) and shared the one order of food they had been able to afford at the expensive beach shack restaurant that catered to wealthy mobile home owners.

"Come to bed with me," she urged him.

"I'm not tired. I'm going to take a walk."

"I'll make it worth your while." She rubbed against him in a feline gesture. "You know you're like catnip to this kitty. Being with you makes me all crazy and lazy."

"Okay. For a little bit." He knew agreeing was the best way to keep his evening plans moving along.

Physically, he stayed with her for the next few hours, but mentally, most of the time he was very far away. Eventually Kit rested against him, still clinging to his body like a limpet on a rock. "Oh, god, you make me feel so good, so respected. I never realized how Denny made me feel about myself until I met you. I love you, Coy-boy."

It disturbed him how often she declared her devotion for him. This was not a forever thing. He couldn't even picture a week from now, let alone a lifetime.

As her breathing became even and relaxed, he finally felt her grip loosen. He slipped out of the bunk and landed lightly on the floor. At the foot of the bed, Diva stretched and nuzzled her face against his shoulder, in a motion that reminded him of Kit's seductive manner.

"You stay here," he whispered to the cat, kissing the top of her little head. "I'm locking you in."

Pulling on his black hoodie, he picked up his empty backpack, locked the cat door and then went out into the night.

As he approached the campground he could see a bonfire blazing on the beach and hear music playing loudly through a portable speaker. He stayed up on the road, making a wide swath around the tent, not wanting the girls to see him. Maybe he would stop and be social on the way back. He moved on in the direction of the private cove where he'd seen the seaplane parked.

There were still one or two lights on in the cluster of RVs. Using his empty backpack as a cushion, he sat down on a rock to wait.

"Hey, stranger. What are you doing wandering around so late?" The voice that called out to him sounded more than a little intoxicated, but he recognized it as belonging to the petite bicyclist. She was sitting on a piece of driftwood waving an empty bottle of tequila in the air at him. The well-endowed friend was stretched out on a ground cloth next to her, propped up on one elbow but looking nearly asleep; the other girl was not with them, probably already asleep inside.

"Insomnia," Myles answered. "Looks like you guys have been doing some partying."

"Yeah, without you though." She stuck the bottle upside down in the sand. "You know where we can get some weed?"

"I probably do. You want to smoke some right now?" He pulled the pipe out of his front pocket.

69

She sat up straighter, weaving a little from side to side. "Si, si, senor. And I will buy some from you too."

His business sense told him that it was best to conduct that transaction before she got any higher. And at least he would have some more cash to put fuel in the gas tank tomorrow.

"Can I give you American money?" she giggled. "I can't remember where I put my pesos."

She got up and unzipped the tent flap. "Come in while I get it. And don't worry about waking Arlene. She sleeps like a log."

He knew it was a bad move, but he couldn't resist seeing her stash of American cash. Crawling inside, he sat on the edge of a silky down sleeping bag, while she rummaged in a saddle bag for her money belt. The tent smelled unfamiliarly feminine, like flowery soaps and scented body lotions.

"I never wear this thing," she laughed as she opened the rectangular pouch and pulled out a wad of hundred dollar bills. "Now how much can you sell me?"

He was tempted to go home and come back with his entire stash, but knew that he might not be able to score again for a while. Instead of answering, he offered her the pipe and flicked on his lighter. "Why don't you try some and see what you think?"

Later, when he tried to remember the progression of events that led him to be still staggering down the beach a few hours before dawn, it was all very hazy and he could only recall the sensations not the details. He wanted to say she had attacked him, but there had been no battle. He had more than surrendered, he'd been a willing participant, and when the second one had joined them, he had been surprised but not enough to protest. He didn't even know their names and he didn't care. It had been as carnal and pleasurable and present as life could get, with two female bodies that were as different as humanly possible.

And when he finally extracted himself from the sleeping heap, there was the money belt, the exposed pile of cash taunting him. Who needed that much to live on in Mexico? He could feed himself and several local families along the way for weeks with half the amount she had with her. Removing several bills, he left the remainder of his pot on top of it before stealthily unzipping the tent and slipping out into the night.

As he finally approached the camper, alone on its remote beach, he was overcome by guilt and then immediately angry with himself for feeling so. What responsibility did he have to Kit, he had no obligation to her. She was a freakin' rescue animal who had attached herself to him. He felt even guiltier for thinking of her like that. They had a relationship, however dysfunctional it was.

Besides, infidelity was the least of the crimes he had committed in the last few hours. Opening the door to the truck cab, he slipped the heavy backpack off his shoulders and hid it behind the passenger seat.

There was no point in going to sleep now. At first light they were driving out of here.

CHAPTER FIVE

Gonzaga Bay, Baja Nord, Mexico
November 2017

"Baby, I think we have a problem."

Myles rolled over in the hammock and opened his eyes. Kit was standing over him, blocking the sun so that he could see her face. She let the heavy plastic bags of grocery fall to the sand at her feet and helped herself to the water bottle that was tucked between his legs.

"What's the problem? No tomatoes left at the store?"

"No, a little tougher than that. The policia were there in the parking lot when I came out. Showing a photo around."

Myles felt the relaxation ebbing out of his bones. "Of who?"

"A gringo. Named Lyle Evans. That your real name, hon?" She pulled her dress over her head and then wiped her face with it. Even her bikini seemed drenched with sweat.

"Uh…no. Shit." He swung his feet to the ground.

"Really? Cause that's whose name is on the truck registration, isn't it?" She pulled a cold can of Corona out of one of the bags and popped the tab. Taking a swig, she peered at him questioningly before handing the beer to him.

"What, you been poking around in the glove box?"

"Don't get pissy with me. This is real."

"I told you, Lyle is my uncle who died and left me his money and his truck. But yeah, I use his identity here most of the time. Shit," he said again. "What the fuck is it now… Did they say what the charge was?"

"It was printed in Spanish. I couldn't understand it. Except for the "Wanted" part." She opened the door to the camper. "I have to put these groceries away. Oh my god, the fucking flies. They're everywhere."

Myles was suddenly sweating violently and not from the heat. He drank half of the beer so quickly that it made him feel like puking. Life in Gonzaga Bay had been pretty chill so far. A white crescent of sand lined with unoccupied vacation homes – he'd counted just three that actually had residents in the last couple of weeks. He only liberated stuff from the ones that clearly belonged to the obscenely wealthy, but there were enough of those here. Even though the handful of palapas at the campground end were nowhere near as nice as the ones at Playa Los Cocos, it was fine.

But where would they go to now... when it came down to it, Baja was a small community in a spacious place.

Kit reappeared with a lit cigarette in hand, and leaned against a pole, studying him thoughtfully. Her skin tone had darkened so much that Myles had decided that she was probably part Native American; he would never be that tan. He was always impressed by the high contrast of the tiny white triangles over her breasts and crotch when she took off her bathing suit, which was pretty much all she ever wore anymore. She wasn't quite as emaciated as she had been at first, and the few extra pounds softened her angles just a little bit. Now she was no longer skeletal, just plain rail thin.

"So I've got an idea. It's kind of radical, but I think we can pull it off."

He looked at her with dubious interest. "And what would that be?"

"Don't condescend to me, lover boy. Your choices are pretty limited. Hear me out." Tossing her cigarette into the sand, she came towards him and with a swift movement held his hair back from his face. Squinting her eyes, she looked back and forth from him to something she had pulled from the back waistband of her bikini bottom.

"What's that – a passport?" he asked curiously.

73

"Yessuh. You, my pretty man, are about to become Denny Laveaux."

"What! That's absurd." He tried to pull away from her but she tightened her grasp on his scalp.

"Don't underestimate my powers as a make-up artist. This is going to be a piece of cake." She laughed hoarsely. "I just don't know if I'll want to fuck you anymore afterwards."

Myles couldn't believe it when she showed him Denny's passport photo. "The dude actually has a face tattoo? Who does that? I mean, that's permanent."

"Well, yours won't be. I actually thought it was cool when I met him. He talked me into getting this, which sometimes now I'm sorry about." Kit touched the dramatic tattoo on her arm and shoulder. Then she started making a list of what she needed. "I can do it with a fine tip marker."

"What is it?"

"It's a fleur-de-lis. It's like the symbol of New Orleans. I've heard you can dye your hair black with strong tea or coffee. We'll try that. And the moustache...hmmm..." She ran her finger over his upper lip. "We might be able to make one out of pubic hair..."

"Ha, you are so whacked."

"And we're going to need glasses. They'll make all the difference. Black ones similar to what he is wearing. And finding them, my light-handed dear, is going to be your job." She brought one of his palms to her mouth and licked it with the tip of her tongue.

The whole thing was crazy – but the adrenalin rush he got from the idea of it was also an incredible turn-on. She was surprised when he pulled her towards him and kissed her. "This is so bad it's good," he said, untying the strings of her bathing suit top.

Over the next few days, Kit worked on him so much that Myles thought it was probably the closest he would ever get to having a "spa experience." He sat motionless for hours while she sketched on his face, eventually lying with

74

his head in her lap, cheek resting against her thigh while she painstakingly colored in the fake tattoo.

"This is one of the most boring things I've ever done," he complained, running a finger up the inside of her thigh towards her crotch.

"Don't do that," she snapped at him. "If I make a mistake it'll be really hard to undo and you'll have to keep still even longer."

When she worked the coffee and tea mixture into his hair, she made him lie face down in the sun while it dried and then insisted that he keep the concoction in all day so it would set. At least he didn't have to hang around while she created the moustache, cursing as she stitched and glued coarse hairs onto a tiny strip of fabric. Instead he shoved his stiff, sticky hair up under a cap and walked towards the one hotel located at the far end of the beach, surreptitiously looking at the handful of tourists for someone that might have eyeglasses or sunglasses that were anything like Denny's.

The closest he found among the limited choices belonged to an overweight German named Klaus who was vacationing with his young Thai wife. She sported a couple of Kit's silver spoon bracelets, the inflated price of which had paid today's grocery bill. Kit had also sold her a purse made out of an old Mexican license plate, a creation of bent metal hanging from a chain strap that she claimed was a "must-have accessory" for any woman with an eye for artistic fashion trends.

"You can make good arts-and-crafty shit out of license plates. I've seen handbags, wallets, placemats, even laptop cases. I'm always collecting them," she had explained, like it was a normal thing to do, like packing suntan lotion or an umbrella. And when Klaus's wife's purchase proved her point, Myles realized he shouldn't question Kit's eccentric aesthetic sensibilities.

Myles spent the next few hours drinking red wine with them and pretending to be interested in Klaus's idea for selling online porn novels that were based on his own adventures. By the third bottle, Klaus was sufficiently wasted, having consumed most of the alcohol he'd bought for the three of them. When Klaus went to the restroom, it was a piece of cake for Myles to slip his black reading glasses into a pocket. Dodging an invitation to join the couple for dinner with a promise to return for lunch accompanied by Kit the next day, he made his way back up the beach.

"The only problem is I can't see a fucking thing with them on," he commented as he proudly modeled them for her.

"Wear them down on your nose like this so you can see over them. Only push them up when you need to." She pulled the cap off to inspect his hair. "You better jump in the sea and wash this gunk off before it gets any darker outside. Otherwise it will be all over our pillows."

Because his hair was still wet when they went to bed, they couldn't really see the color of it until morning. The nights were much cooler now, almost downright cold, and they huddled close under the comforter, waiting for the sun to warm the outdoor air. "Doesn't this camper have heat? What's that vent there?"

"If we had electricity it would. But we don't. Maybe we need to put on more body fat."

"Somehow I don't think that's gonna happen soon. You know, I've been thinkin'..."

"That sounds dangerous. You're gonna have to stop that." He slid a hand between her legs.

""I've been thinkin' us gypsies should head up to New Orleans. A place where we could actually *earn* a living. You could make money just standing on the street playing music there, baby." She grabbed his wandering fingers and held them against her for a moment.

"You mean cross the border? You forget. I'm an outlaw."

"But Denny Laveaux isn't."

He had to admit, the disguise was almost genius. He felt weird as fuck when he looked in the side-view mirrors on the truck because he didn't recognize his own face at all. But that was a good thing, he reminded himself. Maybe he could actually get out of Mexico, start over again. The more Kit talked to him about New Orleans, the better it seemed.

"Okay, I say let's do this thing. I wanna go with y'all to Naw'lins." His mock drawl sounded almost legit and Kit threw her wiry arms around his neck. He gave her a little butt smack and said, "Y'all better start packin', baby."

An hour later, as he was rolling up the hammock, Kit sidled up to him, her hands behind her back. "I've got a surprise for you. Something I've been hiding all this time."

"What's that, baby?" He was getting his Denny Laveaux on now, working the accent. "What y'all hidin' from me?"

She held out a pair of Louisiana license plates, one in each hand and gave that throaty laugh of hers. "These."

He stared dumbfounded. "You just happen to be carrying those around in your luggage?"

"Don't give me that look. You've seen how I can turn this old junk into money."

"You callin' me junk, baby?" As always, he got a funny rush of affinity for her when she came up with these unexpected bursts of creativity. He hadn't even thought about the license plate thing. If he was going with this Denny Laveaux disguise, he definitely needed a Denny Laveaux mobile.

"You know how I feel about your junk, baby." Tucking the plates under one arm, she reached out and gave his crotch a squeeze. "But I thought it might make the camouflage complete if a Cajun couple were driving a Cajun camper."

He felt suddenly exhilarated at the thought of the caper they were about to embark on. He dropped the hammock on the ground and grabbed the hem of her skirt. "You got time for a quickie, baby? Because Denny feels one comin' on."

The involuntary shudder she gave before hiking up her dress made him realize how tricky this impersonation was going to be for the two of them. "Come into my boudoir, honey. I think there's still some empty space on the bed."

He was jubilant after passing the test at the first roadblock. The khaki-clad federales looked into the cab and then let them through with a little bit of macho Mexican banter. Myles knew where most of the checkpoints were. He let Kit do the driving through the next one, partly because he couldn't see the road very well when he put Klaus's reading glasses on but also because she was so professional at flirting her way through any situation.

He was getting used to the disguise. After putting his now darkened hair into a ponytail at the base of his neck and adding a cheap baseball cap from the local grocery store, Kit had made him wear her sleeveless tie-dyed tank top. "Perfect. There's a reason this style is called a 'wife-beater,'" she murmured, more to herself than him.

"It's too tight," he whined. "Don't make me."

Her answer was to rip out the seams beneath the armholes.

They ditched the moustache, deciding that it looked too fake and using the marker she darkened up Myles's own facial hair. But it was the tattoo that did the trick. "Your eye gets fixated by it. You can't stop staring at it and you don't really notice anything else. You're way skinnier than Denny but if anybody asks, we'll just say you've been suffering from a bad case of Montezuma's Revenge."

And every time he looked in a mirror, he saw she was right. The rest of his distinguishing features just sort of fell away, a backdrop to the mesmerizing concept of a cheek tattoo.

At nightfall they camped on a beach somewhere south of San Felipe, planning out what details they had to take care of before crossing the border the next day.

"I need to find a vet in Mexicali and make sure Diva's papers are all in order. No unforeseen problems, you know?" Myles sucked in a big hit off of a joint and passed it to Kit. "Also we need to smoke all this up tonight. Why waste it, right?"

"What'd you say, 'get wasted'?" She held up the bag. "Because we definitely are going to be if we do all of this."

"Kinda too bad, because I am already so naturally high just from how well we pulled it all off today. But, what the hell. Let's party."

"Maybe we should invite the neighbors." Holding the smoke in her lungs, Kit nodded towards another camper parked at the far end of the stretch of beach where they had pulled off.

But the thought of having to keep up his charade all evening in front of other people was too much for Myles. "I say let's just have a little one-on-one tonight, baby." Damn, he couldn't stop talking like his new self now. "Remind me to check the oil in the morning; I didn't like the sound the engine was making this afternoon."

"How about you check my oil in a few minutes? I'm thinking you'll like the sound my engine makes with a little lubrication." She made a little whirring purr.

"Oooh, I do like the sound of that. What do you say to a full night of sex and smoke?"

Even though it was pretty much what they did every night, it seemed more festive and way more intense. In the back of his mind he knew it was kind of fucked up to get more blasted than ever before, but this time he felt like he succeeded. He was still high when they woke up late in the morning and decided he was too stoned to deal with a border crossing without excessive paranoia. Kit sat cross-legged on the mattress next to him, naked except for numerous necklaces and bracelets, her eyelids heavy, her lips puffy and tender from overuse.

"How you feeling, baby?" he asked.

"Exhausted. In a good way." She looked at him in a way that was more loving than lustful. "You're the best thing that's ever happened to me, Coy-boy."

He closed his eyes, unwilling to go to that place with her. "It's fun making you happy," he murmured as he felt her easily responding again to his knowing touch and, then he fell once more down the rabbit hole of carnal sensory overload enhanced by marijuana.

Myles had forgotten all about checking the oil until the truck started making some really weird noises about thirty miles north of San Felipe. "Oh, fuck. I totally spaced out the oil thing. You better pull over at the next turn off."

The dipstick came out of the engine block almost dry, just a little bit of blackened fluid on the bottom. "We're going to have to go back. There's nothing north of here for almost 100 miles." The good mood he'd been in for a few days became suddenly dark.

"Maybe you better drive." Kit stamped out her cigarette and climbed into the passenger seat.

The engine took a staggering amount of oil. Myles could not believe he'd let it get so low.

"You probably need a new head gasket," Kit commented, but kept the rest of her thoughts to herself after he glared at her. He hated that there was a good chance that she knew more about engines that he did.

"Let's go. We've got some time to make up." He slammed the driver's door.

"Why, do we have to be somewhere?"

He gunned the gas pedal and they took off, leaving a cloud of black smoke in their wake.

By the time they arrived at the vet's office, the engine was almost out of oil again. "Oh, my god, we are so fucked." Angrily he picked up the cat carrier with Diva inside, and kicked the door of the truck shut. He didn't want to think about Plan B. Plan A was difficult enough to pull off.

An hour later he was back on the street with the appropriate paperwork to take a pet across the border. Kit was leaning against the side of the camper, lighting another cigarette from the end of the lit one already in her mouth. "Everything good, love?" she asked chirpily.

"Just perfect." Sliding Diva back onto the seat, he pulled out his detailed map of Baja. "We're only ten miles from the border. Let's get this over with. We'll deal with the engine on the other side."

"I put in the rest of the oil we had. Hopefully it will get us there."

As they started off again, Myles asked, "How do you know so much about engines?" He just needed to make conversation, to distract himself from the fear of the upcoming unknown.

"My daddy was an auto mechanic. My brothers and me, we had to help out. We weren't allowed not to." She drummed her fingers nervously on the door handle.

He glanced at her appreciatively. "You never fail to surprise me, Miss Kitty."

"I'll be glad when we get this crossing over with." She fidgeted in her seat and then began digging around in her purse. "If we beeline it, we should be able to make Louisiana in three days probably."

Myles felt a buzzing in his head – he could not even imagine three hours from now, let alone three days.

"Here," she said, handing him a passport. "Better familiarize yourself with birth places and all."

He flicked the dark blue booklet open. "Evangeline Katherine Beauchaine? Your real name is Evangeline?"

"Hey! No one ever called me that. Give that to me." She swiped it back, trading him for the other passport. "Worry about yourself, Dennis Francoise Laveaux."

He peeked down at the information, thankful for the gift of a nearly photographic memory. Denny had been born in the unpronounceable town of Plaquemine, Louisiana. "Shit, how the hell do you say the name of this place?"

"Plack-meen. It's near Lafayette if they ask you."

Road signs began warning them of the upcoming immigration station, and before long they had joined a line of cars waiting to cross over into California. As if on cue, the oil light began flashing wildly on the dashboard, the heat indicator needle moved into the red zone, and the motor began to make ugly grinding noises.

"No, no, no..." he moaned. Ninety second later, steam began rising out from under the hood as the truck from New Hampshire with Louisiana plates died right there in the middle of the lane marked "US Citizens."

It took six people from other vehicles to help them roll it off to the side of the road. "What do you think we should do?" Kit asked nervously. In the distance they could see a pair of uniformed officers walking towards them.

In the intensity of the moment, the sweat began to run down his face threatening to destroy the magic marker tattoo. "I guess we need to get towed to a garage. You do the talking."

And so it was that, twenty-four hours later, they found themselves again headed for immigration and customs, but this time they were walking, very slowly. Kit went first, rolling her suitcase with Diva's carrier riding on top. Myles followed, carrying a duffel in one hand, his fiddle in the other, a heavy pack on his back and a wad of pesos in his pocket from the sale of the camper. Way below book value, but outlaws and gypsies couldn't afford to be choosy.

"Ready, Denny?" Kit murmured over her shoulder.

Myles moved forward, eager to get over the border and on to whatever his new future would be.

CHAPTER SIX

West Jordan, Vermont
November 2017

"Chloe! The water's almost boiled away. Are you making pasta or not?"

With great effort Chloe tore her gaze away from her phone and blinked a few times at Tyler. "What?"

"Dinner. Cooking. You. Remember?"

"Oh, sorry." With a nimble leap, she was on her feet and at the stove, phone tucked into the back pocket of her jeans." I just got a very weird email. Can I use the car tomorrow? I need to drive to Burlington."

"Ohhhkayyy..." Tyler looked at her quizzically but could see that she was not about to share any more information. "Can I ask..."

"You'll know soon enough. Let's just say it's a surprise." She turned her back to him so he could not see the combination of disorientation and joy on her face.

Not until the twins were asleep and she could finally have some alone time, did she dare to look again at the message she had received. The sender's address was "colin@weshipyourpets.com" and she would have ignored it as junk mail except for the subject line that had made her catch her breath.

"Your Cat DIVA Arriving Saturday at BTV."

Was it really possible? Or was this a secret code of some sort from Myles? She had not heard a word from him in more than six months, the last contact being a cryptic Facebook message from Diva Gatotita with a profile photo of a striped cat in a sombrero, which let her know that he was alive and safe somewhere called Bahia de Concepcion in Baja Sur, Mexico. How many times had she looked it up online, trying to imagine where he was and what it might be like. She'd finally had to let him go, immersing herself in the babies and the newspaper work with a feverish obsessiveness that did not allow time for thinking or feeling much about her personal needs. Love was reserved for the babies; romance did not exist.

"Your Cat DIVA Arriving Saturday at BTV." She whispered the words aloud and then reread the body of the email. It said that Diva was being flown in by special courier on Delta Airlines, from Phoenix via Detroit and arriving in Burlington at 5:07pm. The shipment had been paid for by someone named Dennis Laveaux. The cat would be handed over only to Chloe who had to produce a valid ID and proof of receiving this email. She'd had to respond to the email immediately to confirm she had received the message and would be able to accept the pet at the airport at the appointed time.

What did it mean – had Myles actually paid for a person to fly with Diva to Vermont from Arizona? Did it mean he was back in the states or had he somehow negotiated this deal from rural Mexico? And who the hell was Dennis Laveaux? And why...

She could not come up with any answers, and the exhaustion of the day was closing in on her fast. As she quietly undressed, another astounding thought occurred to her – what if this crazy email was actually a hidden message that Myles himself was coming home? And if so, what then?

With one hand resting on her heart, she allowed herself to imagine for just a few seconds what it might be like to have him here with her again. And then she thanked the gods of the universe that Tyler had not found Tucker in Greece.

It would take almost two hours to drive to the airport, which meant she would have to leave the twins for at least five hours. They were eating baby food now, but she would still have to pump breast milk for a separation of that length. Tyler could feed them supper and get them ready for bed – the image of him doing the necessary multitasking to manage the evening routine of the two babies made Chloe laugh aloud.

She quickly sobered up as she stared into her closet, wondering what to wear. It had been so long since she had paid any attention to her personal appearance. Her winter wardrobe was pitiful – the previous year she had been pregnant and wearing stolen oversized sweaters and sweatpants. Now that she was thin again, all she had were a couple pairs of worn-out jeans and some faded shirts with spit-up stains on the shoulders.

What did it matter – she was picking up a cat, not going on a date. Still... Eventually she put together a passable outfit with a stretchy black miniskirt, a pair of funky patterned leggings and a long-sleeve thermal shirt with a low V-neckline. A black beret helped hide the disaster of her hair and a little eye makeup made her feel slightly better about herself.

It took all of her organizational skills to actually get out the door and into the car by three o'clock. The girls were still napping, breast milk was in two bottles in the fridge and George was on call if Tyler freaked out. Chloe breathed deeply several times as she typed her destination into her phone's GPS and then backed the Subaru out of the driveway. Two hours alone in the car was like a mini-vacation; she barely knew what to do with herself when all she had to do was one thing – drive.

She spent most of the ride thinking about the months she had spent living secretly in a cabin in the woods with Myles and the cat who had adopted him. In the rosiness of her recollection, there was only warmth and love and coziness. She had been pregnant with Tucker's child (at the time she hadn't known there were two), and Myles had welcomed her after Tucker had blatantly rejected the idea of parenthood and left her alone in a Greek island village for weeks at a time while he went out to sea. Their relationship had already been on the downslide for the better part of a vagabonding year by then; the ill-conceived idea of getting married on a beach in Thailand had done nothing to repair the damage.

Through Burma, India and Turkey, Chloe had tried to convince herself that things with Tucker would sort themselves out, but then Myles had met them in Istanbul... The fateful three-way that occurred had been her fault, and the trajectory of events afterwards had obviously changed all their lives. And yet, here she was, back in Vermont, a place she was not even from, living with Tucker's father in a small bungalow that seemed smaller each day...

By the time she turned off at the South Williston exit, Chloe had concluded one important thing. She needed to find a place of her own for herself and the twins. Not tomorrow, but soon.

She'd only flown through the Burlington airport a few times and she'd forgotten how tiny it was. Nothing like Changi in Singapore or Charles DeGaulle in Paris. There were only fifteen gates but not even really, because there was no Gate 9 or 10. On a late Saturday afternoon in November it was virtually empty. If she waited at the bottom of the escalator in the baggage claim area, there would be no chance of missing a guy with a cat carrier.

She leaned against a wall and nervously checked her phone. There was only a message from Tyler –*"How much mashed bananas are they supposed to eat? Athena wants more."* Could the man figure nothing out on his own?

A garbled announcement came over the loudspeaker about the arrival of the Delta flight from Detroit and she straightened up, watching the stream of travelers that began to funnel into the moving staircase from the second floor. Most of them had backpacks or small rolling suitcases. And then finally she saw him – a clean-cut twenty-something in a lime green windbreaker carrying a square black case with mesh sides. It was nobody she'd ever seen before in her life.

She moved forward to meet him at the bottom of the escalator. There was nothing shady about this character; his carrot-colored hair and freckled nose shouted

86

wholesomeness as loud as his big silver watch with its steel stretch band.

"Hey." She blocked his path. "I'm Chloe."

"Oh, hey. Mike from We Ship Your Pets." He put down the carrier and extended his hand. "Your cat was a good traveler. I guess she's been a lot of places, from what I hear. If I can see some ID, we'll be all set."

Chloe handed him her passport. "And I'd like to see my cat to make sure she is really my cat." Although she could see some striped fur pressed up against the screening, she had a momentary panic attack that it might not really be Diva.

"Of course." He squinted at her passport photo. "Wow, your hair is really different."

"Yeah, so is my life. Can I see her now?"

"Sure. We had to tranquilize her for the flight so she may be a bit out of it." Mike unzipped a corner of the carrier and Diva's golden eyes gazed up at Chloe in trepidation.

"Oh, Diva!" She fell to her knees and stroked the cat's forehead, afraid to pick her up in a strange public place.

"Okay, so you just need to sign here to prove that you took delivery." Looking up, Chloe saw he was holding out an iPad. Zipping the container closed, she straightened up and quickly scanned the e-document he handed her. There was that name again, Dennis Laveaux.

"So I need to ask you about the person who sent me the cat." She looked up at Mike, who had apparently already moved on mentally and was scrolling through the messages on his phone. "Did you actually meet him?"

"Me? Well, uh, no." He flushed." I'm just the courier. The company did his paperwork. This is just a weekend gig for me; I'm flying back tonight."

"Really?" Her interest piqued, Chloe was momentarily impressed. "Do you make good money?"

"Good enough for just sitting on a plane. And I can get my studying done." He glanced up at the flight board. "I've got to get something to eat. My flight home leaves in an hour."

"So how much does it cost – for a person to ship a cat? I mean, it must be like a few thousand dollars, right?"

"I'm not allowed to discuss that, and really I have no clue. But yeah, it costs a lot. Either your friend Dennis is rolling in it, or this cat must be really important to the two of you. Now if you can just sign… I've really got to go."

Overcome with emotions, Chloe scrawled a signature on the screen with her finger and handed the iPad back to him. "You'll email me that, won't you?"

"Sure. Good luck and thanks for doing business with us." He shoved the iPad into his messenger bag and turned to leave.

"Mike, wait. Is – is there any way I can get a message to Dennis? I – I want to thank him."

He shrugged as he walked backwards towards the concourse. "You can try calling the office on Monday. The number is on the receipt."

Once they were safely locked inside the car, Chloe lifted Diva out of the carrier and buried her face in the cat's soft coat. Whether out of fear or happiness, the trembling animal began to purr in her arms. Was she just imagining it, or could she actually smell Myles in Diva's fur?

An aching in her breasts reminded her of the two hour drive ahead and what awaited her at home. As she buckled her seat belt, the cat leaped out of her lap and began exploring the car. Chloe started to worry about her being loose in the vehicle and then remembered that Diva had traveled five thousand miles by truck and another three thousand by plane. Myles used to carry her with him in his backpack around New Hampshire and Vermont. The journey back to West Jordan would be nothing for this vagabond feline.

Tyler was on the couch listlessly watching another rerun of CSI, which seemed to be his status quo most nights, and his speechless astonishment at Diva's appearance was almost enough gratification in itself for

Chloe. However, when he quickly recovered and began peppering her with questions, she knew she would not be able to live with him unless she told him the truth and enlisted his assistance.

A few seconds after she showed him the email, he was on his laptop looking up the name Dennis Laveaux. "Well, there aren't very many matches in the U.S. and none in Arizona. The only one I can find is in Louisiana. You're sure the cat was shipped from Phoenix?"

"Well, that's where Mike got on the plane with her. And I had to show ID on my end; hard to imagine whoever dropped Diva off didn't have to also. Maybe just paying is good enough." Chloe thought if she sat in the armchair pumping breast milk Tyler might go away, but he was too engrossed in his online search to even pay attention.

"If you look at the bottom of this receipt they sent you it says 'paid in cash.' So that leads me to believe that Dennis did this deal in person. Hold on – let me look him up on Facebook."

Chloe swore under her breath – why hadn't she thought of that.

"Here's one in Belgium. Looks like he races cars...Here's another in Montreal... Oh, here's the one in New Orleans. Kind of a scary-looking dude." Tyler turned the screen so Chloe could catch a glimpse of his profile photo. His most identifying features were black glasses, a handlebar mustache and some weird kind of tattoo on his cheek.

"Huh. Doesn't exactly look like the kind of guy who would pay for a cat to fly to Vermont, does he?" There were few things they agreed on, but this seemed to be one of them.

Discouraged, Tyler shut his computer and stood up. "Well, let's see what happens when you call their office. Meanwhile, I think it's only fair we let the rest of the 'family' know. I'll call Sarah and Hunter tomorrow."

"Oh, good." The last thing Chloe wanted was to be interrogated by Myles's parents. She was the only one who knew that he had ended up in Mexico and whether he was still there or not, she did not intend to betray that trust.

The Sunday afternoon gathering filled the cramped living room and spilled over into the kitchen. Separating herself from the crowd, Chloe opened the French doors to the deck and let the cool air from outdoors spill over her. Mai Li and Jin, the adopted Chinese sisters, each held one of the twins on their laps and were vying for who was the best at playing with an eight-month-old baby. Dylan, Myles's sixteen-year-old brother, was glued to his Iphone and expertly ignored the noise around him. He only resembled Myles in the vaguest physical way, darker in complexion and more introverted, much geekier. Myles had been more like Hunter, easygoing, prone to laughter, and stoned a lot; they'd enjoyed a unique father/son relationship in his teens. The Scupper-Adams clan had been a close-knit family unit, along with Kashi, the adopted older sister who was half-Nigerian and who no longer lived at home but with her boyfriend in Burlington. But both Hunter and Sarah had aged a lot in the last year since Myles had shut them out; even Hunter who was only in his early forties had a few gray hairs now in his thick, honey brown ponytail.

Diva, who was the reason for this informal party, had finally shown herself at the bedroom door, and Mai Li had almost thrown Artemis onto the floor in her excitement to reacquaint herself with her older brother's cat, who scurried with appropriate fear back to the safety of Chloe's closet. Discovering that all the toys had been hastily tossed into that room, the older girls had carried the babies off to play there, leaving the others alone.

Tyler had printed out the emails that Chloe received, and now the adults studied them, trying to decipher any secret messages that might be there. "Who the fuck is this Dennis Laveaux?" Hunter asked the ubiquitous question to which they all wanted the answer.

"We're working on that." Tyler glanced up at Chloe, who leaned against the edge of the open door and stared out into the yard. Contrary to what Tyler might be guessing about her thoughts, she was actually wondering how she could ask Hunter if he had any pot he could leave with them; she hadn't gotten high in months.

"So do we think this means Myles is okay or not okay?" Sarah's worried expression took the question one step further, to the place that none of them even wanted to consider.

"Whoever was on the shipping end knew to send the cat to Chloe. And was willing to pay some ridiculous amount of money to do it."

"That doesn't sound like Myles. He was always very careful with his..." Sarah's voice trailed off as Tyler rolled his eyes at her.

"He's not the same boy who left your home," he said quietly.

"That person has to still be inside somewhere."

"He really loves Diva."

They all turned to look at Chloe who hadn't spoken up until now.

"I mean, he took her with him when he... left. I think he would do anything to make sure she was safe, no matter what it cost." Everybody was quiet now, even the babies.

"So are you suggesting he's not safe?" Sarah radiated tension.

"Relax, Sarah. Maybe he just can't have a pet where he lives or something." To Chloe's joy, Hunter pulled out a pipe and a bag of weed. Tyler stood up abruptly, muttering something under his breath, and Chloe moved into his seat. Dylan looked up for a second to see what was going on and then with a glazed look of disinterest went back to whatever it was he was doing on his screen. He was certainly way different than Myles that way, she thought. She guessed that Hunter had not been able to entice Dylan into working with him during the pot-trimming season after Myles had left home.

"Well, we'll let you know tomorrow if we find anything out when we call the We Ship Your Pets people," Tyler said taking up Chloe's position at the door, obviously not wanting to partake either.

"How's George working out?" Sarah asked.

"George is great," he answered tersely. "Clean as a whistle. We couldn't manage without him."

Chloe tried not to laugh. "They get along excellently. George is here pretty much every day." She lowered her voice to a conspiratorial whisper. "They even do the New York Times crossword together."

Everyone's eyes widened and Hunter grinned and snorted as he held smoke in his lungs, which caused them all to crack up.

Mai Li seemed to materialize at Hunter's shoulder. "Daddy, can we go soon? We're tired of the babies."

Oh, how Chloe sometimes wished she could say that same thing.

In the morning Chloe called We Ship Your Pets and was disappointed to be sent directly to voice mail. "Maybe they're not open yet because of the time zone difference in Arizona."

Tyler clicked a few keys on his laptop. "That area code is from Chicago. Not that that really means anything these days."

George arrived and took charge of Artemis and Athena, bundling them up for a walk in the stroller; Chloe and Tyler moved into the office to work on final layout and proofing of the current week's newspaper. She was pleased when Diva strolled in and hopped onto her lap; stroking the cat's fur helped calm her nerves a little.

It was a long forty-five minutes before Chloe's phone finally rang. It took more than a little sweet talk to convince the guy on the other end, who was indeed in Lincoln Park, that she needed to speak to the Phoenix office. It was another forty-five minutes before the next call came in.

"Yeah, is this Chloe Mackenzie? This is Colin at We–"

"Hey, Colin. I'm hoping you can help me out." At Tyler's frantic gesturing, she turned on the speaker phone. "My cat arrived here safe and sound but there was no message with her. Did Dennis give you any instructions or notes for me?"

"Uh, Dennis... sorry I'm trying to remember this one here... that the guy with the rad ink on his face?"

Chloe swallowed, unsure of how to play this, but Tyler nodded vigorously. "Yes, although he didn't have the tattoo last time I saw him. What color was his hair?"

"I don't know...dark? He was wearing a hat. Nice guy. Not too old. Sure had a hard time parting with that cat." There was some coughing on the other end of the line and then Colin said, "Nah, I remember now him sayin' he didn't need to send nuthin'. You would know what to do."

"Well, I'd like to send him a thank you card. Do you have a mailing address for him?"

"You know it's illegal for us to give this stuff out, lady, but let me see what I can do for you." There was some shuffling on the other end. "Oh, yeah, right. He was the dude who paid me in hundred dollar bills. No address but I got a phone number. You could send him a nice text thank you."

Tyler's eyes widened and he shoved a pencil at her. Chloe couldn't end the call fast enough after that, and with trembling fingers she dialed the number. They listened as an unfamiliar voice with a southern twang came on to deliver a recorded message. "Hey, this is Denny. You can leave a message but don't expect me to answer until next spring because Miss Kitty and me are off to ole Meh-hee-ko. Hasta luego, amigos!"

"What the fuck..." muttered Tyler, sinking back into his desk chair. "What the frickin' fuck..."

CHAPTER SEVEN

New Orleans, Louisiana
January 2018

As he waited on the corner of Ramparts and Esplanade for the next 88 bus headed up St. Claude, Myles's fingers closed around the small wad of bills in his jacket pocket. Not much of a take for an evening's work, but he reminded himself that it was a Tuesday in the middle of winter. The weekend would be better and hopefully he would get to sit in again at the Spotted Cat. A couple of shady-looking characters stumbled out of a bar on the next block, and he clutched his fiddle case a little tighter. The bus only ran about once an hour this time of night, but he didn't want to spend any of his hard-earned cash on an Uber, even if it would probably get him home in a mere ten minutes.

An older woman wearing a food safety hairnet joined him at the curb, and then two adolescent males; beneath their winter jackets, uniforms of white shirts and black pants indicated they had also just gotten off their shifts. More people at the stop were a good sign, maybe they knew something he didn't about the sketchy bus schedule to the Ninth Ward. Soon a white girl with blue hair and a pierced lower lip also appeared, accompanied by a black man in shredded leather pants whose hair was an equally improbable shade of green.

"Isn't the fucking bus supposed to be here by now?" the girl complained, swiping hard at the screen of her phone as she shivered uncontrollably.

Myles couldn't sympathize with these southerners who wore down jackets when it was fifty degrees outside. In Vermont they'd put on flip-flops and shorts when it got this warm in the spring.

"Here it comes," murmured the woman and there was a mutual sense of relief among the disparate group of strangers as the bus approached, the lighted sign above the windshield announcing it as the "88 St. Claude." It was the only way to get across the canal to the Lower Ninth unless you had a car or took a cab. Myles got off the bus just before it crossed the bridge. He headed into the Bywater, a somewhat less dangerous neighborhood than the Ninth, but Myles had been warned that nowhere in New Orleans was actually safe after dark. So far he'd had no trouble, and there had been some very late nights.

Although the path was unlit and the ground uneven, Myles moved effortlessly along the side of the house to the back door and let himself in without making a sound, barely aware of the black cat that streaked past him and out into the darkness. He slipped silently through the clutter of the shared kitchen and turned the knob of the room he and Kit slept in.

The room was illuminated by the warm yellow glow of a candle that burned in a glass on the nightstand, and for a brief second it almost felt homey, the way the cabin in Windfall used to feel when he returned after a gig at the bar. He stood motionless, listening to Kit's even breathing. If he got into bed carefully, maybe she wouldn't wake up. He didn't feel like having sex tonight. In fact he hadn't felt much like it since they'd moved in here with Darcy and Wendell.

It had been the least offensive living arrangement of all the affordable shared houses they'd looked into, passing up cheaper situations with little to no privacy. "I do not want to sleep on a fold-out couch in someone's shotgun apartment just to save a hundred dollars a month," Kit had hissed insistently when they'd viewed the tiny bungalow on Burgundy, although Myles had thought it would be cool as hell to be able to say they lived on the block between Piety and Desire. Mainly they just really needed to get out of where they were, sleeping on an air mattress in the corner of a kitchen in the home of some "friends" of Kit, who she really only knew as mutual vendors on Jackson Square and who, each night, mainlined most of what they made on their phony crystal ball readings during the day. Myles had never known what needle tracks looked like before. Now he could pick out junkies on the bus by what their bare arms and legs looked like.

So they'd ended up on Poland Avenue in a house with Darcy and Wendell, the self-proclaimed "Voodoo Buddhists," and their pair of black cats. Myles had been skeeved out at first by the idea of living with witches and warlocks, even if they did have photos of the Dalai Lama and Tibetan prayer flags amidst their Wiccan amulets and stick-pin dolls. Darcy was a seamstress who worked on an antique sewing machine in a corner of the kitchen; Wendell taught world religions at a community college. Strange as their ways were to him, the couple turned out to be super-nice people, even though they wore exclusively black clothing and kept the skeleton head of an alligator in the freezer.

Kit and Myles had a big furnished room to themselves and their own bathroom; they also had use of the kitchen and an awesome back porch. It was way more space than they'd shared in the camper. Plus there were the cats.

It had been two months and he was still grieving his separation from Diva, but he knew it had been for the best. After making it through customs with little to no difficulty, it became instantly clear that it was going to be extremely hard to hitchhike with a cat and even harder to find places to stay. Without a credit card, they couldn't rent a car. Myles had thought about buying them airline tickets to New Orleans, but then wondered how he would keep Diva safe in a city until they found somewhere to live.

"I wish I could send her home to Vermont," he commented glumly as they stood at the side of the highway, heading east from Yuma.

Once they had arrived back in the States, Kit's cell service worked fine and she spent hours staring at the small screen and viewing Facebook posts. Now she handed the phone to him. "Look at this." It was the website for We Ship Your Pets.

He asked Kit to wait for him outside when he met with Colin in the modern co-working office space in downtown Phoenix. At first her face froze into a grim expression and then he could see it forcibly soften into sympathy. "Sure, baby. I'll have a smoke and then meet you in that Starbucks on the corner." Affectionately, she pushed a lock of hair out of his eyes and stroked his cheek before kneeling down on the sidewalk next to the cat carrier. "Bye, Diva."

He didn't know what he'd been expecting, that maybe he would actually hand the cat over right then and there, but it didn't work that way. Colin took his money, checked flights and courier schedules, and then told him that, after they had confirmed the delivery date and time with the courier and recipient, he could bring Diva back. If it all went well, she would fly to Vermont in two days.

He barely had enough cash left to rent a fleabag motel room for the next two nights. It was an impossibly tense forty-eight hours; Kit painted and decorated her nails, shaved her legs, made a few bracelets, and watched endless hours of TV, when she was not outside smoking. Myles lay morosely on the shabby quilted spread that covered the double bed and stroked Diva's fur, trying to talk himself out of this scheme. But at the same time, he felt good that he was reconnecting himself to Chloe, and when he thought of Diva living happily in Vermont with her and the twins, it warmed him in a way he had forgotten. He liked the idea of all his girls safely in one place together again.

"So Coy-boy, you know, when we get there, you're going to have to stop being Denny." Kit said this in an offhand way as she studied the nail on her left big toe.

"Thank god. Are we gonna be able to get this thing off my face? I'm sick of it."

"And you're not the one who has to look at it every day. Rubbing alcohol should take it off. I'm thinking we could say you're Denny's distant cousin. Coyote Laveaux. Then you can still use his ID if you need to – like your real name could be Dennis too."

He lifted his head off the pile of flat foam pillows and squinted at her suspiciously. "You've been thinking this out pretty carefully, haven't you?"

"Well, people know Denny there. And they know I left town with him. So we've gotta get our story straight." She thumped another cigarette out of the pack on the nightstand, flicked off the TV remote and headed for the door.

"What happens when he comes back?"

"Let's not worry about that until it happens," she called over her shoulder.

"Fine with me!" But after she disappeared, he remained frowning. She was being too casual about this. The last thing he ever wanted to do was run into the real Denny Laveaux, however inevitable it was.

After dropping Diva off, it only took them two days to hitchhike to New Orleans. Myles had not expected to be instantly enchanted by the character and charm of the city, and to his cynical surprise, just as Kit had promised, he was blown away by the music scene. For the first time in his life, he was intimidated by all the talent around him, and knew he was going to have to work hard to prove himself in the Crescent City.

But within a few days, he was busking on the street in Jackson Square for tourists, bringing home a fiddle case full of cash and coins each night after spending the afternoons and evenings playing original tunes for rapt listeners. He was amazed that anybody could claim a piece of the sidewalk for free. As long as you didn't infringe on the space of one of the longtime regulars, you could stake out an area and do your thing.

He started by staying close to Kit, who set up a small table for card readings and an easel with a black velvet display board of silver and beaded jewelry. When she wasn't doing a Tarot interpretation, she would use her time to make necklaces and bracelets. But as he learned how to draw a crowd, eventually Myles moved slightly away to his own zone, where spectators could congregate more easily. Sometimes another musician joined him – there was a Russian backpacker who played a mean mandolin and a guitar player from Baltimore with a short attention span. On rainy days he relocated to Royal Street where there was a good balcony overhead that he could stand under and where the sympathy dollars for a fiddler trying to make a living in the rain were sometimes better than a regular day on the Square.

And then there was Frenchmen Street, musical heaven for those who love New Orleans blues, classic ragtime or washboard music. Between bands one afternoon, he sat down at the old upright piano in the bar at the Spotted Cat and tentatively tested the keys with a couple of his original rag compositions. He hadn't touched a piano since the fiasco in Windfall last spring. But after a few really nerve-wracking flashbacks, he was able to shut down that part of his mind and the room disappeared behind him as he became one with the instrument again in that familiar all-encompassing way. The next band asked him to sit in on a few numbers and from then on he became a regular highlight at certain times of the week, depending on which group was playing.

"Sorry we can't cut you in," one white-haired cocoa-skinned trumpet player explained. "But by the time we divide up the take, we barely make a living here."

Myles totally understood and didn't complain. He was grateful for the hours he spent at the Spotted Cat, as those occasions were some of the first times in months that he'd felt complete and normal, learning, sharing and appreciating from experienced masters in his field. It was almost like going to the music school he never got to attend. Well, almost.

He actually felt proud and happy when Washboard Chaz asked him, "What's your name, boy? I want to be able to tell the audience who our guest piano player is." He hadn't felt emotions like that in longer than he could recall.

"Coyote."

"That's it? Just one name – like Bono?" The old man shook his head. "Guess I'm not one to be talkin'. Maybe we should add something to it, like Ragtime Coyote. You think on it."

His identity had not been as much of a challenge as he thought it was going to be. Mostly because he didn't need one. He had no employer, no car and a cash economy. The Voo-Boos (as he and Kit secretly called them) were happy to receive their rent under the table and he had come up against no other needs for a real name so far. Unlike living in a small town, he could disappear into the daily crush of city dwellers and gawking tourists in Mardi Gras beads and he felt safe in an entirely different way than he had on the seacoast of Baja.

Looming over him, however, was always the threat of Denny Laveaux's return and what would happen if/when this manic depressive man grew tired of Mexico, got a new passport and returned home. A few menacing-looking characters had approached Kit on the square asking about him, eyebrows raising when Kit told them she'd left Denny, lips smirking when she introduced the new "love of her life."

"Y'all is gonna be in big trouble, girl," laughed one lunk with tattoos on his shaven head and thick gold hoops in each ear.

"Fuck off, Chet." She dismissed his comment with a wave of her wrist and the jangle of multiple bracelets. "We weren't married."

"Yeah, but he ain't the kind to stand for bein' dumped for some airy-fairy boy toy musician."

"You don't know nothing about it. Now get out of here or I'll tell the cops you're harassing me." Kit glared at him, out of eyes that were darkly defined by thick black liner and a row of tiny green sequins and then patted Myles reassuringly on the butt in a way that he totally resented but ignored for the time being. "Don't you be worrying, baby. There's not gonna be any problems."

Mostly he felt very secure in his new persona, only shaken badly once when he realized he was being filmed by a TV crew as he fiddled for a crowd in Jackson Square. He had quickly turned away from the cameras, trying not to draw attention to the fact that he did not crave his fifteen seconds of fame like the other street performers did. It seemed like there was always some team making a movie or staging a magazine shoot in downtown New Orleans, and after that mishap he stayed more alert, rapidly learning how to spot the paid extras by their makeup and costumes and avoiding the theatrical crowd scenes that frequently occurred.

One ironic consequence of his new working class/street person lifestyle was that the more he hung out with the disadvantaged folks in underprivileged neighborhoods, his resentment towards the entitled and affluent seemed to fade away. He no longer felt the urge to help himself and others to the excessive possessions of the rich. He had also been discouraged by the difference between the security systems of urban and rural mansions; during a lengthy hike around the Garden District he had barely found a single home that was even remotely accessible. They were all intensely fenced and well-protected from intruders or trespassers. And unlike the poorer communities, nobody sat outside on the front porch on nice days, chatting with family members or friends. Myles realized he was actually way more comfortable in his "bad" neighborhood with its distinctive New Orleans architecture and its eclectic array of characters of all ages.

Still, beneath his Mexican tan, he was a white boy from the mountains of Vermont and he was aware that he was probably not as street smart as he should be. He had grown up in a town where people left their keys in their cars and only closed up their houses at night in the summertime so that black bears wouldn't be tempted to rip through the screen doors and come in. He continued to look passersby in the eye and forgot to keep an eye on the money in the open fiddle case at his feet.

Now, as he slid stealthily under the covers, he was ready to indulge the guilty obsession that kept him alive. Reaching carefully across Kit's sleeping form, he used two fingers to pick up the iPad on her nightstand. With a few silent finger strokes, he logged out of her Facebook account and into the one he had set up nearly nine months ago for Diva Gatotita. At that time he had only used it once, to send Chloe a cryptic message letting her know he was safe in Mexico. But for the last several weeks he had used it to lurk online and stalk her posts and photos.

His vision had blurred the first time he saw a current picture of Athena and Artemis, now gorgeous, chubby-cheeked wonders with giant eyes and two-teeth smiles. But his body temperature had risen by ten degrees when Chloe had posted a selfie with the babies. There she was, slimmer even than when he'd first met her, but looking more lush and lovely and alive than in his now distorted memories. Checking her page became a nightly ritual that he couldn't always perform but seriously tried to honor. Once she even shared a photo of Diva posing with Artemis. Although he knew it wasn't true, he liked to think that she knew he was watching her from afar and that she was posting for him personally.

Tonight he was trying to wrap his mind around Chloe's post from earlier in the day. The caption read, "A and A with their loving caretaker, George," accompanied by a photo of the twins with an old white-haired man who looked oddly familiar. He was lost in thought, trying to figure out where he knew the face from, when he suddenly realized that Kit was resting her chin on his shoulder.

"Whatcha lookin' at, babe?" she croaked in a groggy voice.

His shaking fingers couldn't close the page fast enough. "Nothing. Just surfing the net trying to relax after a long night." When he reached over to put the iPad back in its place, she wrapped her arms around him and pulled him down on top of her.

"I know a great way to release some of that tension." Her hand was already between his legs.

And as he always did in his nightly routine, he closed his eyes and visualized Chloe.

It was probably a week or so later that Myles began to realize that Kit was acting a little weirder than her usual eccentric self. In Mexico when it had just been the two of them, twenty-four/seven in the middle of nowhere, they had developed a way of being that was just short of codependent. Now that he was out several nights a week, they were spending less and less time together. And, as they really didn't have that much in common, starting to drift apart.

Myles had no problem with putting some space between them. He had never really wanted to get involved with her this way in the first place, it had just sort of happened. But Kit became desperate to keep their connection strong in a way that began to feel increasingly smothering. She left casseroles in the oven for him to eat when he came home, even waking up a few times to eat with him at three am, when the last thing he felt like doing was having a meal. She tried to entice him with romantic rendezvouses in bed involving sexy lingerie and rose petal-strewn pillows, all of which seemed to him like ridiculous trappings. And her conversations drifted into bizarre, uncharted territories that made him just want to tune her out.

"Did you ever kill for love?" she asked him one night as she stroked his bare chest after a short but intense sexual encounter.

"What? What are you talking about? I've never killed anyone for anything." He closed his eyes, willing this exchange to be over as soon as possible.

She sat up. "I thought you told me you killed two people."

"Accidentally. Both times."

"Okay, then let me rephrase the question. Would you kill for love?"

He shrugged. "I don't know. Maybe. I guess it would probably depend on the situation."

He knew she was waiting for him to ask her if she would do the same, but he wasn't going to give her that satisfaction. He didn't want to know her answer.

It was the next day that he met Sparkle.

Driving downpours and gusty winds had kept both Myles and Kit home during the afternoon and as the rain continued into the early evening, she settled in with her jewelry making tools as he dressed to go down to Frenchmen Street.

"Don't bother waiting up or making me any food. I'm going to try to sit in on the late set at the Cat." Ignoring her pouting expression, he put up the hood of his windbreaker and went out the back door into a dusk that was exceptionally foreboding.

The bus took longer than usual to arrive at Poland Avenue. When the door opened the smell of damp clothing and wet humans assaulted his senses. Even at this fairly early stage in the route, there was already only one seat left next to a large black woman in a cheap clear plastic raincoat. As Myles slid in next to her, he heard a few snickers and snide remarks from nearby passengers. When he looked sideways he instantly understood why.

Beneath her budget rain gear, she wore virtually nothing at all except for a pair of jeweled and sequined pasties on a set of breasts the size of prize-winning watermelons. If she had anything on at all below the waist he couldn't tell, because the view was obscured by her enormously inflated knockers, which were impossible not to gawk at.

"Go ahead and look, mon, dat is de whole point of dis exercise." The voice had a musical Caribbean cadence to it, like something he might have heard in a Bob Marley tune. "I not charge you since I not officially at work yet."

Myles swallowed hard and tried to act nonchalant, since he knew all eyes on the bus were on them. "Where do you work?" he asked in what he hoped sounded like an indifferent manner.

"De Kinky Monkey Club on Bourbon. We cater to all taste." He found it difficult to look up at her face as she spoke, his gaze still riveted to the colossal dark mounds that he realized now were too large for her coat to close over. "Sometimes I stand on de street to draw in de tourist."

"Do you mind if I ask...are − are they real?" He knew his question was naïve and crass but he couldn't help himself.

Her merry laughter actually caused him to break his stare and look up at her face. Beneath the sparkly makeup and decorative adhesive stars, he could see classic African-looking features, round and strong. "If you tink I was born like dis, tink again. I have dis work done to make me special and extra sexy. In dis city you mus' stand out to succeed."

Her solution was an extreme reaction to the general perspective of the New Orleans work ethic, but he couldn't disagree. "So, uh, you make a lot of money doing...this?" He waved his hand vaguely, not quite sure what exactly it was she did.

"Yes, mon. Some people pay me just to touch dem, to see what dey feel like." She took hold of one lapel and with an inviting gesture, revealed the full extent of the right breast to him.

"Uh, sorry. That's okay. I don't have any money for that." He shrank a little in his hard plastic seat as a woman across the aisle made tsking noises and said a little prayer.

"But you are curious, right? You want to know, dem hard like coconuts? Dem soft like jelly?" Before he knew what was happening, she had taken his hand and held it

105

against her warm skin. "Give it a squeeze, boy. You tell me how it feel to you."

Her joking tone made him understand that as uncomfortable as this was for him, it was just status quo for her. "Can you feel this?" he asked curiously, pressing his fingers into the unsurprisingly firm flesh.

She shrugged a little. "Not so much as before. But dat de price you pay for fame and fortune." As he slid his hand out from under hers, she winked a silvery eye at him. "De rest of me still everything just fine."

Now that his initial bedazzlement was over, he was able to take in the remainder of her attire, or most of it. Beneath an expanse of brown belly she seemed to be wearing a sequined G-string and garter belt with straps that extended over ample thighs to the tops of lacy metallic stockings, only a few inches of which could be seen before they disappeared in black vinyl boots that extended well above her knees. The few times he'd strolled Bourbon Street he'd seen "working women" like her but usually gave them a wide berth, unconvinced by their aggressive sexual behavior.

"Where are you from?" he asked her now.

"Charbonnet Street, Lower Ninth."

The bus jerked to a stop and a few passengers gave her dirty looks as they disembarked, one man hissing as he passed by, "Cover yourself, Jezebel!"

"I meant before here. Where were you born?"

"Kingston, Jamaica. We lucky to get out and come to me auntie's home some years ago. And what about you, boy? You not from here?" As she adjusted her raincoat around her girth again, he noticed her extra-long fingernails, also painted silver.

"Vermont. You know where that is?"

And so began their unusual friendship. He rode all the way to her stop with her, curious to see where exactly it was she worked. In her high spike-heeled boots with hair teased into a spangled do atop her head, she cut a tall impressive figure as she swished down the sidewalk. She turned so many heads that he felt almost invisible as he moved along beside her. Unlike on the bus, here in the Quarter she had plenty of fans and friends, all men, of course, who catcalled and shouted greetings at her as she pranced proudly by.

"Be careful you don't freeze off them famous titties, Miss Sparkle! It gonna be one cold winter night here!" one admirer warned.

"Don't you worry 'bout me, Jonesey. I got plenty on dis body to keep me warm!"

When they reached the Kinky Monkey, Myles extended his hand to her. "It was nice meeting you, Sparkle. Maybe we can do the commute together again sometime."

She laughed and in one motion, swatted his hand away and planted a kiss on his cheek, her spangled nipple covers pressing hard into him as her chest inevitably filled the space between them. "You a nice boy, Coyote. Go play some good music now."

Although he tried to pretend to himself that it was a coincidence, Myles began adjusting his schedule so that he could ride the bus downtown at the same time as Sparkle. As awed as he was by her enhanced physical attributes, he enjoyed her all-encompassing warmth and spunky who-gives-a-shit personality. There was no meanness, spite or jealousy, and he found her a welcome relief from Kit's intensity, which seemed to be growing greater by the day. One night he stayed out until Sparkle's shift ended at four am so they could travel back together and he saw the-end-of-work side of her, tired, subdued, less outgoing, limping along in her uncomfortable four-inch heels, a silver velvet cape wrapped around her massive body against the chill of the January dawn.

"Want to eat some breakfast wit' me? I'm always starving at dis time." They ducked into a tiny all-night diner that was surprisingly alive with the other players of the late night New Orleans scene, most getting off work, a few just about to start. Although all Myles had was coffee, Sparkle ate a huge plate of shrimp and grits and then took two po'boys to go. "One for my momma and one for my sister. Dey's no place to get food near where I live. And our cooking stove is broke."

He didn't usually drink caffeine at any time of the day, and he was feeling pretty jumpy by the time they boarded the bus, thinking maybe he wouldn't bother to go to sleep, just stay up and watch a sunrise, something he hadn't seen since he'd been in New Orleans. "How about I walk you to your house and catch the next bus back?" he suggested as they took their seats on the nearly empty 88. "I'm not feeling very sleepy now."

Her big hand with its flashy nails closed around his. "You tink I don't know you just curious to see where me living, boy? You can't come home wit' me, you know. Me share one bed with my whole family."

He flushed at her suggestion of what was on his mind and embarrassed that he had not thought about the poverty she might be living in. "I just enjoy your company, Sparkle."

"Maybe you invite me to your house some time, sweet man. So I can scare dem Voodoo witches you be livin' wit. And dat skinny-ass woman you tell me about."

The idea of Sparkle's presence was so at odds with his sense of his own living situation that his mind went blank for a moment as he tried to conceive it. "Okay," he agreed, a grin spreading across his face. "We'll do that some time soon."

He got off at his own stop and as he loped home along Poland Avenue, for a brief moment he actually saw the sun on the horizon before it disappeared into the dense cloud cover that hung over the city.

As he rounded the corner of the house he was surprised to find Kit sitting on the back porch wrapped in a blanket and puffing on a cigarette.

"Pull an all-nighter?" She glared at him angrily.

"What's it to you?" Her livid energy offended him and he tried to push past her, but she stood up and blocked his way.

"Word on the Square is you've been hanging out with some tranny whore with fake tits from the Ninth who works Bourbon Street." Her spiteful words seemed to heat the air between them, like dragon's breath.

"You think I'm sleeping with Sparkle?" He laughed harshly. "Kit, you're an insane jealous bitch if you believe that gossip."

"Sparkle? That's a stupid-ass stripper name, if I ever heard one."

He stood still for a moment and stared at her – hair wild, eyes unfocused with sleep deprivation yet still flashing defiantly, cigarette burning between trembling fingers – and then he shook his head. "Kit, maybe we need to take some space."

Forcibly he moved her aside and stepped into the kitchen. Instantly she was behind him, whispering furiously in his ear. "What are you saying, you want to break up with me?" She followed him through their room and into the bathroom, shutting the door behind them.

"Will you leave me alone so I can take a shower? I'm tired and smelly and I can't deal with this right now." He didn't turn around and finally he heard the door slam and then the sound of her howling sobs on the other side.

"Fuck." He dropped his clothing on the floor and turned on the hot water.

When he finally emerged from the bathroom, Kit had composed herself and was sitting calmly on the edge of the bed in her silk kimono. As she gave him a pale smile, he noticed that she'd even brushed her hair and put on some fresh eyeliner. "I don't want to fight with you, baby. What do you say we have some make-up sex?"

He sighed. "I'm not really in the mood right now." Flopping onto his side of the bed, he fluffed up some pillows behind his head and reached for the iPad.

"Okay, maybe later then." She was unusually docile as she kissed him on the cheek, in the same place that Sparkle had kissed him less than an hour earlier.

When he opened the Facebook app he found it was still on Chloe's page – he must have forgotten to log out the night before. Shit, he needed to be more vigilant.

Although he knew it was coming, Myles was thrown off stride when Mardi Gras suddenly descended upon New Orleans. For several days life lost whatever small amount of routine and stability it had, and between parades, parties and general city upheaval, he and Kit seemed to be on parallel tracks that rarely intersected.

Transportation was disrupted and erratic, and there were a couple of nights when he never even managed to make it home and he rarely ran into Sparkle. Unfortunately the one time he saw the most of her was the afternoon that he actually put on a colorful coyote mask and attended a parade route with Kit, who, he had to admit, looked spectacular in a mostly sheer black lace bodysuit with sequins in only the most strategic places and a cat headdress made of feathers.

"We have to do this together," she had insisted and for a few hours he had allowed himself to be drawn into her irresistible spell and let her be his guide to the Mardi Gras.

They were standing on a curb with giant plastics cups of Hurricanes (a local rum cocktail that Myles usually avoided because it was way too easy to get drunk on). Kit was having such a good time that she was laughing at her own full body shivers as cold breezes swept through the street and penetrated the thin nylon of her outfit. She was leaning back against Myles, pulling the front edges of his down jacket around her shoulders, when the Kinky Monkey float passed by. The crowd erupted in cheers as several nearly naked women tossed shiny necklaces into the crowd.

"Sparkle!" he shouted, waving furiously, his drink spilling like a sticky shower over Kit and the sidewalk. He was glad that Sparkle had the most prominent perch, where she sat proudly in all her silver glory atop a high glitter-covered throne where for once she was celebrated in appropriate style for her larger-than-life, parade-sized silhouette. She looked up at the sound of her name and when he realized that she didn't recognize him, he ripped off his mask and beat at the air with it. "Sparkle, over here!"

Finally seeing him, she jumped to her feet and tossed a handful of beads to him, her enormous breasts bouncing so dramatically that the onlookers hooted and applauded in appreciation before the float moved on down the block.

When he looked down he saw that Kit was no longer shaking with laughter but in anger, the remaining droplets of his drink running in slow rivulets down her bare chest and onto her costume. "Oh, so sorry, babe. I had to get her attention." He made a halfhearted attempt to mop up the spill with his sleeve, unable to suppress the smile that still lingered on his face.

"Give me your jacket," she said in an even, controlled tone that sounded nothing like her usual emotion-filled voice.

A week later he came home to find that Kit was gone. There was a note propped up on his nightstand. "*Taking a little trip and giving you some space, baby. I love you so much! See you in a few weeks. K.*"

CHAPTER EIGHT

West Jordan, Vermont
Februrary 2018

Tyler lay on the couch, his limbs as limp as a corpse; the only indication that he was actually alive was in the movement of his thumb as it clicked the channel changer of the remote. His self-imposed rule was usually "no TV until after sunset," but on this gray Sunday afternoon he was making an exception. Besides, there was an NCIS weekend marathon, including his favorite version of the series, the one that took place in New Orleans.

"Maybe you should see a doctor," Chloe suggested as she passed by, carrying a basket of dirty laundry.

"For what – terminal TV addiction? I'm not the only one with this disease; I'd be in the waiting room for hours. I'm just a short-term binger, there are people who can't ever stop watching, even sleep with it on." He lingered for a minute on an ancient episode of Columbo. "Oh, this is the same one that was on yesterday. Besides," he called after her defensively, "I never even owned a television until a couple years ago. Let's just say I'm making up for lost time."

"You could be skiing. Or taking the twins for a walk."

"George is already doing that." He felt too lazy to even get up to get himself a cup of coffee – did he dare ask Chloe to bring him one?

"This is a stupid way to fight depression. It only makes you more depressed to lie around all day." She blew by him with an armful of freshly washed baby clothes and then stopped and turned. "Here." She dumped the load on his lap. "Make yourself useful."

"Wait until you're an arthritic aging newspaper owner. With no love life, a missing child and a houseful of babies," he grumbled sitting up.

"You're not old. And I already have all that except a missing child. And the people I hang around with are either twenty years younger than me or forty years older. But I don't lie on the sofa feeling sorry for myself."

"Well, then I'll just have to do it for both of us." He turned up the volume and picked up a tiny T-shirt. "How do you even fold something this small? In half?"

"Are y'all open yet?"

Sarah looked up from the ice machine to see who was addressing her. Beneath a big fuzzy fur hat and above a colorful crocheted scarf, a woman's face peered out, eyes rimmed heavily with dark liner, cheeks crimson from the cold.

"Not for a few minutes, but come on in and get warm. You can sit by the fire if you want." Sarah nodded towards the couch in the corner.

"Oh, that looks nice. Thank you." The stranger stepped onto the hearth, close to the flames, not even unzipping the long down coat she wore.

"Guess you're not from around here." Sarah moved behind the bar and opened the beer cooler to take inventory of what needed to be restocked for the night.

The woman laughed. "It's that obvious, right? Thought I'd get out of my comfort zone and explore the north for a while. Learn how to ski. I've always wanted to learn how to ski."

"Well, you've come to the right place for that. If you look over on that bulletin board by the door, there's lots of info about what's going on in the Northeast Kingdom. There are plenty of cultural activities that happen here too, beyond the ski industry." Sarah flicked the switch on the "Open" sign in the window and began wiping down the tables in the bar.

"Thanks. Mind if I use your rest room?"

"Round the corner, past the front office there." There was a shriek of childish laughter and then Mei Li and Jin streaked through the room chased by Dylan and one of his friends. "Kids! You know the rules – keep it out of the bar. And Dylan, you're on as dishwasher in an hour. Sorry, we're a family business here."

"Well, that's nice." A little unnerved by the sudden presence of the children, the woman's Southern accent became a bit stronger. "I'm just gonna step outside for a smoke after this and then I'll come back in for a drink."

Sarah smiled a little to herself as she watched the tall figure disappear down the hall in search of the bathroom. You never knew who was going to walk in from where at the West Jordan Inn; sometimes the surprise element was all that kept her sane during the darkest days of winter.

A blast of cold air announced the arrival of a group of après-skiers, ready to finish off their weekend with a few rounds. Busy serving them, Sarah forgot all about the Southern woman until she suddenly reappeared again, apparently a little warmer now, coat unzipped and fur hat removed, revealing straight hair that fell below her shoulders with blonde streaks that looked less than natural. Beneath the outerwear, Sarah could see she wore a long sweeping purple skirt, a white turtleneck sweater and several dangling necklaces with strange silver charms.

"I'll have a glass of red wine," she announced, sliding onto a bar stool.

"Merlot, Cabernet, Pinot Noir or Chianti?"

"Ummm…whichever you think is the best," she replied, trying to cover her uncertainty.

She was clearly not a regular wine drinker, but Sarah kept this thought to herself as she poured a glass of the Pinot.

"So where are you from?" It was the expected question, almost rude not to ask it.

"Louisiana. Cajun country." She took a sip of the wine and choked a little, the way a non-smoker might do when taking a drag of a cigarette. Sarah wondered what it was that she usually drank.

"Really? Most people from that neck of the woods don't venture so far north at this time of year."

"Well, I'm not most people," she declared with a crooked smile that was half pride, half rebelliousness.

Sarah was about to reply when the door burst open again and a steady stream of customers began pouring in, stamping the snow off their boots. "There's about thirty-five of us," a man called out to her. "Can you handle us for dinner?"

She took a deep breath, trying to calm herself. Winter vacation week was always like this; you had to suck it up. It was hard to turn away this kind of business when in a month there would be no one around but the locals again.

"Sure," she said welcomingly. "Just give me a few minutes to get organized." She turned away and popped her head in through the swinging doors to the kitchen. "Hunter, is Rhonda here yet? We just got a party of thirty-five."

Hunter's eyes widened as he wiped his hands on his apron. He waved his phone at her. "She just called. She's got the flu and can't come in."

"Oh my god! Should I tell them to leave now that I just told them to stay?" Sarah pulled on the end of her braid in a gesture of frazzled anxiety.

"There must be someone we can call. One of our former employees who wants to make a quick couple hundred dollars in tips?" Even Hunter, who was normally unfazed by any crisis, seemed a little stressed by the situation.

"Right. Like who do we know who's gonna be able to drop everything and just come over here and jump in?"

"I have to go to work at the inn for a few hours. They have a dinner emergency. Shit, where the hell is my hairbrush?" Chloe started tossing things off a small table in the front hallway.

"What? They think they can just call you out of the blue like that? Tell them no." Tyler stared at her crossly. "George and Robert and I are playing Texas Hold'em tonight, so don't get the idea that we're babysitting."

115

"Well, you're going to be playing Baby Hold'em for the next few hours. Artemis, don't eat that!" Chloe pulled half a page from a National Geographic magazine out of the baby's mouth, as Athena crawled eagerly over to see what the excitement was about. Now that the twins were mobile on all fours, taking care of them had become even more of a challenge. "At least you'll have some help." She deposited the squirming Artemis on Tyler's lap and then planted Athena on the cushion next to him. "Grandpa's going to give you dinner and a bath, girls. Mommy will see you later!" She kissed each of them on the forehead and then darted away before any sticky hands could grab her clean shirt.

"Chloe, wait —"

"Have you seen my other boot? And the keys are in the car, right? Oh, there it is. Later, gators! You too, Grandpa!" she added merrily as she slammed the front door behind her.

"So much for my CSI afternoon," Tyler grumbled as Artemis picked up the remote and began chewing on it. Athena put her thumb in her mouth and nestled against Tyler's sweater, stroking it like a kitten. "Oh, come on. Let's get you girls something real to eat."

Three whirlwind hours later, Sarah said goodbye to the last of the big party of skiers and helped Chloe carry the remaining dirty dishes into the kitchen. "I don't know how we would have done it without you. Can you have a drink or two before you go?"

"Let me just check in with Tyler, make sure everything is all right at home. I never know how he is going to manage." She pulled her cell out of the back pocket of her jeans. "Ha, ha — look at this. Robert must have taken it." She showed Sarah a photo of the twins sitting in their footed pajamas sucking on baby bottles, one on Tyler's lap, one on George's, intently watching the cards and poker chips on the table in front of them.

"Well at least three grown men figured out how to take care of two small babies." Out of the corner of her eye,

Sarah saw movement at the other end of the bar and realized that the Southern woman was still sitting there, nursing a third glass of wine and covertly watching them. "Are you all set, hon?" she called.

"I'm fine. Don't y'all worry about me." An unsteady wave of fingers wearing multiple silver rings was not as reassuring as it had probably been intended to be. As Chloe stepped into the front hallway to make her call, Sarah rang up the woman's bar tab, placing it discreetly in front of her.

"Your pretty waitress there, what's her name again?"

"Chloe? What a dynamo she is." Sarah moved back to the dining room to do a quick check on a final pair of customers who were sitting at a candlelit corner table holding hands and staring romantically into each other's eyes. It was not a moment she wanted to intrude on but she wished she could urge them to hurry up. She was ready to have this night be over.

When she returned to the bar, Chloe was walking back in through the other entrance. Eyes still glued to her phone screen, she said, "Yeah, I guess I have time for a quick one."

Still without looking up, she slipped onto a barstool next to the Southerner, who sat up a little straighter, appraising her with a glittering gaze.

"Oh, sorry, I didn't even see you there." Chloe smiled apologetically and put down her phone. "That looks good – Sarah, can I have a red wine also? God, I can't remember the last time I sat down in a bar for a drink. Like more than a year ago." She settled back into her seat, trying to relax a little.

"Well, that's not right. Why don't you get out more, babe?" The woman leaned towards her as if she wanted to inspire confidence-sharing.

Chloe laughed. "Confinement due to pregnancy and birth of twin girls." As she took a big gulp of wine, her smile faded into a wistful expression. "And I don't really have any barhopping buddies around here."

"Aw, that's hard to believe. What about your husband – or boyfriend – or whatever. He doesn't take you out none?"

At that remark, Chloe gave a tight cynical grin. "Nope. Haven't seen either of them for quite some time."

"Well, I'm not even gonna begin to ask you about that. But it sounds like things can get pretty wild in this picturesque little ski town. Your name's Chloe, right?"

"Yes, sorry." Chloe held out her hand. "And you are…"

"Evangeline. It's a mouthful, I know," she apologized. "You can just call me Angel."

"I think it's beautiful. I like unusual names. You're not from around here, are you, Evangeline – Angel?" Chloe turned, really taking in her appearance for the first time.

"No, I've never been to Vermont before. I just got here today. From New Orleans. But I think I'm gonna stay for a while. You know, hang out, learn to ski, do what you mountain people do."

"Really?" Chloe giggled a little. "How nice for you to just be able to do that. I used to have that lifestyle, but those days are gone now." She shook her head a little, as if trying to dismiss the thought. "So where are you staying?"

"Oh, I actually found a good cheap room on AirBnB. Nice enough, but I have to share the bathroom. I'm not gonna do anything but sleep there anyway." She shivered a little and pulled her down coat up around her shoulders. "Now. Tell me all about those sweet babies of yours, Chloe."

"Well, it looks like you boys managed to have a party night anyway." Chloe stumbled a little as she came into the kitchen. She steadied herself on the edge of the counter on which sat more empty beer bottles than she could count, as well as a large wooden bowl that held the dregs of popcorn kernels

"Shhh! Lower your voice – they haven't been asleep that long," Tyler admonished in a loud whisper, not even looking up from his cards. "I see you and I raise you fifty."

"Oh, really?" George pushed some poker chips into the center of the table. "Looks like you might have had a good night yourself, baby mama."

"I did. And I realized I need to get out more." She stood at the sink watching the water overflow in the glass she was filling. "In fact, I am going out again on Tuesday night."

"What?!" Tyler slapped his cards down. "Four of a kind. Sarah can't expect you to start working there regularly again. You have enough to–"

"I said I was going OUT. Not working." She smiled over the edge of her glass at the three pairs of eyes that stared at her in shocked silence now.

"On – on a date, you mean?" Robert asked.

"No, silly. With a girl I met. Like people my age are supposed to do." A little water sloshed down the front of her shirt.

"Ha, ha – you seem a little drunk, girlfriend," George laughed. "Tyler, you bastard, I've got almost nothing left now."

"Oh, Hunter gave me some weed that I smoked on the ride home." She giggled a little." I actually feel really good. I'm going to bed."

"You drove my car home stoned? You know how I feel about that."

"Only for the two thousandth time. Get over it, Grandpa." Chloe stopped outside the bedroom door, peered into the darkened interior and said, "Oh, look at them. They're so sweet..." and then disappeared inside.

"Well, I'm glad for her. That poor girl needs a social life. Maybe she'll stop working like such a maniac." George yawned.

"I think I better take you home, dear." Robert patted his partner's hand and stood up. "Thanks for having us over, Tyler. This was a riot. We should make it a regular thing."

"Most fun I've had in months," Tyler agreed, wondering if that was pitiful or a good thing. He looked at

119

the mess on the table and shrugged. It would be there in the morning. For now, he might have time to catch the last episode of the NCIS marathon before it was over at midnight.

"Are you going to use the car tonight?" Tyler turned down the volume on the television so he didn't have to shout to Chloe, who was using the hall mirror to apply more mascara to her already heavily made-up eyes. "Because if so, you'll have to put some gas in it."

"It's like you haven't even moved from the couch in three days. No, she's picking me up. So you don't have to worry about me 'driving your car stoned'."

"This is not the first winter you have lived here. You know how I get."

He knew his seasonal depression was worse this year than ever before. With Chloe taking on so much of the work for the newspaper and with the regulated early-to-bed/early-to-rise schedule of the babies, his life had taken on more of a mind-numbing routine than he could ever recall. Except for those years in Grenada that he had disappeared into a bottle of rum. At least he'd been able to swim in the Caribbean then.

"I really don't remember you being such a slug last year. If I recall, you were always jumping in the car and running off to tango with your teacher lady. You used to even go skiing sometimes." The dinging of her phone made her glance down at an incoming message. "Oh, she's here. I'm going to meet her outside since the twins have just gone down. Call me if anything comes up."

"Sure. Have fun." His wish sounded as half-hearted as it felt. What did she think was going to happen in a couple of hours on a Tuesday night? All he was looking forward to was a new episode of NCIS:New Orleans at ten o'clock.

Diva jumped up onto his chest and tucked herself into a neat ball, resting her head on one paw. He watched her relax into a sleeplike position, her eyes never really fully closing, eternally watchful for the tug of a stray baby hand or whatever other prey it was she worried about. Sarah had been disappointed that they had come to a dead end in the investigation of Dennis Laveaux in Phoenix. She had in her mind now that Myles was living somewhere in the Arizona desert under an assumed name. At least she had a delusion she could live with.

Tyler hadn't told anyone how unsuccessful he had been at tracking down his own son, Tucker, even with a big clue like the name of the sailboat he had crewed on. His attempts to contact the captain had gone unanswered and his Facebook searches had come up blank. And since he was still paying off the trip to Greece, with the inclusion of Chloe on the payroll and the added financial burden of the extra bodies in his household, there wasn't a lot of extra money in his accounts to pay for another search expedition at the present time. He just had to hope that his irresponsible offspring was okay for now.

And meanwhile he'd stay home on his couch and feel like a loser.

"So I can't believe you traveled all the way around the world and came back to...here." Angel took a sip of her margarita and looked around. The only place they had been able to find open was not exactly lively at 9:30 on a Tuesday night. "There must have been a man involved." She glanced up coyly from beneath her darkened lashes.

Chloe laughed. "Of course. A couple of them." Her smiled faded. "Plus I had nowhere else to go. Except back to Greece to be with the baby daddy who didn't want me to have his babies."

"Well, I don't know anything about what that must feel like. But you have my sympathies." She fidgeted with an unlit cigarette, clearly wishing she could drink and smoke at the same time. "So what happened to the guy up here?"

"He left suddenly." Chloe shrugged, trying to give off an air of nonchalance. "I don't know where he is now."

121

"Really? No idea? Like not one itty bitty inkling?" Angel leaned closer as Chloe shook her head. "What a rat. You still love him?"

"I don't know. Yeah, I guess. I try not to think about it. He thinks he can't come back." Chloe sucked down half of her own margarita, feeling the whoosh of the liquor go to her brain.

"Now why would he think that? Like you wouldn't take him in, you mean?"

"No. He – uh – accidentally did a few bad things."

Angel giggled. "What – like drugs?"

"No, like murder." She didn't want to talk about Myles and hoped the mention of murder would stop the questioning. Angel's eyes grew appropriately large and she put a finger to her lips before smoothly changing the subject.

"BTW, girlfriend, speaking of murder, that was some killer weed we smoked the other night with that guy Hunter at the inn. I haven't smoked anything like that since I was in Mexico."

Eagerly Chloe picked up on the new thread of the conversation. "I've got some more, if you want to get high after this. So when were you in Mexico?"

"Last fall. I traveled around with a sweet young guy named Coyote." Her gaze drifted to Chloe's face. "Actually I think he was from New Hampshire. Maybe you know him?"

"Now, Angel, if you want to fit in around here, you're going to have to stop saying things like that," Chloe admonished her jokingly. "Everyone thinks Vermont and New Hampshire are the same place, but they're not."

Angel flushed. "Sorry. I mean, it's like just over the river, right?"

"Yeah, and actually my twins were born over there," she admitted. "But I don't know hardly anyone on that side. And certainly no one named Coyote." She looked around the nearly empty room. "Unfortunately most of the guys around here are boneheads. It'd probably be good for me to get out and meet a new one."

"It was his nickname. OB-viously." Angel seemed unwilling to stop talking about her Mexican boyfriend. "He *said* his real name was Lyle – which is clearly not as cool as being called Coyote. Right?!" She lowered her voice. "And definitely not as cool as being a fugitive from justice. Hey." She sat up suddenly. "I know. How about if I read your cards?"

"Cards?"

Angel dug in her bag and then tossed a Tarot deck on the bar between them. "This is what I do for a living. But I'd love to read your past and future for free."

Tyler had almost nodded off when he realized that the opening sequence of NCIS:New Orleans was beginning. He propped himself up facing the television, hoping that a more direct view would lessen his chances of falling asleep during his favorite variation of the popular crime show. There was a fast array of city street shots with quirky characters before the camera settled into a sequence on an open square full of milling tourists watching performers.

A bearded man in striped pants ate fire; another who was painted entirely silver mimed for the audience. A magician slipped out of a straightjacket to the amazement of the crowd and a young fiddler, with his head bent down intently over his instrument, busted a riff with amazing musical dexterity. At the end of the improvised melody, he looked up, clearly realizing for the first time that he was being filmed. He put a hand over his face and quickly turned away so that his features were no longer visible.

"Holy shit." Tyler was wide awake now. "Holy fucking shit."

He reached for the remote, unsure of what to do. It was a new episode, being broadcast for the first time. After it aired, he would be able to watch it again online somewhere, but maybe not until tomorrow. He wanted to call Sarah, but he didn't want to get her hopeful until he was sure. Who even knew how long ago this had been filmed?

123

It had been all of five seconds at the most but if he could just see it again, maybe freeze-frame the shot somehow, just get a chance to actually study that brief glimpse of the musician's face...

He stood up and began pacing back and forth on the living room rug. For the first time in weeks, Tyler actually felt like himself again.

...WEST JORDAN, VERMONT...

As she tossed her cigarette butt out the window into the snow, she realized she hadn't driven a vehicle since Mexico. Memories of that journey blew across her mind with frigid clarity, like the air that filled the interior of the car, keeping her awake after the long hours of travel. There were frightening recollections of abuse by an angry and irrational man that even now caused a tremor of fear to run through her body. She quickly suppressed these thoughts with the subsequent wonder and surprise of falling in love with a boy named Coyote who had rescued her from near-death in the desert.

Their life together on the beach had been a dream she'd never wanted to end. She hadn't been able to imagine going back to life without him. That boy was everything to her, everything she'd never had and always wanted. Generous, kind, talented, beautiful, interesting... he'd help recharge her batteries to full power again and she'd imprinted on him like a baby duck, falling hard and crazy for him. His ongoing devotion to his previous girlfriend and the protective fence he kept around his heart and mind made her want him even more. His lack of reciprocation only caused her to intensify her efforts to win him over in whatever way necessary. By the time they fled north, she had ensured that he was as dependent on her as she was on him. Need was just love in a different disguise, wasn't it?

She was going to have a future with him. She knew how to do that; she determined other people's futures all the time. It was easy once they believed in you. You just had to pay attention to what was important, watch, listen, learn. She'd learned a long time ago how to turn a disadvantage into an advantage. To turn knowledge into power. To change anger into control.

She didn't really have a plan yet but she had some ideas. Although her brain was starting to hurt from so much thinking. Or maybe it was from the freaking freezing temperatures – she'd never felt anything as cold as the subzero weather of this afternoon in Vermont.

Nothing was going to come between them. No one from her past. And no one from his.

125

CHAPTER NINE

New Orleans, Louisiana
Februrary 2018

"Ooh, dis some scary shit. You sure dem welcome my kind?" Sparkle spoke in a hushed voice, as Myles ushered her into the kitchen. She stopped to stare at a shelf that was a mixture of semi-precious geodes, voodoo figurines and Buddhist prayer beads.

"Believe me, they welcome more kinds than you ever even knew existed." Myles made sure the door to Darcy and Wendell's half of the house was closed before turning back to her. "You hungry?"

"What you tink – I am always ready to eat." Sparkle looked dubiously at the rickety wooden stool he offered her. "Don't make me break dat, sugar." He laughed and instead pulled out a sturdy padded chair from beneath the black oak dining table. She sat down heavily, untying her weighty silver cape and letting it fall behind her bare shoulders. "If dees people come in, dey gonna be okay wit me like dis?"

Her concern touched him. "Sparkle, when have you ever cared what people think?"

"Me not want to make trouble for you, boyfriend. Your skinny-ass woman not like me much." Her colossal chest heaved like an earth tremor as she sighed and settled back. "Oh yes, me feet hurtin' me, mon. It feel good to sit here."

"I told you my 'skinny-ass woman' isn't around this week. Look, I've got some leftovers that are begging to be eaten right now at three in the morning." Myles put half of a barbecued chicken on the table along with a large bowl of rice and beans.

"And what you gonna eat, boy?" she laughed.

He added a loaf of bread and a jar of peanut butter to the spread along with a couple of Jax beers before sitting down across from her. "I'm not that hungry anyway." He opened a beer and picked up his fiddle. "I'll play for you while you eat, princess."

He serenaded her with a quiet tune as she ate without speaking. But even with no conversation, Sparkle's jumbo-sized presence dominated the atmosphere, her nearly bare breasts resting on the table next to her plate. Myles wondered if there was any place where she would not be incongruous. He closed his eyes for a few moments as he played, trying to see if it felt different if he was not looking at her.

He was startled when he heard the legs of the chair push back across the floor as she stood up. "Don't mind me, honey, I need to use the little girl's room," she said coyly. "Just point me in the right direction."

Myles led her into the bedroom and flicked the bathroom light on, trying not to imagine Sparkle negotiating the tiny space. "It's kind of small," he apologized, stepping out of the way and sitting down on the bed.

"Not small at all," she reassured him, winking as she shut the door behind her.

Closing his eyes again, he leaned back against the pillows and began to play his own variation of "Summertime." In the days since Kit had left, taking the iPad with her, he'd had to revert to his old bedtime rituals of making music before sleep. Suddenly a sonorous sound filled the room.

"One of these days, I'm gonna rise up singing..." Deep and rich, Sparkle's voice seemed to saturate all the empty space between the ceiling and floor. "I'm gonna spread my wings and take to the sky..."

Myles stared at her with wonder as she belted the lyrics to the popular ballad with the power and vibrancy of a professional singer. When she plopped herself down next to him at the end of the song, she was beaming like a proud schoolgirl.

"Sparrr-kulll! What the fuck! You are good, woman. You should be doing something with that talent." He grinned at her warmly, feeling as though he had just struck buried treasure.

"I don't tink so, boy. I be makin' more money off dees big titties than offa any la-la lullaby singing. Oooh, dis one comfortable bed." Making sure the bottoms of her high-heeled boots didn't touch the quilt, she stretched out full length next to him, filling the space with an expansive landscape of soft dark skin.

"Yeah, but! Let me hear you sing another. Do you know this one? 'Could be a spoonful of coffee, could be a spoonful of tea'..." He led her through the simple words, his mind racing forward. He was not sure why it gave him such a rush of excitement to find out that Sparkle had as much talent as she had stage presence. As she sang, he tried to imagine performing with her and realized immediately that unless she changed her style, nobody would pay any attention to her amazing voice.

For the next hour, he ran her through a repertoire of standards, testing her range and versatility, until she gave a lioness-sized yawn and rolled onto her side, saying, "Honey, me need to go home now or me gone sleep right here."

"You can stay here if you want." Myles's mind instantly sprung through the gamut of possibilities of what sleeping with Sparkle could possibly lead to and whether he was even ready for that. Mostly he didn't want to let go of the dream he had started to spin around her.

"Coyote." For the first time since he had known her, she assumed a serious expression. "Dis part of me–" she waved a hand below her belly– "dis is a business agreement with a big price tag. Me na do dis wit friends."

"I wasn't suggesting..." he started to protest but she cut him off as she leaned across the bed to kiss him on the lips. It felt wet, luscious, overwhelming, and as confusing as the rest of her was, but suddenly all he wanted was to fall asleep wrapped inside a cocoon of her mountainous flesh.

"Just stay," he said, putting down his fiddle and snuggling into her, newly aware of the smell of her sweat mixed with the flowery scent of cheap perfume and makeup, and how different it was from any womanly reality he had ever known.

For a moment she held him against her and then with a motion swifter than any he had seen her previously use, she suddenly stood up. "They be worrying where I be. I need to go. When de nex' bus is?"

"Who's they?" he asked his face still pressed into the pillow where her head had been.

"My momma and little sister. You know I have family." She turned in a circle, seeming to have lost her bearings, perhaps looking for the door.

He reached out to stop her, his hand coming into contact with the solid softness of a thigh. "Let me call you an Uber. You might have to wait an hour for the bus at this time of night. Morning. Whatever it is." He sat up. "Come on. Let me do that for you."

"Okay. Okay. You do that. Please." It was the first time she'd ever seemed the least bit vulnerable. But then she reached out and pulled him to his feet. "But do it now, boy."

"Sparkle, listen." He followed her out into the kitchen. "Do you have any real clothes?"

She turned to him, a hand on one hip, her old sassy, sexy self again. "What you sayin' – you tink dis is a magic cape or some such?" She whipped the silver cloak around her shoulders.

"No, I mean, like a dress or something." But before she even replied, he was embarrassed by the question, already knowing the answer.

"Extra extra queen size is not easy to find," she said proudly. "And special order is expensive."

"Look, I want you to come sing with me this weekend. But..." he gestured helplessly at her skimpy spangles, not knowing how to say what he wanted to without it coming out the wrong way.

"Don't be jokin. I need de money I make at de Monkey. I can't be flouncing around wit you."

"We'll do it in the afternoon, before your shift."

"Why you care so much?" she asked softly. "Why you tink I need to escape my lifestyle. Like I am some slave. I am good at what I do, mon. People love me like dis." She smacked a hand against the side of an enhanced breast and glared at him defiantly.

"And before I came here that's exactly what I used to do," he said slowly. "Help people escape, that is. And I was good at it."

She looked at him bewildered.

"That's what coyotes do. Never mind. Fine. Don't do this for you; do it for me. Where is my frickin' phone..." He moved a couple of black garments that were tossed across the end of the table next to a portable sewing machine and then turned back to her with an expression of triumph on his face. "Say you'll do this for me, Sparkle. And I promise you'll at least go home with a new dress out of it."

A few afternoons later, the two of them were once again in the kitchen, Myles playing music, Sparkle striking a sexy pose while she sang, but this time Darcy was there as well, kneeling on a cushion on the floor, her mouth full of pins, as she pieced two black satin garments together to span Sparkle's girth.

"The skirt is the easy part," the tiny blond woman murmured mostly to herself as she stepped back to survey her work. "But the bodice will have to be a feat of extreme engineering. Using all my witchcraft powers." She gave a crooked smile as Sparkle drew back in alarm.

"I'm beggin' you not put no voodoo curse on me. Dis body have good juju now."

"I'm just kidding," Darcy assured her. "Now hold still so I don't pop anything important with these pins."

Sparkle froze as Darcy began to place shiny strips of cloth along the edges of the halter-style top, trying to extend the coverage to accommodate the vast swell of her chest. "Dat's plenty. My cleavage still need some display, you know."

"No worries, dear. You're going to look tremendous."

Myles turned his head to conceal the grin he could not suppress. He had a really good feeling about this transformation that was taking place, even though Sparkle seemed to have misgivings about covering up her flesh.

"Coyote, go look in the coat closet in my living room, will you? There are some long black gloves that will be fantastic with this outfit. Now Sparkle, you're going to have to carefully step out of this fabulous creation so I can stitch it together."

When he returned, he was surprised to see that Darcy had actually gotten Sparkle to slip on a voluminous embroidered kimono, in which she was swishing dramatically around the kitchen. "It feel so fancy and nice, like wearing just air." She stopped suddenly. "What de time?"

"You're fine. Relax." He held out the glittery spandex gloves. "Try these on, lady."

"Silver look better against my skin color, you know," she sniffed. "But, thanks."

"Sorry, but black is what we have available in this household." Darcy's foot sent the fabric moving at lightning speed through the sewing machine.

"Be grateful," Myles whispered, bumping his hip against Sparkle's.

"Dis your dream, boy, not mine." She waggled a shimmering gloved finger at him. "My dream already come true. In all de unnatural glory." She opened the robe to flash her brown breasts at him, the large nipples dark and shiny in their perfectly crafted roundness. Myles realized he was staring – he'd never seen them totally naked before. "Another dream come true, right? Put you tongue back in you mouth or you will need to pay," she whispered loudly, laughing.

131

He reached over and pulled the front of the kimono together. "You're embarrassing Darcy. We don't want to make her uncomfortable."

Darcy gave a little giggle. "That is so lame, Coyote. I just did the whole dressmaker thing on her buck nude body."

"You so cute when you blush. Now I am going to sit dis big 'buck nude body' down because it need rest before it be standing all night." As she lowered herself into the nearest chair, the front doorbell rang.

"Do you mind getting that?" Darcy nodded at Myles. "I don't want to stop here."

Myles retraced his path into the living room and then pushed through the beaded curtain that separated the space from the front vestibule. He rarely used the street door and it took him a few seconds to negotiate the heavy deadbolt.

There was something vaguely familiar about the brawny man standing on the front porch. He had a craggy face framed by scraggly black hair pulled back in a messy ponytail. He wore a leather jacket and ripped jeans, both of which appeared so perfectly weathered that Myles was sure they had been pre-distressed for a fashionable look. He peered at Myles through thick lenses framed in black plastic.

"I'm lookin' for Kit Beauchaine," he said bluntly, without any preamble.

Something about his presumptuous attitude made Myles instantly defiant. "Really. Because there's no Kit Beauchaine here."

The man studied the house number next to the door and then glanced down at a scrap of paper in his hand. "Yeah, well, I was told this is where she lives now."

"Well, she's not here." Myles tried to fill the doorway with his long arms and legs so that the interior of the house was not easily visible.

"You mean right now. At this moment." A pair of dark eyes narrowed suspiciously behind the hefty glasses.

"That's correct." Myles was not going to be intimidated.

"And when do y'all expect her back? Because I can wait." The visitor lowered himself onto the wooden porch railing and crossed his arms.

"Make yourself comfortable. She's been gone since last week and I have no idea when she'll be back." Myles turned to go inside but instantly sensed movement behind him.

"Hey! You fuckin' with me? Kit!" He shouted over Myles's shoulder. "If you're in there, you better come out right now!"

Myles took a breath and faced the man, who was now red-faced with anger. "Look, I'll tell her you came by whenever she comes back. But remind me, who are you again?"

For a second he thought he was going get a fist planted in his mouth, but then the stranger took a step back and tried to compose himself. "Beau Laveaux. I'm actually trying to find my brother, Denny."

Myles wondered if Beau was sensitive enough to notice the effect his words had on the color of Myles's cheeks, which felt suddenly bone cold. "Denny? There's nobody here with that name."

"Yeah, but Kit probably knows where he is. She left last fall with him for Mexico, but I never heard anything from them again after they crossed the border." Beau's fury seemed to suddenly dissolve into uneasiness. "I figured that was normal, their cells wouldn't work in Baja, right? But then when they didn't come back for Mardi Gras, and didn't call or nothin'... Well, that just ain't like our Denny. He wouldn't miss Mardi Gras. It's a Laveaux family tradition."

Myles just nodded, not trusting himself to speak.

"Then I heard from a friend that he'd seen Kit working Jackson Square again, just like she used to. Denny still wasn't answering my texts or nothing, so I drove down here from the parish a few days ago lookin' for them." Beau glanced unconsciously over his shoulder at a black pickup truck that Myles hadn't really noticed before.

"So who sent you to this address?" he asked carefully.

"Some old friends Kit crashed with when she showed up in town with her new boyfriend. The bitch. Where's my brother, that's what I want to know?" Beau pulled a pack of cigarettes out of a jacket pocket. "Mind?" He lit up without waiting for an answer. "I mean, maybe he ditched her. She is a piece of work, right? Hold on a minute – are you the new..."

Myles shook his head. "No, man. My wife Darcy and I just rent a room to her. Look, why don't you leave your number and she can call you when she gets back?"

"Right. Like why would she do that when I've left her a bunch of messages already. How about you call me when she gets back?"

"Maybe she has a different phone now? It's been a while, hasn't it?" Myles wished he could think of something smart to say that would make Beau go away.

"Maybe. What number do you have for her?" Beau's phone appeared in his hand.

Fuck, Myles thought. "Oh, I don't know, my wife might have it. I never call her."

"Yeah, well, if I was y'all, I would be careful about even having Kit in your house. She's bad news. Couldn't convince my dumb brother that he should steer clear – he was so hot for her. Let's hope he's staying far away from her on purpose."

"Really... so... like what should we be watching out for?" From inside the house he could hear Sparkle calling his name and he tried to speed the conversation along. "You mean she's like a thief or something?"

"Word is she did time for something a while back, when she was still a minor. Her people is a rough lot, no telling there." He shook his head. "You must have noticed how intense the woman is – when she decided she was into Denny, she was on him like a tick on a dog. I knew she was gonna be trouble for him. His old girlfriend, Charlene, she was a good girl that one, but it was like she just disappeared when Kit came on the scene. Somehow she made sure Denny never saw Charlene anymore – it was like she didn't exist or something."

Now it seemed like Beau couldn't stop talking. "A guy like Denny, he don't want no artsy-fartsy girl-power chick," he went on. "He likes a chick that knows her place, riding behind him…" Beau's words trailed off as his eyes focused on something beyond Myles's shoulder. "Holy fucking shit."

"Boy, you just chit-chattin' on de front porch like we got all day here. De seamstress lady say she need your help wit' de fitting." Sparkle moved past him and appraised Beau, who was staring dumbfounded at the sight of the big black woman in the open silk kimono.

"So, yeah, you kind of interrupted us." Myles slipped an arm under the robe and around Sparkle's waist, and then just to make his point, planted a kiss on the sumptuous mound of her nearest breast. "We're kind of busy here, so maybe you can check back in…a few days."

"Yeah, sure, no problem, man. I'll be in town until Sunday." Hands in pockets, eyes still riveted to the sight of Sparkle, Beau started to back down the steps and then stopped. "Oh, so, just let me ask you – have you ever seen this guy with Kit?" He held up his phone so that they could see the photo displayed on the screen.

Even though the last traces of the magic marker tattoo had faded away months ago, Myles had a hard time not clapping his hand to his cheek as he stared at the same image that was affixed to the passport hidden in the lining of his backpack. "Wow, uh no, I think I would remember that. I mean him."

"Yeah, people usually do. Hey, let me give you my number. Could be the bitch will reappear with him in a day or two."

"Just tell it to me. I'm a rain man with phone numbers. Really."

Myles felt Sparkle's hold tightening on him and he realized that his knees were actually buckling. As she held him upright, she gave him a suspicious sideways look. "What dat mean – 'rain man'?"

Beau chuckled and Myles forced a laugh. "I'll show you as soon as we get back to business," he replied with a broad wink at Beau. "Now what's that number?"

It was several minutes before the blood stopped rushing to his brain and he could think clearly. By then Sparkle had already put on her 'work' attire and was getting ready to leave. "What dat person say make you so woo-woo? You look like you seen a duppy man! Now you comin' on de bus wit' me or not?" she demanded.

"You better go without me. I'm not ready. I'll catch up with you tomorrow." He needed a little space to himself before he went down to the club. "I wish we could find a piano to practice with; it would be so much easier."

She pursed her painted lips. "I tink I know a place. You know my stop on de line? Meet me there tomorrow half after one and I take you there."

He blinked, surprised and intrigued that she was actually participating in his plan. He already could feel himself moving beyond the anxiety brought on by Beau's visit. "I'll be there. Good luck tonight – hope you make millions."

The afternoon was sunny and warm and reminded Myles of late spring weather in Vermont. But that was the only similarity between West Jordan and the Ninth Ward. He had enough city smarts now to know that even if the neighborhood did not look sketchy, it was.

He saw Sparkle heading towards him as he stepped off the bus onto the broken sidewalk. She was wearing the embroidered black silk kimono; he hoped Darcy had lent it to her and that she hadn't just walked off with it. Her head was covered with a purple turban and for the first time it occurred to him that she probably wore a wig most days.

"You not to tell anyone you see me so," she warned him in lieu of a greeting, touching the cloth covering her forehead and nodding towards the plastic flip-flops on her feet. "I not even have de foundation makeup on."

"Your secrets are safe," he assured her. "So where are we going?"

Walking at her usual brisk pace, she led him a few blocks in the direction of the river and then stopped in front of a majestic old church. "Dis de place. It always open." Climbing a couple of marble steps, she pulled open one of the heavy front doors.

"Wow." He was stunned to see the structure from inside – the majestic arc of the ceiling, the stained glass windows, the heavy wooden pews. On one wall there was a thick black mark painted several feet above the floor with an arrow pointing at it and the legend "Water line 8/30/2005."

"Yeah, it famous. Dey use it for making movies and de TV shows alla de time. Come." She strode up the aisle and Myles followed, although his eyes still roamed over the cavernous interior. "Here de piano. Since de choir director, Mary Elena die, nobody hardly touch de ting anymore."

Myles was used to funky pianos, he could make virtually any instrument work for him, and this one was actually in decent condition, only slightly out-of-tune. But the acoustics in the church were so perfect that the state of the piano became just a small part of the sound equation. For the next two hours he played and Sparkle sang, sometimes haltingly as she repeated the words he taught her, and sometimes just improvising in her unique way. The previous afternoon he had handed her a sheet of paper with some lyrics on it, but quickly realized that her grasp of written language was not very good and rather than embarrass her, he went with the "call and repeat" method.

A couple of times interested heads peeked around the church doors, curious as to who was producing the awesome sound that could be heard by the passersby who braved walking the streets of the Ward. But Myles and Sparkle were oblivious to the onlookers, caught up in their own reality of music-making and loving every minute of it.

"Me done for today," Sparkle declared suddenly, sinking her bulk into the closest pew and wiping her brow with the sleeve of the kimono. "Me must go on home now to prepare for de Monkey."

"How far away do you live?" He hoped the question sounded casual, but he really wanted to get a look at her house.

"On de nex' block. And you not comin' in. I know you are jus' so curious about me life. You don't want to see it, mon." She heaved herself up again and started towards the door.

He did want to see it, but he knew better than to say so. "Okay, it's a nice day. I can just wait outside for you."

She waggled a finger at him in that way she always did. "You tink me stupid, boy? I come back here for you when I ready to go to de bus."

He continued working on the melody line for "Catnip Boogie," the original tune they'd been practicing, and did not reply as she swished out of the building. But as soon as he thought she was out of earshot, he leaped up and stealthily opened the door. He looked both directions, but Sparkle had already disappeared from view.

Sprinting to the nearest corner, he caught a glimpse of her as she climbed the steps to a wooden shotgun house on the next block of the cross street. He waited until she was safely inside to move any closer, making a mental note of the location, and memorizing the details. Peeling lavender paint, a missing post beneath a sagging porch roof, a pile of black garbage bags tossed outside a metal door with a twisted window frame without a screen. A few weeds poked through the dirt of the small front yard. He moved closer to see more of the side of the small house. There was no foundation and the crumbling cinder blocks on which the structure rested did not look sturdy enough to hold up any building that Sparkle might occupy, especially not if her family members were built like she was. There were two long narrow windows with broken Venetian blinds that obscured the interior from view, or vice versa.

As he turned to go back to the church, he could hear shouts coming from inside and some high-pierced shrieks.

He stopped, suppressing the instinct to intervene, at the same time noticing an old man observing him from his porch across the street. He was shaking his head at Myles, a clear signal that he should go away and not get involved.

"Nothin' unusual goin' on there," the man said in a voice just loud enough for Myles to hear. "Move along and mind your business."

For once Myles did as he was told.

CHAPTER TEN

West Jordan, Vermont
Februrary 2018

Chloe groaned and rolled over as two pairs of chubby hands patted her face.

"Say 'Wake up, sleepy mama. It's nearly ten o'clock!'" George's voice came from the doorway in a high-pitched imitation of what a toddler's voice might sound like.

Chloe's eyes flew open and tried to focus on the lurching room. "Ten o'clock! Why'd you let me sleep so late? Oh, my god, I am so hung over. I feel like shit. Hi, girls, hi." As the twins clamored onto the bed, she folded them in her arms. "Ten o'clock. I am the worst mother ever. Lucky for you we have Georgie."

Struggling to sit up, she looked down at herself. She was wearing only a lacy camisole and boxer shorts that she could not remember even putting on before she went to bed. Her mouth felt like dry scratchy toast and her head pulsed like a gasoline generator.

"So you must have had a great time last night with your friend. Where'd you go?"

"Uh, just to a bar. I don't even think we drank that much." She didn't want to admit that she had only the fuzziest recollection of what had happened after she and Angel had left the bar. She recalled they had smoked a lot of pot, maybe really a lot, and maybe even snorted something Angel had magically produced. Since she wasn't the one driving, Chloe had let herself totally relax and enjoy. It had been so long since she'd been able to not be responsible for someone or something. They'd talked and talked, the girl stuff she hadn't realized she'd been missing, but she didn't remember any of the specifics. She felt a flush go over her whole body and was suddenly anxious at the cause of it; was she just heavily hung over or was there a reason she should be embarrassed? She found herself wondering how much she had shared – had she confessed the intimate details of her sexual experiences? Had she even told Angel about Anabel?

"Here – drink this. And then this." George was hovering over the bed with a large glass of water in one hand and a mug of coffee in the other. He plucked the clinging girls off of her and carried them, still protesting, into the living room.

"Thanks, you are such a sweetheart. I have so much to do this morning." She frowned, seeing for the first time that her clothes were neatly folded in a pile on the floor next to the bed with her phone resting on top, plugged into the wall. She would never have done that; even on a good night her clothes ended up in an inside-out heap. Angel must have come inside with her and put her to bed. The disturbing part was that Chloe remembered none of it.

She looked at her phone – there was a text from Angel. *"Message me when you get up. Your wallet is in the top drawer. Love hanging out with you, gf. How about tonight? XXOOXX"*

She could not go out again; she needed to be with Athena and Artemis, have a normal evening at home with her babies. But there was a part of her that felt so fulfilled being able to giggle and talk with Angel...

She quickly typed a reply. *"Need to stay home. Want to come have dinner with us?"*

For the next few hours, Chloe focused on getting things done around the house. Tyler was nowhere to be seen – George said he had closed himself up in the office for a few hours and then abruptly left. "He was definitely focused on something – you know how he gets. He said he left a to-do list for you by the computer."

Chloe was always a bit put off by Tyler's lists – she liked to think she knew what she was doing when it came to putting the newspaper together – she had done it alone the

141

whole time he was gone – but she tried to be respectful when he advised her. She knew she was part of his future retirement plans, even if she wasn't quite sure if she wanted to be.

She had a sudden flash of a memory from the previous night...tarot cards on the bar and Angel reading Chloe's future. Something about letting go of old relationships and moving on. She remembered now there had been shots of tequila involved. God, had there been kissing too... or had that just been her talking about the Anabel interlude in France?

"Starting to snow," George announced as he pushed the double stroller into the hallway. Chloe knelt down to help him unbuckle straps and lift bundled babies out of seats. She always loved how the girls looked coming in from cold fresh air with rosy cheeks and pink noses and wide clear blue eyes. "As you can see, they didn't fall asleep."

"That's okay, I'll let them nurse and they'll go right down. We're way off schedule here." Her breasts felt heavy with milk – the weaning process was sometimes more uncomfortable for her than the twins.

Maybe because Chloe had slept half the morning away, everything seemed like an endless process today – getting Athena and Artemis out of their snowsuits, changing their diapers, feeding them lunch. It was already well into the afternoon and temperaments were cranky by the time George left and she settled into the couch to nurse them to sleep. Athena was no problem, still easily soothed by a nipple and the warmth of her mother's skin. She always rested one little hand on top of Chloe's breast, patting now and again to reassure herself of the closeness. But Artemis was less interested these days, wriggling and unlatching, poking and playing. When the knock on the door sounded sharply throughout the house, Artemis pulled away and bobbed up, looking expectantly around.

"Shit." Chloe tried to detach Athena but she was still intent on sucking and would not let go. The rapping came

142

again, this time followed by the scraping of the door opening.

"Hello? Y'all home?" Angel's voice was instantly recognizable.

"In here!" Chloe tried to get Artemis back on the other breast but she was too interested in seeing what was about to happen.

"Sorry to come so early, but I'm kind of afraid of driving in the snow. Oh! Sorry, shhh." Angel stopped short at the sight of Chloe, shirt wide open, a baby nursing eagerly on one side, on the other, a large bare breast with a protruding wet nipple and a child bouncing up and down, restrained by Chloe's arm. Angel's mouth formed a large O and she whispered, "You're so beautiful, like a Madonna. Ohh."

"I'm just trying to put them down for a nap, but as you can see it's not working that well." But as she spoke, Athena fell away, snoring lightly, her little lips slightly parted.

"Do you mind putting her in the crib?" she asked Angel, who still stood there, melted snow dripping off her coat and boots onto the floor.

"I'd love to." She came forward to pick up Athena, her cold jacket brushing against Chloe's bare skin as she awkwardly cradled the baby in her arms before straightening up. "In here?" She nodded towards the bedroom.

Angel did not come back for several minutes, and although Chloe wondered what she was doing, she was glad of not having any distractions for the restless Artemis, who finally calmed down enough to drift off. When Angel finally returned, Diva was following at her heels; she leapt eagerly onto Angel's lap as she slipped off her jacket and sat down on the couch next to Chloe.

"That's unusual," Chloe commented, watching the striped cat curl around herself a few times before nestling against Angel's legs and proceeding to lick her paws. "Diva must like you – she doesn't usually take to strangers that quickly. She's been a bit traumatized by the attentions of these two."

"Maybe we knew each other in a past life." Angel gave a crooked smile as she ran her hand along the sleek fur. Diva began purring so loudly that Chloe laughed aloud as she stood up, straining a little under Artemis's weight.

"So I hate to say it, I mean, I'm glad you're here – but I have work to do for the next couple of hours. Can you amuse yourself?"

"Of course! Don't you worry about me." Angel waved a dismissive hand accompanied by the jangle of silver bracelets. "Or why don't you let me help you out – give me a task to do. I'm just happy to be off those wretched snowy roads and in your company again, girlfriend."

Chloe felt a rush of warmth for this unique woman who had already worked her way so deeply into her life. "Can you cook?"

Tyler was keyed up and mentally exhausted by the time he finally stamped the snow off his boots and dropped his laptop bag on the hall bench. He was glad to be home to a house that seemed unusually cozy – some bluesy tune was playing softly and the aroma of something delicious permeated the air. As he cautiously approached the kitchen, he was surprised to see an unfamiliar female figure standing at the stove, stirring a pot and swaying to the music.

"Hello?" he called tentatively. "I'm home, right?"

Long hair and hoop earrings swung into the air and a startled pair of blue eyes turned to stare at him. "Oh, wow. Y'all must be the father-in-law." Her face settled into an expression of inquiring interest that bordered on provocative.

"I prefer to be known as Tyler. And you must be…" This woman in her fuzzy black sweater and sweeping purple skirt seemed too exotic for a snowy midweek afternoon in his not very exciting life.

"Angel. I'm a friend of Chloe's. Want a taste?" She held out a wooden spoon full of a rich red sauce.

The gesture was irresistible and the flavor was as intoxicating as the smell. He closed his eyes, savoring the experience – it had been a long time since anyone other than himself had cooked anything so appealing in this household.

"Jambalaya," she replied to the question not yet asked. "Old family recipe." She leaned towards him. "What do you think?"

"Amazing." Her presence seemed suddenly too close and too overwhelming and he had to take a step backwards, bumping awkwardly into the butcher block table behind him. "I guess I'll stay for dinner."

He realized that, although Chloe had been living with him for almost a year, she'd never invited any friends over before, except for George who was in a category all his own. A wave of guilt washed over him – she was barely more than a girl; of course she needed a social life.

"Oh, I see you've already met Angel. And isn't she one? Did you see what she did for us this afternoon?" Chloe was beaming in a way he hadn't seen in a long time as she wrapped an arm around Angel's narrow waist and gave her a warm squeeze. The energy that passed between the two of them made Tyler feel strangely like an intruder.

"I did. I even tasted it. So how soon do we eat?" He opened the refrigerator and stared inside, praying that maybe there was a beer hidden in it somewhere. His focus had been so clear all day, but now he felt strangely rattled and derailed.

"In a while. After the girls have their dinner and bath. And then later maybe Angel will read your cards for you. She's multi-talented." Chloe's glowing admiration only added to his sense of gatecrashing and he had to turn his back on the two smiling women. Instead he sat down on the floor to play with his granddaughters for a few moments and think about his day.

He'd been up early, searching online for the latest episode of NCIS:New Orleans so that he could watch the opening sequence again. This time he was able to freeze-frame the few seconds that had caught his attention the night before. He stared at it for a long time, until the sounds of Athena and Artemis fussing in the bedroom made him poke his head through the door. Chloe was sleeping soundly and did not wake even when he called her name several times, so he rescued the girls from their cribs. By the time George arrived, Tyler had already exceeded his parenting threshold and was happy to turn the job over, returning immediately to his office to see what he could learn about the filming of NCIS:New Orleans. He was surprised that it was indeed shot on location and that local residents could sign up on a Facebook page to be extras in an episode.

Packing up his laptop, he'd headed over to the West Jordan Inn, needing someone else to corroborate his conclusion that Myles was indeed the fiddle player in this segment of the television show. Although the inn seemed empty, he finally found Sarah doing laundry in the basement.

"Tyler! It's not beer o'clock yet – what brings you here at this time of day?" Her cheery greeting was tossed over a shoulder as she pulled tablecloths and napkins out of the dryer.

"I need you to watch something and tell me what you think." He set the computer on top of the dryer and clicked through the screens until he was on the NCIS page. "It's super short so pay attention."

Sarah's reaction was immediate and extreme. "Holy shit. What is this? Where is this? How did you find it?"

When he explained to her what it was, she sank to the floor, still holding an armful of linens. "So what does this mean? Is Myles in New Orleans?"

"I think he might be. From what I can tell the show is filmed on location. I thought maybe I was hallucinating what I wanted to see, but now that you agree, I'm thinking

I should pursue it. See if I can find out where and when this footage was taken."

Sarah covered her face with her hands. "I'm just so glad to see that he is alive and well. It's almost enough." Her expression was tearful as she suddenly raised her head. "It does look like he's alive and well, doesn't it? I mean, he might be a drug addict or a homeless person, we can't really tell that. Oh, Tyler."

"Sarah, look, I'll go there, okay? Especially if it's New Orleans – I've always wanted to go there. Or you can even come with me."

She smiled through her tears. "Tyler Mackenzie, you mean in all your travels, you've never been to the Big Easy?"

While Sarah had loaded the washing machine and folded laundry, Tyler had sat there in the cellar for the next hour on a broken barstool, searching for contact information and any other clues that might connect them to where NCIS might have shot these few feet of film. Miraculously, by mid-afternoon, he had managed to get through to a production assistant who had been sympathetic to his story and eventually shared what she considered to be public knowledge.

"It's shot on Jackson Square, of course. An iconic and recognizable location for street performers that viewers can identify with. Everyone knows that."

"Of course," Tyler agreed. "That's what we thought. Just wanted to make sure."

"So what now?" Sarah asked. By this time they were upstairs having coffee. "I can't leave the inn for the next few days. But maybe next week…"

They had explored flights and lodging and before long it was time for Sarah to get ready for work and Tyler realized that several inches of snow had fallen and he'd better dig out his car and go home. He'd been so caught up in his thoughts and plans that he'd barely been aware of the treacherous drive along unplowed country roads. He had been still trying to figure out how Chloe would react to the news and whether he should even tell her or not, when he entered the house and the day's events had more or less vanished from his current brain activity.

The sound of a cork popping brought him back to the present. "Who wants wine?" Angel sang out, holding up a bottle of red.

"You brought wine?" Chloe squealed in a giddy tone that to Tyler's ear was over-the-top but that he was beginning to recognize as a "girlfriend voice."

"When I stopped to buy cigarettes it was just staring me in the face. I don't know my wine – is Merlot an okay kind?" She pronounced the last syllable as "lot" but neither Chloe or Tyler laughed.

"In a snowstorm any kind is good wine." Tyler got to his knees to receive the glass she was offering him.

"None for me. Okay, just a little. I'm still recovering from last night." A look passed between the two women that Tyler found hard to interpret. Mischievous... secretive... suggestive... definitely something had been shared.

"Let the bon temps rollez!" Angel said, leaning over to clink glasses with Tyler. He was so startled by the classic New Orleans toast that his jaw dropped.

"You do know what that means, don't you, Tyler?" Chloe teased him. "Our Angel here is from Cajun country. Watch that baby!"

Whisking the wine out of Artemis's aggressive reach, Tyler sprung to his feet. "You're from Louisiana? That's a coincidence," he said without thinking.

He was saved from explaining himself by the ringing of a cell phone somewhere in the room. "Oh, that's mine," Angel exclaimed, diving for a colorful bag on the arm of the couch. "Oh, it's my boyfriend. Excuse me, I have to take this." She stepped out into the front hall and then they heard the outside door closing behind her.

"Fun, isn't she? I'm so glad I met her – she's saved me from the winter doldrums this week." Chloe chattered as she got out the baby food grinder and began preparing dinner for the twins. "I'll be sad when she has to go back."

Tyler was still staring after Angel who had gone out on the porch without a jacket for the sake of privacy; he could see her head through the window, bobbing up and down animatedly. A moment later she was back inside, her thin shoulders quivering from the cold.

"Everything okay?"

"Fine. Just fine. I think I'll have a smoke." This time she did put her coat on, extracting a cigarette and a lighter from the pocket as she stepped out again.

There was not much opportunity for adult chit-chat during the next hour or so, as Athena and Artemis took the full attention of their mother and grandfather. When the babies were finally bathed and snapped into their footed pajamas, Artemis content with a bottle and Athena comfortably nursing at Chloe's breast, the three of them sat down at the kitchen table to begin the anticipated meal.

"You can eat like that?" Angel nodded in amazement at Chloe's ability to feed a large baby sprawled on her lap and still have the use of both hands for eating. Her eyes kept drifting uneasily to the sight of Chloe's naked blue-veined breast.

"You'd be surprised at what she can manage like that. But let's talk about you, Angel. So if you're from Louisiana, you must know New Orleans a little."

Chloe choked with merry laughter. "You have to forgive him – NCIS:New Orleans is his favorite TV show. I'm sure he is going to ask you all kinds of ridiculous questions."

Angel smiled at Tyler. "Of course, I've been there. It's the most wonderful city on earth."

"So you know it well? Like what are some of the best places to hear live music?"

"Why, you thinking about a trip there now, Tyler?" Chloe teased.

"Actually I am. Why not. See the real thing and not have to live vicariously through the TV," he retorted, happy that she had actually given him a good excuse for going there.

149

"All depends on what kind of music you want to hear. Music is everywhere. On the streets, in the clubs, at concerts and festivals." Angel took a big swig of her wine and batted her thickly-mascaraed lashes at Tyler.

"Well, let's start with on the street. Like I've heard of Jackson Square. Is that just super touristy or are there actual good musicians that play there?" Tyler bit into a piece of shrimp and could almost imagine himself at an outdoor café with French doors and rococo grillwork.

"Jackson Square?" Angel's voice squeaked a little. "They got all kinds there. A lot of up-and-comers; most of the buskers try to get a regular gig in a club eventually, but I've heard a lot of great music on the street."

"So where are the best clubs? Don't look at me like that," he said to Chloe. "I'm seriously planning to go."

"Well, maybe you two can travel down together." Chloe's tone was a little huffy and Tyler realized she was probably upset that he was monopolizing her friend's attention.

Angel put a hand on Chloe's arm. "Honey, I'm not going anywhere in this weather. In fact, I'm wondering if I can sleep on your couch tonight."

"Well, that will impact *somebody's* television watching," she replied cynically. "But, really, you're welcome to stay over. If you want, you can join the sleepover party in the girl's dorm. The futon Myles used to sleep on is still under the bed. I'll be back in a minute." Hoisting the sleeping Athena over her shoulder, she disappeared into the bedroom.

"Who's Myles?" Angel asked Tyler quietly.

"Well, he was her boyfriend last year when the twins were born. He was the best friend of my son. Her husband. Yeah, it's complicated." Tyler kept his eyes on Chloe's door, not wanting her to walk in on this conversation.

"So what happened to Myles?" Angel spoke in not much more than a whisper, making little clinking sounds with her fork as she pushed the rice and beans around on her plate.

"He left town rather abruptly after a series of unfortunate events. You mean she hasn't told you anything about him?" He raised his eyebrows as he transferred his gaze to her face. "I'm surprised."

"Well, I get a little confused. And your son is Tucker, right? And they're not together anymore?"

"Apparently not. Nobody's heard from Tucker in almost a year and a half." Tyler stood up abruptly. "Sorry, sore spot for me." He reached up on a high shelf and brought down a framed photo. "Here's a picture of both boys from a couple of years ago."

"Wow. Cute young hotties." Angel studied the photo carefully, taking in the wild dreadlocks and slim bare chests of the two teenagers with arms around each other's shoulders, sitting on the edge of a wooden platform in a tree. "Did you look like him when you were younger?"

"Pretty much. Without the hair." It made Tyler feel immeasurably sad to look at the picture of the missing boys and he put it back on top of the bookcase as Chloe reappeared.

"Has she offered to read your cards yet? She does Tarot for a living. And she's pretty right on. Hey, weren't we going to do some other ceremony tonight, for cleansing of the past? I am so ready for that."

"Oh, please. I do palms too. Among other things." She laughed and winked. "I'm also a jewelry maker."

"Uh, thanks, but I'm good with my future staying a mystery. I like mysteries." Tyler grinned, realizing it had been a while since any woman had flirted with him." I'll go into my office and leave you two alone. Angel, feel free to sleep on the couch. Despite what Chloe thinks, I can live for a night without TV."

"Your father-in-law is still pretty hot for an old guy." Angel sucked in the final toke from the joint they were sharing and flicked the butt away. "This is toast. Let's go back inside."

151

"What! Tyler? Don't even say that. Oh, my god." Chloe giggled reaching for the door handle. "We get along okay, but he can be incredibly annoying sometimes. Especially when he gets depressed."

"I'm just saying. I mean too bad you didn't stay with his son – he probably has good genes."

Chloe slapped her playfully on the arm and then put a finger to her lips as they slipped into the darkened bedroom. The futon she had made up with sheets and a quilt took up most of the floor space and the two of them sunk down on it, leaning their backs against the side of Chloe's bed.

"Oooh, this is pretty cozy." Angel patted the mattress. "Are we okay to talk in here?"

"Just keep your voice down and they won't wake up." Chloe lit a couple of candles. "I thought this might be the best place to chase my ghosts away."

"It's perfect. You need to be comfortable and relaxed." Angel ran her fingers along Chloe's brow and then down the side of her cheek and along the jagged edge of her hair. "Have I told you how much I love this cut? It's so chic."

Chloe closed her eyes, enjoying the feel of Angel's touch. It had been so long since anybody had really touched her.

"Now don't y'all go falling asleep on me." Angel was suddenly all business. "We have work to do. We need a sheet of paper for you to write on. And maybe even an envelope. Yeah, that would be perfect."

Chloe sighed almost imperceptibly and then went out into the other room where Tyler was hovering impatiently. "If you guys are not going to be out here..." he gestured at the couch.

"You're unbelievable. Go ahead, we're good." By the time she had retrieved the stationery from the office, he was already stretched out in his usual position with the remote in hand.

In the candlelit bedroom, Angel had cleared a space on the nightstand and set up a little altar on a flat stone with what looked like a tiny incense burner in the middle of it. Chloe sat down cross-legged next to her, a pen poised over the lined white pad of paper.

"So you need to write a letter to that boyfriend of yours who left you so high and dry here. Tell him you can't wait for him forever and you need to move on. Like what we talked about last night."

Chloe had no clear memory of their conversation the previous night, but since she had certainly had that very thought more than a few times in the last months, she guessed she might have said those words. Maybe she did even feel that way when she let her guard down. "Okay, so what's the point of that if I don't know where to mail it."

Angel's laugh sounded like wind chimes, the harsh wooden ones, not the soft tinkling bell kind. "We're not going to mail it, silly. We're going to burn it."

Somehow it all made perfect sense and Chloe realized she was feeling more than a little stoned. "Ahh, okay. So what do I write? 'Dear Myles,'…"

Angel stroked the back of her neck, gently massaging. She leaned closer and her breath was hot in Chloe's ear. "You know what to say."

Chloe shivered, despite the heat that seemed to rush from Angel's fingers down Chloe's spine, coursing over her shoulders, suffusing her breasts in a way she had forgotten. "Tell me," she whispered. "It's hard."

"It's easy, baby. Just relax. I'll help you. Here, finish this wine and then we'll write it together."

She had not even realized she'd fallen asleep, but suddenly she was awakening from a deep dreamless state. Something was covering her face and she clawed it away, gasping for breath.

"Angel?" She moved an arm back and forth and then forced herself to a sitting position. She was alone on the futon in a room lit only by a single sputtering candle, in some strange state of blistering sweat; her shirt was open and soaked through, her hair felt plastered to her head.

"Fuck, what is going on." It was like she had been hypnotized or something.

As her eyes adjusted to the darkness she could see the little altar on the nightstand with a few burnt scraps sticking out. She could smell it in the air now, the odor of burning paper, and it came back to her. She'd written a letter to Myles, telling him she needed to get on with her life and then they'd had a "letting go" ceremony, where she had stretched out on the mattress and Angel had taken the envelope from her and then laid a warm compress over her eyes with the heavy soothing scent of lavender and something else. Had Angel taken another warm wet cloth and washed her with it as well? She thought she remembered the sensation of the rough damp fabric rubbing over her neck and bare breasts and torso; her jeans were unbuttoned and pulled back and another washcloth had been tucked across her lower abdomen. Was the wetness between her legs just from water dripping down or was it because she had been so turned on by Angel's 'cleansing touch'?

She felt a sudden flood of embarrassment as she recalled begging Angel to be intimate with her and Angel putting a finger to Chloe's lips and shushing her, gently removing Chloe's hands from beneath her skirt and forcing them back to her sides. But the humiliation shifted to irritation as she heard voices and laughter from the next room. Was Angel really out there flirting with Tyler now, after the intensity of what they had just shared?

Chloe staggered to her feet, bumping into Artemis's crib. The baby gave a frightened cry and then began wailing and Chloe quickly gathered her up, holding the little body to her damp chest. The door to the bedroom flew open with a momentary blinding dagger of light and then closed again, and Angel was at her side, one hand around Chloe's bare waist, the other patting Artemis's back.

"You okay, babe? You were sleeping so soundly I didn't want to disturb you."

154

For an answer, Chloe turned her head and ground her lips hungrily against Angel, who gasped and pulled away. "Sweetie, you know I'm not – I've told you– I have a boyfriend – I don't even know how..." But her hand stayed on Chloe's hip as the now-soothed baby was placed gently back under the covers and Chloe turned to face her, shrugging off her drenched shirt.

"Yes, you do. It's easy. Just do what would turn you on." She grasped Angel's fingers and held them against her nipple, sucking in her breath from the sensation.

"No, honey, look I know you haven't had sex for a really long time and are super horny but..." Chloe could feel Angel getting more and more tense.

"Just come lay down with me. Hold me. I need that so bad." She sank down on her own bed, still hanging onto Angel's hand until Angel slowly sat down beside her. Chloe kissed her again, more passionately this time, until Angel turned away, trembling violently.

"Honey, I love you, but I can't – I can't have a woman touch me. Not that way." She ran her finger down the side of Chloe's face in that familiar sensual motion that made Chloe want her even more.

For a moment Chloe felt as though her heart had broken and then she realized it hadn't. She knew what she needed. "Okay, I won't touch you that way. I promise. But will you touch me?"

Sliding out of her jeans, she stretched out on top of the comforter and reached out to Angel. "Please?"

Angel looked down at Chloe's body, an invitation of softness and curves, and her terrified expression finally drifted away until she once again became the powerful Angel who controlled the world around her with a bewitching personality and cunning ways. The calculating look in her eyes scared Chloe, but thrilled her as well, and the riskiness of what she was asking for seemed to make it that much more irresistible now.

"Please," she begged again. "Please, Angel."

155

"Okay, baby." Angel's voice was hoarse and unfamiliar. Fully clothed, she lay down next to Chloe, resting her head on her hand. "You tell me what to do."

Chloe sighed with anticipation.

By morning Angel was an expert at satisfying Chloe. And Chloe was ready to do anything that Angel asked.

CHAPTER ELEVEN

New Orleans, Louisiana
Early March 2018

Myles moved cautiously around the side of the house and then ducked below the railing of the front porch to peer out at the street. The black pickup was still there, Beau's silhouette visible inside the cab, slumped against the driver's door. Every time Myles had gone out for the last two days, the truck had been parked in the same place, about a hundred feet away on the other side with a good view of the comings and goings of the Voodoo Buddhist household. He wondered how long Beau could keep his surveillance up; he had said something about staying in town through the weekend and it was now Sunday afternoon. Myles was guessing he had to be back at his job in the morning and that the creepy stakeout would be over until at least the following weekend.

Taking a deep breath, he strode out onto the sidewalk and walked nonchalantly in the other direction, towards the bus stop. He'd only gone about a block before he heard the roar of an engine idling beside him and the buzz of the passenger window being lowered. The smell of stale beer was strong enough to disinfect a bacterial wound.

"Hey, you seen Kit yet?" Beau looked like hell, dark half moons under his eyes, thick stubble covering his cheeks and chin.

"No, man, sorry. And my wife says she's not expected back until next month. I'll make sure to let her know you came by." He didn't mention the fact that he had spoken to Kit just a couple of days earlier.

"Shit. I hope she's not doin' a runner. There's some new shit I found out about what went down in Mexico and I really wanted to confront her with it. You know, see the look on her face. You need a ride somewhere? Get in." Beau swept several empty Jax cans off the passenger seat and onto the floor.

The last thing Myles wanted to do was get in a truck with Denny's brother, but he was curious what the latest developments were. "I'm just going up to St. Claude to catch the bus downtown, but sure." He climbed inside.

"Where you going? I can give you a lift all the way if you want."

"That's okay. My lady friend is coming from the Ward on the next bus and she'll be expecting me to ride with her. We've got a gig to do."

"Oh, you mean the one..." Beau made a lewd gesture with his hand that replicated Sparkle's outstanding features. "She's something else, bro. I wouldn't have pegged you for that type. Your wife know about her?"

"Well, she knows we work together. She just doesn't know what kind of work." Damn, he needed to be `careful about keeping his stories straight here. "So what more did you learn about your brother?" The pile of beer cans rattled noisily under the nervous jitter of Myles's foot.

"Oh, wait till you hear this. I almost don't know how to say it, it's so fucked up." Beau started sputtering in his excitement to share the news. "I mean if it's true, it means Denny is probably toast, but I don't know, maybe the van got stolen or something. They're talking about cartel shit, man." A six-pack of Jax seemed to materialize between his legs. "Want one?" Without waiting for an answer, he popped the top and handed a can to Myles before opening another for himself.

"So I guess the police here had the cops there run the VIN number of Denny's van," he went on. "And it came up with a match in Baja of some vehicle that was part of an arson hit. Torched with at least one guy inside."

"What? Really? That's totally fucked up, man." The details sounded way too much like the event in Bahia de Concepcion that he had been blamed for – was that like an everyday occurrence in Baja or was this just a weird

158

coincidence? Myles chugged half of his beer as he remembered waking up to the sound of an explosion, Kit watching it from the window of the camper, and the vague recollection of some crazy-ass best sex ever afterwards, before everything started to go downhill in his Mexican existence.

"They told me not to get too wigged out about it – chances are it wasn't Denny, but if that's true then why haven't I heard anything from him for months? I mean, we were never that close or nothin' but still. Mardi Gras, man? He would never not be home for Mardi Gras."

"Well, people change." Myles had never crushed a beer can with his bare hand before, but he tried to now. "Believe me, I speak from experience." He could see the 88 bus at a stoplight a few blocks away. "But hey, let me know how that story turns out. I gotta go now."

"Yeah, okay. I'll see you again; let me know when that freakin' card reader is back in town. Trust me, she knows something about this. If I was you I'd get a few months advance on her rent. Catch you on the rebound." His tires screeched as he pulled away.

Already on the bus, Sparkle was sitting proudly in her new black dress which was beginning to look a little worse for wear even after just a few days, the stitching starting to tear a little in the places under the most weight strain. When Myles had marveled at how the fabric managed to defy gravity and not fall off in the most crucial locations, she had laughed at him. "It be glued on. Dat how we do it in de industry."

And, to the wonder of the spectators and other musicians, for the last two afternoons, she had been right. The magical dress had moved and heaved with her breathtaking bosoms as she belted tunes, first on the sidewalk outside the bakery on Frenchmen Street and then again when they performed at the Spotted Cat. Myles had been blown away by the amount of cash in the tip can after Sparkle had personally passed it around. A trombone player in the band after them had been totally smitten by

159

her and invited them to sit in on a few numbers. He was even bigger and blacker than Sparkle and although she rebuffed his attention in the same superior manner she used with everyone, Myles could sense that the interest pleased her.

"That your woman?" he asked Myles when Sparkle had hastened off to the ladies room to change into her Kinky Monkey attire. "Cause I'm likin' on her."

"She's her own woman. And definitely one in a million." He laughed as the man had the usual eye-bulging reaction when Sparkle streamed out of the bathroom in her silver cape and skimpy sequined attire before threading her way through the crowd to reach the street. Myles followed close behind, his pockets bulging with bills and coins.

"You were fantastic! They loved you!" he enthused as he trotted beside her.

"Yes, mon. But don' make me late now for my regular show." Her steps grew longer and he finally fell back and stopped trying to keep up.

"I'll buy you dinner after work!" he called.

She'd been touched by the bouquet of roses and the containers of Chinese take-out he'd carried back to the Bywater for a feast on his porch. But she had refused the champagne. "I don' touch alcohol. Except maybe a little sip of de gold Appleton's rum on special occasions."

He realized then that he'd actually never seen her drinking. "Well, I wish I'd known that. Because this is a pretty special night." He leaned back in his hammock and held up both glasses and clinked them together. "To your new musical career." Then he drank first one and then the other while Sparkle watched amusedly from the wicker loveseat.

For the next few days Myles's life settled into a pleasant rhythm of practice and performance in which Sparkle played a major role as often as possible. A few nights later he surprised her with a bottle of her favorite Jamaican liquor and she agreed to a toast. Despite her size, it took only few shots for the effects to be obvious and their good night kiss was a bit heartier than usual.

"See, you men all de same – you tink you can get Miss Sparkle drunk and she let your big bamboo inside. Don' look at me like dat – I can feel what going on in your pants down dere. I see you tomorrow afternoon, boy."

"Just sleep here. It's late and you shouldn't be out," he whined, although he knew it was a hopeless dream. These days he liked to go to bed with images of Sparkle in his mind rather than faded memories of Chloe or scary reminders of Kit's imminent return.

Kit had been way too excited to hear from him when he had called her a few days earlier. But when he told her about Beau's visit, the silence had been so long that he thought she had hung up on him. "Kit, you still there?"

"Yeah, baby, I'm just thinking about Denny. I've been so happy he's never showed up in New Orleans, but now I'm wondering what happened to him. You didn't say anything to Beau about the passport thing, did you?"

"You think I'm stupid? Where are you anyway? Can you stay away for another week or two?"

"I'm visiting an old girlfriend up north. Having fun. You know, getting drunk, having sleepovers, doing girl stuff." She giggled in a way that was even more giddy than her usual high-strung self. "But you're always on my mind. Yeah, sure, I can stay a little longer, but I'm missing you, Coy-boy. And don't you worry about that dumbass Beau. I'll deal with him when I get back. Just don't say anything to him about Denny, okay?"

"Kit, you know I'm not a talker. I'm busy with a new music thing so I'm not even around the house much. You might as well stay up there as long as you can."

"Oh, I love you, baby. Makes me all tingly to hear your voice. Wish I could be jumping your bones right now. But we're about to eat, so I gotta go. Love you."

He had been glad to hear she wasn't coming back for a while yet. The only thing he really missed was her iPad.

And she was not going to be happy about how much time he was spending with Sparkle.

"Hey, tell me what troublin' you. You not right today." Sparkle was patting Myles on the hand, an unusual look of concern in her silver-lidded brown eyes. "Say you not finish that bottle of Appleton's after me left you because dis my one night off and I want me some more of dat sweet stuff." She winked at him in her cheerful, seductive way.

"I'm fine. Don't worry about me. I was just talking to a guy who rubs me wrong. But now I'm with a woman who could rub me right." He squeezed her thigh and Sparkle looked over her shoulder coyly.

"What woman dat be? Because you better not be talking about dis one here. We doin' a double shift today at de Cat? Dat trombone man gonna be there again?" She preened a little and turned towards the bus window.

"Sorry, sister, probably not. Unless he stops by to hit on you. And hear our music, of course. You think you're ready to do Catnip Boogie yet? You remember the new verse?" Myles wasn't sure if they were really ready to debut the song he'd been working on, but he was hoping to try it out at least as part of a medley today.

"Dem dirty lyrics makes you so bright when me sing dem? About my girl Kitty tink her pussy can fly when she roll in de catnip and get all kitty-cat high, she doin' de Catnip Boogie..."

Myles laughed. "Yeah that's part of it. Just make it up if you forget the real words."

"Well, how you like this one I made up – My girl Kitty rub some nip on her titty, thought it look really pretty when she nudie in de city, ain't it a pity that her titty's itty-bitty, she doin' de Catnip Boogie..." Sparkle gave a little shimmy of her own chest that was more like an earth tremor and the two men in the seat behind them howled with amusement as loudly as Myles did.

"You good, girl, you real good," one of them praised her.

"Come see us perform at the Spotted Cat this afternoon," Myles invited. And then we'll be out on the street later on."

"I've got a surprise for you." They were back in Myles's bedroom, earlier than usual, due to a sudden rain and wind storm that had whipped up unexpectedly, driving people indoors and turning the two of them into a drenched soggy mess. Sparkle had hurried to cover her hair and Myles shoved his fiddle case up under his jacket as the two of them dashed for the bus shelter through the flash flooding of the gutters and sidewalks. Even Sparkle, usually stalwart when it came to weather, was shivering and daunted by the time they reached the house.

After exchanging his sodden clothes for flannel pants and a sweatshirt, Myles made them hot coffee liberally laced with rum. Meanwhile Sparkle had stripped off her nearly ruined dress and wrapped a fleecy blanket toga-style around her vast body.

"Show me now den. It hard to amaze me, you know."

From a bag next to the bed he began pulling yards of shimmering silver cloth. "I found these curtains at the secondhand store yesterday. I'm going to pay Darcy to make you another dress. In your favorite color."

Sparkle actually squeaked with delight before her expression became dark. "Why you so good to me, Coyote? Every day you be buying me tings now; me starting to feel funny about dis. You expecting Sparkle to reward you for dese kindnesses?"

"Don't insult me, girlfriend. You know me better." He emptied the rest of the Appleton bottle into her coffee cup. "Nobody's making me do this. I'm having fun."

She scrutinized him for a moment before tossing back the rest of her beverage. "Oh, me dizzy from dat already." Sinking back against the pillows she closed her eyes. "I maybe take one little nap before I walk home."

Myles took the opportunity to stretch out and roll up against her soft bulk and was pleased when she did not object to his snuggling. "Sparkle, when was the last time you had a regular boyfriend?"

"Why you want dat information?" she mumbled quietly.

"Just trying to know you better."

"You and everyone. Me never have a steady man since we move here."

"So there was someone in Jamaica?"

"He was not my boyfriend. Don' ax me more about him."

"Did you ever have any babies?"

He was close enough to her to feel the cessation of her breath for an instant.

"You don't need to know nothin' about that. It nobody bizness." She threw a thick arm over him and he marveled at its girth – a log that big around would have heated his cabin in Vermont for hours.

"Ever think about a career in wrestling?" he joked, changing the subject as he squeezed her bicep.

"Ever wash a bed sheet by hand?" She actually mimicked his American accent for a second before falling back to her Jamaican lilt. "Me be doing laundry wit me mama like dat from when I was small-small. In a tub by de pipe, dawn to dark, scrubbin' wit de brush and wringing dem 'round de arm... Carry it wet and heavy on me head to hang in de sun... if it fall in de dirt, she whip me so it hurt and me have to do it again. I de best washer in de parish by de time I ten years..."

Myles didn't move or speak, hoping she would go on with her fascinating story, but instead she groaned a little. "Why you give me dat rum..." She began to snore lightly and then snapped suddenly awake. "You want touch dem while I sleep, you can. But nothing else, you hear?" Then she was out again, leaning heavily on his back, one hefty arm around his waist.

Well he wasn't going to pass up that invitation. He rolled over and buried his face in the musky canyon of her perfumed cleavage, his hands gently exploring the miracles of modern plastic surgery. If he suffocated now, he would at least die happy.

Sparkle was gone when he woke up mid-morning. He stayed where he was, trying to separate his fantasies from the realities of the night – had he really licked her oversized areolas or had he just been imagining it so vividly that it seemed real? No, he remembered it now; in his dreams she had always responded passionately. In reality, her breathing had not even changed. He had thought her giant body parts would bring her giant pleasure, but it was as if she couldn't even feel anything in what should have been one of her most erogenous zones.

He was more curious now about her past than about her physical enhancements. He was sure that her history had probably played a big role in bringing about her current circumstances and he had a feeling that her existence growing up in Jamaica had not been a holiday postcard of palm trees on a beach. He tried to picture her as a skinny girl with stick legs and a torn school uniform that was always too short for a rapidly growing body. He wondered what her home life might have been like – maybe a stifling one room shack in Shanty Town shared by an extended multi-generational family of washerwomen or perhaps a rude hut in the countryside ruled by a father with the bloodshot eyes of an alcoholic and a stern mother who beat her with a stick when she dropped the wet laundry in the dirt.

By the time he got out of the shower, he'd written half a song in his head about Sparkle. His creativity was interrupted by a buzzing on the nightstand; a text message on his phone from Kit. In fact there were several text messages from Kit since last night, all of them pointless and bothersome. *"Thinking of you, baby." "Miss you so much, Coy-boy!" "Love you XXOOXXOO", "Can't wait till we're together again."* They reminded him of those candy hearts he used to eat by the handful on Valentine's Day. So sweet they made you sick to your stomach.

Sparkle had said she had some family "appointments" that day before work so there would be no practicing or performing together. But the unseasonably warm and sunny weather made Myles want to be outdoors, so he decided to head down to Jackson Square with his fiddle and see what was going on.

He hadn't been to the square since Kit had left town but nothing much had changed. The regulars had closed the gap around her space a little, but it was still pretty much the same assortment of artists, psychics and musicians. He caught up with a few acquaintances and played a few tunes before he saw a girl who was a friend of Kit's hanging around listlessly on a bench trying to get his eye. Although she was dressed for belly-dancing in a midriff-baring costume of faded Indian-print material decorated with shimmering coins, she did not seem to be making much of an effort to perform. As he approached her, he noticed her smooth olive-toned skin and jet-black braid actually looked a little dusty, as though she hadn't washed in a few days.

"Hey, I'm Jasmine." Although she was speaking to Myles, her eyes were still moving around the street as though she was watching for someone or something. "You're Kit's friend, right?"

"Coyote. Yeah." Something about her creeped him out and he didn't really want to hang with her.

"You seen her lately?"

"No, she's out of town till next week sometime. What's up?"

"Oh, I sold her all my shit before she left and I wondered if she'd come back with any. I haven't been able to score anymore and I really need a hit."

Myles tried not to show his lack of knowledge about this event. "Sorry to hear that. What was it she bought from you again?"

Her eyes, wide and watery, focused on his for a second. "The good stuff. I mean, she paid me, she doesn't owe me nothing, I was just wondering, you know," she made a

166

gesture with her hand which caused her clothing to jingle a little, "if she might have a hit left."

"I've got some nice weed if you want some," Myles offered sympathetically, starting to reach in his bag. She laid a hand on his arm to stop him and he noticed how dirty her fingernails were.

"No, thanks, man. I just wanted some of that great blow and besides, I don't have any money. I haven't felt much like dancing lately." She scratched at the crotch area of her harem pants. "Just tell her to come find Jasmine when she's back. Hopefully by then I'll have more and maybe she'll want to cop some again. I could use the money. My rent's overdue." Then suddenly she looked up hopefully. "If you want, I can give you a hand job or something if you've got some cash."

"No, thanks. Here." He gave her a twenty and called over his shoulder, "Good luck, Jasmine. I'll tell Kit you were asking about her." Not, he added silently.

He was weirded-out that Kit had bought hard drugs from a street person before she left. Maybe she was trying to impress her New York City friends or something. He left the square and wandered over to Royal where he ran into Vlad playing in the usual doorway with a few guys Myles didn't know, but he stopped anyway to jam a few numbers with them. In a few minutes, Kit was far from his mind.

Cruising around without Sparkle for a night put him into a little bit of overdrive and without the goal of waiting for her to get off work, Myles burned out earlier than usual. After stumbling into his room and falling across the unmade bed, it took him a while to notice the envelope on his pillow with a note attached to it.

"What the fuck is this?" he muttered holding it up to a bedside lamp that had been dimmed by an antique beaded shawl.

"*A girl dropped this off for you today,*" Darcy had scrawled across a sheet from a note pad that announced the 25th Annual Crescent City Wiccan Conference.

The envelope was not addressed to anyone, but the handwritten return address in the left-hand corner made his stomach drop like he was on a carnival ride. *"Chloe Mackenzie, 712 Mountain Road, West Jordan, Vermont."*

What the... who had... with a violent gesture, he tore it open and pulled out the single folded page inside.

"Dear Myles, It's been nearly a year since I last heard from you. I miss you but it's time for me to get on with my life. I can't wait for you any longer, I've got to move on and find a new relationship. I hope you are happy wherever you are and that you have a new woman who loves you as much as I once did." *"Love"* had been crossed out and then so had *"Always Yours"* and finally replaced with *"Goodbye forever, Chloe."*

It couldn't be real – how had it even gotten to him? How would Chloe even know where to send a letter? But it hadn't even been mailed and his name wasn't on the envelope. It had to be some kind of cruel cosmic joke – but even that didn't make any sense.

He rarely crossed the privacy line between his space and Darcy's, but this was an emergency. Pushing aside the curtain, he strode into his landlords' living room, where she and Wendell were sitting in the near darkness watching an old black-and-white movie on their big screen TV.

"Hey, what's up, Coyote?" They both looked at him in mild surprise as he interrupted their seclusion.

"What girl brought this?" he demanded, waving the envelope at them indignantly, like an angry corporate president.

"Whoa, cool down, man. You're seriously wound up," Wendell commented. "And I have no clue what you're talking about."

"Some young girl knocked on the door this afternoon and asked if a fiddle player lived here," Darcy answered Myles matter-of-factly. "Then she told me to give it to you and left."

"What did she look like?" He tried to keep from shouting but he could barely contain himself.

She shrugged. "Kinda cute. Blonde, shortish hair, sorta bosomy. Not like Sparkle, but in a normal way."

"What color eyes?"

"I don't know, she was only here for thirty seconds. I figured she must be some fan of yours. I wasn't going to pry. Who you want to hang out with is your business. Oh, this is the good part, Wendell." She clutched her husband's arm as the dramatic music coming from the television got louder. "Watch how she kills him."

Myles stumbled back to his own room like the victim of a nuclear explosion. It couldn't have been Chloe herself who delivered the letter, what would she be doing here anyway and besides, she wasn't blonde. He leaned against the door jamb and reread the handwritten sheet of paper.

One paragraph that destroyed all possibilities that his life might ever return to almost normal again. The hope that someday he might reunite with the person he loved the most had just blown away like litter in the wind. He couldn't blame her – why should she wait for him forever when she hadn't even heard from him since last spring. But still... He felt a pain in his chest, as though he was physically being ripped apart, and it became hard to breathe. He needed to get outside, get some air.

Still – how the fuck had this letter found its way to him?

Wadding up the page in his hand, he shoved it into his jacket pocket and staggered out into the night.

"Coyote! I knew dat be you when I keep hearin' dis kine music comin' from de church. What wrong wid you, mon? You nah meet me for two full days now and Darcy she say she nevah see you since de night before dat."

Sparkle's voice grew louder as she moved down the aisle of the church towards where Myles sat slouched over the piano, his fingers playing a sloppy rag on the keys.

"Where you clothes, boy? You can't be naked as de day you born here in de lord's house. And what dis?" She picked up an empty bottle that lay on the floor next to his

169

discarded apparel and sniffed it. "Rum? You drink all dis here in the choir box? You lookin' for a one way ticket to hell for sure now."

"Yeah, and this too." Myles kicked at a six pack under the piano bench. "You got a problem with that?"

"Jesus, help us, you one big mess." She piled his clothing on the seat next to him and pulled at his arm. "You stand up now and get dressed. You can't be here like dis."

He shook her grip off and continued to play. "Well, isn't that the pot calling the kettle black. Or do I mean the black pot calling the kettle white..." He snorted at his own joke. "It ain't like you got your church clothes on, Miss Sparkle."

"Dis my normal, boy. You be acting crazy. You forget to take some medication you nevah tell me about or some such ting?" Sparkle began to sound a little frantic. "De choir be comin' in an hour to practice for de Sunday service tomorrow and you can't be here like dis. Get off you ass, you hear me?"

"You told me anyone can be in this church any time of night or day, so here I am. Doin' the right thing. Now just say a prayer for me and go away." Myles banged out some heavy minor chords for mournful emphasis and continued playing.

"What your plan den? You just going to sit here and make music until you die from de sadness of your condition? Because you don't know bad, mistah, if you tink you life is bad now."

"De sadness of your condition..." He sang her words back to her with a Jamaican lilt. "You just be naturally a poet, woman. And I am just naturally a loser."

"If you don' get off dat bench dis minute, you sad life is about to become much worse." Myles could feel her looming behind him now but he purposely ignored her, closing his eyes and swaying to the tempo.

Then he gasped uncontrollably as her washerwoman arms went around his chest and lifted him away from the piano, squeezing the air out of his lungs as she heaved him towards the door, cursing loudly in her native patois.

"You don't tink I can carry you skinny naked white body out dis building? And you not weighing as much as one basket of wet sheets." She dropped him on the tiled floor of the entranceway where he tried to catch his breath as she went back to carry out the debris of his bottles and clothing. "Get up now and walk to de door."

He was suddenly so tired and hung over, he just wanted to curl up on the cold floor and go to sleep, away from everything. "Leave me alone. I am happy to die here."

Sparkle sighed deeply and knelt beside him. "If you tink I don' know how to dress a drunk, tink again." He could feel the warmth of her body against his as she slipped his limp limbs into his clothing. She kept up a running monologue as she worked. "You actin' like you woman just left you or some such ting when me not believe you ever love dat woman anyway, so I don' know why else you might do such ting to yourself..."

"How do you know about Chloe? You don't know Chloe..." He wrenched away from her and tottered to his feet. "I can pull my own pants up very well, thank you. Wait, I was tired of wearing them..."

"Chloe? Dat your witchy fortuneteller woman's real name? I thought she Kit Cat or some name. Don't be pulling dem jeans down again." Sparkle buttoned his waistband and picked up his shoes. "You can walk barefoot out to de sidewalk. Now where dat phone of yours – you gone show me how you call dem Uber cabs."

Myles had only a vague memory of falling into the back of a white car, nodding out against Sparkle's infinitely comfortable body, and then being unceremoniously dumped onto his own bed, where he awoke several hours later with a headache the size of Mexico. When he crawled out to the kitchen for some water, Darcy appeared with a steaming mug of some foul-smelling tea which she insisted he drink, claiming it would not only cure his hangover but get rid of his demons as well. When he barfed it up a half hour later, he decided she was wrong. He would never get over his demons; they were going to haunt him forever.

The next time he awoke, the first thing he saw was a large silver tassel dangerously close to his face. "Be careful you don't poke my eye out with that thing." His voice was hoarse and did not sound like his own.

"Don't tell me what to do wit my body or I will have you arrested." Sparkle's fingers crushed his in a powerful squeeze. "You smell like a he-goat – you need to wash yourself, boy."

Before he could get out a sassy comeback, he heard the pinging of a text message on his cell phone. "It been going off for de last hour like dat." Sparkle reached across him and for a brief second, he suffered the enjoyable sensation of her flesh smothering his face. "Make it stop."

He looked at the screen. Five messages from Kit. "Shit."

"What it say?"

"She's coming back in a couple of days."

"So you be getting some again soon den. All de misery over."

Myles tossed the phone on the floor and then rolled towards Sparkle. "I wish." He wanted to bury himself in the steadfast safety of her presence and forget about the future or the past, but she pushed him away.

"You too stinky to touch me. Go shower now and make yourself pretty. Your woman coming home and me need to go."

"Sparkle."

But she was already in the doorway. "Me see you on de bus tomorrow. De Spotted Cat say we don't come, we back on de street like de garbage we be."

"I owe you big time, girlfriend!" he called after her.

CHAPTER TWELVE

West Jordan, Vermont
Early March 2018

"So when are you doing this New Orleans trip again?" As she spoke to Tyler, Chloe's eyes did not leave her computer screen where she was proofing the preliminary layout of the next issue of the newspaper.

"Next Monday. We should be all ready for press before I leave, and I'll be back by Friday to help with the following week. I'm working on some feature stories for it right now." Tyler glanced up from his laptop. "You good with that?"

"Yeah… it's just… I really want to get away for a couple of days. I haven't spent a night anywhere else for nearly a year." She was embarrassed that her voice actually broke a little with the emotion she was feeling. "And Angel and I were talking about taking a little weekend trip somewhere, like maybe Montreal, before she leaves. Would you mind?" As she saw him considering the possibility, she began speaking faster. "I already talked to George and he said he would be happy to help with the twins, he would even stay over if you want, and I've doubled up on my pumping so that there should be plenty of milk in the freezer for bottles and only Athena is really nursing much anymore, and…"

"Chloe. Chill." She could tell he was amused. "I get it. We'll figure it out. Get out of here for a couple of nights, why don'tcha?"

"You're okay with it? I know it's a lot to ask, especially with Artemis starting to walk and all…"

"Relax. I've got George, the wonder nanny. Go scratch that vagabond itch of yours for a few days, and have some fun. We'll be fine."

She flushed with appreciation; she knew he was already nervous about it, he didn't even like it when she went out for a few hours. "Thanks, it really means a lot to me. I don't know when I'll get to do this again with anybody." She leaped up, gave him an impulsive hug, and then ran out of the office, already dialing her phone.

"And tell Angel I need to get together with her to talk about New Orleans before you go!" he called after her.

It had been an intense week since the night of the snowstorm, a roller coaster of pent-up energy and release, in so many ways. When Chloe had emerged from the bedroom the next morning with a child on each hip, she'd carefully closed the door so Angel could keep sleeping and turned to find George already in the kitchen making coffee. He looked at her suspiciously. "Why are you smiling like that?" he asked. "You're never cheery before coffee."

Chloe knew she was beaming and wondered how long it would be before George figured out why. The man was crazy intuitive when it came to her moods. "I had a good time last night. Angel stayed over. It's been like forever since I had a girlfriend."

He leaned closer to her and grinned. "Honey, you have sex written all over you. Give me those babies and go take a shower."

"George! Stop it!" She tried to sound offended. "Don't say stuff like that."

"Girl, who knows you better than George." It was his turn to pretend to be slighted. "If you got some, I'm happy for you. And if not... well, then there's still work to be done."

She flashed him a warning look as they heard Tyler moving around in the other part of the house. "Don't. Say. Anything."

"Sealed. With a kiss." He made the gesture of turning a key in a lock in front of his lips. "Can't wait to meet this Angel."

But as it turned out, to Chloe's distress, George and Angel were oil and water, swirling around each other like distrustful animals, never connecting on any harmonic level. When Angel finally left around noon, after they eventually managed to dig her car out of the driveway and get it onto the plowed road, George shook his head at Chloe.

"Be careful with that one, darling."

"What! Why do you say that? I love how exotic and different she is. You don't know how I used to be before I was a stupid stay-at-home mom. I used to know *interesting* people."

"I'm just saying. Something doesn't feel quite authentic to me."

"Oh, what do you know about women anyway. Tyler likes her." Chloe walked away from George, not wanting to hear his disapproval.

"And we all know what a good judge of character he is," George yelled after her.

She knew it was true, Tyler had made some really bad choices in his life, especially regarding women. But she wasn't Tyler.

In the days that followed, Angel flowed in and out of the household until she became an accepted fixture in their lives. In Chloe's opinion she was always helpful and always fun. Angel seemed to push the button on the neon arrow that pointed the way towards intrigue, just over the edge of Chloe's comfort zone, and Chloe loved that feeling of risk and adventure she had been missing so much. Sometimes it was just as simple as staying up a little too late, but sometimes it was something that Chloe knew was on the unacceptable meter, like Angel giving Chloe a line of coke to snort in the bathroom while Tyler cooked dinner in the other room. A couple of times they played a dangerous truth or dare game where Angel would get Chloe off sexually if Chloe would do something illicit for her in return, like shoplift makeup or drink from an open bottle while driving.

She always felt kind of disgusted with herself afterwards but somehow the reward seemed worth the transgression.

On a couple of nights Chloe made sure that Angel drank too much so that she would be unable to drive and forced to stay over. But Angel never seemed drunk enough for Chloe to take advantage of her. Somehow she always managed to take control of the situation once they were in the bedroom by seducing Chloe with the offer of exotic drugs combined with a sensual touch or a wet tongue in all the now-familiar right places. Chloe loved melting away in a haze of sex and opioids and before long she accepted the fact that she was a willing addict to anything Angel.

Somehow the days took on a semblance of normality that included Angel, whether it was caring for babies, covering newspaper stories, or cleaning house. When Artemis took her first steps, Chloe videoed her toddling into Angel's open arms and then back out again to chase Diva across the room. Angel didn't make fun of Tyler's nightly TV ritual; instead she sat at the other end of the couch curled up under a blanket and watched NCIS reruns with him. Angel watched with fascination as Chloe nonchalantly pumped containers of breast milk for the freezer and was delighted when given the opportunity to bottle-feed the girls and put them down for their naps. Angel dropped Chloe at the high school to get some photos of an award ceremony and then came back to pick her up with an open bottle of tequila and a small bag of blow.

"This is so much better than when Tyler gives me a ride!" Chloe laughed. "Wow, I'm so high. You okay to drive?"

"Oh, yeah – those were just gifts for you. I only had one shot while I was waiting and I'm not a coke whore like you. Girlfriend."

"I'm not a coke whore! How could I be – I haven't been near any in years until a few days ago." But she knew it was obvious to Angel how much she loved the high and she wasn't going to pass up the opportunity if it was put in front of her for a few days.

176

Once Angel dared her to go grocery-shopping dressed like a prostitute, which gave Chloe a scary thrill and actually seemed to turn Angel on a little – afterwards she recalled the arching of her hips and the sensation of her boot heels pressed into the window as Angel electrified Chloe's body with memories she savored for days.

"I want to go somewhere nobody knows me," she murmured, as they lay in the back of the cold car, Chloe's skirt still up around her waist, Angel's face resting against her bare abdomen, Chloe stroking her hair, the windows frosted over with the steam of their breaths. "I want to do bad things in public and not care."

Angel picked up her head and gazed at Chloe with a gleam in her eyes. "Really? I can think of all kinds of things I would love to dare you to do. Push your limits."

Chloe felt her stomach tighten a little with both fear and exhilaration. "Game on? With prizes?" she challenged.

Angel stared at her, the wheels in her mind clearly turning. "Yes, with big prizes." Without breaking their gaze, she forced a hand into Chloe's push-up bra and tweaked one of her nipples so hard that Chloe cried out in pain.

"Ouch! What was that about?" she asked, pulling away.

"Just making sure you're up for anything. Game on." Angel yanked the bra down to expose the throbbing breast and then got up, opened the door, and climbed into the driver's seat. "Let's go home. And I dare you to leave it like that and get out of the car really slowly and flash those two old people before you get into the front."

"No problem," Chloe declared climbing out into the icy parking lot and defiantly standing outside the passenger door so that the elderly man and woman in the neighboring sedan could get a jaw-dropping eyeful before she got back into the car. "Game on."

Angel threw back her head and laughed as she started the engine. "Oh, baby, you are the best. I can't wait to get you out of this small town."

177

"Let's get out of this country even. How about Montreal?"

"Canada?" squeaked Angel. "Yes! Oh, yes! I've never been. And I've even got my passport. Canada, that's so perfect. Chloe, you're a genius, I love you."

Angel's praise warmed Chloe's heart and eclipsed the fact that her nipple was still hurting like hell from the unexpected abuse. It didn't matter; they were planning a trip. Now she just needed Tyler's buy-in.

The next few days flew by as Chloe tried to organize her family routine enough to leave it for forty-eight hours, as well as find an affordable place to stay in Montreal. "No Air BnB," Angel had warned. "Not enough privacy. Find us some cheap hotel in a bad part of town."

While Chloe buzzed around doing laundry, making lists and guiltily kissing Athena and Artemis so that they would know she loved them, Angel and Tyler poured over maps and websites about New Orleans. When they discovered that Angel was flying back to Louisiana only a few days after Tyler arrived, he was delighted. "Maybe we can meet up and you can show me around."

"Well, uh, Arnaudville is like two hours away, but yeah maybe I could spend a night in town before I go back home." Angel sounded a bit wary of the idea. "I might have a friend I could stay with."

"Well, if you're stuck, maybe I can get you a room. It would be worth it to have you as my local guide."

Chloe did not like the sound of that but, even more, she did not like the idea that Angel would be going home just a few days after they came back from Canada. What kind of monotony was her life going to return to without Angel in it? She pushed the idea out of her mind, determined not to ruin the upcoming weekend with thoughts of their impending separation.

It was late morning on Saturday by the time they finally got going, heading north through the snowy landscape of northern Vermont to a small town border crossing that Chloe assured Angel was "super-easy and super-cute."

"I brought some special treats for you. I guess you better do them now, in case they, like, you know, search us when we go across." Angel held up two plastic packets, one held weed and one with a small amount of white powder.

"Oh, my god, I love you. Let's get this party started." Chloe pulled out a packet of rolling papers. "I'm going to Canada with a buzz on."

"Just a few tokes of pot for me. The rest is for you to celebrate with."

"You want me to snort all this by myself?"

"Do half now and then half right before we cross. That way it'll last you longer," Angel advised. "How many miles is it?"

"I don't know. About forty minutes though. We'll start to see signs." She hummed happily to herself in anticipation of how stoned she would be when they got to Quebec.

"Passports, license and registration, please." The solo border guard leaned out of his booth and peered into the car at the two of them. "Where are you ladies going today?"

"Girls weekend in Montreal." Angel smiled at him. "Y'all are welcome to join us."

Chloe didn't trust herself to speak, just nodded and grinned in agreement.

But the officer was frowning now. "I'm afraid to disappoint you, girls, but this is a rental car. You can't take it into Canada."

Chloe felt as though she were falling off a very high cliff. "But we have to get there!" she blurted out in a breathless voice.

"Shhh. Calm down, sweetie." Angel put a restraining hand on Chloe's arm. "What are our options, sir?"

"You can park the car in that supermarket parking lot and walk across. There's a restaurant and guesthouse about half a mile down the road. They might be able to help you with finding a Canadian rental car. Or you can have yourselves a nice little vacation there. But it's not Montreal."

"Is there a bus or something?"

"You'd have to get up to Magog for that." He handed them back their documents. "Have a good day. You can turn around right over there."

"What are we going to do?" Chloe's enhanced mental state had her bordering on hysteria.

"Shhh, calm down. We can still make this work."

"There's probably a bus if we drive to Burlington." Her brain was speeding through a roulette wheel of possibilities.

"How about we just park the car, take a few things and walk across. When we get out of sight of the guard, we'll hitchhike. Is that illegal in Quebec?"

Chloe shrugged and her shoulders seemed to reach up several feet beyond her ears before falling back down again. "I don't know. How will we get back?"

"Chloe – look at me. Focus on my eyes. Now. I dare you to do this with me."

It was hard to focus on Angel's swirling irises; it felt like falling into the riptide of a seaside lagoon.

"Chloe." Angel touched the end of a finger to the crotch seam of Chloe's jeans and then lightly ran it all the way up to her lips. "I dare you. Game on?"

"Game on."

Thirty minutes later they stood at the side of a Quebec highway, the cold wind whipping through their down jackets and making their hair fly around their heads. "Here comes a car. Unzip your jacket a little and stick out your thumb." Angel turned her back to light a cigarette.

The car rolled to a stop a few feet away and backed up. The driver looked at them through polarized sunglasses and asked something that sounded to Chloe like, "Oooh sone los shoon fees going?"

"Montreal!" they chorused in excited unison.

He patted the back door. "Allons au Montreal."

While Angel chatted in a strange mix of Cajun French and English with the two Quebecois men in the front seat, Chloe slept most of the way into the city, her head in Angel's lap. Angel kept one hand hidden under Chloe's jacket and sweater, resting it against Chloe's breast, occasionally twirling the nipple between her thumb and finger until it was erect and sensitive enough to make Chloe moan a little and jerk awake. After a while she pretended to be asleep just so Angel would continue to play with her while she conversed with the two Canadians, at one point even rolling over and moving Angel's hand to the other breast. Eventually her buzz wore off and after a while Angel started to get rough and Chloe found herself biting the cloth of Angel's skirt to keep from crying out. She grabbed Angel's hand to make her stop and realized that Angel's fingers were wet and slippery with the milk that Chloe's breasts were leaking from so much stimulation. Their eyes met and then Chloe's widened as Angel slid her hand out and pushed the fingers into Chloe's mouth, all the while chattering away with Rene and Francoise.

Confused and disoriented, Chloe struggled to a sitting position and dug in her backpack for something absorbent to put under her sweater. This was not a usual occurrence anymore, maybe it was because she had been pumping so much in the last few days; she hoped it wasn't going to ruin the trip. Looking around she realized they were already crossing the bridge into Montreal and a few minutes later were being deposited on the street outside a rundown-looking hotel that occupied a narrow vertical portion of a city block.

Chloe was so excited that she hugged Angel while jumping up and down. "We made it, I can't believe it. Here we are!"

They climbed four flights to a tiny overheated room barely big enough to hold a double bed and a nightstand – the bathroom seemed to be constructed in a former closet and was accessed by pulling on a piece of wainscoting along the wall. Chloe threw herself down on the sagging mattress as Angel immediately forced the double hung window open and stepped out onto a fire escape overlooking an alley. "Fantastic, I can smoke right out here," she announced lighting up.

"I'm dying of thirst. And it's so hot in here. Do we have any water?" Chloe stripped off her sweater and the camisole beneath that displayed two uneven wet circles on it. "And I need to call home, let them know we arrived. Oh shit. Oh shit. My phone has no service here."

"Honey. Honey. Give me that useless thing." Angel reached through the window and put out her hand. "I'm keeping it for the rest of the weekend. And look what I am trading you for it." Another ziplock bag full of a gleaming white substance was resting in Angel's palm.

Chloe squealed with amazement. "Oh. My God. You smuggled that across? You truly are my angel." As she reached eagerly to make the swap, Angel pulled it away.

"So first, you have to agree that you are going to let me take control of this weekend. You are going to relax and do nothing – I am going to make the plans, and set the agenda and take care of you, my dear Chloe." Angel climbed back inside and sat down on the edge of the bed. "Will you let me do that for you?" She stroked Chloe's cheek lovingly.

The idea of being completely cared for brought real tears to Chloe's eyes. She licked her dry lips and nodded. "Yes. Yes."

"You're going to let me pick out the bars we go to, what street corners we hang out on. I am going to decide what you should wear, or not wear..." Angel reached for the button of Chloe's jeans and Chloe excitedly helped her slide them off as she continued talking in a hypnotic, seductive voice. "I'm even going to dress you and do your makeup. And I'm going to make sure you stay high all weekend. Very very high. In all the ways you like best."

"Yes. Yes." Chloe brought her lips up to meet Angel's but after a brief kiss Angel pushed her away and held up the bag. "Do you want to try some of this? It's different and really special."

"Do you want me try it?"

"Very much. And then I have a really creative afternoon activity planned that I think you will get off on." She traded Chloe the drugs for her cell phone, which disappeared deep into the recesses of her purse. Then Angel kicked off her turquoise cowgirl boots and gathered up her long skirt and sat cross-legged on the dangerously bouncy mattress next to Chloe. She ran her slender fingers along the soft sensitive skin on the inside of Chloe's thighs which parted willingly under her touch, even as Chloe leaned sideways over the line of fine white powder on the nightstand. With a contented sigh of anticipation, she lay back against the thin pillows on the headboard, waiting for the rush to hit her, and opened her legs wider, hoping Angel would move in soon.

The blinding flash of blissful euphoria was like nothing she had experienced before, so intense that she lost all sense of place and time. As she slowly floated to the surface of consciousness, her first thought was that she had never felt so good ever in her life. She blinked and blinked until the swirling room came into focus and there was Angel's happy face grinning down at her and mouthing the words, "Good, right?" Or maybe she was speaking but Chloe just couldn't hear her. She had never felt so loose-limbed and relaxed. Nothing mattered. At all.

"So lovely," she mumbled or thought she did. Angel was holding a pair of scissors and asking her something, and whatever it was, it had to be all right. As if she was watching a movie, she observed Angel begin to trim the wiry curls of Chloe's pubic hair.

"Why? Do they bother you?" Her slurred question seemed to use up all her energy reserves and Chloe's eyelids fell heavily after the effort.

"No, silly. I told you. Couldn't you hear me?" Angel asked gaily. "About the magic marker tattoo I'm going to draw on you?"

"A magic tattoo... draw on me?" A rainbow of neon colors swirled through Chloe's imagination and she let herself be swept along by it. Some part of her felt alarmed and tried to move away as the other part just watched passively.

"Like this." Angel picked up Chloe's arm and turned it so that the inside of her wrist was up. "Oh, look at you now, my ragdoll," she commented, amused by the limpness of Chloe's limbs. Chloe almost fell asleep and then woke up to the feeling of something crawling on her skin. "Don't wriggle. You'll wreck it."

She saw that Angel was sketching with a fine point marker on the smooth surface of Chloe's inner arm. The outline of a little blue image appeared. In a moment she held it up for Chloe to see. "There! What is it?"

"I know! I know!" She looked at the iconic symbol of a halo over a pair of wings but she wasn't able to bring the words to her lips. "Angel. Angel." Chloe knew she was repeating herself but she couldn't help it. She brought the wrist to her lips and kissed it. "My angel." She was feeling both numb and tingly at the same time, almost like having an orgasm.

"That's a big smile on your face, baby. What's going on in that head of yours?"

Chloe was still clutching the tattoo to her mouth and Angel slowly pried her arm back down to her side. "Want another one? How about I do something pretty on your titty?"

Angel laughed at the rhyme she had made and Chloe laughed with her – it seemed like the funniest joke in the world.

"And then maybe something fine on your behind? And something hot on your twat?"

Chloe was laughing so hard now that she was gasping for breath. It felt so good. She had never been happier.

She had no memory of the rest of the afternoon. She thought she heard Angel calling her name from the top of a tall building but she was too far away and then someone was tugging on her nipples like it was time to nurse but they kept pulling and pulling and pulling until she finally heard herself yell "Stop! Stop!" and she opened her eyes. The light was already fading from the room and Angel was sitting on the nightstand next to the bed, hovering over her.

"Time to get up, Sleeping Beauty. We have places to go and bad things to do."

Chloe's mouth was so dry she could barely speak as she struggled to sit up. "Why do my tits hurt so much? They feel sharp like tacks, like someone put clothespins on them." Her voice was a harsh whisper as she explored the tender soreness that radiated from her chest.

Angel held a bottle of water to her lips and Chloe guzzled it greedily. "Y'all look like a young calf drinking. Now let's put some clothes on you and fix your face." She helped Chloe to a standing position. For a moment the room turned upside down and Chloe broke out in a sweat and then everything fell back to its normal orientation.

"I don't feel so great anymore." She gulped at the cold fresh air coming in from the open window and then realized her whole body felt like ice. "I'm cold, Angel."

"Well, you're not wearing anything, honey. Let's get you dressed." She held up a strange piece of clothing that seemed to be made of leather and laces. "Now help me get this garment of mine onto that sexy body of yours. I had to open it up to the largest setting but I'm sure it will work."

In obedient wonder, Chloe stepped into the bustier that Angel held out for her. "Ouch, it's tight. The cups are too small. My nipples are half showing. I look like I should work in a German beer garden."

"Or on a street corner. Oh, it will totally work. They'll stay in as long as you don't bend over too far. And if you do...then ooh, la, la! And that rose I drew right above your left nip is totally visible. See it?"

Chloe did not remember the red flower peeking saucily over her neckline. "When did that get there? You drew it, right? It's not real, is it?"

"You are such a riot when you are high, Chloe," Angel teased. "Now where's that fur miniskirt you packed?"

"Ohhh, my fur skirt, I love my fur skirt. Thank you for including that in my outfit."

"You're going to need something to keep your bare butt warm. Not to mention that smokin' hot twat." Angel grinned broadly and winked.

Chloe slapped at her playfully, but Angel sidestepped the potential embrace. "You be okay with bare legs? Because it'll make things so much easier. Well, I suppose we could cut the crotch out of these tights."

"I don't know what you're talking about, but you're turning me on."

"That's what it's all about, right? Now sit here and let me do your eyes." She patted the nightstand. When Chloe sat down, she felt the skirt ride up above her crotch and Angel quickly tugged it down a crucial inch or two, patting the fur. "Like a bunny." Angel giggled. "Oh that's a perfect name for your weekend persona. Bunny. I love it."

An image of a vulnerable pet rabbit came to Chloe's mind. "Um, I don't know..." She stroked the soft skirt lovingly.

"Chin up, Bunny, don't look down." Angel came at Chloe's lids with a black eyeliner.

Chloe was starting to feel depressed and headachy. "When can I have some more of that fabulous whatever it is. That was the most amazing high of my life."

"As soon as I'm done here. I need you to sit up straight and hold still. And you gotta take it a little slower, babe. I mean Bunny. We've got some walking to do, Bun-Bun."

It was like floating down the street in the embrace of an electric river. She had never felt so calm and so alive, everyone staring at her, lots of men smiling, Angel's arm around her keeping her steady and guiding her forward.

"Oh, I think Bunny is going to get some dick tonight," Angel said conversationally.

"What?! Don't be growth. I mean gross." Chloe stumbled and started to slowly fall, but Angel caught her and stood her upright.

"Everything all right, ladies?" A concerned citizen who had seen Chloe start to stumble, looked first to Angel for confirmation and then his gaze roamed fixatedly over Chloe's body.

"She's fine. Just not used to her new shoes." As she steered Chloe on down the block, she murmured again, "Oh, yeah, I definitely see some dick in your future. We're going to find you a boyfriend tonight, Bunny girl."

Chloe stopped walking and the street seemed to tilt sideways like a big slide. "Why do you keep saying that? I want to have sex with you." She leaned towards Angel who had to throw both arms out to keep her from toppling again. "Right here. Right now. Standing up on the street."

"Later. I'm sure there will be no problem getting you some standing-up sex later. But we have a few stops to make before we get to the club."

"Club? Like drinking and dancing?" Chloe sighed as they moved forward again. "I love you, Angel."

It was almost like sleepwalking. She knew they went first to some kind of lingerie store where a woman put a tape measure around her chest and Chloe couldn't stop giggling from the sensation of it, even as she signed the credit card slip.

"How did they get my credit card number?" she asked Angel in wonder. "I mean, we're in a different country."

"You gave me your card to use, sweetie." Angel patted her on the head and exchanged an apologetic look with the saleswoman.

"Did we get the red one? Do I sound drunk? I sound drunk, don't I?"

She actually thought she might have fallen asleep walking because the next thing she knew Angel was squeezing her arm and asking her loudly, "Which one do you want, dear?" And she thought she was hallucinating because it looked like a wall of giant penises was about to fall on them.

"Where are we?" she whispered in awe.

"Sorry, my friend is a little high. Just give us a big one that vibrates. You take credit cards, right?"

Some part of Chloe's brain registered what was going on. "Wow. Are we in a... sex toys store?"

"Yeah, she really is stoned, isn't she?" The clerk behind the cash register stared at Chloe. "She's got a nice set of knockers too. Are they real?"

"How can you even ask that?" Chloe demanded, pulling down the neckline of the leather bodice. "Look at them!"

"Oh, my god, now we've got to stuff them back in there!" Angel was laughing as she guided Chloe to a chair.

Had she actually blacked out or just lost track of time? Now they were in a bar and doing shots of tequila and there were a lot flashing lights that made everything a trippy neon purple color. She saw Angel several stools down, talking to a bald guy with tattoos on his head and pointing at Chloe. Then somehow she was on the dance floor surrounded by sweaty gyrating bodies and a big black guy was holding her hips and grinding on her and it felt really good. She lifted her arms and reached behind her to grasp her hands behind his neck and her breasts came free of the tenuous hold of the leather cups and began bouncing in the air. Her partner put his big hands over them and said, "Oh, baby," and pulled her closer.

"Do you wanna do a speedball with me?" he shouted into her ear.

She had only the vaguest recollection of having sex in the bathroom with him – she felt like she was barely in her body as he groaned, "Ride my cock, ride it harder. Oh, bitch..."

When she staggered back out into the club, Angel was at her side almost instantly. "Oh, my god, you fucked him, didn't you?" she said as she pulled the bodice back up into position. "You finally got a big dick in your smoking hot twat."

Chloe thought she had tried to smack Angel across the face, but instead had somehow ended up hitting her own head against the wall.

"Baby, isn't this what you wanted? To be wild and do bad things? You just got an A plus on the pop quiz."

"Yes. Yes, I did. Am. Angel, Angel, I'm so high. I want to sleep but I want to dance. And I'm really really thirsty."

"Good. Because there's some guys at the bar who want to buy Bunny a drink."

The next thing she was conscious of was the glare of the mid-day sun falling across her face. She knew if she lifted her head she would be a goner but she had to see where she was. She was relieved to find herself sprawled naked across the wrinkled sheets of the saggy mattress, wearing only her boots. Everything from her skull to toes ached like she had the flu, and her crotch burned like it was on fire. She panicked when she peered down and saw that there were, in fact, flames coming out of it. But then she realized it was Angel's artwork, the orange and red blaze was a magic marker drawing of triangular little flames; one larger one that licked up the side of her belly was a little smeared from sweat. Chloe only had a flickering memory of the tickle of the pens but she could hear Angel's voice loud in her mind repeating the words "smoking hot twat" and the two of them laughing. She tried to suppress an overwhelming flush of shame – had anybody else seen her cartooned up like this? Had she actually showed people?

"Angel?" She couldn't even sit up to look around and she thought she might vomit all over the nubby yellow polyester blanket. "Angel? I need you. Where are you?"

She couldn't remember feeling this awful ever. But she couldn't remember much of anything. A big sob welled up in her chest and suddenly she was bawling, choking on the tears and snot running down her throat.

She was crying so hard that she barely heard the door to the room open. She felt Angel's touch on her forehead and face, heard the whisper in her ear. "Don't worry, baby.

I'm going to make it all really better for you now." A warm washcloth was placed gently across her eyes, just like Angel had done at home. "You're going to be okay. Now let me have this arm. There we go."

Chloe tried to breathe slower but could not stop hiccupping. Her head was pounding too much to turn it. She thought she heard Angel speaking softly to someone else, and then she felt her bicep being squeezed. She started to pull her arm away but something heavy held it down. Her back suddenly arched in reaction to a sharp prick followed by an icy cold sensation.

And then she was completely filled with the biggest rush of euphoria ever and all the pain went away.

CHAPTER THIRTEEN

Montreal, Quebec, Canada
Early March 2018

"You sure that's her name? How come she doesn't answer to it?"

There was a throaty laugh followed by an attack of raspy coughing. "Of course, I'm sure. She's just so wasted on your awesome shit that she doesn't want to come back to reality."

"Yeah, damn. I've known some crack whores but she seems kinda different."

"She's fresh. Like a virgin." More hoarse cackling. "She's alive – watch this. Bunny, baby. Bunny."

A tickling that felt like spiders crawling up the inside of her thigh caused an involuntary shudder and then suddenly Chloe was awake and trying to remember where she was. A cracked cement ceiling with a dirty square glass light fixture pulsed overhead. She nodded her chin just an inch so she could see better and the effort made her want to go back to sleep. She didn't understand what she saw.

One of her legs, still dressed in a black knee-high boot, was resting on the iron headboard; her other leg was splayed across the laps of Angel and a stranger with tattoos on his bald head that looked vaguely familiar. The two of them were propped up on the pillows sharing a joint, resting their elbows on her thigh and staring intently at her. She didn't like her head being jammed up against the foot rail and her crotch being wide open like that in front of a guy she didn't know. She tried to move the leg that was in the air but nothing happened. For a moment she panicked, thinking she was paralyzed or something; she willed her muscles to move and felt a small motion in her knee. Then she saw the studded leather belt that strapped her ankle tightly to the railing.

"Why? Why?" she asked plaintively in a repetitive way she couldn't seem to control.

"What's she asking?" The man was looking at her like she was a zoo animal and Chloe felt intense venomous hate for a second before the feeling drifted away and she forgot all about it.

"Oh, sweetie. You have Restless Leg Syndrome or something. You kept kicking us with your sharp heel so I just got it out of the way. Plus I wanted to show Zoltan my artistry." Angel drew a triangle below Chloe's abdomen with her fingernail, letting the tip of it come to rest on the most-sensitive place in her vagina, just out of Chloe's line of vision. "And of course we've been admiring your sweet spot too. So soft and pink and juicy. Zoltan, don't you just want to eat her up?"

Angel licked her lips and the sight of her wet tongue combined with the sensation of her feather-light touch sent a jagged jolt of electricity through Chloe's brain. She actually felt her eyes roll back into her head before she passed out again.

Her next conscious awareness was the sound of Angel crooning some song about a ragdoll and the smell of a lavender scented washcloth. She tried to move her leg again and discovered her limbs were no longer spread-eagled and there was no bald-headed man staring at her. She was curled up in a tight ball against the wall and Angel was gently washing her brow. "Let me get you cleaned up, baby. You're a mess."

"I'm sorry I'm wrecking our day." Chloe was surprised to hear her own apology came out in a full clear sentence.

"It's all about you, baby. I just want you to feel good. AND do bad things. Right? That's our goal. Now lay back so I can get this washrag into your sticky places. You kind of left earth for a while there. How'd that feel?"

"Beyond... beyond..." Chloe couldn't express the experience in words. "Who was that man?"

"What man? I'm the only one here, baby. You must have been dreaming, Bun-Bun." Angel stepped into the little bathroom and ran the washcloth under the hot water tap.

The sudden clarity Chloe had been feeling was instantly clouded by doubt. "The – the – bald one…"

Angel ran the warm wet cloth down the length of Chloe's arms, scrubbing the back of her hands and between her fingers. "The one we met at the bar last night? He wasn't here. But you must be psychic, because we are going out to meet him and his friend later. You remember – the little one who really liked you, Bunny? You don't remember?" She smiled indulgently at Chloe's blank look. "The one who did you on the pool table?"

Chloe tried really hard to bring up a face, but she didn't recall anyone except the guy she'd had sex with in the bathroom, and him only sort of. "Pool table guy? What did he do to me?"

"All I know is when I walked into the back room you had a leg-lock around his neck and everyone was cheering you on." Angel slapped her butt playfully with the wet cloth a couple of times. "You really made up for lost time last night."

Chloe felt as though she was losing body parts – she had no idea what Angel was talking about. "I did?"

Angel gazed at her thoughtfully before saying, "You really don't remember? I mean, how many guys did you fuck? Five? Six? I lost count when I found you in that three-way." She went back to the sink to warm the washcloth again. "You were unstoppable. Like a sex machine." She grinned mischievously at the lost expression on Chloe's face. "Aw, what's the matter? Want me to tell you all about it?"

Chloe closed her eyes and searched deeply in the recesses of her mind but came up with nothing at all. Angel ran the wet toweling up and down her thighs and then vigorously between her legs. For a brief second Chloe thought she was going to have a mind-blowingly fast orgasm, but then the sensation passed and all she felt was lightheaded. Angel was chattering away about some hard-bodied cowboy. "... thought I was your pimp... gave me a hundred dollars for you to suck him off in the alley... how was that anyway..." and then a Frenchman with a hairy chest and gold chains. "... let him finger-fuck you right there at the bar while his friend played with your tits... Don't tell me you've forgotten all about it? That was when the bartender threw you out. You had such a good time being a bad bunny. Oh, baby, don't cry. You were such a bad girl and you loved it. You told me so. You know it's what you've been really wanting for so long. Ever since that undependable boyfriend dumped you and ran away. Yeah, you really showed him you didn't need him anymore."

Chloe pressed her face into the blanket and tried not to hear what Angel was saying. "I'm really thirsty, Angel. I need a drink."

"Of course, baby. What was I thinking... " There was a suspended moment in time and then she heard Angel commanding her to sit up. Chloe upended the plastic cup into her mouth and choked on the burning sensation in her throat and nose.

"That's not—" Wooziness descended over her like a thick crocheted net.

"Vodka, honey. You said a drink. Oh, I'm sorry, did you mean water? We're all out."

"Food? Hungry." Chloe couldn't remember eating in Montreal.

"You haven't had much of an appetite. Except for one thing, of course. We'll get something later when we go out. You know, I've been thinking Bunny would look really good as a blonde."

"So would you." She leaned forward to kiss Angel's lips and tipped over onto the floor. A wave of depression rolled over her as her face met the filthy wall-to-wall carpeting. She dragged herself into a kneeling position. "Angel, can I please have some more of those great drugs you brought?" She realized she was begging.

"Oh, Bunny, dear." Angel chucked her chin affectionately. "You blew through that stuff last night. But I scored something even better, didn't I? It was amazing watching you get off on that. It was like – pow! Didn't you love it?" She stroked the underside of Chloe's left arm and rolled it over to examine it in the light, pressing lightly on a faint blue bruise just below the elbow. "I'll get better at this. Do you want to try again?"

Chloe tilted her head trying to comprehend Angel's words. "Did you... what... inject me?" She knew this was a really awful thing but she couldn't recall why.

"Your nose started bleeding so badly, it was the only way – I mean, I have heard of people dying from bloody noses."

"But... so..." What was happening? She leaned her forehead against the edge of the mattress. "I'm really starving."

"Look, how about I give you a little more of Zoltan's awesome shit and then I'll do your hair and we'll go out." Now Angel was putting a pillow on the floor and gently coaxing Chloe down on to it. When Chloe tried to resist, Angel straddled her hips and sat back, slipping a hand between Chloe's legs as she tried to get her to make steady eye contact. "There's my girl. I know how you like it. Stay with me now. Yes, baby, yes, baby, yes. Here, you do it to yourself, while I do this. That's it, you know what you like. Eyes open, Bunny. Bunny! Watch me." Angel held up a colorful Mexican belt and then slid it around Chloe's upper arm. "Come on now, we're doing this together. You rub while I tie this tight." She pressed just below the elbow again. "Thank god your veins are as beautiful as the rest of you."

Chloe was breathing hard, unable to take her eyes off the spectacle that was taking place, as the fingers of her free hand moved faster and faster against herself.

"That's it, that's it, you're almost there, take yourself higher..." Angel kept up a steady stream of supportive phrases as she fiddled with something on the floor beside Chloe. "Go on, girl, go on, let's make this a double whammy.

195

Watch me now. Here we go... You won't believe how fast you are going to get off."

Chloe wasn't sure when or how they left the hotel room that night, and she certainly didn't care. She was almost certain she had felt the cold tiles of the bathroom floor against her back as Angel massaged her scalp and poured scalding water over her head. She had a terrifying memory of looking in the mirror and seeing another woman look back at her – a blonde in a tiny red lace bra with projectile bosoms and a rose tattoo.

She dreamed someone was pounding themselves into her so hard that she was vibrating like an engine, but when she opened her eyes there was only Angel at the foot of the bed, smoking a cigarette and nodding at her with an encouraging smile on her face. There was a hazy recollection of a cab ride and falling down on snow-covered steps. A smoky noise-filled space, she was wearing only Angel's down coat, and then she was wearing only her boots, dancing naked in a roomful of gaping strangers before melting into a clumsy heap on a wet wooden floor. Unfamiliar hands groped her and dragged her lethargic body down a hall to a dimly lit place where she was rolled unceremoniously onto a hard mattress that rested a few inches off the floor, and where she gratefully drifted off again into unconsciousness.

Once she did wake up choking and coughing to laughter ringing loudly all around her. A blindfold was quickly tied over her eyes as somebody held a bottle to her lips. She sucked down tepid water and then it was pressed to her mouth again, but this time it was something fiery and alcoholic that made her sputter violently.

At some point, when she felt like she was breaking through the surface of the ocean and gasping for breath, she was cognizant of Angel and two strange men looking down at her. "Good. I like them to be awake," someone said.

"I like them to be tied up," said the other.

196

"Well, who wants to be first?" asked a voice that sounded like Angel's.

Chloe screamed but no noise came out of her mouth. She tried to roll away but her arms were caught in something above her head.

"If she kicks me in the balls I'll beat the shit out of her. Hold her down."

She heard a shrill shriek coming from somewhere, high-pitched and keening. Then someone smacked her hard across the face and the sound disappeared into a well of blackness.

"Bunny. Bunny."

Her eyelids fluttered open. She was back at the hotel. The room was quiet. It was morning. Angel was standing next to the bed, hands on her hips, looking down at her.

"It's time to get up."

When Chloe didn't respond, Angel grabbed her by the hands and jerked her to a standing position, forcing her to be upright as her head spun and her knees buckled.

"Everything hurts, Angel. I can't." She fell to her hands and knees, and then vomited a gush of pale liquid onto the rug.

"Oh, my god. You are disgusting." Was somebody else there? This did not sound like Angel. A hand grabbed her by the hair and pulled her violently backwards. "It's time to get dressed."

"Angel?" she asked in disbelief.

"I'm sick of you, you crack whore." A piece of clothing with a sharp zipper grazed Chloe across the cheek.

"I'm not a crack whore. I love you, Angel."

"Shut up. You do not. I've been watching you fucking and sucking men for the last two days. Just to spite me."

"No, that's not true. I didn't do anything!" Her tongue was so thick she could barely speak, and her brain felt like it wanted to split into a thousand pieces.

"Oh, really?" The new angry Angel held up a cell phone. Chloe saw a photo of herself, spread-eagled beneath

197

a man she didn't recognize. Angel touched an arrow and the frozen frame turned into a video with sound. Chloe burst into tears.

"I don't remember that! I didn't mean it. Forgive me, Angel, please forgive me." She buried her face in the dirty jeans that Angel had tossed at her. "I'm so hungry and thirsty, I feel like I'm going to die. Help me, please."

"Put some clothes on, bitch. I'm tired of looking at your ugly naked body and your puffy saggy tits, you nymphomaniac. And here." Angel threw a dirty towel at her. "Clean up your puke so I don't step in it."

Chloe was so stunned that she couldn't move. "Why are you being so mean to me, Angel? I thought you were taking care of me."

"Why are you being so mean to me, Angel?" The words were flung mockingly back at her in a high-pitched mimic. "Well, game over. It's Monday morning and this is the real world."

Chloe was so scared now that she broke out in a cold sweat. Her hands were shaking too much to find the waistband of her pants. When she tried to pull them on, she realized that she was still wearing the black boots. Had she really been wearing them all weekend? She stared at her footwear, trying to figure out if she was supposed to unlace them or unzip them, but it was just too complicated.

She didn't see Angel's fist coming but, even if she had, she probably couldn't have moved out of the way fast enough anyway. Chloe fell backwards, holding her mouth, howling with pain. Angel came at her again, this time dragging her sharp fingernails across Chloe's shoulder and down her chest.

"No, please! Stop!"

Angel kicked her hard in the stomach and Chloe fell over on the rug again, retching bile while Angel smacked her hard on the butt over and over again.

Then, as suddenly as the attack had started, it was over and Angel was cradling Chloe's head in her lap and

198

stroking her cheek and bruised lips. "I'm sorry, baby girl. But I had to do it."

"Why?" she sobbed. "Why did you have to hurt me?"

"Because you've been so very, very bad. You had to be punished." Angel ran her hand over Chloe's scratched breasts and then gently teased her raw nipples. Chloe sucked in her breath, waiting for the now familiar painful twist she knew was coming. This time Angel kept tugging until Chloe started writhing away. "Bunny loves it rough, don't you, Bunny?"

"No, I don't. Stop calling me that. You know I don't." The ache seemed to shoot through her whole body. She was too exhausted to fight anymore. It was only pain.

"Yes, you do. Say 'hurt me, Angel' and I will stop. Say it, baby. 'Hurt me, harder, Angel.' Let me hear you say it. Are you passing out again? Do I need to use the clothespins to keep you awake? Stop screaming and say it. Don't pass out on me."

Cold water splashed across her face and she spluttered into consciousness again. Her breasts ached like they had been clamped in a vise. "Sit up, whore, so I can get this shirt on you." Angel jerked her to a sitting position. "Hands up." The tight stretch lace fabric made Chloe's skin crawl with that bug-like feeling again and it felt like needles were poking into her sore nipples. "Stop whimpering and pick up your ass so I can get this skirt on." She pulled something small and black up over Chloe's legs.

"Where's my fur skirt? Can't I wear that?"

Angel's harsh laugh hurt as much as her punches. "You traded that a few nights ago for the line of crack that made your nose bleed. You'll have to wear this now."

Chloe sobbed again inconsolably.

"Do you want me to smack you another one? Thank god this is the last time I have to do this. Can you put your own coat on or do I have to do everything for you, you dumb Bunny?"

"My name is Chloe and I want to go home to my babies. How are we going to get home, Angel?" She tried to stop her nose from running and then stared in horror at the fresh blood on the back of her hand.

"You're so stupid you don't even know who you are. Here, let me do this for you." Angel was writing something on a card with a red magic marker. Then she pinned it to Chloe's shirt with a paper clip. "In case you're too dumb to read – it says 'My name is Bunny and I fuck like a rabbit.' Now let's go."

She opened the door and dragged Chloe out into the stairwell. "And don't fall going down these steps like you have every other time. I'm tired of picking you up."

Just looking down the stairs made her so dizzy that Chloe fell to her hands and knees. From somewhere below came the sound of a door slamming and Angel suddenly became cautiously quiet. When she knelt down, her tone was the kind soothing one that had once melted Chloe's heart.

"Baby, stay with me. Look what I have for you when we get to the bottom. Here, you hold the pretty belt that helps you feel good. But first put your coat on so you don't get cold when we get out on the street."

Chloe felt so weak that they had to stop three times to rest before her feet finally touched the ground floor. As they passed the front desk, Angel held her tightly, her palm pushing Chloe's face into her shoulder,

"She's not feeling well this morning. We're going to the doctor right now," she heard Angel explaining to somebody.

Then the air was cold and they were on the sidewalk and icy sleet was falling intermittently from the sky. Angel was tugging her impatiently along, yelling at her to stop crying and walk faster.

"Angel, please, I can't breathe, I need... I need a dose..."

"I can't shoot you up on the street, idiot. We have to find someplace more private." She continued to drag Chloe behind her, making a sharp turn into an alley between two buildings and then picking up the pace. Finally she came to an abrupt halt by a pile of black garbage bags beside an overflowing dumpster. "Here we go. Exactly where you belong."

With just the slightest nudge in the right direction, Chloe toppled over onto the heap of bulging trash bags and closed her eyes. "Take off your jacket," Angel commanded, prying the belt from Chloe's fingers. "Hurry. I need your arm."

She tried to obey the orders as quickly as possible, afraid that her clumsiness might cause Angel's anger to flare up again. "Thank you for helping me, Angel," she whispered.

Angel did not respond. Although she seemed intent on getting the job done, her hands were trembling and she kept glancing over her shoulder every few seconds as she tied the belt just above Chloe's elbow and then snapped it so tight that Chloe felt an explosive pressure right down to her fingertips.

"Jesus, I hope there's enough left," Angel murmured. "Please, Jesus, help me finish this here and now. Find me a vein with a hard-on. I hope this hurts, bitch."

Chloe cried out as Angel stabbed fiercely through her skin and into her bloodstream. And then once again everything was intensely beautiful.

She was cold and wet and something smelled really awful. She managed to open one eye and saw gray clouds swirling overhead. Looking at them made her dizzy, so she drifted off again until the throbbing of her breasts brought her back to semi-consciousness. It felt like mosquitos were biting her all over and she clawed at the neckline of her shirt, stretching it downward until she managed to free one and then both of her raw nipples from the offensive bug-stinging fabric. The frosty air felt good on the fiery soreness and she drifted off again but the rancid odor wouldn't go away. It seemed to cover her like a blanket that wasn't a blanket at all, it was goose bumps all over her body. Why couldn't she stop shivering? There was a piercing pain in her left arm – did a dog have its fangs in her flesh? She tried to move away but her limbs would not listen to her mind now.

Something bumped into her hip, tentatively the first time, more forcefully the second. She heard words in a language she didn't understand and then the blissful sound of English. Why did it sound so sweet, she wondered objectively.

"Ne dormez pas ici. Wake up, you can't sleep here."

"Her name's Bunny. Look at this. Can you hear us, Bunny?"

"Bunny, parlez vous?" Strong hands shook her by the shoulders and then swore. She couldn't understand the rest of his words. She opened her mouth to answer him but she didn't know how to talk in his language.

"Bunny, listen to me." Chloe struggled to open her eyes. She saw four policemen and then three and then two. "You speak English, yes?"

She nodded and the two policemen became six. Her eyes grew wide and her teeth began to chatter. "Jensen! Brown! Ici, maintenant! Anglais! Drug whore."

Footsteps approached. "Bunny. Can you hear me? Bunny, oh my god, you left the needle in your arm." A calloused hand grabbed her bruised jaw and she moaned. "Her pulse is weak. Call the EMTs. She needs a hospital before we lock her up. She's a mess. Looks like heroin and hypothermia for starters. And serious dehydration no doubt. Get a blanket to cover her up."

"Hold on. Holy shit – have you ever seen anything like this? What are those – flames?" Fingers probed roughly between her legs, poking and exploring. Chloe involuntarily moaned again as one found its way inside her vagina.

"What the hell are you doing, Jensen?"

"Looking for drugs. Contraband." There was a crude laugh. "Why should the prison matron be the only one who gets to do this?"

"Well, put on a freakin' glove. You might catch something."

"Bunny, can you feel this? She's getting wet. How much you wanna bet I can make her come before the ambulance gets here. I gotta warn you, I never lose at this game." His tone became suddenly compassionate. "Poor girl. She didn't do this to herself."

Although his one hand was still rhythmically stroking, the other was checking out her cuts, bruises and abuses. She flinched reflexively when he touched one of her cold swollen nipples, whimpering softly when he tried to warm it with his palm and giving an instinctive howl as he tried to pull her thin lace shirt up over it. The effort of blocking out the memory of Angel's cruelty was too much, and she felt her head loll to one side as she blacked out again.

"Bunny, are you still with us?" The pain streaking down her chest brought her abruptly back to consciousness and she gasped and gagged. "Are you getting that blanket? Her tits are like blocks of ice. Hurry! Somebody's been doing some nasty shit to you, haven't they? Stay with me now, Bunny."

Hadn't Angel said the very same thing to her... when was that? Why were people always asking her to stay and then leaving?

"Let me see your eyes – that's it. Keep looking at me." Chloe was back on the soiled rug in the hotel room feeling pathetically gratified that Angel was finally touching her sexually to distract her from the fix she was about stick in her arm. It was Angel who was here stroking her so sensually while a man talked to her calmly and firmly. Angel was trying to make her feel better now. "Brown has a blanket to keep you warm while I test your reflexes. Can you feel this? And this? How about this? Is this a sensitive spot? How about when I use my spit like this? Yeah, that's good, right. My girlfriend likes that too."

"Dude, this is so very politically incorrect. I'm having nothing to do with it. You could lose your badge in an instant over this warped obsession."

"This is a prostitute's dream, Brown. They spend all night making other people come – it's never about them.

Besides, I'm keeping her alive by raising her heart rate. Look how fast she's breathing. It feels fucking fantastic, right, Bunny?"

"Then why does she look so terrified?"

For a brief instant Chloe focused in on a pair of steely blue eyes gazing intently into her own, searching earnestly for a response to something. She felt a rush of love for this stranger and then a rush of something else. Was she so pathetic that she was actually having an orgasm just because somebody was looking at her with kindness?

"That's not terror, it's ecstasy. She's pushing up against me like there's no tomorrow. Look at her." The blanket flapped up over her face for a few seconds and she thought she might suffocate as the scratchy wool covered her mouth and nose. Her numbed senses felt enormously confused – everything was wrong but right, bad but good, paralyzed but alive.

"She's fucking delirious with fever or something. Hyperventilating. Stop this nonsense – here's the ambulance now."

Chloe could hear the soundtrack of the voices overhead, but a protective curtain seemed to have closed in around her brain. She knew her body was doing something but she could not feel or control her physical responses. A warm tingling sensation seemed to suffuse her whole being and she heard an animal growling and panting like it was giving birth.

"There you go, Bunny. What a release. Wow. Way to go. You must really be something when you're actually conscious. Give me five more minutes and I could probably fall in love with you."

Then she was floating away into strong arms; warm hot air surrounded her. A strap was tightened around her waist and fingers tentatively touching the shaved vee below before moving quickly away. There was a flurry of exclamations in French and then a couple of bright flashes seemed to burn their way through her eyelids before the exquisite heat of soft blankets enveloped her. Someone was examining her arms and there was more shouting until finally she felt a gentle prick. As she waited for the comforting woosh that would take her away, a man spoke quietly into her ear.

"You did a great job, Bunny. Unforgettable. A high point in my career, really. I'll check on you in the hospital later, before they take you to lock-up, make sure your heart rate is still good. You'd like that, wouldn't you? Be strong, girl..." His voice faded away.

Where was the woosh? It should have happened by now, but the only sensation she had was a nauseating one of moving through space at a very rapid speed.

CHAPTER FOURTEEN

New Orleans, Louisiana
March 2018

When Tyler landed at Louis Armstrong International Airport, his only intention was getting to his hotel and going to sleep. But after spending the last several months in a tiny Vermont village, the energy of New Orleans was so revitalizing and intriguing, that his second wind came easily. His quaint guesthouse on the edge of the Treme was located on the Esplanade, which turned out to be a boulevard with a wide median strip of shade trees that ran through a neighborhood of historic antebellum mansions. His room was furnished with over-the-top antiques and featured French doors that opened onto a classic wrought iron balcony. He took a quick shower in the refurbished claw-foot tub and headed out for some food and downtown nightlife.

As he walked along Bourbon Street towards the famed tourist area, he checked his phone, realizing he had forgotten to take it out of airplane mode after arriving in the city. Several text messages and a few missed calls were quickly displayed. The first one of significance was from Chloe.

"Hi, we had a mishap with the rental car and it looks like we are not going to make it back tonight. Really sorry! I contacted George and he is going to stay over with the twins. Will be home tomorrow. No worries, enjoy New Orleans." An additional message read, *"Angel says she will still be able to meet you there tomorrow night."*

The next was from George. *"Did you hear from Chloe? She sent me a text – apparently not able to get back tonight due to car troubles. Robert and I have this covered. Just wanted to let you know."*

Shit, how could he have waited until now to check his phone and how could everything go to hell so quickly? He reassured himself that it was all okay, in her usual capable way, Chloe had all bases covered. He tried to call her, but was bounced instantly to voice mail. He sent a text instead. *"Hope all problems are resolved and you get home without any additional issues. Tell Angel I'm looking forward to a night on the town with her when she gets in!"*

Then he called George. "Everything is copasetic, dude. The girls think I am both their mother and father anyway so there have been no incidents. Robert is here now, cooking dinner for me, I'm drinking a nice glass of Pinot Noir and all is calm. Don't worry, I'll even change the sheets on your bed before you get back."

"You're the best, don't worry about the sheets. Did you actually speak with her?"

"No, I don't think she is getting real cell service there. I think they may have broken down outside Montreal somewhere on the way back. It's all good. In another day it will be just one more story to tell. Now go find that bad boy of Sarah's."

"Tomorrow I will. Tonight I'm just going to enjoy the metropolitan buzz. But call me if you have any questions at all. We owe you. And say goodnight to my granddaughters for me."

Shaking his head, he shoved his phone deep into his pocket and then ducked into the nearest bar. Life shouldn't be this complicated.

He got off to a late start the next morning but he figured that was okay. He was not going to let any kind of drama disrupt this expedition. When he turned on the GPS navigator in his phone to figure out the best route to Jackson Square, he remembered that he had forgotten to plug it in the night before. It was probably going to die on him in the next few hours. There was a text message from George saying all was well and another from Chloe saying she was catching the once-a-day bus from Burlington and that George would pick her up. He downloaded the map of New Orleans, uploaded the photo of Myles that Sarah had provided him with and then put the phone in airplane mode again. At least it would die slower that way, even if he couldn't get any calls. Probably better like that anyway. He'd traveled around the world for years without a cell phone; he could get by for a day. Even so, he couldn't keep himself from putting the charging cord in his daypack before he locked the door to his room and headed off into the city.

The weather seemed perfect compared to the grayness of late winter in northern Vermont and he questioned his sanity for continuing to live there. He chose a route that wandered through quiet residential streets with classic houses still festooned with the remnants of Mardi Gras decorations. Spring flowers that would not be seen for months in West Jordan were already blooming in a few yards and window boxes.

Jackson Square actually looked familiar to him after having watched that particular opening sequence of NCIS:New Orleans so many times. But it was fairly quiet at noon on a Tuesday with only a handful of tired looking artists and fortunetellers. There was a small crowd gathered around a performer doing magic tricks featuring a little dog. He sat on a bench for a while trying to decide who to approach first, waiting to see if any musicians showed up.

He finally decided to start with a man in a battered top hat who was sitting by a small table that featured an arrangement of large crystals. His bored attitude was off-putting and Tyler thought he could use a lesson in customer service. He peered with disinterest at the photo of Myles.

"Yeah, probably. There was a fiddle player hanging around the Square for a few months, but I don't think I've seen him lately. Been doing this for nearly ten years, it's basically a blur now. So you want a reading?"

Tyler moved on to a woman selling painted tiles against the park railing and then to a girl who sold beaded jewelry. "Looks like Kit's boyfriend. She hasn't been here for a few weeks, and I haven't seen him for longer than that. Maybe they're not together anymore."

"Kit? Who's Kit?"

"Another jewelry maker. She does fortunetelling too. She can be a bitch; steal a customer right out from under you, she doesn't care. No morals that one. Hope she never comes back."

It was his first lead, but not a very positive one. A few of the other vendors wouldn't even speak to him unless he was shopping for something so he returned to his bench, surveying the people around him. There was the usual motley assortment of city vagrants, slightly more colorful in a locally flamboyant way. He spoke to a guy with a 70s style Afro wearing a fringed purple shirt and another in a Confederate uniform jacket with a bandana tied around his head.

"Yeah, I know this dude. I sold him some weed once. Cool cat, awesome musician."

Tyler hadn't heard anyone use the expression "cool cat" in decades, but he hadn't seen anyone with an Afro for a long time either. "Do you know where he's playing these days?" he asked eagerly, but both men shook their heads.

"No place we've been hangin'. Ask Jasmine, she used to keep track of all the pretty boys. Not so much anymore." He nodded towards the other side of the iron fence that surrounded the grassy area next to the square. A dirty waif of a woman was sleeping on the grass wrapped in a woven blanket, her head on a striped knapsack.

"If you can wake her up," said the other. "Come on, I'll help you." He led Tyler over to where Jasmine was passed out like a street dog, clearly stoned on something. "Jazzy, wake up. There's a guy wants to talk to you, and he looks like he's got money."

The girl jerked to a sitting position, her almond-shaped eyes struggling to open more than halfway. Her ragged harem costume hung loosely on a nearly skeletal frame. "Are you a cop? 'Cause I didn't spend the night here, I was just resting."

"She's gonna be picked up by the end of the day," the Confederate-jacket guy murmured to Tyler. "So if you want a blow job, you better ask for it now." He walked back to join his companion.

Tyler knelt down beside her and Jasmine's expression became hopeful for a second. "No, no, neither," he quickly assured her. "Not a cop, no sex. Just got a question. Do you know who this is?"

He could see that she recognized the photo of Myles. She raised an eyebrow, but said only, "You got anything to eat?"

"I'll buy you lunch if you can tell me anything about him."

Despite her obvious hunger, she stiffened defensively. "Why do you want to know? He's a super nice person and I don't want to get him in any kind of trouble."

Tyler couldn't decide what was the best lie to tell a girl like this. She would probably protect a runaway, but might want to help an aspiring fiddle player get a break.

"I've heard him play and I want to offer him a really good-paying job. I own a club. Do you know where I can find him? I don't even know his name."

"Coyote." She tightened her lips and looked away. Tyler realized she was waiting for some money and he pulled out his wallet.

"Coyote? What's that – a place?"

She smirked a little. "That's his name. He came back from Mexico with Kit. But he doesn't work the square anymore."

"This guy? His name is Coyote?" He was going on the word of a stoned street gypsy, but it was more than anyone else had told him so far. "Where does he work now?"

Jasmine rolled her half-closed eyes. "How the fuck should I know." She took the handful of bills Tyler was holding out and started to slump down, stopping halfway. "But I did see him last week. I think. I don't know. Maybe.

210

Yeah. I'm really tired and I have to pee." She curled up in a ball and reached futilely for her thin blanket. Tyler covered her with it and got to his feet.

The prospect of talking to anyone else was too depressing right now. If she could be believed, at least Myles was still alive and in the city. Tyler looked around and spotted a restaurant with a second story balcony overlooking a corner of Jackson Square. It looked like a great place to have a beer and watch the street.

A few hours later, as he climbed the outside steps to his room, he reminded himself it had not been a totally fruitless afternoon. Another vendor had confirmed that there was a fiddler who called himself Coyote who was playing the streets of the city; a guitar player mumbled something about the bars on Frenchmen. When Tyler's phone died completely, he decided it was time to take a break, maybe have a shower and a nap and recharge his own batteries while juicing up his cell.

He had completely forgotten about Angel until he reached the balcony and saw her sitting there in the wrought iron chair next to his door, her long skinny legs encased in black jeans, one tucked beneath her, the other pulled up against her chest with her cheek resting against it as she gazed at the phone in her hand.

"I'm so sorry, have you been here long? My phone was in airplane mode all afternoon before it died so I wouldn't have gotten any messages." As he leaned forward to kiss her on the cheek, she turned her face so that their lips met briefly. As he hastily pulled away, he noticed the rolling suitcase stashed neatly under the outdoor table. "You must have come directly from the airport. How was the trip?" He fumbled in his pocket for the room key.

Angel unwound her limbs and stood up stretching. "I wondered why y'all didn't answer my text. That dyke who runs this place wouldn't let me in but she agreed to let me wait out here for you."

She looked different and Tyler realized he'd never seen her in anything but her colorful ankle-length skirts and heavy sweaters. She looked like a sophisticated beanpole now in tight pants and a fuzzy white top that kept sliding off one bony shoulder. Her hair was tucked up into a black beret and her ever-present hoop earrings had been replaced by pearl studs. "Wow, you look... great." He felt awkwardly attracted to her and wasn't sure why it seemed so inappropriate.

When she smiled at him in that crooked Mona Lisa way, he had second thoughts about the prudence of their evening plan. "Thank you, Tyler." She dragged her luggage behind her into the darkened interior and Tyler quickly flicked the light switch that illuminated the ceiling chandelier. "Ooh, I steered you right, didn't I? Good choice, it has plenty of local character, even if the owner is a bull bitch."

"Yeah, it's nice." He watched her gliding around the room, inspecting its accoutrements before he turned his back on her to begin the search in his pack for his phone cord. "So everything work out okay with your car mishap in Canada? Chloe texted that you dropped her at the bus this morning – I assume she is home safely by now. I haven't been able to check my messages all day."

As his fingers closed around his charger, Tyler was suddenly aware of Angel's presence behind him, near enough to feel the heat of her breath on the back of his neck as she spoke. "Yeah, Chloe's all set for now. She got just what she needed in Montreal."

He stood motionless, unsure of how he felt about what was going on. He cleared his throat. "Really. Because I kind of thought you two were sort of..."

She laughed hoarsely. "Not me." She placed her hands lightly on his shoulders. "I've been looking forward to a fun night in the Big Easy with you before I head home tomorrow. You good with that?" she whispered in his ear.

"Angel..." He didn't know why he was in denial about this. "I'm twice your age."

"And incredibly attractive for an older man. Don't tell me you haven't felt the energy between us." She leaned into him until her hips pressed against his buttocks, making a little grinding motion. Tyler closed his eyes, trying not to accept the inevitable.

"Don't you have a boyfriend?"

"What he doesn't know won't hurt him. I'll be home tomorrow." She reached around his body and slowly slid the phone charger out of his grasp. "You know you want this as much as I do." She pulled him by the hand until he was turned towards her.

The first kiss was like a freshly lit fire; by the second one he was a burning building.

"I need a shower," he said as she unbuckled his belt.

"Me too. Let's go."

It was not how he had anticipated they would start off the evening and it certainly changed the game. "You still want to get something to eat and hear some music?" Angel asked, running her fingers through the damp curls on his chest. "We could just order a pizza."

"I was thinking about Frenchmen Street. It's not far from here. There's actually a musician I was hoping to hear." He had never told her the real reason behind his mission to New Orleans, knowing that she and Chloe shared everything. Chloe, shit. He sat up. "Where'd you put my phone charger? I need to check in with Chloe."

"Relax, babe. All is cool, she texted me a few hours ago. Look." She held up her phone so he could read the message. *"Made it home at last to my sweet babies. Thanks for the rockin' weekend, gf. Tell Tyler to chill – all is well here."*

He kissed the top of her head. "Thank you. Now I can just enjoy the rest of this night. So do you know a place called The Spotted Cat?"

He felt a little tremor run through her body. "Oh, that's a touristy spot. I know a much better place across

213

town. I'll order us an Uber. Do you want to hop in the shower again or should we just go?"

She took him to Tipitina's where they drank sugary frozen alcoholic beverages in place of dinner and danced to some of the best music Tyler'd ever heard in his life. He was very drunk by the time they stumbled back up the steps to his balcony and sprawled once again across the four poster bed.

"Don't expect much of a performance out of me for a few hours," he apologized as Angel peeled off her jeans. "Wow, nice red lace thong. I always wonder how woman can stand to wear one of those. I mean it looks really sexy but it must be so uncomfortable to have that in your crack."

She laughed and put an unlit cigarette between her lips. "I'm still hot so I'm going outside for a smoke like this. Think of me on your porch with no pants on and maybe you'll get hard again."

"Yeah, you don't get it, I'm very turned on by you but..." He couldn't remember the last time he'd had so much to drink – he was going to pay for this tomorrow. "Do me a favor and plug my phone in, will you? I promise I won't look at it until morning. Okay, later this morning."

"Okay, look. Here it is, over here." From across the room, she showed him his Iphone attached to a white cord that ran into an outlet on a far wall. It might as well be a mile away – there was no way he was going over there now to look at it. "It will be waiting for you in the morning. I'll be back in a couple of minutes."

"Wake me up when you come to bed." His words sounded slurred like somebody who'd had too much to drink. Oh, right, he was that person. "I want to have sex again."

He didn't know how long he'd been sleeping when he felt her mouth moving against him and he was surprised to find he was already aroused, like a teenage boy. He had not had an intense one-night-stand in a long, long time, and he didn't think he'd ever slept with someone so much younger;

the idea made him feel youthful and vibrant, even as the beginning stages of a hangover began to set in.

"Oh my god. Nothing like the tongue of an experienced man," she gasped. "I could get used to this."

He tried not to think of what it would be like if Angel ever came back to visit them again in Vermont. It would probably never happen anyway.

The thick velvet drapes that covered the windows of the French doors were so effective that Tyler had no idea what time of day it was when he finally opened his eyes. He ached all over - he was definitely too old for nights like that very often anymore. His lower back, his left shoulder and, for some reason his right thumb, were all killing him. Not to mention the throbbing in his temples and the explosive pain in his forehead.

"Angel?" he called. There was no answer. She was probably having a smoke on the porch. He staggered into the bathroom to take a leak. It was hard to believe his headache could get worse but it certainly felt more painful when he was standing up. He put his mouth under the sink faucet in the bathroom, not caring if New Orleans water was safe to drink or not.

When he emerged into the darkened bedroom again, he could see an old-fashioned digital alarm clock with a red LED readout that told him it was 9:55. He dragged one of the curtains back to peer out onto the empty balcony. Shit, had she left without even saying goodbye?

He found his eyeglasses on the nightstand and of course that helped him to focus a little better. Angel's suitcase was gone from the closet; if, in fact, there was no trace of Angel left in the room except for a crumpled cigarette pack in the trash can and the faint lingering scent of lavender.

Depression washed over Tyler as he fell back on the pillows and he tried to let it run by him, like dirty rainwater in a gutter. There had been no commitments or expectations beyond an evening of pleasure. But he should at least send her a text and thank her for making his vacation memorable.

He looked over to where he'd seen her plug in his phone when they'd returned from the club, but there was nothing on the table. Thinking it might have fallen, he dropped to his hands and knees and searched below. The charging cord still hung from the outlet like a forlorn white snake, but the cell was nowhere to be seen.

Shit. She must have taken his phone. Probably by mistake, thinking it was her own. He would just have to contact her somehow to get it back. She would not have done it on purpose, right?

He lay on the bed trying to think what he knew about Angel. She had virtually lived at his house for nearly two weeks as Chloe's constant companion, taking care of his grandchildren, cooking meals, even watching TV with him. She had shared anecdotes of growing up in rural Louisiana and tidbits about the culture of New Orleans. She'd read his palm and painted a dresser for the girls in a colorful folk art pattern. He'd watch Chloe fall headlong into girlfriend love with her and George circle her like a wary dog. And yet he could not come up with any actual facts about Angel – he didn't even know her last name.

He was such an idiot when it came to women.

Shit. His whole life was on that phone – in his present condition, he could barely remember his own number, let alone any of the other important players in his life.

So much for Frenchmen Street. He needed to find an Apple store.

It took pretty much all afternoon to get a new phone. He finally found an electronics place on Canal and had to settle for a refurbished outdated model since the prices were so outrageous. The sales clerk helped him restore the data that had been saved on the Cloud but by the time they got around to that part, his account had already been seriously hacked, many of his contacts erased or compromised, messages and emails deleted, passwords

216

changed and photos simply gone. He wondered if Angel had done all that damage or if she had sold it on the street to somebody who had wiped it clean.

Finally he leaned against the outside window of the store and called the only number he had committed to memory years ago.

"West Jordan Inn. Sarah speaking."

"Hi, it's me. I need your help with something."

"Tyler, where the fuck are you? Everyone's been trying to reach you for the last twenty-four hours. I was seriously thinking of calling the New Orleans PD." He had rarely heard Sarah sound so worked up.

"Why? I thought everything was fine. I had a message yesterday from Chloe saying she was home and all was well." A jolt of nervous energy ran through him and he started walking in the direction of his guesthouse, just another guy on the sidewalk talking on a cell phone as he moved through the city.

"What? What planet are you on? The last thing we heard was that she was on the bus from Burlington. Hunter went over to stay with the girls while George drove to Montpelier to pick her up, but she never showed. And that was more than a day ago!"

"But – I swear…" He ground to a halt and the two women walking behind nearly ran over him. "It was…" But the text hadn't been on his phone, had it? Angel had showed him the message on hers as they lay sweaty and spent in a state of post-sex satiation.

"The police won't put an APB out on her until she's been missing for forty-eight hours and we've been going out of our minds here trying to get in touch with you. Why haven't you been checking your phone?" Sarah did not wait for his answer, but continued hurling an avalanche of words at him. "The only thing they have done is find out that she did buy a ticket for that bus – I guess you have to show your driver's license to purchase a ticket now, and she used her debit card for the purchase. But she never got on it."

"What the hell does that mean – she decided to stay in Burlington and not go home? It doesn't make any sense. I just spent the night with…" He couldn't bring himself to tell Sarah about another one of his serious misjudgments of character. "I went out with Angel last night. She said she dropped Chloe off and everything was fine. My problem is that I – I lost my phone so I am totally out of touch. It's been a nightmare, everything's been hacked. The only number I could remember is yours."

He heard Sarah sigh in exasperation. "Okay, what do you need to get your ass back here as quickly as possible?"

He stepped into a shop doorway and leaned against a window to pull out his notebook and pen as she dictated phone numbers and checked airline schedules. As they waited for her computer to boot up, he told her what he had learned about her son. "This all totally sucks. If only I had another day down here, I'm sure I could track this Coyote guy down – I'm almost certain he's Myles."

By the silence on the other end, he could tell Sarah was as torn about the decision as he was. Finally she said, "Athena's got a cold, but George has been a saint through all this."

"Thank god, because I never know what to do for sick babies." For a moment, Tyler's fear of parenting overshadowed anything else he might be feeling.

"You just take care of them, Tyler. That's the easy part." He could hear her sniffling a little as she tapped away on her keyboard. "So the only affordable last minute option flies through Cincinnati and Detroit and takes seventeen hours. You might as well wait until tomorrow afternoon. Do you want me to rebook this for you?"

"Sarah, did we ever put our parents through what these grown kids have done to us? I mean, no one worried when we didn't call home for a week or a month. They couldn't right?" He started walking again, looking for a quieter through street than Bourbon for getting across town.

"You're asking the wrong person. I was a responsible child raised by my grandmother, remember? Not an entitled gallivanter like you. Look, I just want to know Myles is okay, whatever he's doing with his life, that he's not a drug addict or street person."

Tyler swallowed and kept quiet, not sure exactly what constituted a "street person" in Sarah's mind and whether he would find out that Myles was that now.

"And I also hope Chloe is okay – this is so unlike her. There's so much sick shit out there in the world. I'm scared for her safety. We want this flight, right?"

"Yes. Yes, we do." Neither of them had brought up Tucker – the blackest sheep of their extended family. He swore to himself that as soon as this current nightmare had subsided, he was going to find his own son and... he didn't know what.

Sarah gave him his new flight info and promised to call him in a few hours with any updates on the situation. As he dialed George's number, he felt a pelting of cold rain drops on his face and head. He hadn't noticed how dark the skies had become in the last hour. He either had to find an umbrella or get inside fast.

Tyler looked up at the signposts so he could pinpoint his current location. Royal and Frenchmen. Well, at least something was in his favor.

The shoulders of his denim jacket were pretty well soaked through by the time he ducked into The Spotted Cat. He joined a damp crowd of people like himself who had taken shelter from the storm but were also enjoying some seriously good music. He ordered a beer and leaned against the bar looking at the odd trio on the stage; a chubby white guitarist in a tartan driving cap, a lean black trumpet player and a gargantuan dark woman with a mammoth set of mammaries and a pair of lungs to match. At the end of the number, the trumpet player leaned into the microphone and announced, "Sitting in for Sparkle and McCoy today since McCoy could not be here, we are Sparkle, Lawson and

Ledbetter, not a law firm, but we will take all your cash. Miss Sparkle will be coming around with the tip jar so please be generous and remember, this is how we make our living, so if you love the music scene in New Orleans then help keep it alive with your donations."

The big singer began moving through the crowd. As she came closer Tyler was able to appreciate all the details of her appearance, from her glittery silver eye shadow to the hand-stitching of what was clearly a custom-made black dress. She reminded him of a girlfriend he'd had years ago when he'd washed-up on the shores of Grenada and her lilting West Indian accent confirmed his intuition.

"Where's your cute piano man?" the woman on the next bar stool asked her. "I love him."

"Him girlfriend just come back so him need take de day off to satisfy her, you know what me talkin' bout, sistah." Miss Sparkle winked one big shimmery eye.

"What? You not his woman? What wrong with that man?"

"Coyote and me, we partners. And me can't be having any boyfrien' in my line of work. It scare de money off." She held the can out towards Tyler and winked again.

"Did you say Coyote?" Tyler froze, a five dollar bill held aloft.

"Him de Coy-boy of Sparkle and McCoy. Catch him here tomorrow, Mr. Fine-Looking Man." Sparkle leaned forward to take the cash out of his hand and brushed her solid chest against him. "And if you want to see more of Sparkle, come down to de Kinky Monkey in a few hours. De price is right, as dey say on dat TV show."

"So he's a good piano player?" Tyler asked the fan sitting beside him. "What kind of music does he play?"

"McCoy? He's like some kind of savant. Boogie woogie, jazz, ragtime... he plays it all. Plus he's as pretty as he is talented. Enjoy him now, before he gets so famous he don't play here no more, that's what I say."

"So what time are they on?"

"Graveyard shift – afternoons, before things really get going. When only tourists, drunks and music fanatics are around." She upended whatever was in her plastic cup and Tyler signaled the bartender to buy her another. "Thanks, hon. Mark my words, he'll be the evening headliner here before long. I seen 'em all and I know."

Tyler celebrated by staying at the Spotted Cat for the next few hours, watching Lawson and Ledbetter join a seven-piece jazz band for another set and witnessing Sparkle's flamboyant exit. He marveled at the amount of skin she displayed beneath a long silvery cape, staring in awe along with the rest of the customers as her augmented breasts caused the crowd to part in a less-than-Biblical version of the Red Sea as she made her way to the doorway.

He looked up the Kinky Monkey on his phone and decided that, after his debacle of the previous evening, he didn't want to visit a place like that. He doubted that Sparkle would divulge any more information.

He checked his phone and saw that a call had come in from Sarah. Stepping outside, he dialed her number.

The first thing she said was, "I can't talk; I've got a full bar and Hunter is at your house."

"Listen, I've got great..."

"I wanted to tell you that the police did check the border crossing records and they found that Chloe and Angel entered Canada on foot last Saturday at Beebe Plain, but there is no record of Chloe's reentry to Vermont on Tuesday, only Angel's."

"Beebe Plain? That's nowhere near Burlington. Why–"

"None of it makes sense, Tyler. But Angel looks really suspicious right now. If you can get a hold of her, please try. She's got some 'splaining' to do. Three Sam Adams and a Pinot? Yeah, one sec."

"So Chloe might still be in Canada?" Tyler couldn't fathom the labyrinth of complications that was settling in around his family.

"Look, I'm super busy. Just get back here. I'll call you in the morning if anything changes."

Sarah hung up before he could tell her that by tomorrow afternoon he hoped to be reunited with her son.

CHAPTER FIFTEEN

New Orleans, Louisiana
March 2018

Myles sat bolt upright in bed and looked around, his heart pounding in accelerated two/four time. It sounded like someone was in the room going through his drawers.

"Hey!" he called out. "Who's there?" He felt around, looking for something hard or heavy.

"Shhh. It's me, silly. I just got back and I was trying not to wake you, baby." The bedside light flicked on and there was Kit, pulling a black beret off her head and shaking her hair out. Flinging her arms around him, she knocked him back onto the pillows, kissing him all over his face.

"Oh, hey. You scared me." She smelled strange, some familiar scent layered over perfumey soap. "What time is it?"

"Too early for you, obviously. Show me how happy you are to see me." She rolled on top of him. "I've missed you so much, baby. I couldn't wait to get back."

Myles sighed, realizing he was not ready for such a large dose of Kit on just a few hours of sleep. "Yeah, yeah, I bet." He closed his eyes again, knowing she was not going to let him get off that easy.

"What's the matter? You sad about something?" She ran her fingers across his forehead. "Something bad happen to you while I was gone? It did, didn't it? I can tell."

He wished she wasn't so damn intuitive. He didn't want to think about his grief over Chloe's letter with her right there; it still hurt too much. "Yeah, I have been kind of blue." He rolled away, hoping it was a good enough excuse but knowing it wouldn't be.

223

"Oh, don't be depressed, baby. Kit's home to make you feel better now." He felt her hand slither quickly under the covers. "I gotcha now, baby."

He knew there would be no shaking her off easily. He might as well get it over with. His self-loathing made him realize there was no getting around the truth – he was going to have to end their relationship sooner than later.

The next time he awoke, Kit was standing beside the bed grinning broadly, holding an old-fashioned picnic basket. "I have a great surprise planned for you today, baby."

Myles rolled his eyes. "Kit."

"No, really." She snuggled up next to him. "It's going to be like going back in time. To when we first met."

He said nothing, knowing she would go on.

"So get dressed. We're going to the beach for the day."

He had to admit that she still had the ability to intrigue him with her creativity. "And how are we doing that?"

"Darcy is lending us her car. She was totally sympathetic to the idea that we needed a little honeymoon adventure to lift your spirits. We're going to Shell Beach."

Despite himself, he actually smiled at her. "The beach? Really? Okay, I'm in."

"It's not going to be as warm as Mexico," she warned. "But it's as close as we're going to get in Louisiana in March." He saw that she was wearing all white clothing, like it was the middle of the frigging summer, except that it was actually multiple layers – an airy skirt on top of white jeans, a fuzzy sweater over some sort of long-sleeve tee, a gauzy cream-colored scarf flung around her neck and shoulders.

"I need to get a message to Sparkle, let her know I can't do this afternoon's gig." He frowned, trying to figure out how he was going to solve that problem.

Anger passed over Kit's face like a dark storm cloud and then the sun came out again. She kissed Myles on the forehead. "Okay, be quick, baby. I'm going to pack the car."

He was alone in the bedroom, pulling his jeans on, when he saw the iPad sitting on the nightstand again, plugged into its usual electrical outlet. Swiftly he picked it up and logged onto Facebook as Diva Gatotita. Her only friend, Chloe Mackenzie, was the first post that showed up.

"Chloe Mackenzie updated her profile picture," the Newsfeed announced. The accompanying photo showed a very stoned-looking Chloe puckering up and posing for the camera, cheek to cheek with a dark-skinned, tough-looking man whose large hands were visible just above the bottom crop of the pic. He seemed to be tightly grasping the pale soft flesh of Chloe's nearly naked breasts. Myles's stomach lurched as he stared at the picture. Chloe's face was heavily made-up in in a new unbecoming way and she was wearing a garish necklace that looked like a medieval collar for a pit bull; it reminded him of something he'd seen before.

He clicked on the picture and Chloe's personal timeline came up. "How do you like my new look?" her most recent posting asked. A platinum blonde with half-closed eyes and a pouty mouth, she was proudly displaying tits overflowing a red lace bra that coerced them up into an abnormal and obscenely provocative angle. Beneath it, in the first comment box, Chloe had added– "To see more of the hot new me, check out this video link."

Myles could not look away; his finger hovered over the link as he heard the outside door slam and Kit say something to Darcy. He quickly clicked the screen off, replaced the iPad in its customary spot, and sank slowly down onto the bed.

"Come on, honey, let's go. It's going to take us an hour and a half to get there anyway. What's wrong, babe? You all right? You're not going to be sick, are you?"

It took enormous mental gymnastics for Myles to be able to violently push all images and thoughts of Chloe out of his mind. He forced himself to look ahead – to spending the day at the beach with Kit, who reminded him in no way of the old, or new, Chloe.

"I was just... going to check my email. I haven't been online since you've been gone." He hoped she didn't notice the visible shaking of his hands as he pulled his shirt on, but he knew she always saw everything.

"Well, you can get online tonight when we get back for as long as you like. Now let's go; I can't wait to get on the road with you again."

They fucked in a sheltered spot behind a bush – Myles did not want to think of it as anything other than "fucking." It was raw animal rutting, purely physical, not involving his mind and especially not his heart. He did not respond in any way other than sexual when Kit murmured over and over how much she loved him, crying silently behind her back as he pounded into her. They smoked all the pot he had brought with them and despite how high he got, the pain was still present, even under the open sky, wrapped in a blanket against the stiff breeze that wafted in the fishy odor of the Gulf of Mexico and blew thick puffy clouds across his expansive view.

"This is the best day ever. And you're the best. I love you, don't ever leave me." Kit's legs squeezed his thighs in a stronghold that left no room for argument or doubt.

Myles pretty much didn't care whether he left her or not. It might be love to her, but to him it was just fucking. No matter how they did it.

After a while they both fell asleep and did not wake up until the rain began pelting hard against their faces. "How did we not see this coming?" Myles groaned as they hurried back to the parking lot. "Wasn't it a beautiful sunny day when we started napping?"

Inside the car they blasted the heater and stripped off their drenched clothing. "Should we fuck again? It will probably warm us up faster."

"I don't know. Let's wait a bit. I'm getting kind of sore," Kit said in an uncharacteristically petulant tone.

"You've really been an animal today. Don't get me wrong – I love it," she added quickly. "But I've had a really long night and day." She leaned closer to the heating vent, letting the hot air blow on the gooseflesh of her prepubescent chest, the hard points of her nipples softening and expanding a little in the warmth.

But now that their Bacchanalian excursion was in full swing, Myles didn't really want to stop. He might start thinking again. "But the party's still going on. Look at me – I'm ready for you now. What a stud, right? Got any ideas?" He reclined his seat and put his hands behind his head.

"Oh, my. Don't y'all worry. I know how to take care of that, baby."

When they stopped at a roadside food truck for crawfish po'boys, they had to jam themselves back into a few pieces of wet apparel to get out and place their order. As darkness fell, a full stomach and the uncomfortable dampness of his pants broke the mood for Myles, and he leaned against the window in sulky silence as Kit chattered idly on the drive into to the city.

He was relieved when, back at the house, she took a hot shower and fell instantly asleep. He wondered how Sparkle had managed without him this afternoon – he had sent a message to her through the Spotted Cat. He didn't know how she would react, but he didn't think she would be surprised. Part of him wanted to go downtown right now and wait for her to be finished with work so they could talk about their respective days. But really he didn't want to admit to Sparkle how he had behaved today.

Instead, with a sinking feeling of inevitability, he reached over Kit's slumbering form for the iPad and then slipped quietly out of the room and onto the back porch.

The tablet went instantly back to the photo he had abruptly left it on that morning. It still looked as sleazy as his memory of it had been all day. He scrolled down to see if this was really the same Facebook page Chloe had always had. Sure enough, there were photos of Vermont and

Athena and Artemis flying quickly by. Maybe she'd been hacked – maybe someone had cloned Chloe's features onto someone else. He knew it could be done.

"To see more of the hot new me..." He could not keep himself from clicking on the video link.

It was an amateur phone video that captured all the necessary details from the neck down. It started with the red bra falling away and a close-up of a rosy red tattoo above the prickly puckered skin of a nipple being roughly massaged and tweaked. Okay, it didn't seem probable, but maybe she had gotten a breast tattoo in the last year. The camera panned across a pale rib cage and Myles swallowed hard as he caught sight of the familiar twinkle of the jeweled stud that pierced Chloe's bellybutton.

Continuing down, the video zoomed out a little to display what almost appeared to be cartoon artwork of flames on a smooth canvas of skin where pubic hairs usually curled. It was a small bonfire really, that licked up the soft curve of her abdomen from a fiery start somewhere between her legs. He stared in disbelief – this could not be real. It had to be someone else. But when she lay back and opened her thighs to display the red and orange lines that disappeared into the area he was so personally intimate with, he felt himself flush with a sickening sense of humiliation and disgust. Chloe was wonderfully uninhibited, but this was beyond any place he'd ever imagined she would go.

Until a new scene came on the screen, involving the black man in the profile picture. Chloe was backed up to his chest as they faced the camera just like in the photo, only this was alive with action, Chloe bracing herself with arms locked behind her and around his neck, top pushed down and skirt hiked up, her flaming crotch grinding with shameless enthusiasm as the man thrust himself into her from behind. The shot zoomed in for a close-up as Chloe seemed to collapse from pleasure or exhaustion, her partner clinging to her bouncing breasts and continuing to plunge in and out of her until he finally finished with a convulsive tremor. When he released his hold, the camera followed her as she tumbled limply to the floor at his feet, her legs splayed wide for one final public exhibition as the man zipped his oversized organ back into his pants and walked away.

Myles tried to be a dispassionate observer, noticing that this must have been filmed at a different time than the first video because Chloe's hair was still dark and her makeup was not the same. But as he attempted to separate himself from his feelings, his initial visceral reaction began to deepen into a sense of fierce betrayal and a defensive hatred for how she was behaving. What would her daughters think about her conduct when they grew up?

He closed the pop-up box with the pornographic video and found himself back on the Facebook page. His index finger was trembling so hard that he could barely keep it on the arrow key as he moved slowly down the screen. He wanted to see the time frame of when this change had taken place in her. The photos of the "new" Chloe had been put online only a couple of days earlier. Before that, was a posting that threatened to break his already very wounded heart.

"*Artemis takes her first steps! #mybabywalks*" was the heading above another video that he could view right here. There was the chubby golden-haired child clutching with one hand at the edge of the coffee table in Tyler's bungalow, reaching with the other for something off-screen. A patch of tiger-striped fur moved into view and Myles realized it was Diva strolling by. He felt his fragile psyche dissolving as he watched Artemis let go and toddle across the room reaching for his cat. Diva streaked away and Artemis was caught by someone's outstretched arms and fell into what looked like a purple curtain. Then the video looped and started over again.

Myles sobbed into his knees until he felt empty and dead inside. Nothing in his life mattered anymore. Nothing at all.

In the morning he pushed Kit away when she reached for him, curling into a defensive fetal ball and not moving until he heard her actually leave the house. When he knew it was past noon, he forced himself to get up and take a shower. He didn't feel like eating and he was out of weed. Hair still wet, he grabbed his fiddle case and walked out to the street. Maybe he would take the bus down to Sparkle's stop and meet her there. It was better than hanging around in his own world.

The black truck pulled up next to him as soon as he was on the sidewalk, the electric window gliding ominously down. "That witch back yet?"

The irony of Beau's question put Myles into a familiar rebellious mode. "You do know we are a household of Voodoo Buddhists, don't you? We don't take kindly to insulting remarks about witches."

He was glad to see he'd made Beau instantly uncomfortable and he used his advantage to deflect the inquiry back on to him. "Any news about your brother?"

Beau leaned across the seat and opened the passenger door. "Get in. I'll take you where you're going."

"What are you doing here on a..." Myles couldn't even think what day it was but he was pretty sure it wasn't a weekend.

"Got a phone call from a friend in Opelousas and decided I ought to take the day off and get back down here. I learned some shit about that gypsy bitch you might be interested in. So she back or not?" He pulled a can off the twelve-pack of Jax that rested on the seat between them and offered it to Myles, who declined, shrugging.

"I don't know. She might be. My schedule's different than hers, come in late, get up late, so we don't intersect much." He wondered where Kit had gone off to this morning; she could possibly show up at any second. "I'm headed over to the Ninth. You okay with driving me there? 'Cause I'd like to hear what you found out."

"Should be all right in broad daylight, shouldn't it?" The pickup began moving down Poland Avenue towards St.

Claude. "Although I hate crossing the fuckin' canal. I can't believe they stop all the traffic just to raise the bridge for one freakin' boat. And you never know when."

Although he hardly knew Beau, Myles did remember how quickly the man could sidetrack himself in a conversation. "So what's the word on Kit? She an axe murderer or something?"

Beau swallowed half a can of beer in one long gulp before replying. "Yeah, just about. The guy who called me, he works for the parish, he did some research on her. Turns out she spent most of her high school years in juvie. But those records are sealed since she was underage."

"Huh. Really." Myles did not know what 'juvie' was, but he could guess. "What for?"

"Well, so this guy asked around to see if he could get the local lowdown. And you know who found out the story for him?"

"No – who?" There was nothing to do but play along.

"This is priceless. His wife's hairdresser knew all the details. Turned out she went to the same high school as fuckin' Evangeline Katherine Beauchaine. You gonna tell me where to turn, right?"

"Two blocks. Go down to the big church on the left." Myles was thinking about the day in Mexico when he had seen Kit's real name on her passport.

"So anyway, seems that she tried to kill her father and her older brother. They say she locked them in their repair garage and set it on fire. How about that shit." Beau pounded the rim of the steering wheel triumphantly.

Myles felt dizzy. "Why – why would she do that?"

"Who the fuck knows – what matters is it's a lot like what probably happened to Denny. Well, the rumor was she was kinda bat-shit crazy because the old man had been, you know, abusing her since she was a kid. I mean, you know, he did more than just slap her around."

"Wow. That's – that's an intense story." In fact, Myles could barely process what Beau was saying. "So when you say 'tried to kill'…"

231

"Well, they didn't die. Someone saw the smoke and they got saved – don't know those details. But I guess the father was so ripped at her afterwards that the judge sent Kit away partly to save her own life. They were a freakin' nutso inbred bunch of swamp animals, her family." He looked at Myles like he was waiting for an affirmation.

"Yeah, sounds like it. And she was how old when she did this?"

"I don't know, like fourteen maybe. Oh, yeah, and there was also a rumor that she was pregnant when they sent her up and that it was probably the father or the brother." As he pulled into a parking spot in front of the church, Beau's animated dissertation became even more excited. "I mean, it's totally fucked up, you gotta feel a little sorry for her, but not really if she killed my fuckin' brother. And I'm guessing she might have had somethin' to do with Charlene, the ex-girlfriend's so-called 'disappearance'."

"Yeah, but...how would you ever prove that?" Myles had an image in his head of the night that he and Kit had made a run from Playa Los Cocos, trying to stay one step ahead of the vigilante force of campers after the Canadian had accused Kit of flirting with the dead guy. Who Beau was now saying was Denny.

Holy fuck, he thought. Was this for real? And if it was...

"I don't know, but I'm going to do my damndest to–" But Myles didn't hear the rest of what Beau had to say. He was already out of the truck and reeling down the side street in the direction of Sparkle's bungalow.

He knew she would freak if he knocked on the door, so he collapsed on the bottom step, hoping he wouldn't get any splinters in his ass from the rough, unpainted wood. From inside the house he could make out some faint shrieking, like you might hear coming from an insane asylum and he tried to block out the noise, as well as the curiosity to see what was going. Sparkle would never forgive him if he pried into the shadows of her home life, and he had convinced himself he didn't need to know more than she was willing to share.

These women and their dark pasts... he stared blindly at the empty lot across the roadbed from where he sat. His own childhood with two loving parents seemed safe and sheltered in comparison to Sparkle's and Kit's. And if what Beau had just told him about Kit was true, then that was pretty scary. She was weird, but she had never displayed any behavior that had made him fear for his life. Other than maybe smothering him to death with too much attention. She'd told him snippets about her life growing up in bayou country and he knew she'd run away to New Orleans as soon as she could, but there were definitely big gaps she'd never talked about and he'd never asked because he really didn't care that much. He recalled how beat up she'd seemed when he picked her up in the desert; and how he'd figured anybody would be a little crazy after that experience. But he'd been living in isolation for nearly six months at that point – he didn't know what was crazy or not.

Then again, he'd never hurt Kit in any way, at least not physically. Why would he even worry about her turning on him. He could imagine her hurting the people around him out of jealousy perhaps, but even that seemed a bit improbable. He knew she was aware that she couldn't compete with his enduring love for Chloe, but he was pretty sure Kit didn't think Chloe posed any actual threat to their relationship. Not that it mattered anymore... the video of Chloe screwing started playing in his head again and he forcibly suppressed the images and made himself think about Kit.

Kit had been mad when he started hanging with Sparkle, but she hadn't done anything aggressive; in fact she'd left town. Most of the time she was just the usual over-friendly, extroverted Kit, the one who easily made new acquaintances and charmed strangers enough that they trusted her to tell their futures.

Still… he wondered if he should call her and tell her to watch out for Beau. Just as he pulled out his phone, the door slammed behind him.

"Bumba clot, brudda. What you doin' in me yard? You know I axe you not to come here." Sparkle gripped his arm and yanked him to a standing position. She was wearing her turban and robe, but only one eye sported the usual silvery shadow; he had obviously interrupted her makeup session. But when she saw his face, she softened her hold and dragged him out onto the crumbling sidewalk. "What wrong wid you? You lookin' like some crybaby chile, lost him best toy."

Her rough sympathy reminded him of how sorry he had been feeling for himself, how much he missed his dysfunctional Vermont life – his family, his cat, his relationship with the girl he'd watched give birth to his best friend's babies. "I think I just want to go home."

"Go on den, why you come here anyway if dat how you feel."

"No, I don't mean the Bywater. I mean up north."

"Me thought you couldn't go back for some such reason." She crossed her arms beneath her massive chest. "Don't be like dis, Coyote. Sparkle and McCoy have a show to do. Dere's people dem come yesterday want see you. And me not ready. Sit back down here and pull you-self together. You can't be letting whatever woman blues dis is be getting in your way."

She pushed him back down on the step and disappeared inside.

Myles buried his head in his knees and tried to think of nothing.

Losing himself into the piano keys at the Spotted Cat felt better than anything he'd done in the last forty-eight hours. He kept his back to the crowd, looking only to his left on occasion to check in with Sparkle at the microphone on the stage. When the set was over, he accepted a beer from someone in the audience who obviously didn't know he wasn't old enough to legally drink. Leaning against the keyboard, he stared blankly out into the street, waiting for Sparkle to bring him the tip jar which he would count during the time she changed into her Kinky Monkey clothes in the ladies room.

When someone touched his shoulder, he glanced up indifferently. An older man with thick gray curls and wire-rimmed glasses who reminded him of Tyler was gazing expectantly at him. West Jordan was seriously on his mind this afternoon.

"Myles," the man said.

He stiffened at the sound of his given name and focused on the face in front of him. He was so emotional today; he had to be hallucinating. Holy shit, it was Tyler. What was he doing here? How had he found his way to the Spotted Cat?

"Myles," he heard him say again. Shit, he couldn't have people hear him being called that. He'd left that identity behind more than a year ago. He had worked hard at not being that person anymore. He knew his way home – if he had been capable of going there, he would have.

He stood up blindly and Tyler hugged him in a bone-crushing embrace. For a mere second Myles allowed himself to feel the amazement of the reunion, before trying to tear himself away. He couldn't deal with this today, not after everything else, it was just too much.

But Tyler held on to his shoulders, searching his eyes. "You doing okay? You making a good life for yourself here?"

Myles nodded, still afraid to speak, poised to run. He cleared his throat. "How'd you find me?"

"Long story. Doesn't matter." There was a buzzing and Tyler looked down at the phone in his hand. "Shit, my Uber driver is going to be here in one minute. Your parents just want to know that you're fine. And they want you to know you are welcome to come home any time."

For the umpteenth time that day, he lost control of his emotions, still so close to the surface. Shit, he didn't want the customers and staff of the Cat to see him crying. Tyler kept talking as Myles wiped his nose on his T-shirt sleeve. "The twins are almost a year old now – Artemis is walking..." The phone buzzed again. "Shit, he's here. I've got a plane to catch." He squeezed Myles by the shoulder. "I'd really like to stay but we've got an emergency at home. Have you been in touch with Chloe at all?"

"Um, no." He couldn't tell Tyler about the letter he'd mysteriously received or the photos he'd been stalking. Not in the next two seconds standing here. "She all right?"

"We don't know. She kinda flew the coop – that's why I have to go back so soon." Myles realized that Tyler was straddling a small rolling suitcase between his legs. "Can you come outside with me? I have to find this ride. He says it's a red Fiat."

"What do you mean – she left? The babies?"

Sparkle was suddenly at his side, looming larger than both men, her big eyes narrowing suspiciously at Myles's demonstrative state as she pressed the tip jar into his hands. "Dis de man from yesterday me tellin' you about. Him botherin' you?"

Tyler nodded towards the door to the street and began to push his way in that direction. "No, it's okay, I know him." He could not let Tyler leave without finding out what he meant about Chloe.

"Your girlfriend's something else," Tyler grinned appreciatively. "Great voice too."

"She's just my friend. And musical partner." There was no time for explaining. "So where is Chloe?" He could not keep the rising concern out of his already quavering voice and it was enough to make Tyler turn to look at him as he waved to a car.

"We don't know. She went off to Montreal last weekend with a friend she met and apparently never came back." They stared at each other, the seriousness of the situation sinking in. "Listen, bro, if she tries to contact you... you've got to break your silent treatment and call home. You get it, right?"

He nodded, swallowing hard. "Yeah, but she's not gonna call me – she's – she's probably got a new boyfriend, right?"

Tyler was already in the back seat of the Fiat, his suitcase next to him. "Seriously? When would she have time for that? Look, really, just call home anyway. People who love you want to hear from you. Be safe, buddy. So glad we connected for a sec."

Myles stood on the sidewalk just staring in the direction of the car as it drove away. He was still there, clutching the tin can full of cash when Sparkle emerged in her silver cape.

"Boy, somebody gone take dat money, you just stand on de sidewalk wid it. You not well today. Put dat cash in your pocket and go home. Me check wid you later."

CHAPTER SIXTEEN

Montreal, Quebec, Canada
March 2018

It was two days before the fever broke; three days before they took her off the ventilator. Chloe passed in and out of consciousness, sometimes hot, sometimes cold, unable to speak or eat. She felt hands examine her, heard voices talking, saw kind faces and cold judgmental ones. Something dripped into her arm that kept her from feeling pain and turned her brain into a rolling ocean of constantly crashing waves.

When they finally removed the tube from her mouth and throat, she felt hoarse and sore. That night she woke sobbing and begging for something nameless that she needed more than life itself and was finally rewarded with a shot that took her away again.

The next time she awoke and felt actually conscious, two men in uniform were standing next to her bed. They looked familiar, especially the one who was stroking her hand. "Bunny. How are you?" he asked. "Feeling better, I hope."

"Bunny, are you well enough to answer a few questions?" The taller, cocoa-skinned man had a steel-backed notepad in his hand.

Why were they calling her that name? "Not me," she croaked, unable to say more.

The one with the icy blue eyes squeezed her fingers comfortingly. "It's okay, Bunny. We'll come back."

But his partner persevered. "We just want to know who did this to you. Do you have a pimp? You can tell us. We're going to move you to a safe place as soon as they say you can go."

A pimp – was she a prostitute now? An image of sex with a stranger hovered just out of reach and a few other hazy memories flew violently by.

One of them was reading randomly from the clipboard at the end of her bed. "Blonde, 125 pounds, 5 foot 7 inches, identifying marks include tattoos on left breast and arm, fully shaved genitals marked with what appears to be felt-tip pen, stretch marks consistent with pregnancy, multiple needle entry marks on left arm, tested positive for heroin and cocaine, tested negative for HIV/AIDS, contusions on face, neck and buttocks... cuts and abrasions... mastitis and infection... answers to the name of Bunny, suspected of private enterprise prostitution in exchange for drugs... Blood pressure 120 over 70..."

"Jensen, she's crying. Why is she crying? Bunny, you need to tell us who you work for or who did this to you. It will help us save other girls from this."

"Don't cry, Bunny. We'll come back later when you feel better."

"I want to go home and see my babies," she whispered.

"Oh, Jesus, what is she talking about. Does she have kids? That's going to make things way more complicated."

"Calm down, Brown. She could be talking about cats or parakeets. She could be hallucinating." The one named Jensen stroked her brow and wiped at her tears with a tissue.

"Well, I can't come back later – I've got my daughter's school play tonight. We've got to find out how soon they're going to release her." Brown strode swiftly out of the room.

Instantly she felt a slight breeze and then Jensen's hand was somehow resting on her abdomen beneath her hospital gown. "Don't worry, Bunny," he murmured in a low comforting voice. "We're going to put you in a good place when you leave here."

She sensed it was wrong for him to touch her bare stomach, but it felt warm and reassuring. She was sorry when he quickly withdrew his hand at the sound of

239

returning footsteps. "They say they need the bed. They'd like us to get her out of here tomorrow if possible."

"That seems too soon, doesn't it? She's probably not ready to go cold turkey without drugs either. Let me make a few calls."

"I want to go home." Chloe's voice wasn't strong enough to get their attention as they left the room. A nurse arrived and came briskly to her side.

"Okay, we need to get you up, dear, get you moving around. You need to be able to go to the bathroom on your own. That's it, take it slow. You're going to be a little dizzy." Dizzy was an understatement but Chloe was determined. She walked slowly to the toilet and the nurse closed the door partway behind her. "Call me if you need help."

The hospital gown was open at the back and falling off one shoulder. Chloe let it drop to the floor as she sat down to pee. She felt like she could go to sleep sitting there but she managed to stand up again. Holding onto the sink she looked at herself in the mirror. She choked at the sight of the pasty gaunt blonde who peered back at her. When had she become that person? One side of her jaw was black and blue and there was a nasty looking bruise on her neck and chin. She looked down at her naked body. Deep scratches ran the length of her breasts which looked smaller than she remembered, one nipple still red with infection, the faded fake rose tattoo looking distorted now. But the sight of the smeared flames rising from her exposed vagina made her gasp again. She suddenly remembered Angel stroking her in front of the bald guy – or had it been the bald guy playing with her in front of Angel... Either way they'd both laughed at her as she'd come uncontrollably in full close-up view, feeling shameful and ecstatic at the same time... Angel boldly encouraging her to say how much she loved it, how she always ALWAYS wanted more... or had that been the drugs she had been talking about...

She fell to her knees as another sharp clear memory seemed to sock her in the gut. She'd been at a party, begging for another hit and been promised the needed gratification if she would do both some guy and his girlfriend. She'd refused at first but gave in after only a few minutes, yet afterwards they still wouldn't give it to her and somebody (had it been Angel?), tied her hands above her head with a belt while the woman had pushed her tits into Chloe's mouth and the man ground himself into her crotch, and... oh god, no, had she actually orgasmed during this forced experience? Maybe even multiple times? She remembered Angel snapping photos and praising her again for being such a bad dirty girl, and then finally she'd been rewarded with the drug she wanted so much...

She was a horrible person, she enjoyed terrible things, and she didn't deserve to ever go back to mothering her beautiful babies in a peaceful Vermont town. But if someone offered her a hit of smack right now, she would willingly do anything for it.

"You all right in there, dear?"

When Jensen came for her the next day, she went with him docilely, accepting that whatever punishment was in store would be totally justified given her true shameful nature. He brought a bag from a thrift store with a short fleecy black dress and a red quilted jacket. The soft dress was the coziest garment she'd worn in days and gave her a new sense of hope and security.

"Is that a smile?" Jensen teased. "Here, this is yours, right? It should make it fit better." He held out the woven Mexican belt to her and the sight of it gave Chloe a flashback of disappearing into intense pleasure. She grasped at it like a lifeline, wishing she could be floating in that euphoric place again, even just for a moment, forgetting all the trade-offs that went with it.

Jensen took the belt gently from her and fastened it around her waist, tightening the strap through the metal buckles. "There, now we can see your nice shape." His hands lingered for a moment on the curve of her hips before he reached for her black boots in the bottom of a narrow empty closet. Chloe's pleasant expression faded as she looked at the footwear she'd been forced to wear during all the weekend activities, her feet painfully swollen and blistered by the final march to the street. Her heels were still raw wounds that had not healed yet.

"No, please, I can't." She curled herself into a ball on the hard white hospital bed.

"Her feet are still quite sore," the nurse murmured quietly to Jensen. "Can we find her some slippers perhaps?"

From somewhere in the building a pair of colorful knitted socks was produced – they had rubber grippers on the soles that made them slightly more durable. Soon she was in a wheelchair being pushed to an elevator and down to the lobby and out onto the street where she was then ushered into the back of a police car. She felt a momentary panic when she saw the doors had no handles on the inside.

"Don't worry," Jensen assured her. "It's just because you can't sit up here with me. You're not under arrest."

Chloe realized she had no idea where she was – during the weekend in the city with Angel she had been led around like a pet on a leash without a clue of direction or destination. She put her hand to her throat – there *had* been a necklace with loops on it... and matching cuffs... she shuddered at what she was imagining...

Jensen was asking her a question. "Do you have any I.D. or a wallet somewhere? I mean you had nothing when we found you."

"I... I..." Of course she had those things. Where had she left them? Were they still at the hotel? She tried to remember where she had left her purse, but she couldn't even recall the last time she'd seen it. "I'm from Vermont," she said falteringly.

"You're American? Hell, let's not tell Marie that – she won't want to get involved with an international runaway. Where have you been staying? Any place regularly or just on the street?"

"It was a hotel. We just came for the weekend and then..." She felt the springs of the mattress poking against the small of her back and saw Angel poised between her legs with the scissors. She caught her breath and was suddenly lost in a bronchial coughing spasm that made her chest hurt.

"Bunny, stay calm. It's okay. I've heard so many stories that started the same way." Jensen had a very soothing manner and Chloe felt her heart rate slow down as the wave of panic went by. "So we might have to sell Marie on you. Tell me about your experience – are you good at what you do?"

She had no idea what he was talking about. "I'm a decent writer," she said, trying to recall what her job actually was.

"A decent rider?" He laughed heartily. "So your customers are usually satisfied after you ride them? You're precious, Bunny."

Chloe put her head down on the seat and closed her eyes. She was tired and confused.

"You okay back there?"

"Are there drugs where we're going?" she asked sleepily. "I really could use just a tiny little fix right now."

"Bunny! You've got to promise to be clean at Marie's house. You can't ever say you're using, understand me?"

She nodded off, stroking the end of the woven belt.

They went into a nondescript concrete building and up a few flights of stairs to what seemed like someone's living room. It was warm and comfortable and Chloe sat on an old leather couch while Jensen carried on a long conversation in French with a middle-aged woman whose short gray hair and conservative cotton dress made Chloe think of a bank teller. She didn't understand most of what they said, but they looked over at her a lot and the woman made disapproving clucking sounds with her mouth.

"Bunny, honey, we need to look under your skirt so I can show Marie what I'm talking about. We need to figure out how to clean you up."

Chloe felt a sense of alarm and tried to disappear into the soft cushions of the sofa.

"Marie understands you've been traumatized, but you need to cooperate with us now if you want to stay here. We don't want you to end up back on the street." When she still didn't respond, Jensen leaned over and pulled up the hem of her dress. "It's not like half of Montreal hasn't seen this already – it was the talk of the hospital. Allez, Madam. "

She closed her eyes as Marie examined her, exclaiming over the flames. When she moved away, Jensen stayed there, holding the fabric up and staring at Chloe's crotch as Marie continued to give instructions in French, until Chloe grabbed her skirt and tucked it around her legs.

Eventually the woman left the room and returned with an armload of bedding, which she dumped in Chloe's lap. To Jensen she also gave a couple of bottles and towels in exchange for a fat wad of Canadian cash.

"You are lucky girl. You go. Up. And up again." she said to Chloe pointing at the stairs. "He go too."

"Merci, madam." Jensen kissed Marie on the cheek and took Chloe by the arm.

The room was on the top floor, a narrow cement box, like a monk's cell; two twin beds displayed ticking-striped mattresses on either side of a slit-like window. Chloe sank down on one bed, exhausted by the climb, feeling feverish again, and Jensen took the sheets and blankets from her and made up the other bed.

"The bathroom is across the hall. I'm going to get these rags wet. Why don't you just lie on this towel right where you are; this could be a messy job."

Chloe pulled her knees up into a fetal position and shut her eyes. She still didn't feel very well. All she wanted to do was sleep, even just for thirty seconds.

"Come on, work with me, girl. Spread your legs." She blinked awake. Jensen was rolling her onto her back, pulling up her dress again, holding a damp cloth out to her. She could smell something strong, like bleach or rubbing alcohol. "Here's one for you to use. Let me know if this burns or anything."

He began scrubbing at the flames on her belly, working his way downward. Embarrassed as she was, she watched in grateful fascination as most of the offensive artwork disappeared, leaving her exposed flesh as raw and pink as a newborn baby animal. The magic marker had created a sort of camouflage for the sensuous folds of her vagina, which now seemed unprotected and vulnerable. "I don't know about this part." Jensen said, changing to a new rag soaked in warm soapy water and watching Chloe's face closely as he slid the wet cloth around the edges of her tender crevices. "Does this feel all right?"

She had another flashback to Angel washing her in a similar fashion but much more vigorously as she told Chloe the graphic details about all the bar sex she didn't remember having. She felt her stomach muscles convulse at the memory and she tried to sit up.

"Stop, please, stop." She didn't want him to do this, no matter how it was beginning to make her feel.

But Jensen wasn't listening. He seemed mesmerized by his own slow erotic strokes and their effect on Chloe. "Women are so amazing. Look how beautiful this is as you become aroused. We can see it so well now. I've been thinking about this all week, Bunny. And it's even better than I imagined."

She didn't feel strong enough to struggle and what he was doing to her was so different than the violations that were haunting her. It reminded her of what sex was supposed to be like, of something she used to know a long time ago. "It's going to be all right for you here, sweetheart. I'm going to visit you often and until you're better, it will be just me."

She had no idea what he was talking about, but she didn't care now. He touched her lightly with his tongue and a sigh escaped her lips as he pulled away and spoke again, his breath hot against her. "I know I'm not supposed to get involved, but I want to treat you well so that you aren't just doing me, you're wanting me too." There was more warm licking and she felt herself floating away into remembrances of lovers she had actually loved. "Do you want me to stop? I didn't think so."

He was unhurried and gentle and even though she didn't know him at all, he made her feel wonderful and when he finally entered her, she rode him slowly, savoring the experience, finally generating enough heat to let him peel her dress off over her head and explore the wonders and damages of the rest of her body.

"It's not supposed to be like this," he said afterwards, stroking her hair, as they lay entwined and relaxed on the unmade mattress. "Cops aren't supposed to fall in love with prostitutes."

"I'm not a prostitute," she murmured into his shoulder.

"Well, soon you'll be paid in cash instead of drugs and yes, you will be."

She started to protest but he held a finger to her lips.

"Don't worry. Marie treats her girls really well. But I don't like the idea of other cops who come here sharing you. You're too special to me now. I made a deal with her for the next week but maybe…"

She started crying. "I need to go home."

"Shhh. You are home now. You're safe here." He sat up abruptly. "What time is it? I need to go. My shift starts soon."

"Don't leave me. I'm afraid. I don't know anybody here. Will you come back?" She started shivering again and he helped her into the other bed and covered her with the sheet and blanket.

"Of course, sweetheart. As soon as I can. Maybe tonight even."

"Jensen? Can you maybe bring me a little bit of… something when you come back?" She hated the pitiful way she sounded but her need was stronger than her pride.

"No, darling. You need to let that go if you want to stay here."

246

The first night a pale thin girl with waist-length strawberry blonde hair brought a bowl of chicken noodle soup to Chloe's room. After she spent sleepless hours sweating and shivering, Jensen arrived at dawn with a cup of coffee and a bag of donuts. The sex seemed more urgent this time, she wanted to fill all the empty aching places inside her in any way possible, and she felt gratified that her responsiveness seemed to please him.

Afterwards he explained to her that she would be taking the rest of her meals downstairs with the other girls in the house and that, as soon as she was well enough, she would be assigned some daily tasks to be performed along with the nightly duties she would be assuming.

"But – when can I go home?"

He kissed her on the forehead, tucked the blankets in around her and told her he would be back that evening.

In the days that followed she spent most of her time sleeping. She stumbled down the stairs three times a day to eat at a dining room table with a dozen housemates who spoke a variety of languages from French to Russian and who observed her with varying degrees of wary unfriendliness. There were men who came and went, most of them wearing uniforms and she learned that this was a special house for policemen only and that the majority of the customers had specific girls who they visited on a regular basis, although some liked to rotate. There were no privileges or wages granted for the first thirty days and cell phones were prohibited. After that you were allowed to go in the yard, smoke cigarettes, and use the house computer, but one of the girls told her if you got tips during the probationary period you could keep them.

As her health returned, Jensen's visits became the only break in what seemed like a monotonous existence. After a few days she was assigned a roommate, a teenage redhead from Serbia who wouldn't speak to anyone, and then she and Jensen had to use one of the downstairs bedrooms like everyone else and their time was monitored. He was still as attentive as ever to her sexually, and once after an especially satisfying session, she was warned by Marie that she was not there for her own pleasure, but for his. She wasn't sure how Marie knew what went on after they closed the door, but she tried to be quieter after that.

Chloe was given the job of managing the "wardrobe room," which was really just an oversized walk-in closet full of secondhand sexy lingerie and robes, as well as a few shelves of other used clothing. The girls who'd been there longest had their own apparel that they themselves had purchased, but the newer girls, and especially the ones that were fresh off the street like Chloe, would borrow garments and sometimes required her help with adjusting straps, laces and garters. Chloe was also responsible for laundering the clothing and keeping track of inventory. Some of the women treated a visit to the closet like a shopping trip, trying on different sizes and styles, preening in front of the full-length mirror to see which outfit showed off their assets or covered their flaws. Chloe liked being able to choose the most flattering designs for herself; her favorite was an electric blue teddy of satin and lace that covered the stretch marks on her hips but displayed the curves of her butt and the fullness of her breasts. It always gave her a little sickening thrill to see how provocative it made her look.

There was a pretty Romanian girl name Rania who always complimented Chloe's appearance, one of the few housemates who was friendly. Her eyes were dark and bright and she had a dimple in one cheek when she smiled. "Sweet. Sexy," she would say, using the few English words she knew. Rania had clear skin and a lithe figure; she could have worn the skimpiest outfits because her high upturned breasts needed no support and her bum was smooth and muscular. But Rania did not seem at ease with displaying her body and her choices were modest by house standards. Still she was very popular with the clients and Chloe would have felt a little jealous if Rania wasn't so nice to her.

And then one morning Chloe was informed that she had a customer who had paid for a half hour with her on his lunch break. He was an overweight man with a bulbous nose and puffy lips who breathed heavily and slobbered on her and Chloe managed not to cry until the repulsiveness of the experience was over. But after he was gone, she saw the cash he had left on the bedside table and realized what it could mean. Within twenty-four hours she had managed to score some coke from one of the longtime residents and spent an afternoon snorting herself into a blissful, if temporary, high. For a brief hour or so, she forgot about how much she hated who she'd become.

Jensen was livid when he found out that Marie had let someone else have sex with her, and Chloe could barely calm him down with assurances that she was fine and that he was the only man she cared about. "Did he do this to you? Or this? Did he make you feel the way I make you feel?" he demanded.

"No, you will always be the only one who knows how to take care of me," she promised him.

"Do you like this, Bunny? Do you want me to keep going? Or should I leave now?" She knew how he played – tantalizing and pausing, building the anticipation to an explosive crescendo – and she gave him the physical response he craved so that he would continue. But this time, even as her pleasure grew, she found her eyes wandering to the pair of pants hanging over the back of a chair and wondering how much money might be in his wallet.

Within a few days, she had acquired another client, a beefy officer with hands like hams who offered her a small bag of crack in exchange for a few extra favors. "I heard you might be interested. I have lots of access to this stuff." She eagerly acquiesced to his requests and he soon became a regular customer. He had kinky tastes but she knew she was capable of anything when she was high and he took full advantage of the opportunities her desire for drugs offered. One evening she was sent to a room where he waited for her, still fully dressed, but with Rania who was already naked on the bed and looking rather frightened as he stroked one of her smooth pointy nipples while watching Chloe's reaction to the situation.

"She asked for it to be you," he said, and she could guess what was going to happen. Her eyes met Rania's and she could see inexperience and pleading reflected back at her. "You'll get a bonus for a good performance."

There were handcuffs involved and a lot of girl-going-down-on-girl action in a long session for which she was rewarded with an extra bag of white powder to take back to her own room. She needed it to get her mind off the scene which would not stop replaying itself in her head. Her non-communicative roommate rolled over to face the wall and give Chloe the privacy she needed to get high and drift off to sleep in the dark.

Later that night there was a tiny knock on the door and a narrow shaft of light fell across the floor. "Bunny?" a female voice whispered and Chloe sat up quickly and turned on the light. The other bed was empty and Rania stood in the doorway, wrapped in a shiny leopard print robe that billowed around her slight frame.

"What's the matter? Come in. Close the door." Rania didn't need to understand the words to know what she was saying. Chloe patted the bed and Rania sat down next to her, shivering. Chloe lifted the quilt and tucked it around her lap. "Are you okay?"

"Okay. Yes." She rested her head against Chloe's shoulder for a moment and Chloe knew she was thinking about what they had done a few hours earlier. "You are good…" she searched for the phrase.

"Friend. You too." Chloe slipped a hand under the mattress and pulled out the plastic baggie that contained the remainder of her 'bonus.' "You want to share this?"

Rania put a restraining hand on Chloe's arm before reaching under her robe and extracting a similar bag. "You show me?"

High together in bed with a beautiful girlfriend… it seemed like a perfect dream to Chloe. She thought she had never felt anything as lovely as Rania or tasted anything so sweet. At times the sensory pleasure came into intense focus out of a cloud of floating warmth and Chloe hadn't ever experienced anything like it. Time stopped and started and disappeared and suddenly it was morning and the roommate was back in her bed, face to the wall and Chloe was curled protectively around Rania's naked body in a tangle of damp sheets.

She kissed her neck until the girl's eyes fluttered open and an expression of alarm set in. Making no sound at all, she slipped out from under the covers, swept her robe off the floor, carefully turned the knob on the door and was gone.

For a moment Chloe thought she had never been happier or felt more satisfied. A minute later she wanted more – more drugs, more sex, more Rania.

The following day the roommate was gone for good, apparently a bad match for Marie's establishment, and Marie allowed Rania, whom she clearly considered a treasure, to move in with Chloe. Jensen got a strange look in his eyes when Chloe introduced him to her new roomie. She was already aware her young friend had that effect on most men, but it made her feel a little threatened. Jensen had been her lifeline, and the thought that he might abandon her for someone else made her realize the precarious balance of her current existence, out of touch with the outside world, without a real identity, and with a past life that seemed like a fantasy slipping through her fingers.

They were a twenty-four hour operation, catering to around the clock shift changes, and the long-termers usually got the best shifts which were evening and late night hours. The newbies got the daytime customers because there were fewer of them and they were not as free with their money. This meant that Chloe and Rania usually both had the night hours off together, unless there were special requests. Chloe lost track of what day it was because it didn't matter. Her life was determined by whether it was "fat cop's coffee break" or "kinky man's afternoon," which wasn't so bad now because she and Rania got to do it together. She didn't like the domination games or being cuffed to the bed, but she always offered herself up so Rania wouldn't have to, although that strategy only worked some of the time. Often they would go back to their room afterwards and have a good cry before losing themselves in the "haze du jour" as Chloe called it. They never knew what drug they'd be paid in, probably whatever he'd managed to bust someone for in the last few days, and the high could vary anywhere from miserable to spectacular.

Then came the afternoon when Chloe spaced out that Jensen was coming to see her. She and Rania had free-based some really good shit, stripped off the small amount of clothing they wore and were dreamily kissing and cuddling on top of Chloe's bed, when there was an impatient rapping on the door.

Jensen took in the scene – two naked girls wrapped around each other, stoned out of their minds... a tarnished spoon, lighter, and empty baggie on the nightstand – and his jaw dropped open before his expression hardened.

"Jensen. You're not supposed to be up here." Chloe wasn't sure if she spoke the words or not; but she knew it felt weird to be talking to him while she had two fingers up inside of Rania.

"Looks like we're all doing things we're not supposed to." He picked up the plastic bag and sniffed it. "Oh, Bunny. You're in big trouble now."

He was staring down at them with a look that was both disapproving and fascinated. Chloe could see his rising rage and wasn't sure if she should be scared. Rania was so high she just peeked around at Jensen and giggled before going back to nuzzling on Chloe.

"Oh, no. Did I forget about you?" Chloe started to feel a little desperate, afraid that she was about to lose him to his anger. "Of course, I didn't. We've just been waiting for you. I knew you'd come." Had she really just invited him to have a three-way with her and Rania? Well, why not. It was the two people she loved best right now, it could be a terrific time.

Rania's eyes opened and she sat up. "We share Bunny?" she asked Jensen in beautiful wide-eyed innocence before falling dizzily back to rest on Chloe's chest.

Chloe could see his hard-on growing even as his lips tightened and he crossed his arms. "How old do you think she is?" It was not what she was expecting him to say. "How old are you?" he shouted at Rania.

"Don't yell at her. She's Romanian, not deaf." Chloe wrapped an arm protectively around Rania who looked bewildered. "What difference does it make how old she is?"

"Because I'm not going to jail even if you are. Can't you see how young she is?"

"What I can see is that the idea of this turns you on." Chloe was coming down from her high like an avalanche on a mountain. "How does age even matter? Come to bed with us." When he didn't respond, Chloe could feel terror tightening her rib cage. "You know you want to touch her the way you touched me when you met me." She looked up at him provocatively, stroking Rania between her legs.

Jensen's face turned purple as he tried to control himself. "I am not fucking a fifteen-year-old. And you, Bunny, are under arrest." He pulled the handcuffs off his belt.

"I am not," she laughed although the words "fifteen-year-old" started ringing in her head like a school bell signaling that recess was over.

"For use of a controlled substance and sex with a minor." She could not believe he was handcuffing her to his own wrist. "The holiday is over. Get up. I'm taking you in."

CHAPTER SEVENTEEN

New Orleans, Louisiana
March 2018

Darcy looked up in surprise as Myles came through the back door. He was almost never home at this time of the evening and it felt a little awkward to walk in on his landlady finishing her dinner and working at the kitchen table.

"Sorry, I wasn't feeling well," he apologized.

"No problem, you live here too." She held up the garment she was stitching and he recognized the silver fabric he had bought for Sparkle. "What do you think so far?"

"She's going to love it. Kit around?" He noticed that the bedroom door was ajar and there was no light on.

"You just missed her. She stepped out for a bit. I'm surprised you didn't pass her." Darcy frowned and picked up some of the scraps, searching for something. "Balls, where did my sewing shears go? I just had them a second ago..."

Myles grabbed a beer out of the fridge and went into his room. He was glad to have a few minutes more to himself without Kit. He was still freaking out about seeing Tyler and hearing about Chloe; he'd almost forgotten what he'd learned about Kit earlier in the day.

Chloe. The iPad seemed to draw him to its blank screen, mocking his inability to resist the urge to look her up again. He ought to contact Tyler and tell him about the photos – Tyler might be able to figure something out from them. But he was probably still on a plane, flying back to Vermont. Myles couldn't believe he was actually considering making that call.

He was surprised to see that Chloe had posted a new photo just a few hours earlier. It was a side view of her naked to the waist, laughing hysterically as someone held a tape measure around the widest part of her breasts. In the background, racks of colorful lingerie could be seen hanging on a wall. *"Ooh that tickles!"* read the caption. Beneath her chin, the riveted metal choker gleamed in the camera's flash. He didn't understand why woman thought that kind of necklace was sexy; he remembered Kit had worn something similar once in Mexico. Beneath the post was a comment line that read, *"Suck or be sucked? Yes, please!"* with a clickable link.

This time it lead to a series of very graphic still photographs of Chloe with a woman, Chloe with a man, and then a rather comatose-looking Chloe with both at once. She was not laughing or even smiling and it occurred to Myles for the first time that maybe she wasn't okay with what was going on. He exited back to the Facebook page and changed his mind again; she was totally posing for the measurement pic, there was no way she hadn't been fine with it. She was looking right at the camera, eyes wide, dimples deep, as uninhibited as ever.

He thought about his brief conversation with Tyler and how he had mentioned that Artemis had started to walk. Myles scrolled back down the page to watch the video of Artemis toddling across the living room floor. This time he unmuted the sound. He was flooded with emotion when he heard Chloe's voice speaking.

"Go, on, you can do it! That's it, Artemis, Auntie Angel will catch you!"

Who the hell was Auntie Angel, he wondered, and why did she get to be there for this momentous occasion? A pair of arms reached out to catch the unsteady Artemis and he heard someone speak in a disturbingly familiar accent.

"Come on, baby. Look at y'all go! Angel's got ya – good girl!"

It couldn't be. He was definitely losing his mind today. He watched again as Artemis fell into a shadow of textural purple cloth...and then lifted his gaze to the purple silk skirt hanging in the closet across the room.

He was on his third beer when Kit came swirling in, breathless and a little sweaty, one hand inside her big slouchy bag, the other clutching a loosely woven shawl that she'd tossed over her shoulders.

"Oh!" She stopped short at the sight of Myles propped up against the pillows. "I thought you'd be at the Cat." She swept quickly past him and into the bathroom.

"Yeah, no. It's been kind of a rough day." He picked at the edge of the label on the bottle, waiting for her to ask why.

He could hear the water running and some splashing in the sink before she materialized next to the bed, somewhat more composed. "What's up, baby? Tell me about it." She perched on the edge of the mattress and placed a hand on his hip.

"Did Beau find you?" He tried hard to keep any emotion out of his voice. "He was looking for you again."

"Beau?" She looked quizzical as though she expected him to believe that for a moment she didn't know who he was talking about. "No, I never saw him. I've been down by the Square all day." She jumped up suddenly. "I can't wait to tell you about the new hypnosis piece I've added to my fortunetelling. Just stay right there, let me get a glass of wine."

She disappeared into the kitchen as though their world was exactly as it had always been. Myles gulped his beer, feeling frightened and uncertain; confrontation was not his strong suit and he wasn't sure he was ready to take her on yet.

Kit returned, sipping from a large green goblet decorated with glass gargoyles. "There, that's better." She slipped the strap of her carryall over her head and tossed it on the floor. Kicking off her boots, she curled up next to him, paying no heed to his chilly reception. "So did I tell you about how I've been studying hypnosis in the last month? It's super amazing."

"So what's that mean?" he asked lazily. "Like you can get people to do stuff when they're asleep?"

She laughed. "Kinda. Sometimes. It's more about getting them to relax and open up to their own issues. Most of the time they don't even know I'm doing it."

"That's kind of... weird. So you never told me about your trip to New York. Who were you visiting again?" He had watched the video of Artemis walking a dozen times in the last half hour and still could not reconcile what he had seen.

"An old girlfriend. I told you that. Why – aw, what, do you think I was cheating on you? That's so sweet." She stroked his cheek.

"So like what'dja do – you stay in the city the whole time?" Did he sound as suspicious as he was?

"Well, we went up to the mountains for a little while. I skied for the first time in my life." Her fingers were still on his face, rubbing his forehead, running through his hair.

"Really? I'm impressed. Where'd you go?"

"I have no idea. Some place cold and snowy north of the city. Why you asking me so many questions, baby? You never talk this much. You trying to avoid telling me about your day?"

Shit, of course she could tell he was not acting normal. She was too smart; he was never going to be able to get any info out of her. He was going to have to play her own game with her. "Drink up," he advised, putting a hand on her wine glass and holding it to her lips. "I didn't get a chance to score any more weed so we're going to have to get drunk tonight."

"I used to love drinking tequila in Mexico with you." She snuggled in close to him as she downed her Cabernet, and then glanced over at the iPad. "You have a chance to get online today?"

"A little bit." Had he logged out? He couldn't remember. "I didn't get home that long before you. So tell me about your New York friend. Single? Married? Kids?

257

You need more wine?" He was on his feet and back with the bottle so quickly that she stared in amazement.

"Coy-boy! What is up with you? Lay down here and let me do a little bit of my relaxation technique on you." But she let him refill her glass and then watched as he sat back expectantly, arms folded, waiting for her to reply to his questions.

"Okay, you want to know about the friend I visited. Her name is Bunny. She has a couple of kids, but she's separated from her husband. I helped her get out and meet some new guys. It was fun." Kit gave a strange smile. "But it made me horny for you. As you know from yesterday." She patted the crotch of his jeans. "We had fun too, didn't we?"

"So like what – you did girl stuff, like makeovers? And you went to bars and drank a lot?"

Kit shrugged. "Kind of. Yeah. Actually she liked doing drugs more. You ask too many questions." She climbed onto his lap and kissed him as she undid the waistband of her skirt. "Did you play music today?"

"Sparkle and I did a couple of sets and then I ran into an old friend."

"So how exactly do you perform with that tranny with the gigantic tits? I mean, I know this is New Orleans, but... they actually let her be on stage at the Spotted Cat?"

He pushed her off of him and stood up. "What do you know, anyway? Sparkle is the next big thing about to happen in this city."

"Well, you got the big part right anyway. So what – you riding along to stardom on her fat coon ass coattails?"

"You're disgusting. I don't need to listen to your bigoted ignorant racist comments." As he moved quickly out to the back porch, he was surprised at how shaken he felt by her last remark; it made him realize how little he actually knew about her beliefs and values.

She was at his side before the door had shut behind him. "I'm sorry, baby. I was just kidding – making a tasteless Southern joke. It's hard to take the white trash out of a bayou girl." She clutched his arm. "I guess I'm a little jealous that's all. You spending so much time with her, saying nice things about her talent." She kissed him on the cheek. "What can I do to impress you like that?"

"Oh, come on, Kit. You're one of the most creative people I know. You can do anything you put your mind to." He pulled away from her and sat down on the wicker love seat.

"Then how come I can't get your full attention anymore?" She was not going to let him off that easily. Plopping herself down next to him, she put her hand on his thigh.

"I've just been... distracted these last few days. Been thinking about home." Might as well bring it up, see what happened.

"You're not still thinking about that old girlfriend, are you? It's been almost a year now, I'm sure she's moved on and found a new relationship, just like you have." Kit's words echoed in his brain, like a repeat of something. It came to him almost instantly – he had memorized every sentence of the "Dear Myles" letter he had received from Chloe. Holy Jesus shit.

"You're so tense, baby. Listen, I know you're out of pot, but I've got something else you can smoke if you want. I guarantee it'll make you feel good. Along with a little relaxation therapy, massage, sex, you know... Mama Kit will take care of you."

Her offer made him feel even more on edge, although he was beyond curious as to what she was referring to. "Like what do you have?"

She hopped up, displaying her obvious delight that she finally had his interest and attention. "I'll go get it."

She returned with her big bag, rummaging around inside its contents until she emerged with an Altoids tin. "You ever do anything harder than weed? Because you know it's easily available in this city."

Images of Jasmine sleeping wasted in the park and needle tracks on the arms of bus passengers came instantly to mind. He'd always avoided anything beyond super-strong strains of grass. A memory of Chloe 'copping hash' in Istanbul floated through his consciousness; it had been the turning point for everything that had followed in his life.

"Only some hash once in Turkey." He didn't have a clue as to what he was looking at inside the little metal box. "What is this – cocaine? Heroin? Crack?" He realized he was totally inexperienced in this method of getting high. "Have you been doing this shit?"

Kit laughed hoarsely and lit a cigarette. "No, no. I mean I have done it, but not anymore. I had scored this coke for my friend up north. She really liked it, but then she moved on to stronger stuff and when we went away for the weekend, I stashed it some place safe and forgot about it until afterwards. You want to try some?" She leaned towards him and whispered, "I guarantee it will take fucking to a new level."

He looked at her through half-closed eyes, trying to figure out what was going on. Was she just being mischievous? No, he had to get real – there was some serious shit going on here, and Kit was more than a little demented. "You go first," he said.

She shook her head and blew some smoke out into the night. "Nah, this is all for you, baby. There's not enough for us both to get a good buzz."

"Yeah, no. I'm going to pass. Just not in the mood tonight." He was beyond being fooled by her seductive ways.

She sucked down the last of her cigarette and stubbed it out in the ashtray. "Suit yourself." The metal container snapped shut and disappeared into the depths of Kit's bag of tricks. "I'm going to get some more wine; can I get you another beer?"

"Sure." She left her purse on the floor as she went back inside, leaving the door open behind her and Myles stared intently at it, wishing he had x-ray vision. There were answers in that bag, Myles was sure of it. He had never pried into Kit's possessions, mostly because he could have cared less to know any more about her, but now he wanted to go through her things, see what he could find. Since she'd been back, all the highway signs were pointing towards danger and deception. He needed her to go to sleep so he could do some snooping around, confirm his suspicions. If he wasn't insane, if she was really the "Auntie Angel" of the Artemis video, then his whole world was about to genuinely implode.

"Here you go, babe. It was the last one in there, so drink up." As she held it out to him, the sound of police sirens a couple of blocks away made them both pause. Flashing blue lights lit up the hazy blackness of the city sky.

"Sounds close," Myles commented.

"Probably just another shooting. I've heard this neighborhood is getting even less safe than it used to be." Another pair of cop cars went whizzing down the street. "So much for a peaceful night hanging out in the Bywater. Come on, let's drink up and go to bed before we get caught in the crossfire." She scooped up her bag, waiting for him to follow her inside.

"You go in. I'm going to sit out here for a few minutes more. Don't make that face; I'll be in soon."

The beer tasted weird; after a few sips, he poured it over the side of the deck and then went down the steps to pee at the edge of the garden. He heard some shouting out on the sidewalk and then footsteps hurrying in the same direction as the police cars had gone. Curious to see what was going on, he moved stealthily around to the front of the house and out into the road. The flashing lights had congregated a block away on a cross street, creating a barricade so traffic couldn't pass through. Myles joined the crowd of spectators that hovered on the sidelines.

"What happened?" he asked a couple of guys who he recognized as neighbors.

One of them motioned to a place behind the NOPD squad cars. "Some guy got stabbed to death in the throat in that truck over there."

261

"Hell, how do you know that?" another bystander asked him in wonder.

"'Cause we were the ones who called it in. We walked by and saw him leaning against the window all bloody."

Myles had a really bad feeling about this latest unfortunate event in his ongoing ill-fated day. "That sucks. Does he live in the neighborhood?"

"Probably not. It's a big shiny black four-by-four – not exactly a city vehicle."

His heart began pounding so hard he couldn't hear anything else they said. With a lingering horrified glance back at the scene of the crime, he moved blindly away.

It could be a coincidence, right? It could happen to anyone sitting around in their truck on a back street on a dark night in the Bywater. But it hadn't happened to just anyone on any night. There was no question in his mind who had done it to whom.

What was he going to do now... he couldn't go home and sleep with her. But if he didn't show up, she would know he was on to her and would probably track him down. Shit, she had even managed to find Chloe and now Chloe had disappeared.

He needed to call Tyler. Now. But when he reached for his phone he remembered he'd left it charging in the bedroom. In the outlet next to the iPad.

Okay, so he had to go back. He walked slowly in the direction of the house, thinking about what his game plan was going to be, reminding himself she had never done him any harm. Yet. Maybe her madness was just setting in, maybe she had forgotten to take her meds or something. He'd lived intimately with her for almost six months – he'd never seen her take any prescriptions. But if what Beau, the very recently departed Beau, had said was true, Kit had been an abused child who had tried to kill her own father and then had murdered her ex-lover within weeks of moving in with Myles in Baja. Virtually under his nose.

Shit. And why had she gone after Chloe? Did a crazy person need a real reason? How had Kit even found her?

Obviously Myles had somehow left a trail that led back to West Jordan; he hadn't really thought Kit was a threat.

He stood in the backyard for a long time, trying to decide what to do. Through the glass doors he could see into the kitchen of the house and he relaxed a little bit as he remembered he was not actually alone with Kit. He lived with witches who kept odd hours – Darcy was back at the sewing machine on the table, working on Sparkle's dress; Wendell was cooking something on the stovetop that looked like pancakes. There was a support system of sorts if he needed it. He went inside.

"Look." Darcy held up her scissors. "They were here all the time, of course. Under this pile of cloth."

"Huh. How about that." Did stabbing a human arterial neck vein make scissors dull, he wondered.

"Tell Sparkle we'll be ready for a fitting tomorrow."

"Okay. Not sure if she'll have time to swing by." Tomorrow might as well be twenty years away.

He was hoping maybe Kit had fallen asleep but she was sitting up in bed, wearing only the embroidered shawl and a look of angry impatience. "Where have you been? You disappeared. I was getting worried."

It was not a time for sassy retorts. "Sorry. I needed a walk." What he needed was his phone, but he couldn't get it without reaching across her. "I've got a gig tomorrow night at the Trois Maisons and I don't know what time it starts." Wow, that lie had floated effortlessly to the surface. Maybe this wouldn't be so hard.

"Well, I'm ready to go to sleep so don't be long," she said crossly. "I thought you would be sleepy too by now."

He started to retort that his usual bedtime was hours away but thought better of it. "Go ahead and nod off. I'll wake you up when I'm done." He slipped outside again.

Myles took a deep breath and forced his memory to recall Tyler's number. He swore when the call went to voice mail; Tyler must still be in the air. "Hey, it's Myles. Um, I need you to call me back. There's, uh, something important that's going on. And it might have to do with Chloe. But I need your help." He paused. "Thanks. And it was good to see you."

He stepped back into the kitchen, quiet now that Darcy and Wendell had retired to their side of the house. He peeked into the bedroom; Kit had dimmed the light and was lying quietly under the covers and he backed noiselessly away, hoping she was asleep.

It felt strangely cathartic to have broken his silence and actually reached out to his extended family. He thought about the phone numbers from his childhood imprinted in his brain – there were only a few he had actually memorized; the rest had disappeared when he had tossed his first cell away when he left for Mexico.

On impulse he dialed Chloe's number. Wherever she was, maybe if he left a message it might have an effect. As he listened to the ringing in his ear, a buzzing vibration started up in the next room. What the fuck... He quickly ended the call and slid back into the bedroom.

Kit was sitting up again, looking sleepy and dazed. "Oh, I thought I heard... Must have been dreaming..." She fell back against the pillows. "God, I already feel hung over from that cheap wine. Come make me feel better, baby." Eyes closed, she held out her arms to him.

Could he do this? He was too scared not to try. The sooner she fell back to sleep, the sooner he would be able to get on with what he really needed to do.

He got through the sex – his mind racing to the future, when Kit would be asleep and he could conduct a silent search through her bag, drawers, and other things. When he finally heard her breathing settle into an even pattern, he slid quietly out of the bed. He knew exactly where she'd left her purse – his hand closed around the strap and he carried it into the bathroom with him and locked the door.

Careful not to make any noise, he dumped the contents out onto the soft fluffy surface of the bathroom rug and stared in amazement. Amidst the chaos of what had been contained within, which included everything from tarot cards to Mardi Gras beads to a skimpy red lace thong, was not one, not two, but three cell phones. He recognized Kit's own phone immediately by its purple leopard-spotted protector. But there were two others – a basic black and a sparkly blue. He started with the black, tried first to call his own number, but immediately got a message that the phone had been deactivated. He scrolled to the contacts and rocked back on his heels in disbelief.

Names and places he knew from Vermont whizzed by as he moved down the list. He switched the screen to view the recent text messages. The last messages were dated a couple of days earlier from a contact identified only as George. *"Where are you? Please call." "Call as soon as you can! Chloe is MIA." "Chloe not on bus and not answering phone. What now?"*

And then one that made his head swim. From Sarah S-A. *"So how is it going in New Orleans? Any sightings?"*

A quick switch to the email button confirmed his suspicion. He was holding Tyler's phone in his hand. But how was that possible – he'd seen him just hours ago, texting his Uber driver. Still, there was no question about it. Tyler's phone was in Kit's bag. What the hell did that mean?

He picked up the blue phone and pressed the display button. *"One missed call,"* it read. The unidentified number was his own. He swiped the home screen open. The wallpaper photo was of two baby girls with blonde curly hair. With a trembling index finger he touched the Photo Gallery page.

There were dozens of pictures of the "new" Chloe, some posed headshots mugging for the camera, but most were more raw and graphic than anything he'd seen posted online. He had to scroll down several times before the photos became normal snapshots of life as a young mother in Vermont. And then finally he found what he was looking for. A shot of two women with their arms wrapped lovingly around each other, cheek to cheek, as they sat on a familiar-looking couch, blowing kisses to the camera. Chloe wore a pink shirt he recognized as Kit's, a single button straining to contain her chest within its narrow confines. Kit wore a fuzzy white sweater that he remembered Chloe wearing, in fact he recalled lifting it from Madison Carter's drawer himself during his months of "liberating" the belongings of the conspicuously wealthy in Windfall. In fact, it was the same sweater Kit had worn just yesterday, that he had pulled over her head before they had fucked in the car at the beach...

Sucking in his breath, he told himself he could not freak out now. He counted thirty long seconds and then sent himself the photo. His phone made a quiet ding that, to his heightened and frightened senses, sounded as loud as a cannon exploding. Then moving carefully as to make no noise, he began to put everything back into Kit's bag, when he came across her passport. Evangeline Katherine Beauchaine... the "Angel" in the first name jumped out at him now. He wondered if that was what her daddy had called her as a child. He finished replacing all the items he'd taken out, with the exception of Chloe's cell. Let Kit freak out. There was just no way...

He hid it behind the clawfoot tub, tucked into the crook of a water pipe against the wall. Turning off the light, he glided back out into the bedroom to replace the bag where he found it.

What now...

For a long time he sat on the rug at the foot of the bed. If he wanted to save his own life, he needed to go. But really he didn't think he was in danger; it was everyone else around him who should fear for their lives. When he thought about what she might have done to Chloe, he felt panic grip every molecule of his being. He needed to get in touch with Tyler. He needed to pack and be ready to run. And he needed to confront Kit about the trip to Montreal.

It took almost no time to throw a few pieces of clothing into his backpack and move it and his fiddle next to the door. Then he returned to his watchful position on the rug and contemplated his situation again. He loved his life in

New Orleans; he was meant to be here in the music scene and it wasn't fair that he had to leave because of Kit.

Even muffled by his pocket, the sound of his phone ringing was like a fire alarm. He looked back and forth from the flashing screen that told him Tyler was calling to the specter of Kit stirring under the covers. Then Myles leaped to his feet and ran from the room and didn't stop until he was down the steps and into the backyard.

"Hi." Breathless with anxiety, he doubled over for a moment, trying to focus.

"Myles, what's up? I just barely got to my car in the airport parking lot when I heard your message." Tyler sounded fatigued.

"I... I... don't know how to say this. But... the woman I live with... well, she's the one who Chloe went to Montreal with."

"Angel?" There was a long pause. "You live with Angel?" Tyler's incredulity was audible even from fifteen hundred miles away.

"Yes, but she goes by Kit here." The damp grass was cold on his bare soles as he moved farther away from the house. "I found Chloe's phone in her purse – I think Kit's been posting and messaging from it. There are all kinds of awful sex photos on it." There was still stunned silence on the other end of the line. "And I guess she stole your phone too somehow?"

"Um... yeah, she did." Tyler cleared his throat. "Let me get this straight. You're telling me Angel is your girlfriend?"

"Look, I'll explain another time. I'm afraid she's going to come outside and find me. The chick is dangerous – she's killed two guys that I know of, one of them just tonight, and I'm scared. For myself, and for you and the girls, and especially for Chloe. We need to find her."

He could hear Tyler holding the phone away from his mouth and swearing. "Myles. What are you saying? Who did she kill tonight?"

267

"A guy named Beau Laveaux who's been looking for her for days. Tyler..." Myles lowered his voice and pressed himself into the shrubbery of the garden. "She stabbed him in the neck with a pair of sewing scissors. He was looking for her because when we were in Mexico she set his brother's van on fire with him inside."

"Woah, woah, woah. This is crazy shit you're saying. If it's true, you need to get out of there now. Go be anywhere else. And get Chloe's phone and take it with you. And then call the police."

The police. That was beyond his comprehension. "I can't prove anything. Let's just find Chloe. If you can't go to Montreal, I will. Somehow." The realization that he had no passport or ID suddenly sunk in. How could he go anywhere? He wouldn't even be able to buy a Greyhound bus ticket.

The chill he felt at the sound of the porch door opening made the cool night air seem warm. "Coyote?"

"I'm out here. Talking to... Sparkle. Didn't want to wake you."

"Myles!" Tyler's voice hissed in his ear. "What's going on? Get out of there now."

"I'll see you in a few, Sparkle. Just hang in there." Myles put the phone in his pocket and turned to face Kit. "She's in some trouble downtown. I've gotta go help her."

"In the middle of the fucking night? You need to tell that bitch she needs to find someone else to bail her out of a tight spot. I need you here with me." Backlit by the inside light and wrapped in a long robe, Kit loomed threateningly like a wicked sorceress, but Myles pushed passed her into the house.

"This is usually the end of my work day right about now," he retorted, heading directly for the bathroom to retrieve the phone from where he had stashed it just a short while earlier. He shoved it deep into the pocket of his jeans and turned around just as Kit appeared to block the doorway. Myles forced a smile to his lips. "Isn't this what you love about me? That I'm always helping people in

268

distress?" He put his hands on her waist to move her aside. "I mean, that's how we met, right?"

There was something not quite right about the look in her eyes. He recognized that there had always been something a little off about her gaze – but now he saw it was not just endearingly cuckoo, it leaned towards dangerously psycho. "I love everything about you," she murmured leaning in towards him, resting her head against his shoulder. "You're my goal in life. You know I'd do anything to be with you, don't you?"

He did know that now. And it scared the fucking shit out of him.

"Go back to bed. I'll be home in a couple of hours."

"See if y'all can score us some more pot. I like you better stoned. Let me get you some cash." Before he realized what was happening, she was reaching for her purse to search for her wallet.

"I've got money. No worries." He took the bag away from her and led her over to the bed. "Get some sleep."

She smiled warmly at him as he slid the robe off her body and tucked the covers up to her chin. "I like it when you take care of me. But now I'm kind of awake. I think I'll get online for a bit before I turn in again. Hurry back, baby."

His heart lurched as she reached for the iPad. Slinging his pack over his shoulder, he swept up his fiddle and his sneakers and moved quickly towards the door.

CHAPTER EIGHTEEN

West Jordan, Vermont/New Orleans, Louisiana
March 2018

Tyler actually stopped the car and vomited twice on the drive home from the airport. It might have been the three shots of rum on the plane, or maybe it was the deep-fried shrimp he'd bought while running through the terminal in New Orleans to catch his flight. But more likely it was the realization that he'd allowed himself to be seduced and duped by a murderous woman who was also the lover of his son's childhood best friend and who'd led the young mother of his granddaughters so far astray that she'd disappeared. Or worse.

Halfway back to West Jordan, his phone rang, bringing him out of the driving stupor induced by a moonless sky over snow-covered fields.

"Okay, I'm out of the house with the phone. I'll start hitchhiking north in the morning."

"Why don't you catch a plane?" Just saying the word plane made him want to pull over and puke again.

"I can't. You forget I've been an outlaw. No license, no passport."

"Hold on, I'm putting you on speaker. I need you to keep me awake. Outlaw, right. Tell me what you've been doing for the last year. And how you met, uh, Kit?"

So Myles told him. About his trip to Mexico with Diva the cat, his solitary life on the beach in Baja, and his work "assisting" illegal refugees. About picking up Kit and how she insinuated her way into his existence, the van fire, the accusations, the flight across the border disguised as Denny. Spending every cent to send Diva home and then starting a new life in New Orleans. How it had all been just a normal roller coaster ride until it wasn't anymore.

"You still awake?"

"Oh, yes, definitely. Sounds like quite an adventurous year." It was a lot to absorb and he was trying to memorize the bullet points so he could recite them to Sarah in the morning. "Diva is great, by the way. The girls drive her crazy sometimes, crawling and toddling around after her." An image of the cat curling up in Angel's lap settled disturbingly into the front of his mind. "So Angel. Kit. Did you send her to West Jordan?"

"No! Oh, my god. No. I never even told her my real name. I think it was because…" There was a pause and then Myles seemed to be choking on his words. "I was using her iPad to stalk Chloe on Facebook. Looking at posts of her and the twins. I don't know what I was thinking. Kit is a freakin' genius when it comes to finding out info about people, she does it all the time for her card readings. I must have forgotten to close out of my account at some point."

"So she knew about you and Chloe?" Tyler was remembering how Angel had cozied her way into their home life, filling an empty space in Chloe's heart the same way she apparently had for Myles.

"Yes. She knew… she knew she would never be a replacement… for Chloe. So instead she's being trying to… make Chloe hurt me and make me hate her. Did – did Kit actually stay with you?"

Tyler immediately thought of the night in New Orleans, although he was aware that wasn't what Myles was asking about. "In West Jordan? Yes, she met Chloe at…" – Shit, how was Myles going to react to this one – "…at the inn. I don't know if she actually knew that was your home or not. But I'm sure she does now. She and Chloe shared… everything."

"Kit met Sarah and Hunter too?" His response was a stricken whisper that Tyler could barely hear.

"Look, don't stress about that. She spent all her time here. Chloe was clearly her focus. It actually seemed…"

"What? What did it seem?"

"Romantic. They got drunk and high together a lot and Angel was always doing weird treatments and therapies on

271

her. George and I thought they were kind of... in love."
When there was no reply, Tyler's tone became brisk. "Tell
me about the photos."

"They're gross. There are videos too. But Kit isn't in
any of them. They are all of Chloe with – other people. I
don't know where they were taken. And it's really hard to
talk to you about this."

Tyler could only imagine. "Look. Here's what I want
you to do. Go to the post office as soon as it opens and
overnight that phone to me. Insure it, do whatever you have
to. Or even better, Fed Ex it if you can."

"Okay. I can do that. Although I have no idea where
the post office is. But I'll find it."

"And then we'll figure out a way to get you back here."
Tyler made the final turn that brought him to the Main
Street of West Jordan. "I'm almost home so I'm going to
hang up now and go inside and get some sleep. I'll talk to
you in the morning. Keep your phone charged and in your
pocket." Unlike me, he added silently.

Myles's answer was hesitant. "Okay. I will. So here's a
question. When did Chloe dye her hair blonde?"

"Blonde? Chloe?"

"So not before she went to Montreal then, I'm
guessing. Look, I'm going to text you a couple of these
photos so you have something to work with until the phone
comes. It will help you understand what I am talking
about."

"Good idea." Because Tyler was totally coming up
blank when he tried to picture Chloe with light hair. "So
where you going to sleep tonight, buddy?"

"I don't know. I'll find a place. No worries, it's not my
bedtime yet."

But Tyler was worried.

The house was quiet, except for George's snoring.
Tyler was surprised it didn't wake the twins; the sound was
as loud and uneven as a lawn mower. He drank several
glasses of water and then crept into his own bed, still too

272

wired and exhausted to sleep. He heard his phone ding and saw that Myles had sent him a couple of messages with attachments. Tucked under the covers, his head propped comfortably on his own pillows, he downloaded the photos.

The first one was of Chloe and Angel sitting out in the living room, looking all goofy and girly and cozy with each other, the way he remembered. The next was of a very stoned and laughing Chloe dressed only in a treacherous-looking necklace with spikes and hooks and the fur mini skirt he'd seen hanging in her closet, a tape measure tucked tightly around her bare chest.

The last one made him catch his breath – Chloe with pale platinum hair evenly trimmed in a shag around her face, the opposite of her usual off-kilter style with one side longer than the other. She was wearing a red bra that seemed to be barely there except for the structural way it seemed to levitate her breasts towards the camera. Her moist lips were the same color as her underwear and her heavily-lidded eyes were surrounded by an extreme amount of makeup. It seemed like a Halloween version of the girl he knew, not Chloe the mother of his granddaughters or even Chloe the nature goddess.

Another message from Myles came through as he studied the photo. He clicked on it. "*Brace yourself. A link to the video on her Facebook page.*"

Tyler had seen a lot of bad things in his lifetime, but this was one of the hardest he'd ever watched. Something had gone very, very wrong on Chloe's trip to Montreal. He opened a new page and searched for the phone numbers of the Montreal police department.

"I already called those damned Montreal gendarmes yesterday." George poured Tyler another cup of coffee. "They are useless. The name Chloe Mackenzie brought up nothing in their system. Of course I didn't ask them whether they monitored the dozens of kinky sex clubs across the city. But from my personal experience..." he waved a hand dismissively. "I seriously doubt it."

Tyler held Athena to his chest with one hand and his coffee cup with the other. She had not let go since she'd first set eyes on him at dawn; now, with her head against his shoulder, she sucked her thumb and stroked his cheek in an endearing but heartbreaking way.

"So you know that side of Montreal then?"

"I used to twenty years ago. Before border security got so sticky and they stopped letting my kind come and go so easily. And now you need a passport, which I don't have." George's gaze met his own. "So you know what that means."

"That I'm going to Montreal alone."

"Artemis, sweetheart, no." George pried the greasy butter knife out of her chubby little hand and replaced it with a slice of apple. "Give me a few hours off today to get my affairs in order and I'll be fine. I've gotten pretty good at managing this zoo."

Diva hopped up on the table and began defiantly licking the butter dish. "Diva, really? You trying to prove me a liar?" George swept the cat indignantly to the floor.

"George, you deserve sainthood. And the only place I'm going today is over to the inn to talk to Sarah and Hunter. And these girls are coming with me."

George's lighthearted demeanor darkened. "She's been gone for a week tomorrow. We can't wait any longer. We've got to do something. Minutes count in a situation like this and it's been way too many minutes." He placed a sheet of paper in front of Tyler which Artemis immediately made a grab for.

"What's this?" Tyler lifted it into the air. "A bank statement?"

"Charles at the bank is a friend of mine. He printed out the record of Chloe's debit card purchases for the last two weeks. It's a place for you to start." George leaned forward and pointed at a couple of lines. "Here's the hotel where they stayed; the reservation was made a few days earlier. And here's the ATM where she took out three hundred dollars in cash. Twice. There are a few purchases at the Triple X – it's a sex toy store on St. Catherine.

Another hundred some at Le Monde du Lingerie. A club called Le Chat Rouge. A Tim Horton's on St. Laurent. That's like the Canadian version of McDonalds. It's all in one area of town. And then it gets weird."

Tyler's eyes followed George's finger. There was a charge for the bus ticket on Tuesday, several gallons of gas at a Shell station in Williston, a meal at the Burlington airport. The last two charges made Tyler's breakfast rise in his throat. One was to a cab company in New Orleans; the last was at Tipitina's. "There's only sixteen cents left in the account," he commented weakly.

"From the first moment I laid eyes on that bitch I knew she was nothing but trouble. I mean, I could smell the shit sticking to the bottom of my shoe." George wiped his hands on a dish towel. "But I never imagined it would lead to this."

Tyler suddenly felt more tired than he'd ever been in his whole life.

Myles hadn't meant to fall asleep in the diner booth but suddenly he was waking up to someone violently shaking his shoulder. "Open All Night doesn't mean this is a hotel. If you need a bed, get a room." The waitress slapped his bill down on the table.

He'd been hoping Sparkle might show up after work at their favorite late night haunt, but she usually didn't stop unless Myles coerced her into it. Stumbling out onto the sidewalk, he headed in the direction of Bourbon Street thinking maybe he'd run into her until he realized it was too late; she'd probably already gone home. Not knowing where else to go, he headed for Jackson Square. At least he could crash on a bench until daylight came in a few hours. Then he had to find a post office.

Even at this time of night, or morning, whatever it was, there were still people on the street and in the square. Reveling tourists wearing Mardi Gras beads, drunken business men who would need to look sharp at a conference in a few hours, the usual crackheads and prostitutes. A couple of cops stood at the corner, legs spread apart, idly watching the activity. Myles nodded at them as he passed by.

"Hey, I heard you play at the Spotted Cat the other day," one of them called out to him. "That was some radical ragtime, man."

Was it a good thing or a bad thing that a policeman knew who he was and where to find him? He was going to take it as a positive sign. He sat down on a bench and then draped his body protectively over his backpack and his fiddle case. In the semi-darkness around him, there were a few shapeless lumps curled up on the grass under blankets and he could see a couple of other bodies occupying benches along the path. Exhausted as he was, he could not imagine how these people could relax enough to sleep in a public park.

The next thing he knew he was waking up, sunlight streaming across his face. Holy shit, how long had he been sleeping? His shoulder and ribs were sore in the places where they had been awkwardly covering his possessions, which amazingly were still there. He pulled out his phone and saw that it was nearly ten in the morning. He'd actually been out for five hours. He was surprised he hadn't been rousted from his bench by the cops in the rough way he'd seen them treat so many homeless vagrants here.

Looking about, he saw that some vendors were already setting up around Jackson Square in preparation for a sunny weekend day. His dread grew as he realized that Kit could show up at any moment with her fortunetelling gear; she never missed a Saturday or Sunday opportunity to sucker gullible tourists.

As he got stiffly to his feet, he was startled by a buzzing vibration in his left pocket. Chloe's phone. He forgot he had to get to a post office or some sort of shipping store. He pulled the cell out of his pocket and looked at it. *"New message from Angel."*

Uh-oh. What the fuck. There were actually three messages.

The first one read, *"I know you took this phone out of my bag last night."*

Then an hour later, *"Come home. I can explain. Everything I do is for love of you."*

And then finally, *"Don't do anything stupid, Coyote AKA Myles."*

Fuck. Fuck. Fuck. He had to get this phone into the mail now. As he began rapidly walking towards Decatur Street, there she was, coming across the corner, pulling her rolling luggage cart of equipment behind her, skirt blowing, jewelry flashing. Myles took off running in the opposite direction.

"It's been a week since they went to Montreal." George was writing bullet points on a large sketchpad propped up on the kitchen table. "Since the credit card was used all weekend there, we can assume that they really did go to the city. However, it was also subsequently used in Vermont, where we know Chloe did not return to AND by someone in Louisiana, which we do not, in fact, know was NOT Chloe, although we can pretty much assume it was not." He drew an arrow to a new box. "And, given the fact that we think Angel stole the card and used it, then it is possible that she wasn't even with Chloe in Montreal when she used it."

"But look at this picture." Tyler held up his phone. "I'm thinking we can say that, judging from the content and the background, this photo was probably taken at Le Monde du Lingerie. And I'm guessing the red lace brassiere in this photo was part of the purchase. I think we should make a few phone calls to see if anybody remembers them, starting with the hotel."

The desk clerk on duty at the Hotel Strasbourg definitely recalled the two American women. "If you know them, please have them call the hotel as soon as possible," he said in French-accented English. "They owe money for room damages. We are going to have to replace the mattress and the carpet."

277

"So sorry to hear that," Tyler apologized. "I guess they partied too hard?"

"Party is a, how do I say, weak word for what they did. Tell Mademoiselle Chloe Mackenzie that we will be charging the credit card."

Perhaps because it was exactly a week earlier, the same cashier as the previous Saturday was on shift at the lingerie store. "I would not forget that one easily. She was enjoying herself, if you know what I mean."

"Like...how?"

"You know, super high on something. Screaming and laughing, like everything turned her on, even the measuring tape. I remember it was hard for her friend to get her knockers back into her shirt, she just kept shaking them out again. She could've been a contestant on a funniest porn videos show. But I shouldn't be telling you any of this. You never heard it from me."

The Triple X was more respectful of their customer's privacy and Le Chat Rouge was downright rude. "Well, I guess we confirmed that Chloe was actually in Montreal. Diva, get off the bank statement, I need to look at it again." George swatted the cat onto the floor. "Do we think maybe she flew back to New Orleans with Angel, perhaps with the intention of visiting Myles?"

"Doubtful, there's no airline ticket charged here."

"You've got Angel's number, right? Wasn't there some talk of her showing you around New Orleans? Did that ever happen?"

"Yeah." Tyler hesitated, wondering how much he needed to admit to George. "We went to Tipitinas."

"What?! Well, the plot certainly thickens, doesn't it..." George eyed Tyler suspiciously. "Anything else I need to know?"

"Let's just say she managed to steal my phone and will not be expecting a call from me anytime soon. Why don't you call her from your cell and see what she has to say about Chloe?" He scrolled through his contacts and held up the number for George to see.

Still gazing askance at Tyler, George pulled out his phone. "What do I call her – Angel or Kit? I'm not going to call her anything. Yeah, hey, this is George from West Jordan, you remember me, I take care of the twins?... Right, how you doing? So, we've been wondering if you've talked to Chloe since your trip to Montreal... Uh, huh, and when was the last time you saw her?... The bus station in Burlington..." George raised his eyebrows and smirked. "And you haven't spoken since then?... Why? Because she never made it back here, you two-faced deceitress, in fact, she never even made it back into this country – hello? Hello? Damn, she hung up on me."

"Nice job, George. You did about as well with her as I did."

"It's not like I told her anything she didn't know. Except for the fact that we're on to her. She had to know we'd be freaking out when Chloe didn't come home." George looked up at the clock. "We've got about another half hour till naptime is over, and then I promised Robert that he and I could have a romantic supper at home for just the two of us. So what's our game plan now?"

"What she doesn't know is that we've got Myles on our side now. Damn, I hope he got that phone into the mail."

Luckily the nearest "mailing center" was just a couple of blocks away on Royal, because the next closest was a few miles distant. Myles paid the maximum amount for overnight delivery, but still the package couldn't be guaranteed to reach West Jordan until Monday afternoon. If he stole a car and drove, he could probably get it there sooner. It took him a few minutes to let that idea float away into the ethers where it belonged.

As he walked back out onto the sidewalk, his phone dinged. Kit again, trying a different phone and different tactic. *"Where are you, baby? I've been worried sick about you. You all right?"*

He shoved it back in his pocket. He was dirty, hungry and tired, and couldn't deal. He needed some money and he needed to get on the road. And he was expected to perform at the Spotted Cat afternoon show with Sparkle. He had to do it – he couldn't leave the city without talking to Sparkle.

Ducking into a nearby café, he ordered a bowl of gumbo and a beer. The thick spicy soup revived him and after washing his face in the bathroom sink and running his fingers through his hair, he felt almost human again. He might as well head over to Frenchmen and make a few bucks playing on the street before the set.

He picked a well-trafficked spot outside of the bakery and opened his fiddle case.

"Hey! Coyote!" Myles recognized the person hailing him as a saxophonist who performed regularly in Jackson Square.

"S'up, dude." He looked into a pair of eyes that were a roadmap of bloodshot veins bulging behind a pair of oversized wire-rimmed glasses.

"Kit's been looking for you today. Asking everyone if they've seen you. You two fighting or something?"

"Or something, yeah. Want to do a few numbers with me?" Myles figured if the guy's mouth was on his instrument he wouldn't be able to ask any more questions.

"Uh, sure. Wanna have a few tokes of this killer weed first?"

Even in his highly vigilant state, it was hard for Myles to refuse a pipe full of pot. It helped take the edge off his anxiety and he was able to relax into the tunes without acknowledging the raggedness of performing with someone he didn't really know or like. But the man was a passable player and his sound helped attract the attention of pedestrians.

Approximately an hour passed in the usual fashion, and coins and bills began piling up in the open fiddle case, when a murmur began to grow among the onlookers, their attention diverted by something else down the street. A dazzling specter of shimmering light reflected the afternoon sun as it moved towards them and Myles finally recognized what it was. Wearing her newly fitted silver gown, Sparkle glided statuesquely through the sidewalk crowds like a goddess holding court. A matching turban of the same glistening stretch fabric was wrapped around her head and fastened in place with a glittering green glass brooch. She stopped in front of Myles, a hand on one magnificent hip, the other waggling in front of her face in his direction. He played an appropriate finishing flourish and bowed towards her.

"The great Miss Sparkle, everybody!" he announced. "Her pipes are as robust as the rest of her. Come see us later at the Spotted Cat across the street."

"Don't go ro-busting on me, boy. Where you been since me last lay eyes on you?"

Laughter rippled through the bystanders who were close enough to hear her scold him.

Had it only been last night that he'd left her right here on the same street after watching Tyler drive away in a red car? It seemed like a week had gone by since then.

"That dress looks fabulous on you. I didn't realize Darcy was that close to finishing it." He hoped he had smoothly changed the subject with his flattery.

But Sparkle preened for only a couple of seconds before becoming stern again. "Darcy say dat woman was cray-cray dis morning, woke dem up swearing and shouting about you, so Darcy she got up and finish de sewing. What gone on in de night, McCoy?"

Instead of answering, Myles knelt down and divided up the tips in the case. He gave half the cash and coins to the saxophone player, who smiled approvingly at the take and offered Myles another toke on his pipe with a nod toward the alley alongside the building. Under Sparkle's reproachful eye, Myles declined. Touching her on the arm, he said, "We need to talk before the set."

"Hmmph. You not be rockin' our boat, now, would you, mistuh?" They walked down the sidewalk to Washington Square Park, a block beyond the bar.

"Yes, aye, missus. Dis boat haf to sail away for a spell," he replied in his best imitation of a Jamaican accent.

She slapped his hand. "What choo sayin' a me, boy?"

There was no way to tell her without telling her everything. They sat on an iron bench and he ran through his whole story beginning with leaving Chloe in Vermont. Sparkle clucked and tsked in all the expected places, grew appropriately solemn at the story of Kit's visit to West Jordan and Chloe's subsequent disappearance, and then suitably outraged at the murder of Beau. "What – you tink she use de same scissors dat Darcy cut dis dress wit? De costume have a curse on it now, me sure of it." She stared down in distress at her silver gown.

"We better get going, they'll be looking for us." Myles stood up.

"Me afraid for you, McCoy." Sparkle spoke in a tone he'd never heard her use.

"I'm more afraid for you, Sparky. She's going to want you out of the way next." He didn't realize the truth of the words until he spoke them.

Rising to her full impressive height, Sparkle's indomitable personality returned as she scoffed at the idea. "Dat pesky little fly not going to bother me. Me swat her down like de inseck she be. But you, you wispy music man, you need de eyes in de back your head now."

Sarah and Hunter were like ravenous jungle animals, unable to stop looking at Tyler's photos of Myles playing piano at the Spotted Cat.

"He looks great. He's in his element," Hunter said for the third time.

"I'm so glad we don't have to worry about him." Sarah's voice indicated that she would always worry.

"Well, actually we kind of do." Tyler told them the Angel/Kit story and watched their expressions slowly sink into shock.

"Wait, you're telling me that Southern woman who came to the inn...the same one who took Chloe to Montreal..." Sarah shook her head in disbelief. "Her and Myles?"

282

Tyler was glad that so far nobody knew of his part in the Angel/Kit saga. Although Sarah, of all people, would totally not be surprised.

"Sarah, that's not important right now." Hunter tried to put the situation into perspective. "Tyler, what about Chloe? Any new developments?"

"Not really. We've been getting nothing from the Montreal police. I think I'm going to have to go up to Montreal as soon as her phone arrives with the photos on it. And my twin-sitting relief forces manage to get here."

"Who's coming? Lucy?" Sarah asked.

It would never have occurred to Tyler to ask Tucker's mother, the twins' grandmother, for help. "Good god, no. Myles is coming."

...NEW ORLEANS, LOUISIANA...

Everything was going to shit. She'd worked so hard to make it perfect but somehow the situation was spiraling way out of her control.

When he didn't come back last night, she thought she might go crazy right then. She'd been so careful to cover all the details, leaving no tracks, even compromising her own morality to make sure that there was plenty of time for all the cogs to fall into place. But something had gone way wrong.

Now as she strode rapidly up Decatur in the direction of Frenchmen, she thought maybe she had overdone it. After their day on Shell Beach, she was sure she'd already been successful in turning him. He'd made love to her all day – she probably could have stopped posting the nasty photos then. But she had just wanted to make sure he would continue to be disgusted by what the love of his life had become.

Up till this morning she had considered her trip north to be an amazing success, a testament to the persuasive powers of suggestion that she had cultivated in her career. Chloe had been textbook; succumbing so easily to her own weaknesses and desires. It had been hard not to enjoy exploiting her sense of adventure and her wide-eyed adoration. At first the sex part had been an unthinkable concession, but once she had separated it from her own feelings, it had become just another lesson in manipulation. The weekend in Montreal had been an unexpected windfall of genius – after that it had been easy to set the trap.

The aftermath had been way more complicated than she had imagined, but the night with Tyler had been a piece of cake after Chloe, and it had bought her some much needed time and space. It had all seemed like smooth sailing until Beau had come into the picture. And then suddenly her neat package started to unravel – just like it had when Denny had shown up in Playa Los Cocos looking for her. Beau could have ruined everything. She'd reacted swiftly and desperately.

But by the time she got home something had already been off. Coyote had already been on guard and suspicious, asking questions. Knowing how independent and resistant he was to her hypnotic powers, she'd slipped a sleeping pill into his beer, but even that didn't seem to work. And despite her efforts, she had fallen asleep before he did. When she discovered that Chloe's phone had disappeared along with him, she went ballistic with distress.

Was it a coincidence? She couldn't remember the last time she had seen or used the phone. Had she dropped it during the struggle with Beau?

To calm herself down, she'd decided to act like it was a normal day and just go to work in Jackson Square. Maybe she was blowing the whole incident out of proportion. She'd taken care of all the loose ends now. He loved her and it was going to be fine.

Except that there was still that big black Jamaican whore with the colossal cartoon bosoms. What if they... him and her...

She couldn't concentrate on making necklaces; she wasn't interested in reading anybody's cards. Especially not after she took that phone call from the fag babysitter in Vermont. That fairy had made her even more nervous than she already was.

Where was he? She had to locate him. He didn't answer his phone. He didn't answer Chloe's phone. Someone said they'd seen him sleeping in the park earlier but he wasn't there now.

But there was still one place she knew she could probably find him. "Will you watch my stuff for an hour?" she asked the vendor next to her. "You can keep half of whatever sells."

She walked faster. Maybe she could get there before the first set began.

CHAPTER NINETEEN

New Orleans, Louisiana/ West Jordan, Vermont
March 2018

They were only halfway through the first set when he looked over his shoulder at the audience and saw her standing there. You couldn't not notice her – her purple silk skirt, blue velvet blouse and embroidered green shawl, the peacock feathers in her hair, the intensity in her eyes. Like she was casting a spell on him, but more like a curse than a blessing. Her icy gaze sent a chill up his neck, and he worked hard not to let it affect his playing.

As soon as they stopped for the break, she was at his side, up in his face, close enough that he could smell the wine on her breath. There was no avoiding a confrontation.

"Hey," he greeted her. "Decided to finally catch a show?"

"Why didn't you come home? I've been worried sick." The concern in her voice did not match the daggers he could see in her pupils.

"Really." He couldn't hide his sarcasm. "And why would that be?"

She was almost purring now. "Don't be silly. Because I love you. You're my everything."

He had a sudden vision – the bed in the camper, desert sky outside the window... Kit asking him something like if he'd ever loved anyone enough to kill for them. "Why'd you do it?" he asked.

"Do what?" She was all innocence.

"Kill Dennis. Kill Beau." When she looked at him blankly, he went on. "No, you know what? I don't even fucking care about them. I want to know what happened to Chloe." Despite his best efforts, he choked a little when he said her name.

"Chlo-e." She stretched the syllables out, as if stalling for time. She took another sip of her wine and looked at him thoughtfully.

"Don't act like you don't know what the hell I'm talking about. I know what you did." His words sounded as hateful as he meant them to be. Somebody handed him a beer and he was grateful to be able to concentrate on taking a few deep swigs rather than paying attention to her.

"I didn't do anything. I just wanted to get to know her. She did it all to herself." Kit sneered smugly at him. "She's a drug addict and a sex fiend. She's a victim of her own vices."

He was floored for a moment by her quick retort, but rapidly regained his mental equilibrium. "Don't think you're fooling me for a minute. I know Chloe and I know how you are. There's no way you weren't the influencer here."

"You're better off without her. You've got me now." She reached out to put her hand on his neck and he flinched away. Her hurt was visible.

"Where is she and what did you do to her?" he hissed. "You might as well tell me, because you are going down. The phone is on its way to Tyler and he knows what you did."

"Tyler." She spat his name out like a wad of tobacco. "He's classic. Men are such fools." She tipped her plastic glass up to finish the rest of her wine. "So what does Tyler 'know' about?"

Why was she acting so fearless? She should be scared shitless that she was going to be arrested. It had to be the "Chloe card" that she still held and knew they needed. "He knows Chloe never crossed the border back into Vermont, even though you bought her a bus ticket to West Jordan. So where did you leave her? Or did you kill her too?" Myles couldn't believe he had actually asked her that. Over her shoulder, he could see the bartender signaling him that it was time to start playing again.

"She loved me," Kit leaned forward and hissed in his ear. "She wanted me so bad she would do anything I asked her. Remember our catnip joke? Well, I was *her* catnip. All she ever wanted to do was roll around in me." A fleeting smirk crossed her lips. "You abandoned her, she fuckin' hated you. Wherever she is, she's in love with me now, bro."

Myles wasn't sure if his cheeks were burning with shame or outrage. "Don't you understand, you selfish queen? It isn't about you or me, it's about those babies. They need their mother." His eyes met a gaze that seemed to be lit with a strange smoky blue fire; that same intensity, once oddly attractive, now seemed like the color of the sky before a tornado. "So if you can't tell me where you think she is, then I have no use for you. I'm turning you in, Kit."

"What de problem here?" Sparkle's shadow was suddenly looming above, thrusting a solid wall of bosoms purposefully between the two of them. "What dis bitch doin' here beside spoilin' de show for us?"

Kit took a few steps back. "Careful you don't knock someone over with those things, you freakin' illegal alien freak."

Sparkle glared at Kit with so much venom that even Myles could feel the electricity in the air from where he sat on the piano stool a few feet away.

"We'll talk about this when you get home tonight," Kit said to him, crossing her arms defensively over her chest.

"How do you not get it, Kit? 'This'... "he waved his empty beer bottle back and forth between their two bodies. " 'This' is over." Shoving the bottle into her hand, he spun around on the stool. "Sparkle, how about let's start with Catnip Boogie?"

Her hostile expression dissolved into one of mischievous approval. "Yes, mon. I tink so."

Myles leaned into his microphone. "Welcome back to the second set of Sparkle and McCoy," he announced. "We're going to open with an original tune that we think you are all going to like. Well, most of you. It's called Catnip Boogie."

288

Myles ran through a musical rendition of the catchy tune before Sparkle launched into the lyrics, starting with the version that Myles had written. "My girl Kitty tink her pussy can fly, when she roll in de catnip and get all kitty-cat high, she doin' de Catnip Boogie, de Catnip Boogie, Catnip Boogie make my baby a ho' every night."

He glanced over his shoulder to see if Kit was still there. He couldn't see her face, just the peacock feathers in her hair above the heads of several women who were now jiving to the boogie woogie beat.

"My girl Kitty like a roll in de hay, catnip make her like it every which way..."

Myles wondered when Sparkle was going to launch into her own song lyrics, because he knew she eventually would.

"My girl Kitty put some catnip in her hole, ask me to catch it with my fishin' pole..."

Okay, that was a new one. Myles looked sideways at Sparkle who gave him a big naughty stage wink as she launched into her own version of the refrain.

"My girl Kitty rub some nip on her titty, thought it look really pretty when she nudie in de city, ain't it a pity that her titty's itty-bitty..." Sparkle did the appropriate shimmy to demonstrate she was not talking about herself and then reiterated the words she thought were important in a speaking stanza. "Kitty's itty-bitty titties, yes, oh, my, dey is so tiny her mon can't find dem in de dark, dey be like mosquito bites, only smaller, like flea bites maybe or how you call dem – no see 'ums..."

Myles had never heard Sparkle riff like this before and he could not keep himself from shaking with laughter, even if it was at Kit's expense. The customers were loving it, some of the regulars hooting wildly. Much as he felt a little bit sorry at mocking her, it felt really good to finally let Kit have it in a public place where she could not get back at him.

He was so caught up in the energy generated by the song, he never suspected what might be coming next.

Somewhere, behind his back, he heard the sound of breaking glass followed by a few shrieks. The crowd was getting a bit too rowdy; maybe he needed to bring it down a notch.

He felt something tickle the nape of his neck and then there was a tug on his hair, like it was being grasped to make a tight ponytail. Then suddenly somebody was up against him, jerking his head back, and something sharp and pointy was touching his throat, just under his chin.

"You ungrateful fucking bastard. I dare you to keep playing that song while you watch your carotid artery bleed out over your goddam talented fingers." Kit's voice in his ear was like something from a horror movie, an eerie quaver, low and threatening.

Myles felt his eyes roll back as his brain went black with fear. Then some pheromone of bravery kicked in. Kit was so close to him that her body hid the incriminating hand that pressed the jagged edge of a broken beer bottle against his esophagus. His playing flagged for only a second, before he sucked in his breath and went into a double time that mirrored his terror, just as he felt something wet dripping down his neck onto his shirt.

"Like this, Kit? In public? With all these witnesses?" Myles realized he was still speaking into the microphone.

A strange hush spread out across the crowd and there were a couple of horrified screams from people close enough to see what was actually happening. Myles hadn't realized that Sparkle had still been rapping all this time until suddenly she stopped. There was a brief second of utter silence and then what sounded like a primal war cry rang out over the club as Sparkle leapt from the stage and onto Kit's back.

With a karate-like movement she flicked Kit's forearm away from Myles's neck, the broken edge of the bottle raking across the underside of his chin, taking the top layer of skin with it. He knew it was a superficial wound, but the amount of blood that began spurting over the keyboard made him feel instantly dizzy. Holding his chin with his hand, he looked away from it, just in time to see Sparkle lift Kit up above her head with those powerful washerwoman arms as easily as a load of laundry. Her thick fingers grasped and twisted Kit's narrow frame like a wet sheet that needed the dirty water wrung from its soiled surface.

"Ya bumba clot voodoo womans, keep de evil hands away from de one true good mon!" Sparkle was yelling patois invectives with a vengeance as terrifying as her strength.

"Sparkle! No!" Myles shouted as he realized what was happening.

There was a yelp that became a screech and then a snapping sound and suddenly Kit's legs flopped limply, like old clothing tossed over the back of a chair. For a brief second Sparkle held Kit's sagging body against her silver gown before raising her up once more and then slamming her into the floor, skull first. A collective gasp went up and then an unprecedented quiet descended over the music club for a few seconds before all hell broke loose.

Myles tried to rise and careened sideways, landing on the keyboard with a discordant crash. The last thing he remembered was a crowd of anxious faces forming a canopy over him that left only a pinpoint of light as he disappeared into a flickering filmstrip featuring Sparkle as King Kong holding Fay Wray off the top of the Empire State Building...

He woke up as he was being strapped to a stretcher by a pair of burly EMTs. When he tried to sit, he was immediately restrained. "Where's Sparkle? Where's my backpack and fiddle?"

"This it?" Someone in a uniform held up his gear and then he was whisked out the door and into a waiting ambulance.

"Where's my partner? What happened to Sparkle? And Kit?" But all of the EMTs were busy tending to his vital signs and to his wounds and didn't seem to hear his questions.

Finally a nurse told him to stay calm and try not to talk because he was losing a lot of blood. "You're going to be fine," she assured him. "Don't worry about anybody else right now."

He didn't really think he was going to be fine – his chin hurt like fucking hell.

Five hours and fifty-five stitches later, he was released from the emergency room with a dramatic bandage around his chin and neck. Dazed and confused, he tried unsuccessfully to get information from the front desk regarding Kit and Sparkle. Finally, with the assistance of the young intern who had sewn him up, Myles learned that Kit was in critical condition in the ICU and no one matching Sparkle's description had been admitted to the hospital. Then again, why would she be, nothing had happened to her.

"Do you have someone who can give you a ride home?" he was asked by the orderly who escorted him to the exit.

Home... he'd been on his way to Vermont. Now all he could think about was the bed back at Darcy and Wendell's house. He needed to get some sleep and regroup but he also needed to find Sparkle. He had a feeling things might have not ended up well for his protective bodyguard.

"Thanks, I'll call an Uber." He sat down in a chair and pulled out his phone. There were texts and there were voice mails... messages from musician friends and acquaintances, from the Spotted Cat, from Darcy, from Tyler... and one from his parents.

Hunter arrived forty-eight hours later in the family Honda. They hugged for several minutes without speaking until Myles's chin started to ache and he had to let go of his father.

By then he had learned that Kit was in an ongoing coma from a life-threatening head injury and that her pelvis had been broken in three places. Sparkle was being held in the parish jail without bail for attempted murder.

Myles had tried his best to get in to see her but no one would listen to his story. He had no way to easily prove that Kit was actually the murderer, that she had killed at least two people, probably three, and had tried to add him to the list. There were, of course, the dozens of witnesses to the fact that Kit had attacked him and Sparkle had been merely defending him in her own over-the-top way.

"We'll call the ACLU and get Sparkle a lawyer," Hunter assured him. They were sitting on the back porch eating the leftover shrimp jambalaya that Darcy had so generously offered.

"I'm worried about her family," Myles confided. He had forgotten how steadfast and comforting his Dad's presence was. "I think she is the sole provider for some very dysfunctional situation with a mother and a sister. I know where the house is, but I've never been inside. Sparkle's been gone for two days now and they probably don't even know where she is. Unless they saw it on the eleven o'clock news."

"Look, I need to get you out of here as quickly as possible – remember we've got our own situation back home. But if you want, we can go over there in the morning before we leave. But I've got to get some rest now. Where can I crash?"

Myles was content to just sit next to his father and watch him sleep. Hunter still wore a ponytail that hung halfway down his back; Myles didn't think Hunter had ever cut his hair, always a little vain about his thick chestnut mane. Much younger than Sarah, Hunter had few signs of gray yet and could probably have passed as Myles's older brother. His lean jaw was rough with unshaven stubble from his non-stop cross-country journey. A faint aroma of lingering wood smoke had merged with the smell of two days of unwashed travel and Myles felt a little overcome by the forgotten familiarity of it all. Hunter had been his closest companion during his childhood; he'd shared more with his father than with Tucker, his best friend. Until he and Tucker had shared Chloe.

He couldn't believe that disturbing thought had interrupted his paternal reverie. He had not yet asked anyone about Tucker and assumed that there must be no news on that front. Finding Chloe was clearly the priority right now.

All these women, all his fault. Engulfed with guilt, he curled up next to Hunter, and for a few precious moments, pretended he was just a boy from West Jordan who'd never left home.

"This is it." They sat in the Honda looking at the decrepit shotgun bungalow in the Ninth Ward.

"You sure? It doesn't look like anyone lives there."

"Trust me." Myles had a fleeting sense of amusement at Hunter's naivety. "Although, I've never gotten farther than the front step and apparently even that was too close for Sparkle's comfort." He unhooked his seat belt. "You coming?"

"Um, yeah, sure, I'll be your back up." Hunter had been an intrepid traveler in his youth but decades in a Vermont village had apparently undermined his worldliness.

There was no answer to their insistent rapping on the door, although they could hear a television playing in the background. They looked at each other, and then Myles tried the knob.

"Locked. Let's see if there's a back way in."

The rear door opened stiffly and although there were no steps, they were both tall men and climbed easily onto the sill and then the rotten linoleum floor on the other side. The kitchen was tiny with aqua metal cupboards above and below a chipped Formica countertop covered with used restaurant take-out containers. The rusty sink overflowed with dishes that looked like they had been there for several days.

Then the smell hit them. Like the inside of an uncleaned outhouse, thought Myles, dreading what they would find in the next room. On the other side of the wall they could hear a rhythmic humming accompanied by a steady thumping sound. "I don't know if I can do this," he murmured.

"Yes, you can." Hunter physically moved him towards the doorway.

On one side of the room was a sleeper couch that had been folded out into a double bed; the fitted sheet had come off one corner to reveal the stained and sprung mattress beneath. A shriveled and comatose woman slumped against the upholstered sofa back, her frizzled gray hair matted against her head, her withered limbs extending from a faded sleeveless nightdress. Her gaze shifted from the TV to stare dispassionately at Hunter and Myles and then without a word she looked back at the screen.

Against the opposite wall in a worn-out Barcalounger sat the source of the repetitive noise and the horrific odor. A girl, probably ten or eleven, with a strangely twisted body was strapped into the reclined seat, her face contorted into a distorted expression, a string of drool coming from her mouth.

"Oh, my god, poor Sparkle." Myles spoke unconsciously, but at the sound of his voice, the woman turned her head towards him.

"Sparkle she be where nah..." These were the only understandable words as she launched into a string of incomprehensible Jamaican patois. And then her last phrase was clear as day. "You bring suppah?"

Myles sat on the hood of the car still trying to fathom the living situation of his best friend as Hunter explained the circumstances to the pair of officers who arrived from Social Services. This escalating avalanche of bad events seemed to be an ongoing series of outcomes due to his own poor choices, and he felt as though he was drowning in the consequential guilt. But once the Social Services people had gone in to the house, he pulled Hunter aside.

"They're illegal aliens, I'm sure of it. What's going to happen to them? What if they deport them to Jamaica? And Sparkle. Will they send her back too?" The more questions he asked, the worse he felt.

"Myles, whatever happens in the future, they can't stay here in this squalor. You probably saved their lives by coming here, but now we need to go. We've got twenty-four hours of non-stop driving ahead of us."

"But we still need to get a lawyer for Sparkle."

"We'll do it from the car. I promised Sarah we'd be home by tomorrow night. Come on."

Myles didn't get up. Instead he leaned back until he was lying against the windshield and put his hand to his forehead. "Hunter – she saved my life. I can't abandon her."

Neither of them spoke for a long minute and then Hunter sighed. "Okay, let's find her a lawyer. Get out your phone."

Another grueling six hours and they were finally on the interstate headed north. Not only had they found representation for Sparkle, the eager young attorney had connected them with a web developer who had, within an hour, started two fundraising campaigns for her defense fund, linked both to a Facebook page, and sent the story to several blogs, TV stations, and alternative newsfeeds. Myles felt they had done all they could and left New Orleans with the lawyer's promise to call as soon as he had met with Sparkle.

"You know I'm eventually coming back here, right?" Myles accepted the joint his father passed to him and took a long toke, staring at the endless stream of cars on the highway ahead of them. "Musically, this is where I'm meant to be."

"Absolutely. Now give Tyler a call and see if there is any news on Chloe."

296

Myles felt like he was tumbling out of one black hole and into another.

Two weeks later, life in West Jordan had fallen into a comforting rhythm, despite the growing anxiety over Chloe's disappearance. Myles moved in with Tyler and the twins, who took to him instinctively, despite the fact that they had no recollection of his departure when they were only a month old. He was reunited with Diva, who actually spent every minute with him for a couple of days before returning to her usual feline independence.

Within hours of Myles's arrival, Tyler departed for Montreal, indefinitely leaving the care of Artemis and Athena up to George and Myles. "The truth is, we're way better at this than he is," George confided to Myles a few evenings later as he got ready to go home. "Let's just hope he succeeds at what he does best now."

Five days later, Tyler returned, defeated and depressed. The only good news was that no bodies matching Chloe's description had turned up at any morgue in Quebec province. The police were still uncooperative and he could find no one who had laid eyes on the young woman in the graphic photos since she'd staggered out of the hotel on Angel's arm that Monday morning.

With a few well-placed bribes, Tyler had actually managed to dredge up identities of a couple of the men in the pictures, but even after some extreme coercion and threats, the situation remained the same. Neither of them had any recollection of ever seeing Chloe again after that weekend.

"It was just another Saturday night in Montreal. You think I know anything about all the chicks I've fucked over the last year?" The dark-skinned man was knocking back top-shelf whiskey like he was drinking iced tea on a hot day. "She might have been there last week looking all hot in a different way, high on some other drug. Who knows. It's like Halloween every day around here. But there is one thing I do remember about this chick." He tapped the photo on Tyler's phone with a fingernail that seemed excessively long and sharp. "She was fucking zonkers and loving it."

Tyler visited more sleazy bars, clubs, and businesses than seemed possible could coexist in one city. He checked hospitals and jails, but no one would release any info to him. He waited outside emergency room doors, showing Chloe's photo to employees. Most of them spoke only French and he had difficulty communicating his problem. There was one older cleaning woman who nodded when she looked at the picture on Tyler's phone. "Oui, je recuerde, mais je ne sais pas. She prostitute, yes? You want prostitute? I can get."

Prostitution was an area he needed to explore, but he was not sure how. The street hookers he questioned just shrugged and walked on when he was not interested in purchasing their services. The trouble was that prostitution was legal in Montreal, and the police pretty much looked the other way on all issues connected to it.

Given the clues to Chloe's drug use, crack houses definitely should be on his list of places to visit. But drug abusers tended to be exceptionally skittish and trying to corner them to answer questions was a losing proposition.

Eventually a trip to the American Embassy elicited a promise that the Consulate General would open an investigation into the disappearance of the young lost mother from across the border and Tyler drove back to West Jordan, more disheartened than when he'd left home.

Back at the house, the mood was only better because nobody could be depressed for very long around the two lively golden-haired toddlers. Their first birthday had come and gone, but celebrating had been postponed in hopes that Chloe could soon join them. Despite the dark funk that Myles seemed to sink into at times, Tyler found him a joy to have around because he was as easy with the girls as George was.

"Now if only you could write and edit newspaper articles," he joked halfheartedly, but they all knew the hole Chloe had left in their lives was not a humorous thing.

Even though he was in a safe place, Myles barely slept at night, haunted as he was by his recent past. He was glad he was not in New Orleans for a while, the uproar raised by the events of the last month put him at the center of the kind of attention that nobody really wanted.

The fundraisers for Sparkle's defense had raised nearly $100,000 and she had been released on bail pending trial. But the charges against her hung precariously on Kit's condition. Kit's vegetative coma continued and the doctors had little hope of her recovery. As long as she stayed alive, Sparkle could not be tried for actual murder. The lawyers were pushing for a quick trial, but Myles dreaded it, knowing he would be called to testify. Sparkle had lost custody of her family and Myles had no way of knowing what the future would bring for them. The attorney said she was not working at present, that she was living off a portion of the donations, and that she had declined the opportunity to speak to Myles on the phone.

And then there was the matter of Beau's murder. And Denny's. There was apparently a warrant out for Kit's arrest should she ever regain consciousness. The Laveaux family wanted justice for the death of both brothers, but it was a complex and tricky investigation, particularly in light of the fact that, although Beau had been working on proving Denny's demise by fire in Baja, it turned out that Dennis Laveaux was documented as having crossed the Mexican border into Arizona in late November. Myles heard from one of his musician friends that an FBI man had been to the Spotted Cat looking for Coyote McCoy, said to be the boyfriend of Evangeline Katherine Beauchaine with whom she had traveled from Mexico to New Orleans.

An underground cell phone video of the Catnip Boogie performance had been posted to Youtube for a few days until it had been shut down by the legal teams. But during that time Myles had been able to relive the drama of the event over and over as the music came to its unexpected finish with Sparkle's attack of Kit, followed by footage of himself fainting dead away.

His neck and the underside of his chin were healing into a dramatic scar that he knew would fade over time. But for now the red line of stitches appeared as angry as he felt inside. He had made such a mess of his life. He wondered if he would have to lay low forever.

Myles played on the floor with Athena and Artemis, watching through the living room windows as the snow melted in the backyard. Day by day the chances of Chloe ever coming back grew slimmer and he wondered how long it would be until they all finally accepted the inevitable truth.

CHAPTER TWENTY

Montreal, Quebec, Canada
April 2018

She had no idea how long she spent locked in the windowless jail cell in what seemed like an abandoned building. Jensen was the only one who visited and she began to suspect that no one else knew she was even there. Once a day he came by and pushed a sandwich and a bottle of water through the bars. He wouldn't speak to her. She was cold and hungry and dirty, but worse she felt her sanity slipping away. He ignored her when she finally fell to her knees sobbing and pleading with him to let her out. He did not unbolt the door until he was sure she was completely broken.

She could not stop crying as he led her out of the basement and into the night, pushing her roughly into the back of the squad car. She didn't care where they were going as long as it was away from the hell of being alone with herself in that place. She was surprised when they ended up in a small sparsely furnished apartment; she did not complain when he shoved her into a tub of scalding hot water and handcuffed one wrist to the tap.

"Clean up," he commanded. There was no gentle washing or scrubbing; he gave her a bar of soap and left her alone. At first she relished the comforting warmth of the bath, but after a while the water cooled off and finally she was shivering, unable to get out until he returned to release her. "Dry off." He tossed her a towel.

"Jensen. I'm so sorry…"

The eyes that had once gazed at her so compassionately were stony and psychopathic. "Yes, you are sorry. A sorry mess. But you're mine now, Bunny. You'll do what I say and if you don't, you'll go back."

The bedroom had burglar bars on the window and a padlock on the outside of the door. Everything in it was white, the walls, the furniture the bedding, the linoleum tiled floor, and after the dark dankness of the basement Chloe felt blinded by the lightness of it.

When he told her to lie on the bed and spread her legs, she did as she was told. Even in his chilling uncompassionate state, he still made love to her in the same slow methodical way. But what had once seemed erotic now seemed clinical, and yet she knew he wouldn't stop until he had witnessed her climax and then satisfied his own.

"Was that good for you, Bunny?" he asked getting up immediately. When she didn't answer he put his face in front of her own. "I asked if that was good for you."

"Yes, Jensen. Yes."

She couldn't decide if she was more hungry or more tired. He made the decision for her when he cuffed one of her hands to the headboard and left the room.

When he went to work she was locked in the white bedroom for hours, but able to move freely within the claustrophobic space. When he was home, she was allowed out under his watchful eye. She was his servant in every way; she scrubbed the kitchen floor and the toilet, fed him Chinese take-out food and satisfied his sexual needs.

He was obsessed with whiteness; everything had to be white, bleached, or purified in some way. He brought her white clothing to wear – a T-shirt, boxer shorts, stretch leggings, and a strange sheer nylon dress with a full skirt and buttons down the front like a 50s housewife might wear over a slip, except she had no undergarments. The seams were scratchy against her skin, but when she timidly mentioned this fact, Jensen punished her by not allowing her to take the dress off for two days and nights, not even during sex.

Her dark roots had begun to show beyond the blonde dye job Angel had given her, and now he forced Chloe to

302

bleach her hair. She was afraid it might fall out, but instead it became the palest shade of platinum straw, like an old-fashioned Barbie doll. He insisted she pull it back into a short tight ponytail; the look was a strangely eerie one that she might have enjoyed for a while under better circumstances.

What wasn't white in the apartment was beige – the couch, the rug, the kitchen cabinets, the curtains. It was a colorless world, a monochrome backdrop for whatever this bizarre fantasy was that Jensen was keeping her in.

He liked her to watch television in the living room with him like a typical married couple before they went to bed, at which time he would handcuff her again for the night while he slept. He wanted sex when he arrived home, before bed, and again when he woke in the morning, and she had to enjoy it. There were punishments if she disobeyed or did not perform well, withholding of "privileges" such as being allowed to eat breakfast or sit down or even use the bathroom, and there was always the threat of being returned to the cell.

Jensen became obsessed with cleanliness; every few nights he made her wash down all the walls and surfaces with a solution of bleach and vinegar, while he drank a few beers and watched her work. She was not allowed to have supper until the job was completed, and after not eating all day, she sometimes felt faint and weak-kneed by the time he permitted her a cold slice of pizza or what was left of a bean burrito.

There was no consistency to his treatment, and she knew that was part of his strategy. Kindness one night, cruelty the next – when he allowed her to share a meal at the table with him, she had to control herself from eating too much too fast for fear of him changing his mind. Once he'd brought home a steak dinner, permitted her to have two mouthfuls and then dragged her from the chair and locked her in the bedroom. He wanted her to fear his unpredictability and she did. Just when she might begin to relax and trust him, his bipolar personality could change in a heartbeat and he would be the cruelly cold Jensen again. His days off were the best and the worst; she didn't have to be locked up, but she had to endure endless hours of his erratic mood swings and she was always on edge.

One day he came home with a stationary exercise bike that he set up in the bedroom. "I don't want you getting soft and fat. I want to see that you've ridden this five miles every day." She acted as if he were disciplining her by making her exercise; inside she was ecstatic at the opportunity to move and stay fit. It was less pleasant in the evening when he made her lift weights to keep her upper body toned, pushing her beyond her limits, until her arms shook and her shoulders ached, but secretly she was pleased to be regaining her physical strength.

Because somewhere between the forced detox of the jail cell and the monotonous degradation of her current circumstances, she had regained her sense of self. She knew who she was again. She was Chloe the survivor, not Bunny the sex slave, and somehow she had to get out of here and get home to her babies.

The furnished apartment did not have many personal belongings and she wondered if Jensen kept his possessions elsewhere, or if he just didn't own anything. There were a couple of police procedural manuals, a Gideon's Bible, a copy of Canadian Motorcycle Monthly magazine and a few ancient dog-eared issues of Penthouse from the 1980s. Beneath this small pile of reading material she found an empty wirebound school notebook that she managed to hide beneath the mattress. Luckily cops still had to write tickets by hand and in a nearly empty kitchen drawer she came across a package of cheap pens. The following day, when she had been securely padlocked into the bedroom, she opened the notebook and began to write.

It was a cathartic process, trying to remember the sequence of events and the details of what she'd been through. Starting with Angel and the weekend from hell, she described everything she could recall, forcing herself to

304

admit the nitty gritty details and hazy recollections of sexual encounters and heavy drug use. She sweated through the acknowledgment of Angel's betrayal of her love and the physical and mental abuse she'd made Chloe endure. She went on through what she could dredge up of her time in the hospital, of Jensen's obsession with her, of life at Marie's, and of her eventual descent again into addiction. More difficult was the retelling of her horrific imprisonment and her subsequent existence as Jensen's slave. When she got to the end, she went back, adding as many embellishing specifics as she could bring herself to put down in print. She wrote about Rania's beauty, the perversions of Kinky Man and her nausea at discovering Angel's defilement of her body.

One night she timidly asked Jensen if he would tell her about how damaged she had been when he found her.

"You had been tossed out like a piece of garbage." He seemed to enjoy the recounting of her disgrace. "But those trash bags actually saved your life; you would have frozen to death if you'd been discarded on the ground. You still had a needle in your arm and you were so wasted you couldn't speak or move."

When he realized he had her rapt attention, he went on with the narrative, enjoying how she flinched at the humiliating particulars that he physically demonstrated on her body as he spoke. "Your shirt was pulled down so we could see your tits, all red and ripped up and cold as ice cubes. Your skirt was high enough to see your painted-up cunt and you loved it when I got you off right there in the street in front of my partner, Brown." She bit her lip as he replayed his invasive violation of her, trying to memorize what he said and how it made her feel. "There was a note pinned to you that said, 'My name is Bunny and I fuck like a rabbit.'"

She had not remembered that demeaning detail, and made a mental note of it before turning off her mind so that she could endure his unloving repeat performance of the event.

I made you come even though you were dosed up to within an inch of death, that's how good I am at what I do. I brought you back to life, Bunny. You owe me everything."

The reminder of the encounter made his present behavior more intense than usual and, lost in memories, he seemed preoccupied and unaware of the fact that the recap of his ministrations had become painful to more than just her ego. Chloe seized the feeling, committing it to memory along with realization that Jensen had done a very unacceptable and deplorable thing to her inert body and she had just gone along with it.

Absorbed in capturing her own sordid tale, the daily hours of imprisonment passed much more quickly now, interspersed with intensive pedaling on the bike. She tried to keep Jensen from being cognizant of how alive and aware she felt when he unlocked the door, allowing him to think she had been frightened into submissiveness under his bizarre regimen, rather than flourishing and gaining strength to rebel.

From the junk mail flyers that Jensen brought in from his mailbox, Chloe was able to learn that the address of the apartment was 272 Ste Adrienne #300. His work schedule was not consistent, but once she was able to ascertain the day and date from the evening news, she kept track of time in her journal. She recorded what days he worked and for approximately how long. She counted up that she had been gone from home for almost two months – fifty six days that felt like a thousand lifetimes, so far from any reality she had ever known.

When she cleaned she tried to imagine what she could use to help herself escape this ruthless captivity. The dishes and cutlery were plastic. There were no cooking implements; all the food they ate was takeaway that Jensen brought home on a daily basis. He used an electric razor. Even though the man wore a knife, a gun, and a Taser on his belt, he always locked them in a combination safe whenever he was home. Maybe if she was still and subtle enough to position herself perfectly, at some point she might have an opportunity to see the numbers he turned on the dial. But he usually locked his weapons up before he released her from the bedroom. He had a cell phone that he kept in the pocket of his pants, which he hung away from her reach when she was tethered to the bed at night. He was meticulous in his methods, never forgetting the necessary details to make her captivity complete, rarely letting down his guard for more than a few seconds.

But she could see the vigilance was taking its toll on him. The more cranky and exhausted he became, the less often the kinder Jensen seemed to surface, and she feared what the future might bring if he became too mentally stressed. She needed a plan soon. She paid diligent attention to the police dramas he was so fond of watching, looking for inspiration. But there was so little available to her – no ropes, no matches, no hammers or steak knives. Just a broom and a mop, a bucket and a bottle of bleach...

A movie about trench warfare during World War I got her thinking. She tried to recall some specific lessons from her high school classes in American History and Chemistry. There were a few things she remembered learning that might help her.

And then one evening she saw herself on the eleven o'clock news. "Police are still searching for a missing American woman, Chloe Mackenzie, last seen in March when she checked into the Hotel Strasbourg ..."

She tried not to gasp, and looked sideways at Jensen. His mind seemed to be elsewhere, he was staring blankly at the screen in a kind of TV coma and did not recognize the photo of her with dark hair and fuller features. "If anyone has any information, they are asked to call the police hotline at this number."

As the newscaster moved on to a story about a shooting in the Latin Quarter, Chloe repeated the ten digits of the hotline phone over and over to herself until they became a comforting mantra. Somewhere people were still looking for her, she had not been forgotten.

"Bedtime." Jensen rose abruptly from the couch and motioned for Chloe to go into the bathroom. He stood in the doorway and watched as she used the toilet, brushed her teeth and then got into the bathtub for a quick wash down with a handheld shower. She was still damp and shivering when he clamped one of her wrists tightly to the bed. But something in her demeanor made his gaze narrow. "Ankle also." She swallowed hard and closed her eyes as he cuffed her to the footboard as well before returning to the bathroom for his own nightly rituals.

She had to get out of here. A hot tear trickled out of the corner of one eye and with her free hand she dashed it angrily away. She had to be strong and smart. Stronger and smarter than Jensen ever imagined she could be.

There were two locks on the outside door but she had never seen him use the keys. She didn't even know where he kept them – he always locked her in the bedroom before going out of the apartment. Chloe had only the vaguest memory of climbing two flights of stairs and standing in a small dark landing – she had been so traumatized on her arrival to this place that she had not made note of any details. There was never any noise in the building, she did not think there were neighbors, at least not directly below.

When she had first been left alone, she'd tried banging on the floor but there had been no response at all. The barred windows looked out on a fire escape and a brick wall, a small square of sky visible above if she craned her neck and looked over the neighboring building. The windows themselves were sealed shut and sometimes Chloe thought she would suffocate from the claustrophobia of not being able to breathe fresh air or feel a breeze on her face.

One Saturday afternoon he tilted his head sideways and looked at her. "If I took you outside would you behave?"

"Yes, oh, please, yes, Jensen," she begged.

"Nah." He laughed. "I don't think so. Not going to happen."

Her disappointment was so visceral she could taste it, and she turned away so he could not see her expression. But her body language was enough to let him know he'd struck a fresh nerve. It soon became a new way of taunting her, a childish game of carrot on a stick.

"I'd have to walk you with a leash and a muzzle, like the dangerous pet animal you are. Would you like that, Bunny?" he teased. His suggestion reminded her of Angel leading her around the city, and she felt nauseous with fear. When she didn't respond, he made his tone stern. "What do you say?"

"Yes, oh, please, yes, Jensen," she repeated robotically, forcing her mind to be elsewhere as he laughed.

"Why don't you bleach the bathtub and then we'll decide if you deserve that reward."

Her breaking point finally came one night when they were having sex. "You forgot the condom." She spoke quietly in a reticent voice.

"I didn't forget. It's time for you to have my baby." He began pounding himself forcefully into her as she squirmed and shrieked beneath him. "Stop that!" He slapped her hard across the face. It was the first time he'd ever actually hit her. "Now pull yourself together, and get ready to be the mother of my child."

But she continued to sob silently into the night, long after he had rolled over and begun snoring. By morning she knew it was now or never.

"The floor needs cleaning. Oh, and I'll take another beer." Jensen put his feet up on the coffee table and clicked the TV remote. "After that you can do some reps with ten pound weights – pecs and lats. Shirtless – I want to watch your tits while you work out tonight. And I'm thinking you need to start an ab routine. Important that those muscles get toned for childbirth."

Chloe turned her back and popped the top of the beer can, covertly spitting into the opening and shaking it a little before she handed it to him. Then she got the bucket and mop from the closet and reached beneath the sink for the container of bleach. Next to the bleach was a bottle of vinegar and a bottle of ammonia. She had not been a star student of high school chemistry, but she remembered something about ammonia and bleach.

She put the bucket into the sink and then, moving the spigot so that it just missed the edge of the bucket, she turned on the water, soaking a clean rag until it was sopping wet. Glancing over her shoulder at Jensen, she saw that he was much more interested in Jeopardy at this moment than her mundane cleaning. Emptying the rest of the Chlorox into the bucket, she placed the pail on the floor at a good distance from herself before adding the remainder of the bottle of ammonia.

She stood back and turned her head, hoping that the immediate reaction of toxic fumes would not reach Jensen across the room. She let the mixture subside a little, and took a deep breath, feeling both unsure and certain of what she had to do next. Picking up the mop and the bucket, she moved slowly and carefully across the floor until she was behind the couch.

"What's that smell?" Jensen lifted his nose to sniff at the air. With a flexing of her well-exercised biceps, Chloe hoisted the bucket high above her head and heaved it at Jensen's face, aiming for his eyes.

The sound that erupted from his throat was unlike anything she had ever heard. He leapt to his feet clawing at his burning eyes as she covered her own face with the wet cloth and then flung the remaining liquid at him again. As he convulsed in pain, she thrust her hand deep into his left pocket and pulled out his cell phone. Her own eyes were beginning to burn as she raced into the bedroom and dialed the hot line number she had committed to memory. As she waited for the call to go through, she grabbed the spare set of handcuffs from the nightstand, and blinking with pain she peered into the other room.

In the few seconds it had taken her to flee, Jensen had fallen to the floor, blinded, gasping and choking. He was

310

trying to crawl to the bathroom, his hands groping at the searing chemical burns on his face. Chloe heard the operator speaking in French as she clamped the cuffs around both his wrists while he screamed in agony. Her own skin was beginning to feel as though it were crawling with fiery snakes and she darted back into the bedroom and closed the door.

"272 St. Adrienne #300. Hurry please." Her throat was so tight she could barely speak. "Help me. This is Chloe Mackenzie and I'm being held hostage by a mad man."

"Officer Jensen?"

She realized that the name associated with the phone number had come up and the woman on the other end sounded confused.

"This is Chloe Mackenzie, please hurry."

She hung up and dialed 911, not sure if that worked for emergencies in Canada or not.

She realized she was stretched out on the floor now, feeling dizzy and nauseous. In her plan, she had not really expected that she too would be affected by the toxic gas caused by the combination of chlorine and ammonia. All she really wanted to do was to close her eyes until help arrived, but she forced herself to dial the most important number of all.

"Hello? Yes?"

"Tyler, it's me." Her voice was muffled by the wet cloth over her face and she wasn't sure he could hear her.

"Chloe? Chloe, is that you?"

"Montreal. 272 Venue St. Adrienne. #300." She whispered the last word before she faded into unconsciousness. "Hurry."

CHAPTER TWENTY-ONE

West Jordan, Vermont
May 2018

The sun cast a wide swath of golden light across the pair of red Adirondack chairs on the porch, bestowing the painted wood with a heat that heralded the summer afternoons to come. Sarah and Tyler sank gratefully to sitting positions, ready to enjoy the long-awaited warmth of spring.

"So how do you think they're doing?" Sarah nodded towards the two figures that were disappearing into the distance, a double stroller rolling along the road in front of them.

"Hurting. Healing. I don't know. He spends a lot of time making music; she's been trying to write a memoir. She's still in really rough shape mentally." Tyler tried not to pick at the peeling paint on the armrest. "I'm not even sure what's going on between them."

"Sharing a bed?"

He nodded. "They're always together, but they don't talk much. Except to the twins. He smokes a lot of pot; she goes to AA meetings. That's one divide they may not be able to bridge."

Sarah sighed. "It hurts my heart to think of what she's been through. Does she talk about it at all?"

"No, not since that one interview. But she let me read some of the journal she kept. It's pretty tough stuff." Despite his best efforts, a long strip of red paint came off in his fingers. "I think when she gets through this patch, she wants me to help her do some exposés. I believe someday she's going to become a powerful advocate for sexually abused women. I just don't know how soon."

"Well, that one television appearance she did was pretty incredible. She's a great speaker."

"Yeah, but it took her days to recover from the stress of it. There are others waiting for her when she's ready. But I'm afraid she's going to backslide. She's the first to admit how much she loves doing drugs." He didn't mention how painful it was at times when Chloe tearfully verbalized how much she wanted something to numb her inner pain.

"What about that horrible cop…"

"We don't know anything more." As soon as Chloe had been extradited to the states, a silence had descended on the case, enforced by the Montreal police department and the Canadian government. "If he survived, the long-term effects of being exposed to gassing are horrific."

"He deserves whatever he got," Sarah said darkly.

Tyler did not argue and they sat in silence for a few moments, waiting for the sunshine to lighten their mood.

"What about my boy? How is he doing with his demons?"

He knew Sarah was still hurt by the fact that, other than occasional trips to use the piano, Myles did not visit his own family very often. "His demons are still real. He has to go back down to New Orleans next week to testify at Sparkle's trial. And to play a fundraiser for her family that he's headlining. You know he's kind of a celebrity down there."

"Well, I've heard that. Famous or infamous?"

"Probably both. He promises he'll come back by June to help with the girls so I can head out to the Caribbean."

"Finally?"

He shrugged, trying to appear noncommittal. "We'll see…"

"You know I have to go down there next week. For the trial." Myles looked down at the gravel beneath the stroller wheels as they pushed the twins up the hill at the end of Main Street. His gaze shifted to the ridge of mountains in the distance and then to the cloudless blue sky… to anything but Chloe.

313

"But you're coming back, right?" The edge of insecurity in her voice tugged at his heart.

"Yes. But..."

"Don't say it."

They walked in silence for a minute, their feet crunching on the road. "Look, I've gotta say it. Sooner than later, I'm going to live there. I'd like you to come, but it would be a big deal with these two guys." He waved a hand at the sleeping figures of Artemis and Athena.

"I know. But you'll be back before you go permanently, won't you? I just feel like, well, I'm just not myself yet and..." She touched the back of his hand almost shyly. "I want it to be like it used to be between us."

"I know what you're saying. But... shit, we aren't the same people we were a year ago."

"That's an understatement." A little sarcastic chuckle erupted from her throat and for a second, she was totally the old Chloe, sharp, cynical and witty, before her current apprehensive personality surfaced again. "What about *her*?"

She didn't have to say any names for Myles to know who she was talking about. "She's in a permanent coma. I don't think you have to worry about Kit." But he knew Chloe's anxiety was not going to evaporate quickly when it came to Kit. Even though he had to admit that he should be more open-minded, especially given the fact that he was the root of all this evil, he still had a little trouble with the idea that Chloe had initiated a sexual relationship with her.

"You don't get it – what she did to me was..." She seemed to choke on her words.

Myles stopped walking and pulled her close to him. "Chloe. I'm so sorry."

They stood that way, embracing in the middle of the road, for a long time before Chloe spoke again. "Also there's another thing I'm afraid of."

"What's that?"

"What if Tyler finds Tucker and brings him back? What happens then?"

314

"I have no fucking idea." Myles could not even begin to imagine the awkward bizarreness of that possible situation. "It's not like you would just be together again. I mean, he doesn't even know he has twin daughters. He hasn't even called home once in a year and a half."

"Not unlike someone else we know…"

"Okay, you're right, I'm so busted." But he was glad she had actually made a little joke. It was a good sign. "But that's different – he wasn't a fugitive from justice and besides, I was stalking you online." He laughed and pulled on a strand of her hair, dyed back to a more natural color than the white blonde it had been when she'd come home.

"So how do we know Tucker isn't doing the same? And don't forget, I'm the one who left him." Consumed by an all new aspect of guilt, Chloe extracted herself from his arms and began to push the stroller again.

"You can't worry about that; it might never happen. You have way more stuff to think about." As soon as he said this, Myles knew he had put it the wrong way. "I mean, you have the girls. The newspaper. The story you've been working on. Yourself. You're going to help other women. You've got a cause now."

He could see she was blinking back tears again. "Thanks. I hope so." She waited for him to fall in step next to her. "Did I tell you Artemis said your name this morning?"

"What! No, really?"

"'Mi -ya.' She pointed at you outside in the yard. Her second word after 'Di-da.' She loves that cat more than anything." Chloe laughed with what sounded like genuine glee.

"Don't you think maybe she's a genius or something? She's so quick with everything. Like you."

"Yeah, I don't feel very smart right now. I did some really stupid things, Myles."

"Me too. But I think we're gonna be okay now, Chloe."

"You think?"

"I do."

315

"Great news about George, isn't it?" Tyler accepted the mug of tea that Sarah held out. He'd been hoping for coffee but somehow tea seemed appropriate on this spring afternoon. "Chloe should feel proud of what her story instigated."

As of the previous week, George had received word that he no longer had to register as a sex offender in the state in of Vermont for a crime he had not even committed more than thirty years earlier. "I know, I'm so happy for him. There was lots of talk about it at the bar, and unfortunately there are still some haters out there. Probably always will be, I guess."

"Well, I think it will open some doors for him." Tyler grinned mysteriously. "Did I tell you I've decided to retire from the Jordan Times?"

"Really." For once, Sarah appeared suitably impressed. "You're sure about that?"

"I'm done with it. I just can't be married to that paper anymore. I need to move on with whatever my next phase is. Starting with finding Tucker."

"So you're just going to close it down? What are we going to do for local news?" Sarah looked pensive. "The Jordan Times is an institution around here – we don't all want have to read Facebook to find out what's happening in town."

"I didn't say it was going away. I'm selling it. And I've already got a buyer." He hoped she would ask the appropriate question, but instead she just raised her eyebrows and took a sip from her ceramic mug, waiting for him to go on. "Okay, it's George."

"No!" She laughed with delight. "That's fabulous."

"George will be the owner and Chloe is going to be editor-in-chief. I have a feeling the local news is about to get much more radical than anything West Jordan has seen in the past."

"Well, I'll drink to that." Sarah clinked her cup against Tyler's.

"Drinking tea on the porch with you makes me feel like we're old people. No, don't say it. I'm actually starting to be okay with my age."

"Now that you've shirked your adult responsibilities again. Just kidding." She stood up." You want a real drink? We should celebrate this."

"No, sit down. I hate to admit it, but I'm actually enjoying this tea. It will be a pleasant memory to carry with me when I'm frustrated as hell in some hot, hurricane-ravaged boatyard in the Virgin Islands showing pictures of my irresponsible son to sailors and sea captains."

For a moment they sat there, basking in the unusual mid-afternoon heat, thinking about Caribbean beaches with white sailboats and turquoise waters. Then the sun dipped suddenly behind the treetops and almost instantly the air became cool.

"And we're still in northern Vermont." Sarah rose again. "Must be time for me to start prepping the bar. Buy you a beer, old man?"

"Hell, yeah. I'm not dead yet."

ABOUT THE AUTHOR

A lifelong lover of travel, mysteries, and creative expression, Marilinne Cooper has always enjoyed the escapist pleasure of combining her passions in a good story. When she is not traveling to warmer climates around the world, she lives in the White Mountains of New Hampshire and is also a freelance copywriting professional. To learn more visit marilinnecooper.com.

ALSO BY MARILINNE COOPER

Night Heron
Butterfly Tattoo
Blue Moon
Double Phoenix
Dead Reckoning
Snake Island
Windfall
Catnip Jazz

Jamaican Draw

Made in the USA
Middletown, DE
10 July 2021